Money Shot

BLUE IVY PREP
BOOK FOUR

HEATHER LONG

*For everyone who has ever had my back.
You know who you are.*

Foreword

Dear Reader,

Thank you for picking up this book, and for taking a chance on a new series. If I'm a new author to you, welcome. If you've read my previous works, hello there, it's good to see you. Money Shot is book 4 of Blue Ivy Prep, so if you haven't read the first three, I would recommend pausing to grab those and start with *Problem Child* as this series needs to be read in order.

Previously at Blue Ivy Prep, Lachlan returns to Ramsey's suite and is very aware that it smells like sex. It doesn't take long for Lachlan and Jonas to identify *who* their brother had sex with and the tension between the three ratchets up. However, a voicemail left by KC on Lachlan's phone reveals she didn't run away or take off—she wanted to talk to all three of them but someone attacked her.

The guys track her to where she "vanished" and they get campus security involved. A ransom note is sent to KC's father Gibs. The guys learn because their mother wants them to make her stop whatever "games" KC is playing with Gibs.

Eventually, they convince Gibs to pay the ransom and they

are given a location. Their relief is profound when they find her, and she's transported to the hospital. Aubrey and Yvette are there for her and the guys are being very protective, in the short amount of time leading up to graduation and then the girls take KC back to California.

The guys elect to follow her this time. They also learn more about how sick Pen is and get tested to see if they could also be matches. They are truly realizing everything they thought about the gulf between KC and Gibs is not at all what they thought it was.

Lachlan manages to hook up with KC at a club, the guys reach out to her, she isn't sure she wants to do this anymore especially after everything that happened. Her focus is very much on Pen. With Davina's encouragement, KC invites the guys over for dinner and they all confront some truths—including KC and Ramsey ending up in bed together.

Eventually, KC chooses to go back to Blue Ivy for college classes. She moves in with all three guys—Ramsey is now a full-time instructor while Lachlan and Jonas are going to classes as well.

They are testing the waters to see if a relationship between her and all three will work. In the meanwhile, KC finally gets ahold of her sibling Trace and learns that Trace is now Tracy, and Tracy was worried that KC may not approve of her being trans. KC is just happy Tracy is all right, but she fills her in on Pen's condition.

Tracy gets tested and to everyone's relief, Tracy is a match. As they get Pen ready for a transplant, it's full steam ahead to continue raising money and awareness with a benefit concert.

They travel to California to perform, only for KC to end up on stage with Gibs, an ambush she didn't see coming when Party Crashers wraps up and that brings us to here—Money Shot.

Whew.

Triggers to be mindful of: There is some stalking, and I will give a warning for a severe health diagnosis concerning a side character. A couple of assaults occur including an attempted SA.

If you have read this far, thank you. Money Shot is the fourth and final book in the series following Kaitlin Crosse as she attends Blue Ivy Prep, an exclusive boarding, prep, and college school for the wealthy and the privileged.

The series is reverse harem/why choose. This means the female main character will not have to choose between the guys in her life. This series is also slow burn, and begins with bullying, secrets, lies, and complicated family ties.

While the first book was told exclusively from Kaitlin's viewpoint except for the prologue, all other books in this series contain multiple points of view.

Thank you again for taking a chance on this series, I can't wait to hear what you think of KC and the douchebags three. Be sure to join us in my reader group on Facebook where we talk books, book loving, some spoilers, teasers for the future, and bonus scenes. Don't forget to sign up for news and updates on my website to get all the latest news, releases and more emailed right to you.

xoxo

Heather

Prologue

KC

MORE THAN A DECADE EARLIER...

"Juliet," I called as I slid down the banister. The long slope of the fat wooden banister gave me time to pick up speed before I whipped around the corner. You had to jump at just the right time to hit the thick padding of the rug in the living room.

"Kaitlin Crosse," Juliet scolded, but since she was also laughing, I just timed my jump and landed it. Laughter escaped me and I caught Juliet shaking her head even as she smiled. "You need to be careful. I don't want to have to be the one to tell your daddy you hurt yourself."

I grinned, but I didn't make a promise I didn't want to keep. "Good morning, Juliet."

That just earned me another half-laugh, half-sigh. "Charm will not work."

"Are you sure?" It had taken me time to master that line,

but I had all the practice with Mom when she was working on her last movie. Since then, it had become my get out of trouble catchphrase—well, that was what Davina called it.

"No," Juliet told me with a light swat from the dust cloth she was carrying. "Your daddy is in his studio and I'm going to have breakfast in thirty minutes. So go tell him for me?"

I loved the studio. "On it!" I promised and then raced for the door, half-skipping when I remembered I was not supposed to run in the house. Once at the door though, I hurried down the stone steps, then through the garden, and around the pool where I could follow the rock wall to the bungalow that housed Daddy's studio.

When he was actively recording, the red light on the door would tell you to wait. If he was just working, the red light wasn't on. No red light. I let myself in and danced to the music spilling out of the work booth.

Spinning on a chair, Daddy grinned at me. "Sweet Kaity," he called, and I skipped right over to him. He was seated at the control panel and after a hug, he lifted me up into his lap. "What do you think?"

His hair tickled my shoulder. Daddy had hair almost as long as mine. His wasn't as pretty, or at least that's what he said. I liked the longish waves, especially when he let me brush it. I leaned forward to stare at the sound board and the mixing. Music flowed from the speakers. A steady rhythm, keyboard, and sweet metal from the electric bass, but it was the acoustic guitar that made the piece really sing.

I pointed to the mixer board and tapped the guitar control. "Needs more."

"Yeah?" Daddy nodded and I nudged the switch upwards a half-degree. It gave a little more focus to the mournful notes Daddy teased out of the guitar. The song had a good beat, but it made my chest hurt. "Yeah, I like that," he answered.

"It's sad," I told him after we listened to the full piece. It was almost eight minutes long and it made me want to cry.

"Music is life and life can be pain, Sweet Kaity," Daddy told me. "But we can flip that sound around..." He tweaked the dials and started it over. The tears in the music gave way to something almost taunting. "How is that?"

"It's meaner," I told him and then looked at the controls. "Can I play with it too?"

"Yep," he said, shifting to put his guitar on the stand and hooking a chair to drag it over. "On you go." He lifted me right onto it and then knocked out a cigarette before he touched the controls to explain them. "Pitch. Tempo. We can also fade or increase..."

The flick of his lighter was a familiar sound, so was the crisping of the tobacco catching fire. The blue smoke he exhaled made me grin, especially when he blew little rings.

"Got it?" he asked and I pointed to each dial, repeating back what they did. "That's my girl," he said with a grin before he tugged my ponytail. "What do we want to do with the song?"

I hit play again after I switched the dials back, and then I nudged up the violin a little more. That took the sad and the taunt and kind of tied them together. I played it three times before I touched the dial for his guitar. Bit by bit, I nudged it up until the guitar became the dominant thread. The other instruments came and went but Daddy's guitar set the tone and there—it went from sad to mean to almost a real dare that climbed at the end.

"Hey," Daddy said. "Do that again."

He picked up his guitar and began to tap out the tempo on it, cigarette between his lips and then on the next go through, he played along and I practically vibrated in the chair as the new thread made it seem like a contest—a fight between Daddy's guitar and the guitar on the recording.

When the song came to an end, he flicked off the ash on his cigarette and eyed me. "What do we think?"

"I love it," I told him. "Can I play with you?"

"Hell yes, you can." He stubbed out the cigarette and then settled the guitar on my lap. I loved this guitar, it was so much bigger than me but if he put my hands in the right places—there we go. "All right, one second..." He grabbed his second guitar and then rolled the dials around before he eyed me. "Ready?"

I grinned. "I'm always ready, Daddy."

"Yeah you are..."

When he hit play, I tapped out the first two beats then jumped in on the third.

Daddy never stopped grinning.

One

KC

I was going to throw up.

"*Kaitlin Crosse, you're up. We had a slight change, your girls are coming on right after you, but you're up first.*"

"*Go straight out—*"

"*Kaitlin Crosse on stage in five, four, three...*"

The roar hit me like a tidal wave as the spotlights picked up my arrival.

Movement had me turning to the man waiting out there in his own spotlight.

"*For the first time ever, Gibson Crosse and his daughter Kaitlin, from Torched, will be performing together right here for you tonight...*"

I was going to do more than throw up.

A thousand thoughts collided in my head as the crowd lost their goddamn minds. This—wasn't supposed to happen. Nothing on the schedule indicated Dad had even been invited much less agreed.

Why the fuck hadn't Teddy warned me?

"Hey, Sweet Kaity," Dad said, his smile warm as he gazed across the stage at me. If not for the microphone, I wouldn't even have heard him. As it was, I had to wonder if I was making it up. His guitar was plugged in, so he wasn't exactly walking toward me.

That meant I had to go to him.

The slam of my heart was not the metronome I wanted to perform against. In the rush to get me out here, they'd pressed a microphone into my hand. But I didn't have a guitar. That sent another spasm of pain through my chest.

It was just the two of us on the stage. No band to back us up or hide behind. Staring at Dad, I couldn't tell if I wanted to scream or to cry.

Maybe both.

He'd pulled his long hair back into a tail, keeping it out of his face. There were streaks of gray that caught the lights. Those, along with the lines around his eyes, were a testament to the passage of time. I didn't remember the crow's feet being so pronounced.

Then again...the stage lights had never been kind to anyone. It was why we did makeup and hoped we didn't sweat through it.

"Dad," I said, only half-remembering to raise my microphone. The single syllable triggered another wave of applause and wild screaming. I was going to gut Teddy with a spoon.

If I turned around and stalked off this stage right now, the girls would back me. I was pretty sure the guys would too. For one, seemingly endless and painful moment, I wondered if they'd known he was coming.

If they'd...

No.

I closed my eyes, forcing myself to take a long breath.

No, they hadn't known.

Their anger and regret had been tangible. It *was* real.

I couldn't leave.

Whatever we ended up doing out here would set the tone for the rest of the night. Tonight wasn't about me. It wasn't about Dad. It wasn't even about all those people out there in the audience or watching on screens...

Tonight was about *Pen*.

My throat locked up, but I kept putting one foot in front of the other. Moving across the stage, fueled by the practice of performing on so many stages over the years. The only difference right now?

I was flying solo.

Dad definitely didn't count.

But if I faltered, my girls would be here. Aubrey and Yvette weren't more than a few dozen steps behind me.

"I hope you have a plan," I said, not quite trusting my voice not to wobble. But it came out a little husky. "Cause I didn't even know you were going to be here."

"Yeah," Dad said, his smile almost sheepish. Enough that I might have bought it if he hadn't glanced at the audience. "The producers wanted to go for a real moment."

I snorted.

A *real* moment.

The audience had started to quiet some as if they hadn't expected us to talk.

Well, they weren't alone in that. "This is Hollywood," I reminded us both as I came to a stop just a couple of feet away from him. We had to put on a show. "Nothing here is *real*."

His gaze locked on mine and I lifted my chin. There were cameras. They were all over the place... including one guy who was all but crouched at our feet. Every nuance of this interaction was going to be available fucking everywhere.

But I could play my damn part.

"Maybe so, Sweet Kaity," Dad said, the slow roll of his

voice looping around me like a hug he wanted to offer. "Never was a big fan of Hollywood. But you're still my girl, right?"

The urge to snort in his face was right there. His girl.

That wouldn't help Pen.

So, I summoned a smile and then chuckled. If not for the flashing lights, the hum of the crowd, and the cameraman four feet away from us, I could almost pretend we were alone.

Right, I couldn't even sell that line to myself. "Might have to work on that," I finally said by way of an answer. "I kind of grew up."

Tapping a hand against his guitar lightly, Dad nodded. "You'll always be my sweet Kaity, though."

This time I snorted and the audience lapped it up. "Sorry, Dad. You might have to settle for sassy rather than sweet."

Their laughter rolled up and onto the stage as if to egg me on. But it was Dad I kept my focus on. If I did that, controlled my breathing, and remembered where I was—I wouldn't hyperventilate or throw up.

Mom used to tell me the easiest way to overcome stage fright was to remember that on stage, you were someone else.

That advice trickled through me and I lifted my chin. "Speaking of being sassy..." I deliberately paused to let the word sink in. "What are we singing? Since we've never done this before."

I braced myself for whatever he picked. I assumed they'd picked *something* for this performance. I might not gut Teddy. Maybe I'd just kick him square in the balls.

"Thought we'd do something we both know pretty well..." Dad gave me a side-long look but the ease in his eyes had gone guarded and his smile had definitely faded. Maybe me keeping my distance finally got it through his head how unhappy I was with him.

He ignored me *for years* and to show up tonight of all nights?

Right.

"Well, won't know until we try," I suggested and I glanced at the camera man who was about to look right up my skirt. He shot me a grin and backed off.

Asshole.

Dad tilted his head down as he adjusted his hands on the guitar. First chord.

Second.

The music washed over me as he began to play. The shouts and cries from the audience faded away as the only sound was the guitar as he pulled the music from it.

And he wasn't wrong...

I recognized the song.

He made it through the first stanza with neither of us singing a word before he lifted his gaze and met mine. Eyebrows raised, he asked me if I knew it.

I nodded once.

How could I forget it...

It was one of his earliest hits. A song he'd written for Mom.

Well, that was the rumor anyway.

He flashed me a grin, then started over at the top and I started to tap my foot. There was no percussion out here, but this song had a definite beat.

By the time he made it to the second note of the intro, I lifted the microphone and packed it all away. This was going to be as sotto voce and unplugged as it got—save for him playing on the guitar.

"Oh my god, my dear..." Singing the words was like ripping off a bandage. It stung and it felt good in the same breath. "Oh my god, my dear," I continued. "Don't waste time, don't waste thought, because you are the reason I have no fear..."

Tears clouded my eyes, and threatened my voice, but I

pushed it all away. Out here, I was Kaitlin Crosse, part of Torched. I was a sister. A friend. And a lover. I was *me*.

The audience clapped, measuring the beats for us and it wasn't until I headed for the first chorus that Dad jumped in. "Oh my god, my dear," he rasped into the song and his deeper baritone lifted my alto and I caught him staring at me.

It was a challenge.

So I kicked it up a notch.

"Don't waste time, don't waste thought, because when you're here, I have nothing to fear..."

The song started out with the idea of love, to the commitment, to the part where love was as much a battle as it was a balm. I followed his lead as he played. When we hit the finish, the crowd roared.

His grin should have been contagious, but he didn't wait for the accolades as he transitioned into another song of his. One he'd recorded when I was eight. It was one of the first of his I learned how to play on his guitar. It reminded me of sitting in his lap with his guitar braced in front of us as he put my hands in the right places.

It was a song about love, and not wasting it on the wrong people.

What a dick.

But I matched him measure for measure. Even when he switched it up to play an old cover his band used to perform. It was a wildly uptempo song, not his usual style these days, but much more like the type of rock I enjoyed performing. It didn't hurt that the female vocals were right in my range.

Pride seemed to shine in his eyes as we faced each other toward the last stanza. His voice and mine matched. There were definitely some wobbly moments, but the live on stage atmosphere seemed to overwrite that.

That pride was like a knife in my gut.

Why the fuck was he here? Had he actually come for Pen?

Or was this something else? Why hadn't he answered my calls? Why...?

So many damn whys. All the questions and none of the answers.

It was hot out there, and the sweat gleamed on my skin as we wrapped up our fourth or fifth song. The crowd was well and truly wired. When he raised his brows at me as if to ask did I want to do another, I said fuck it.

At least, internally, I did.

Externally?

I took ownership of the stage.

Raising my hands over my head, I started to clap to get the beat going and the audience responded. Dad cut a look at me, but I ignored him as I focused on the audience and getting the fever pitch up.

On the fourth beat, I started to sing. Dad was quiet behind me as I went for the pure melody. This was one of the first songs Torched recorded. It started out as a mini solo for me, but it wasn't meant to stay that way. Any of us could start it.

We used it on stage whenever we needed to change up the mood. Change the focus.

I knew what I was asking for...

Though I damn near stumbled when Dad fell in and started playing the song on his guitar. He didn't miss a stanza and when we hit the first bridge to the real chorus, Yvette and Aubrey strode out on the stage. Lights flashed. The audience screamed. And when the next lyrics fell from my lips, their voices lifted mine.

It was the three of us and they bracketed me—one on each side as we performed it like we'd been practicing every day. The only real shock was Dad matching us. The song itself was fucking personal. It explored the impact of fame on our personal lives, about being trapped between the demands of life on stage and life at home.

Life with the people we loved.

It was fucking impossible to find that balance, but it never made me stop wanting it. I caught Aubrey's eye and she grinned as Yvette took the lead on the song. We traded it around easily, the three of us *trusted* each other. That trust elevated me, buoying me above the pain of betrayal and so much abandonment.

My girls were here and they'd *never* fucking abandoned me. My next smile burst out of me as I took the lead back then passed it to Aubrey, then it was all three of us. Dad had stopped singing, but he kept playing, the chords of his guitar a screaming accompaniment to the moments of profound loneliness reflected within the lyrics.

He cut off at the closing outro, leaving the three of us to carry the song to its conclusion. One by one, Yvette and Aubrey fell away until it was only my voice on the last, elongated note that I held for the full thirty seconds then dropped as I fist-pumped.

Tears and sweat poured down my face, but I could survive it.

I had survived it.

The lights cut away from us and I lost my smile, pivoted on one heel and strode off the stage with the girls right behind me. Somewhere, the announcer was introducing the next act. But I made a beeline right for Teddy and his excited face.

Ramsey caught my fist when I would have punched our manager. "Hang on, Siren..."

Lachlan's fist slammed into Teddy's face a split-second later.

It wasn't quite as satisfying as doing it myself, but Ramsey tugged me against him and ignored the sweat as he hugged me. There were cameras back here and probably press and more.

Teddy stared up at me as he rubbed his jaw dazedly, at least he was until Jonas stepped between us and blocked him off.

"Torched," the stage director moved toward us. "You have fifteen, then you're back out there..."

Fifteen minutes... I needed the break. The time.

Dad was suddenly there, but rather than let him get close, Lachlan and Jonas, along with Aubrey, blocked him off. They put themselves between us. There were too many eyes and ears back here.

Then a screech ripped through the backstage, despite the pound of music coming from it. Mom. I knew that sound. She was just there, flying at Dad, in a pure fury.

Oh, this wasn't going to end well.

Especially when the cameras started clicking.

Two

LACHLAN

"For the first time ever, Gibson Crosse and his daughter Kaitlin, from Torched, will be performing together right here for you tonight..."

"What..." Aubrey and Yvette exhaled in the same breath.

"...the fuck," Jonas finished for them as we all stared out on the stage. Now that my eyes adjusted to the lights out there versus back here, I could see Gibs clearly.

He stood out there on that stage like he owned it and his attention focused on Ace. "How the hell did he get on stage?" Ramsey muttered.

"It's fucking genius," someone said from behind us and I cut a glance over my shoulder to the woman with the headset. "We want all the eyes and the attention on this benefit, putting father and daughter on stage for the first time? It's gonna make a killing."

Anger flooded my veins as I jerked my gaze back to the stage. They were talking. Her voice didn't waver or warble. If anything, she gained in strength as she spoke. I curled my

17

hands into fists as she met his challenge with one of her own. She was in no way prepared for the shock of that meeting—on a stage in front of thousands.

She didn't let an ounce of it show. She was a goddamn professional. The way her voice sounded when they sang together was going to haunt me. Yvette and Aubrey had become statues as they remained laser-focused on the stage.

Torched was supposed to go on next, they were originally the opening act. So... Yeah, time for getting those answers later. As it was, I had to physically restrain myself from stalking out there to at least *stand* with her and back her up. But she had to do all of this on her own and I hated every damn second.

Listening to her sing with Gibs ripped at my heart. She didn't close the gap between them, if anything, she held herself firm, standing in her own pool of light. Microphone in hand, she owned the stage. I'd never listened to *her* sing, alone. I'd heard her stuff with Torched and there were definitely solo moments in some of their songs but...

"Her voice is..." Ramsey exhaled the words and I felt every inch of that sigh. Because her voice was something else. The weird part though, when she first came to the school—all I'd seen was the arrogance and take no shit attitude. How much of that had been an act? How much of that had been her putting on a brave face?

There was no mistaking it right now.

"Should you go?" Jonas asked and it pulled my attention off the stage briefly where Gibs and Ace segued into an entirely different song. It was one of his older ones, I thought. Why the fuck would he assume she knew his music? Then again, she did seem to know it.

"Not yet," Aubrey said, her voice stiff and it kind of matched her posture. For once though, her "get-fucked" face was not aimed at me. She glared out on the stage.

"She'll let us know when she needs us," Yvette said, her accent feathering over the words but doing nothing to rob her tone of pique. They were both angry. Angry for Ace. Angry at Gibs.

Goddammit, I hated being one of the last to know something. The frost out between Gibs and Ace, we'd always blamed Ace for it. Ace and her mother. That was what Mom said. But more and more, all I could think was the person who didn't want Ace around *was* Mom.

Who the fuck hated a kid?

"I can't get over it," Jonas said. "I've heard her sing alone before but that's—haunting."

Yeah. It was and I wasn't sure how much of that was the music she was singing or the person she was stuck out there singing with. Forcing my fists to uncurl, I slid my hands into my pockets. I rocked back and forth on the balls of my feet.

I wanted to be out there.

Fuck that, I wanted her back here, with us and off that stage. I wanted to put her behind me where no one got to do this shit to her again.

An image of her glaring at me from the pond where I'd shoved her crawled out of my memory to flip me off. Right, the only ambushes she needed were the ninja kisses from me. She liked those.

The rest of this...

It seemed an eternity that they performed but it couldn't have been more than twelve, maybe fourteen minutes tops. I wasn't sure. But she started a song without Gibs playing.

"Microphones," Aubrey snapped to the stagehand.

"Please," Yvette added a little softer layer, but not by much. As soon as they had microphones in hand, they were striding onto the stage and into the lights. The audience roared to greet them and Gibs started to play, his solo accompaniment to their three powerful voices.

He was so outclassed.

Though, I had to admit, the moment those girls hit the stage with her, I saw their friendship live and in full color. It was in how they sang together, how they passed the lead of the song, the way they moved together, and how Yvette and Aubrey framed her to put themselves between everyone and her.

To make this relationship work, I was going to have to get them on my side. Jonas shifted next to me and Ramsey moved up to stand on my other side. Fine, get them on *our* side. That would be easier said than done. Dragging my hands out of my pocket, I folded my arms.

Waiting was not my strong suit. Patience was something the coach always gave me shit about. My dad too. This was not how I wanted to master patience. Finally, they were done and the girls were striding off the stage as the crowd went absolutely ape shit.

The ferocious look in Ace's eyes had me straightening and I wasn't the only one. She stalked right toward their manager and her sweet little hand curled into a fist. Oh, she wanted him punched?

Even as Ramsey caught her fist to keep her from hurting herself or maybe from getting an assault charge—what did I know? I went ahead and finished the move for her. The collision of my knuckles against the asshat's face sent pain flashing over my hand. I enjoyed the way the guy went down like the sad sack he was.

Gibs suddenly showing up—it made sense he'd come back stage, but I'd kind of hoped he'd gone the other way. Still, there he was and I moved to block him. This? This I could do. Ace didn't have to deal with a damn thing she didn't want to.

All around us, stunned workers stared at the unfolding tension. Guess there weren't a lot of brawls at these events. Not like there was going to be one now.

Then a screech of sound that didn't remotely belong to anything human pierced mine and everyone else's ears. "You son of a bitch..."

I twisted in time to see a woman not much taller than Ace, with platinum blonde hair, and delicate features, charge right at Gibs. It took a split-second to register that it was Jennifer Crosse. Not that I knew that much about her.

Actress. Gibs' former wife.

Ace's mom.

She was slapping Gibs over and over again. No one moved. Gibs barely defended himself, he lifted his arm as if to just block her blows but he didn't make a move to touch her.

Now would be an excellent time for security to show up. Music pounded out on the stage, the drums and bass, hopefully covering the inhuman noise Jennifer Crosse released as she cursed at Gibs.

Warmth brushed my side as Ace pushed past me and I was right behind her as she stalked toward her parents. Just as she got there, a guy stepped in, but Ramsey all but shoulder-checked him.

Didn't know him.

Didn't care.

Not getting near Ace.

"Mom," Ace said as she finally got there. She did grab her mother and drag her away from Gibs. "Mom, *stop it.*"

The actress whirled to face her daughter, all at once her eyes filled with tears and she was clutching Ace. "I'm so furious for you. How dare he ruin your night for you..."

"Oh my god, shut up," Ace said, then glanced around. She blinked at Gibs once, then shook her head. "We don't have time for this Mom..."

"Baby, I wanted you to meet—" Jennifer's tone and manner had changed entirely from furious to almost simpering. So not Mom.

"I've met him. I didn't like him then, I don't like him now." The he had to be the guy Ramsey blocked. Good to know. "Where's Dix?"

"Why do we need Dix?" Jennifer asked. "I came here to support you—"

"Yeah, no. You need to go, Mom. Both of you do. Tonight is not about you or your drama or any of this..."

"I'll take her." It took me a minute—Jackie. Her name was Jackie. She was Bronson's mother. She was also Penelope's guardian. The dark-skinned woman reached out to wrap an arm around Jennifer.

"Jackie..." All of a sudden Gibs seemed to have found his tongue. More security and the backstage handlers were suddenly flooding the area.

"You should know better, Gibson," Jackie said to him in a tone that was clearly dismissive. "Now, Jennifer—let's get you out of here."

"I'll take her..." The guy offered but Ace rounded on him,

"You shouldn't even be back here, no one cleared you. In fact, where is security..."

"You want him gone?" I offered, but security was already taking the guy by his arms and marching him out. Jennifer stared after him then looked at Ace almost helplessly.

"Go with Jackie," Yvette said as she slid up to the woman. "Let her look after you. We can come see you when we're done with the show."

"Boys," Gibs said and I cut a look at him.

"Not the time," I said, then Ace's hand brushed mine and I gripped hers lightly. If she wanted to pull away, she could. "Tonight isn't about this—drama."

"If not now then..."

"How about you answer messages," Ace said, sliding her fingers in between mine as she glared at her father. "How about you do it anytime that isn't ambushing me on a stage like we planned this as an event."

"Kaity—"

"No," she said. "I can't do this right now. Jackie, can you take my mom home? I can send Dix to get her or I'll come find her after the benefit."

"Don't worry about it, I'll look after her. You take care of yourself." Then the woman pinned a look on me. "You look after my girl."

"Yes, ma'am."

"I'll help you get to your car," Jonas said, then he glanced at Ace. "I'll be right back. Promise."

"Thank you," she said, leaning into me and I let her. How did she sound both powerful and lost at the same time?

The music from the stage hit another crescendo and the applause bled back to us. Teddy had made it to his feet and there was another agent trying to get Gibs' attention. Mom wasn't here and that was weird, but right now I didn't care.

"What do you need?" I asked Ace. "Besides some water?"

"A quick break," she told me. "We have to be back on that stage in ten—"

"Five," a woman with a headset on told her. "Here, we've got water for you guys. Do you need a touch up?"

Five minutes. Jonas and Jackie were getting Jennifer out of here. Gibs was still there. So was a bloodied Teddy. Maybe I should punch him again.

"We got this," Yvette told Ace and when Ace turned away from her dad and just leaned into me, I wrapped an arm around her. Ramsey shifted to her other side. Right. We were going to have to do this the hard way and that was fine.

"We do have this," Aubrey said, her assurance nearly as strong. "We're gonna need headsets for this..."

Headset microphones. That made sense.

"We have them," the handler said.

"KC—" Teddy started but cut off when she raised a hand and I glared at him.

"Not now," she told him.

That was all she needed to say. Awareness of Gibs watching her kept the hairs on the back of my neck standing up. I didn't leave him an opening. Too soon, the girls had their headsets on and Ace looked up at me with the saddest eyes.

"Thank you," she whispered and I touched two fingers to my lips then to hers. A faint smile curved her mouth and I nodded. Better.

"We'll be right here, Siren," Ramsey promised her and she squeezed his hand before she pulled away from both of us. Jonas wasn't back yet. But then, maybe crazy Jennifer came out to play after docile Jennifer was ushered out. Still, Gibs stood there and when I spared him a look he was studying us with a hundred questions in his eyes.

Questions I wasn't going to answer. Not right now.

Then the girls were striding out together, their playful voices and banter a far cry from the painful display back here.

She really was a rock star in more ways than one.

Three

KC

Returning to the stage let me flee the internal chaos provoked by the presence of Dad, Mom, and that insane guru she was engaged to marry. Tonight wasn't supposed to be about any of them. Goddamn Teddy.

I couldn't believe he set me up like that. As angry as I was and as twisted up as I felt on the inside, I couldn't take that emotion out there. Not internally. I needed to channel it and pour it into the music. With every step, I shed the weight of their presence. I abandoned the uncertainty.

I embraced the pain and let love and friendship carry me the rest of the way. The guys were all right there for me and they hadn't moved to back up Dad. If anything, Lachlan and Ramsey kept themselves between me and them.

"Are you guys ready to rock?" I challenged the audience.

"Of course they are," Yvette answered for them as she pivoted to face me. "The question is, are you?"

"Am I?"

"You heard her," Aubrey peeled off the three words like she had all the time in the world. "Are we rocking it tonight?"

The crowd roared.

"Sounds like *they* think we should," I quipped. "Think we still got it?"

The longer we stood out here, the easier it became to breathe. The stage was where I'd grown up. It was where I'd found myself. It was where I could be myself.

"What kind of question is that?" Aubrey snarked and then eyed the crowd. "Did we sound like we still had it earlier?"

The roar of hell yes and the cheers answered for us and I grinned.

We weren't looking at the audience anymore, but at each other. Hands on my hips, I met Aubrey's gaze, then Yvette's. Our backup band was here. The crew we'd toured with. They knew us. Knew our music.

Yvette raised her eyebrows and Aubrey tilted her head. Tells. Tells for me anyway. Tells that asked me what I wanted to do. Asked me how I wanted to do it. Old school? First album? Second?

Third album had been our most popular, but the first? The first had a lot of classics on it. Songs we'd written together. It wasn't like they didn't have opinions, but they were giving me the lead.

"I think something classic," I speculated aloud and the audience shouted their approval. They were also shouting their suggestions. A laugh broke free because yeah, that was exactly what we needed to do.

Challenge us.

"You wanna pick a song for us?" I said, trusting the mics to carry our voices. We were rolling with the impulsiveness and the spontaneity. The minute they started chanting the Bangles song, I cracked up.

We'd done a cover of one way back in the beginning. It was

theatrical rock, and a hell of a lot of fun. So we let that kick us off. Hell yes, our guys back there fired up on the drums and the acoustics. Keyboards were coming in too. I missed my guitar right now.

Missed it like I'd miss my arm. And as spontaneous as the performance appeared, we followed the one cover with a set list we'd rehearsed earlier. All old songs, first two albums with one from the third.

When we finished that, we held our pose, fists up as the applause rose in a crescendo and splashed over us. After we dropped them, I took two steps forward. Here, we formed a triangle.

"Are you guys still having fun?"

Their applause, shouts, and catcalls assured me they were.

"I can't say thank you enough for coming out and there are so many more great performers here for you. Don't worry, we'll be back before the night is over with a brand new song—"

I had to pause cause the screams rose. It was kind of humbling to feel their excitement throb in the air around us.

"You like that, huh?"

I chuckled but I let them get their shouting, stomping, and clapping out. Sometimes, you just had to feed the moment.

"Thank you—as I was saying—the three of us will be back out before the evening is over. We're going to perform a brand new song for you. A song that I wrote for a very special some-one. That someone is part of the reason we're here. This concert is about raising funds to help find a cure for childhood cancers. Someone very close to me was diagnosed last year and that sweet angel has been fighting ever since. We're lucky, because we have access to great doctors and she has an amazing medical team that I am so grateful for."

Tears clogged my throat, but I took a deep breath.

"I am so grateful for that team and for our team—our fans and our listeners who got tested when we said we were looking for a donor. The fight is far from over, but tonight is for all of those kids fighting that battle. We can do this, to help arm them to do that. So—before we go—one more song and then we'll turn the stage over. Stick around though... and we'll see you later tonight."

I had to blink because of the tears but what was more was the shouts and the applause and the just simple caring. Yeah, they were here for the show and for all the acts that weren't just us. But they *were* here.

That mattered.

Aubrey took point and I followed her lead even as I threw her a grateful smile. We ended up doing three more songs and we were gonna run this show over. The producers could yell at me later.

When we finally headed backstage, I was dripping sweat. We needed a costume change, thankfully, which meant I could peel the spandex and sequins off. Dix was waiting with the guys when I got there. Teddy was nowhere to be seen.

Good.

Jonas cracked open a bottle of water and held it out to me. We needed to vacate the area because we were going to create a roadblock.

"Dressing room?" I said *after* our mics were turned off and removed. I needed a break for real. The chaos back here was everything I was used to. Hell, it was something we all thrived on. But after the performances and the confrontations, I was feeling... *raw*.

Dix straightened. "You bringing everyone?"

"Yes," I told him. "Did Mom get out of here with Jackie?" I focused on Jonas who fell into step with me as Ramsey moved ahead of us with Dix and Lachlan—I twisted to see him motioning both Aubrey and Yvette forward before he moved behind us. We had other security, they were in black t-shirts emblazoned with security on them.

Still, it twisted my heart to see Lachlan looking after my girls.

"She wasn't happy about it," Jonas said pulling my attention back to him as I took another drink of the water. The problem with shows was between performing and the lights, we ran the risk of dehydration. I followed the maze back to our dressing room. There were acts everywhere.

The fact so many had turned out just made my chest tight all over again. I didn't want to start crying out here and I just needed to stand in front of some air conditioning to cool off. We had an hour? Maybe less.

Dix opened the door to our dressing room and Ramsey paused to let us go in first. The smell of the flowers rushed out to envelop us in a garden of scents from roses to wildflowers to orchids and what had to be honeysuckle. I downed another long drink of the water.

"You guys need to change?" Ramsey asked and that was when I realized they were in the hall and it was just the three of us in here.

"Actually," Yvette said. "We should. We'll shower real quick and change outfits. Give us ten minutes."

"You got it." Ramsey locked his gaze on me and I summoned a smile as I glanced from him to Jonas and then to Lachlan.

"Thank you," I mouthed to all of them. We didn't waste time after the door closed. I was peeling off the sticky spandex as Aubrey ducked into the shower first. We weren't washing our hair or anything, mostly just rinsing off the sweat.

I went second, and we were looking at the costumes for our last set when Yvette finished hers.

"I say we go sexy as hell," Aubrey said, nodding to the silver and blue sequined outfits that would look more painted on. "But we can hang out for another twenty in something comfortable before we change, and you need to talk to your guys."

The last she directed at me.

"Agreed," Yvette murmured, pressing a kiss to my cheek. "We're going to be next door in the other dressing room..."

"Guys, you don't have to—" But they were already opening the door to let Ramsey and the others in. Not Dix though, Yvette hooked her arm through his and tugged him away.

In the blink of an eye, I was alone with the guys and Ramsey cracked open another water bottle. "You need to hydrate."

I chuckled because Lachlan was cracking open a sports drink too. "And you need electrolytes."

"I can go get you food," Jonas offered. "But I'm not sure you eat between sets."

"No," I told him with a grin. "I barely eat on concert days. Just too much moving. We can eat after...like breakfast food with huge pancakes and waffles."

Jonas frowned and when I sat down on one of the sofas, Jonas took the table in front of me while Ramsey sat down next to me. Lachlan folded his arms and leaned back against the door like he needed to make sure it stayed closed.

"How are you doing?" Ramsey asked. "I know Gibs being out there..."

I shrugged. "Well, I can honestly say that I've seen him—I guess that's something."

Ramsey frowned but Jonas knocked his knee against mine lightly.

"You sounded amazing out there," Jonas said. "You have never sounded so raw or so pure before. Or maybe I just needed to come to a concert."

"Thanks guys...I'm just—I shouldn't be surprised that my parents made it about them. Yet, I am."

Sliding an arm around my shoulders, Ramsey pressed a kiss to my temple. "Tell us what you need, Siren. We'll make it happen..."

"Or not happen," Lachlan said flatly. "But Ramsey is right. Tell us what you need."

"I need Pen to get better," I told them. "I need this relationship between all of us to work. I need my best friends..." I leaned into Ramsey even as I caught Jonas' hand and met Lachlan's gaze. "That's not too much to ask, is it?"

"What about your Mom?" Jonas asked.

I shrugged. "Mom is Mom. She will always be a little too dramatic and a little over the top. But with her home, maybe I have a chance of getting her away from that so-called guru she is engaged to..."

Lachlan's frown deepened. "Need me to call my dad? He does a lot of legal work."

"I appreciate that," I told him and I did. "I have lawyers too and if I end up needing his help, I will ask. I promise."

He nodded, then knocked his head against the door lightly.

"You okay?" Because where Ramsey and Jonas seemed concerned, Lachlan was furious. It radiated in the air around him.

"I'm fine. We're not worrying about me," he said flatly, then straightened. "You don't have that long. Drink up and then we need to get you girls back out there." He scanned the room. "In fact, you guys stay with her, I'm going to get more drinks."

The door closed before I could say anything. What the—

"He wants to beat them up for you," Ramsey said.

"Who?"

"Everyone," Jonas answered with a shrug. "Me too. But he

already got to punch Teddy...I'll take care of hitting the next one."

I opened my mouth, then closed it again as a bubble of laughter escaped. "You guys do not have to fight my fights for me...I am quite capable of punching someone."

"Beautiful hands with a beautiful job," Ramsey informed me before lifting one of my hands to his lips to kiss the knuckles. "Besides, Jonas and Lachlan live to fight."

Rather than argue, Jonas just grinned.

We had five more minutes, so I closed my eyes and just leaned into Ramsey while Jonas kept a hold of my free hand. I'd drink more in a minute.

Ten minutes later, I let Yvette do up the back of my outfit while Aubrey did hers, then it was my turn to do up Aubrey's. The skin-tight suits were a combination of spandex, mesh, and sequins. They left our legs and our arms bare.

A knock on the door warned us that makeup and hair were here. Lachlan came in with them and his gaze burned me up as he swept it over me. Ramsey and Jonas were out in the hall with Dix.

We had three minutes to spare, barely, when we made it back to the stage where we had to pause to get fitted for our headsets and mics.

Thankfully, there were no parents or managers here to deal with.

Bowing my head, I took several deep breaths.

"Sixty seconds," our tech said.

"Thirty..."

I lifted my head and then it was time. The roar of the crowd as the last act left the stage redoubled as we strolled back out.

"Bonjour," Yvette said in a silky tone. "Miss us?"

Four

"This way," Dix said as the girls strode out on the stage. I cut a look at him. Ramsey stared after KC a beat before he frowned at Dix. For his part, the bodyguard motioned to the back. "We're going around again. Better to be where they exit the stage than over here and in the way."

Yeah. He had a point. Still, I shot a look toward the stage as the three of them got the audience revved up again. I hadn't realized how they handled the stage together. They traded off who took the lead both in vocals and in charming the crowd. I always thought of KC as the star—

Or maybe I'd just decided she had to be. When you thought about Torched, you thought about Kaitlin Crosse— her blue hair, her stunning blue eyes, and the tangle of tattoos decorating her arms. Yvette and Aubrey were both good look- ing, I supposed. They seemed to get attention, but I couldn't take my eyes off KC and I didn't want to even try.

I scanned the backstage as we followed Dix around the

stagehands and others who were hustling. It was a constant hive of motion back here. Made sense... Once we arrived at stage right where they would exit, Lachlan began to pace.

His agitation made me itch. Where Lachlan kept moving, his attention divided between the monitors that let us see the stage from the audience angle and looking out onto the stage itself, Ramsey was absolutely still. Arms folded, he stared at the stage with a nearly expressionless face. Anger thrummed through me.

Gibs.

Her manager.

Her mother.

Did anyone come through for her that wasn't here to get something for themselves?

"You better not be here to talk to any of them," Lachlan said abruptly and I pivoted to face Teddy. Speaking of scum sucking pieces of shit. A red mark marred the underside of his right eye and part of his cheek. That was going to leave a bruise.

Good.

Lachlan was closer, but since he already got to belt the manager once, maybe he'd let me have the second go-round.

"What do you need?" Dix asked when Ramsey just fixed a cool, impersonal gaze on the guy. Yeah, Teddy ambushed KC. I didn't give a damn what he wanted.

"They need to do press," Teddy said, barely sparing us a look, though he was keeping his distance. "Soon as they come offstage, we need it for the behind the scenes look and for the special that's airing."

I wanted to argue against that.

Lachlan clenched his fists.

Ramsey, however, sighed. "We'll tell them when they come off. But if they don't want to, we're not making them."

Them.

Her.

It was the same thing. Those girls were a team. More, they were friends. I could wish I was worth that kind of loyalty.

"Agreed," Dix said, then faced Teddy. "You won't get them there if you're the one who tells them."

Of that, I had no doubt.

The man sighed. "She'll figure out soon enough that it was business. Those few minutes out there were golden and will fuel online discourse and more for months."

I snorted.

"You really believe that?" Ramsey sounded disgusted. Probably hard not to sound annoyed and disgusted by that behavior, it was reprehensible.

"I know *that*. My job isn't to pat them on the head or look after their feelings. It's to look after their bottom line and their contracts. That ten minutes on stage to open with her dad— the first time they've *ever* performed together? That's a gold mine."

"She's never going to thank you for it," Lachlan warned him and his knuckles were white.

"She doesn't have to," Teddy said as he smoothed back his hair. "Press room, as soon as they are off stage. This isn't negotiable. They know about the drive by and we're going to need at least five minutes with all three of them and possibly another five or ten individually."

"Like I said," Ramsey stated coolly. "We'll let them know when they leave the stage."

But if KC or any of them wanted to leave, then we were leaving. Somehow, I doubted she would go though. This event was too important. It was why she'd stayed out on that stage. Why she'd gone right back out there now. The transition as she shook off the sadness and defeat to strut onto that stage had to be seen to be believed.

"Dix," Teddy said, switching his attention.

"Yep," the other man said without a look at Teddy, his expression was less friendly than Lachlan's and he hadn't been there for the ambush. Then again, he wanted KC to himself and he really didn't like us.

The feeling was utterly mutual.

"Yeah, you know—" KC's voice drifted back as they took a beat after their last song. "We promised you something brand new tonight. It's a new single, our first to be released since we took our break. Music is a passion. It gets into your blood, sets you on fire, and never lets you go. Sometimes, I think music is the best thing I've ever experienced and others...I worry that it's the cruelest of mistresses. I love music. I want to give it my everything and sometimes it takes everything from me. As much as we needed that break from touring, the music was still there."

"She's also got a way with words," Aubrey teased. "If you haven't noticed." I caught KC flipping her off on stage and the roar of laughter and cheers from the crowd said they didn't miss it either.

"Thank you," KC said with a grin then she stared right into the camera like she was looking at me. "Just so you all know, songs, like a lot of creative works, aren't made in a vacuum. Even when I write the music, the girls listen to it and offer tweaks and suggestions. I do the same with theirs. It's collaborative. We're lucky, the last couple of years I've gotten to work with someone who is—gifted. Let's just say, his music? It gets you right in the heart and it doesn't let go.

"The best part is he isn't just a gifted songwriter, he's my friend—"

"Our friend," Aubrey agreed and KC shot her a dazzling smile.

Then they both looked at Yvette who made a show of huffing a long sigh. "Fine, *our* friend." Then she winked at the camera. "Don't let this go to your head."

I couldn't help my own smile. They were playing with the audience, with each other—

"Jonas Dekkar was there when I was writing this next piece and he helped bring it to life. So, while this is our new single—it's Jonas' first to be recorded, so you should all keep an ear out. He's gonna do amazing things."

My heart stopped.

"Thank you, Jonas," KC said. "I'll talk to you soon."

Then the music started as the crowd cheered and I forgot how to breathe. Ramsey clapped a hand on my shoulder and I cut a look up at him. All at once, KC's voice rose above the music and jerked all of my attention back to the stage. I couldn't take my eyes off them.

The interweaving of their vocals was the final piece to crown all the elements that had gone into the song. KC had written the music and the lyrics. Yes, I offered some advice, but this piece was all her.

It was her heart.

Her talent.

Then their voices lifted each other and it was—pure ecstasy. In all the times I'd heard them practice the last few weeks, they hadn't performed it like this. They'd worked on shifting the bridges and building in the chorus where they would blend their voices. I thought they were singing it in three parts, separately, but their harmonizing took it to a whole new level.

The power in the ballad held their audience riveted. It gripped me. There was one thing to write the music, to hear it in my head, and it was entirely different to hear it coming from them. KC was so damn magical. I never wanted to just listen to her on a recording again.

The real thing? So much better.

By the time the last note drifted away, the silence held the crowd hostage for a few seconds. They had to be as equally stunned as I was, but not for long. The cheering rose like a tidal wave, the sound echoing all the way back to here.

They didn't linger on the stage this time, blowing a few kisses before they jogged off stage, even as a new act strode out there to pick up the proverbial baton. Sweat gleamed on her arms and her legs. The light danced over the glitter and rhinestones decorating KC's face as she made a beeline right for us.

My heart fisted at the directness in her approach. I had no words. None. She was the one who wrote the lyrics, but the song in my soul was one thousand percent for her. When I held out a hand, she glided her palm over mine and then I was hugging her.

"Thank you," I whispered against her ear. The soft brush of her lips to my throat sent a shiver over my spine and when she pulled back a little, I dipped my head to hers. I wasn't big on the public displays. Kissing KC wasn't about notoriety, hell, far from it.

She tasted like sweet lemons and a hint of sweat. There was a muskiness underscoring her scent that I wanted to bathe in. But more, I wanted to drink in her nearness as her lips parted under mine. I tested the welcome with one swipe of my tongue and she fisted my hair as she sucked my tongue deeper.

I wanted to drag her somewhere quiet, steal away with her, and kiss her until the hint of tears in her eyes and the ragged notes in her breathing were gone. But even as the thought took purchase in my brain, I had to let her go as she leaned her head back and then her smile at me was everything.

"Hi," she whispered.

"Hi." Yeah. I was good with "hi." Still a little dazed, I needed to take a step back to remember where we were. As it was, Aubrey was grinning at me. So was Yvette. KC wrapped her arm around mine and I'd rather break my arm off than pull away.

Lachlan wore a brooding look that Ramsey mirrored.

They didn't look pissed, just worried. Dix, however, looked furious. I wanted to smirk, but I didn't. 'Cause kissing KC was about KC and about me. No one else.

"You need to swing by the press room," I said quietly before the dick brought it up. "Your manager told us that they were going to need five or ten to talk to you three about tonight."

"Promotion," Yvette said with a sigh as she accepted the water bottle Ramsey handed her. KC took one as well but she didn't drink it yet, instead she glanced at me then nodded to the hall.

Yep, time to go.

"How much do you want to bet they're going to ask about who we're dating?" Aubrey said.

KC groaned. "No takers. Though I bet my dad is at the top of the list they want to talk to me about."

"Or your three boyfriends," Yvette teased, but she lowered her voice so it didn't carry, Dix had begun striding ahead of us as if to clear the way.

"Who I'm dating isn't for public consumption," KC said, then she stole a look up at me, then over at Lachlan and Ramsey.

"Not planning on giving an interview, Ace. But can we get out of here after you talk to them?"

He was still antsy and hadn't stopped moving. Not that I blamed him. It was irking me too. There were so many people back here. I recognized a lot of the acts, but they were all moving, either heading for the stage or heading into dressing rooms.

Gibs was coming out of the press room as we got there.

"For real?" Aubrey muttered and I was right there with her. KC's hand tightened on my arm and I shifted to put myself slightly ahead of her. Not that I needed to bother,

Lachlan moved right in front of both of us and Dix even dropped back.

"Fuck," Ramsey muttered and it didn't take me long to realize why. Gibs wasn't alone. Mom was right there with him.

Her expression went from smiling to thunderous as she locked eyes on Lachlan. Nope, not just Lachlan. She glared past him to me and then to Ramsey before she stared at KC.

Gibs pivoted, cut off her laser glare and he studied all of us before he looked at KC. Teddy was there too, wading into the fray. Great, the only one missing was her mother and I really hoped she wasn't here. She'd ranted all the way out to Jackie's car and even then she hadn't wanted to get in.

It was a stand-off with Mom and Gibs standing between us and the press room. "C'mon, sweetheart," Mom said as she rubbed her hand down Gibs' arm. "We should go. I think you've donated more than enough of your time." Her tone clearly said he shouldn't have.

Fine, whatever, as long as they left KC alone.

"Actually," KC said, letting go of my arm as she stepped forward. Lachlan stilled as she put a hand on his back before stepping out from behind him. "Dad—do you have a minute to talk?"

"This is probably not—" Mom began.

"I wasn't talking to you," KC said, never once taking her gaze off Gibs. "Dad?"

Gibs glanced at Mom then KC. "I always have time for you, Kaity. Do you need to talk to the press first? I'll wait."

"It could be a bit if I go in there..."

"I won't leave," Gibs promised.

"Gibs—"

"No, Linzi. If you're tired, you can go. I'll catch up with you later. I want to talk to Kaity." Gibs pulled away from Mom and oh boy, her expression...

"Mom," I said, throwing myself on that fire. "I can walk

you out if you need it." Not that I wanted to leave KC, but maybe getting Mom far away from her was a good idea.

"No, I don't need it. My place is with Gibs. So if he's waiting, I'm waiting... for Kaity."

"My name is Kaitlin," KC told her, in a cool voice, "Only Dad calls me Kaity. And you're..."

"She's my wife," Gibs said gently.

"Yeah, that doesn't mean that much to me Dad. She can't stand me and the feeling is probably going to be mutual. But I do want to talk to you."

"Then go talk to the press, Sweet Kaity, and I'll be here when you come out."

KC hesitated and who could blame her. I'd hesitate too.

"He'll be here," Ramsey said.

"Yep." Lachlan backed him up. "We'll be right here too."

Translation, we would keep an eye on them. Yeah, I could do that. "You guys got this?

I checked with KC as well as Aubrey and Yvette.

"We have her," Yvette said. "Dix can come in and keep an eye on things in there."

Good. The press wasn't going to do anything, right?

"C'mon," Aubrey said, taking KC's hand and then they were heading for the door. Mom had to back off and so did Gibs to get out of their way. As soon as the door opened, cameras went off and questions began to fly. Dix stayed at the door, holding it until all three were through. Teddy didn't follow them.

The door closed again, leaving us out here with Gibs and Mom. The manager excused himself and then it was just the five of us.

"How can you—" Mom started but Gibs shook his head.

"Linz," he said, his voice quiet. "Not now."

Impatience creased her face and she glared at us before she wrapped an arm around him. She was really unhappy. For the first time in my life, I found it really hard to even care about that. Gibs didn't react to her contact, his gaze was on the door to the press room.

Arms folded, I moved to lean against the wall and a moment later, Lachlan dropped back to lean next to me. We weren't going anywhere without KC.

Period.

Five

KC

"How do you approach the balance between maintaining your privacy and connecting with your fans?" The question came from Mike Reader. He was a familiar face in a sea of strangers. Far closer to Dad's age than ours, he'd interviewed us before. I was actually kind of surprised he was here.

"Not well," I admitted. The three of us split who spoke into the microphone. I could have let them answer, but I could handle this. "But we love our fans, so we do our best."

Not that the press let us have that much in the way of privacy. Kissy Kat, for example, happily made up all kinds of stories with her speculation. She didn't need to talk to us to come up with the doozies she liked to report.

Then again, Mom and Dad hadn't always been that circumspect either. Mom liked it when they were talking, because as long as people cared about the scandals,or lack thereof, in her life, the more she stayed in the public eye.

At least that was her theory.

"Are any of you dating currently?" There came the question.

"Maybe," Yvette answered with an easy smile. "We don't kiss and tell. We leave that for the gossips." The fact she added a saucy wink earned us some laughter.

"You took a break to go to school, but you've graduated now, right? Are you looking at another tour soon?"

"We've been discussing it," Aubrey said, keeping it noncommittal. "Trust us, when we're ready to announce, you guys will probably be amongst the first to know."

I bit back a smile.

"Miss Crosse," someone called from the back and I focused on the woman standing there. I didn't remember her name but she worked for one of the billboard sites. "Can you tell us more about the inspiration behind tonight's new release?"

"Let's just say that she's very close to me and I adore her. While we put ourselves out there and sacrifice our privacy, I don't want to do that to anyone else, you know?" At her faint nod, I plowed onward. "That said, she does love it when we sing to her and tell her stories so that's why I wrote the song the way I did."

"Two more questions," Teddy said as he appeared next to us. "We need to get these girls going again and we have more acts for you to talk to... Jet?" He nodded to one of the reporters in the room who was more of a celebrity podcaster than a reporter these days. We'd sat down with Jet before and been on his show.

"Thanks, Teddy. I have a question for all three of you. Aubrey and KC are both attending college, but Yvette isn't. Are you ladies planning to break the band up permanently?"

"Never say never," Yvette commented. "And I am going to college, I just prefer my classes online. As for the rest of it, these ladies are my best friends and my sisters. Whatever we choose to do, we'll always have each other's backs."

That was an excellent answer.

"KC," Demi Brown got her hand up next. "Throw us a bone. You performed with your dad tonight, it was a first on stage together...what was that like for you? Performing with a legend while being a legend yourself."

Despite the fact I was aware they'd have questions about it, I still took a moment to consider my answer. Teddy shot me a look but I shook my head. No, I didn't want him cutting anything off.

"That's hard to answer," I said, choosing as much honesty as I could. "I used to imagine what it would be like to perform with my dad. You know, hard not to when he's the one who taught me to play half the instruments I know. That said..." I touched my tongue to the roof of my mouth. "Nothing I could have imagined even touched the reality of it."

And I was leaving it at that. Let them interpret the answer how they wanted. "Thank you," Teddy said as he moved in to take over the microphone. "We've got more coming up for you."

Dix got the door opened and held it to let us out. Relief coursed through me. I was still sweating from the stage, and my stomach had been doing flip-flops since Dad appeared in the hallway with the new wife.

I half-expected Dad to be gone when I got out there but he was present along with the guys and... what the hell was her name? Linzi. Her name was Linzi.

Fuck, I hated her name. Worse than being Dad's wife, she was Jonas, Lachlan, *and* Ramsey's mother. Which meant as long as they were in my life, so was she.

Ick.

Lachlan brushed his knuckles down my arm before he

offered me another fresh bottle of water. Belatedly, I realized Ramsey was holding out bottles to Yvette and Aubrey as well.

"All good?" Lachlan asked softly.

"Yeah," I said slowly even as I locked eyes with Dad.

"Where do you want to do this, Siren?" Ramsey asked. He and Jonas moved in closer to form a semi-circle around me. We were still in the hall, Linzi glared daggers at me. Dix and the girls were right there and the guys were firmly on my side.

This was—a lot.

"Dressing room," I said after a beat. "Somewhere quieter."

"We can do that," Dad said as he pushed off the wall. "Lead the way..."

I nodded and pivoted. Rough sympathy waited for me in Jonas' eyes and I gave him a small smile. I could do this.

"No, Linz—this should just be me and Kaity..."

The comment had me pausing to glance back to where Dad was facing Linzi.

"The boys are going—"

"To wait for Kaity, if you want to wait for me," Dad said, his slow tone lingering on those last few syllables. "But I'm gonna talk to my girl now. Alone."

"I guess I'll wait then," Linzi said, her expression blanking.

"Oh boy," Lachlan muttered under his breath and when I shot him a look, he shook his head.

Dix took lead again, with Aubrey and Yvette right behind him. I followed with the guys and Dad trailing us. I didn't know if Linzi followed to wait outside or if she stayed right there.

Frankly, I didn't care.

I'd downed about half the water before we got to the dressing room.

"You wanna change first?" Dad asked me when I pushed open the door. Oh, I glanced down at the sparkly outfit and shrugged.

"If you can give me another five minutes?"

"Not going anywhere."

"I'll help," Aubrey said as she and Yvette slid inside with me. Undoing the zippers, I stripped out of the sequins and spangles, then pulled on a tank top and panties, before sliding into capri pants.

"You wanna do your makeup now or later?" Yvette asked as she zipped up her hoodie.

"Later, it feels like the longer I make him wait, the more I'm chickening out."

"You aren't chickening out of shit," Aubrey said. "You also don't owe him a damn thing."

Their support was everything. "Maybe not," I said, agreeing with them. "But the thing is...I have questions. Like, why is he here? Why now? He hasn't even asked about Pen. I know Jackie sends updates so maybe he doesn't care but..."

"He paid your ransom," Yvette said softly.

"And he knew our music," Aubrey added. I caught their hands and we formed a small circle together. "That's something."

It was something.

"I'll try not to take too long," I promised them.

"You take as long as you need. And keep hydrating. We'll be next door." Yvette kissed my cheek and then Aubrey.

"Hey," I said before they opened the door. "Tonight? I loved being out there with you two again."

Aubrey grinned. "We still got it."

Yeah, we did. "And we'll talk about that later," Yvette said with a wink. Dad was waiting just outside and the girls let him in. I found a smile for Ramsey before Dad closed the door and it was just the two of us.

"Hey, Sweet Kaity," Dad said and my heart squeezed. He really was one of the only people who called me Kaity. Dad and Tracy. They were it.

Sweet Kaity had been his nickname for me forever.

"Hey, Dad," I welcomed him inside and waved to the sofa. "Want to sit?"

He moved over to the sofa and dropped down. There were more water bottles, cold ones in the room and I passed him one before I took a seat on the end of the sofa. Dad's eyes were red, and his pupils were a little blown.

It hit me, all at once. He was high.

"You on a lot? Or just weed?"

"Just a little weed," he said. "Nothing more than a relaxer. I'm good."

Uh huh.

"You?" The question made me raise my eyebrows.

"Do I sound like I'm on drugs or stoned?"

Dad's fingers twitched. The smell of tobacco and smoke lingered around him. He probably wanted a cigarette. Or a joint.

Or both.

"No," he said, before he unscrewed the top of the water bottle. "Wasn't sure about how you partied...it's been a while."

"I try not to party," I admitted. "Bad for the reputation and for the brain." When I needed to cut loose, I ran or I went out dancing.

Or I had sex.

But I wasn't having *that* particular conversation with him.

"Yeah, I guess...biz is a lot different from when I was coming up."

I shrugged. Sure, that was it. "Dad..."

He looked at me again.

"Thank you for paying the ransom."

"You were really in trouble?" His frown deepened. "We thought—or maybe I hoped it was a prank for attention."

"It wasn't a prank," I promised him. "And they still don't

know who took me. And why would I prank you for attention? You barely notice me now."

"That's not true..."

"I've called you three times in the last six weeks." The hurt was there and it burned in me. "I called you over the summer. I called you last spring after they found me."

Dad frowned.

"You have *never* called me back." It was hardly the first time and as much as I promised myself I wouldn't cry, the tears were right there. "If you never wanted to see me or any of us—fine. I've gotten used to that. But why are you *here*?"

"I've never said I didn't want to see you," Dad argued. "I'm so damn proud of you. But I know the demands, I thought that was why..."

"Why what?"

Dad pulled out his phone and stared at it for a minute.

"What number are you calling me at?"

Was he for real? "Did you change it?" I climbed to my feet and went over to the duffel where I'd stored all my stuff when we got here. Taking out my phone, I walked over to show him the number.

And the messages I'd sent.

Some of the sleepiness left his manner as he stared at the screen on my phone and then at me. When he unlocked his phone and studied the screen, I gave him a minute but he kept scrolling.

"Dad?"

"This doesn't make sense. That's my number," Dad said. "But I don't have any messages from you."

I stared at the blank screen where voicemails went. "You don't have any messages."

"Nah, Linzi cleans it out for me. The numbers make me nuts but I don't always want to listen to all the messages, you know?"

No. "So, Linzi gets my messages and just deletes them?"

"She wouldn't do that, Sweet Kaity." His protest didn't sound all that believable though. "She's—she's a good woman. Puts up with me. Never judges... maybe she should have. But she's been there. Those boys..."

Resentment unfurled within me.

"The boys you have time for when you don't for your own kids?"

Dad stared at me. "I've always had time and respect for you . It's why I told you that I wasn't going to make you go back and forth anymore. Jen was getting too damn pushy and always trying to put you in between us. I didn't want you feeling pressured..."

"You told me I didn't have to come anymore and then to call you if I wanted to see you before you went on a world tour and I never heard from you." I stared at him. "And it's not just about me. It's about Tracy and Bronson and Pen..."

"Trace cut me off a long time ago," he said, shaking his head. "Jackie doesn't want me around Bronson unless I get clean. I make sure they get their money though, or my people do. I've always been good for that."

"And Pen?" I threw down. "Allie? Cam? Zeke?"

Fresh confusion clouded his eyes. "Who's Pen?"

"Give me my phone," I said, holding out my hand. He passed it over and I switched to photos then pulled up pictures of her. When I held one up, he stared. "This is Pen. This is my baby sister—*your daughter*—who has cancer. She is the reason we're doing this whole damn event."

He stared at the picture then down at his own phone a minute before he looked at it again.

"Pen... short for Penelope?"

"Yeah, ringing bells now?" Anger flash-fired through me.

"No, sweet baby, I don't—I've never seen her before." He studied the picture. "I didn't—she can't be that old. That...

maybe one of the last tours. Linzi...she got mad at me for hooking up and told me if I couldn't keep it in my pants, I could at least just keep it on the road. So...yeah that's what I did."

I dropped into my seat.

This was not information I wanted to know about him.

"Who are..."

I flipped through the photos. "Cam." I held it up. Then scrolled to find Zeke. Allie took me the longest. "They don't have our eyes. Just Pen and me."

"And Trace," Dad said. "Bronson got his mama's eyes. Jackie is—a good woman. Hell of a woman. She knew about Jennifer and she...told me I had to choose, not between you kids but between her and Jennifer." He sounded almost bewildered. "Never liked having to make that choice...but then we had you, and I can't regret that."

"Could have fooled me. Because you never chose us... your kids."

"That's not true," Dad argued. "I told Linzi that I was putting you first. Always. Ask her. She knew that. You kids all came first with me. But I'm not always good at the dad stuff and that's why I wanted you to not have to worry about it if you didn't want to see me. Your mamas are—mostly good."

Mostly good.

I rubbed a hand against my face, then belatedly remembered the glitter on it. "You have four kids you don't even seem to know about, and the three you do know, you never talk to...so tell me again how you put us first? Or is Linzi the gatekeeper there too?"

Because I didn't like her before.

I could hate her right now.

Six

RAMSEY

The night spiraled radically through varying layers of intensity. Excitement for the performance. The thrill of getting to see them on stage again. This had been so next level compared to the first time I saw them perform. More, as much as I enjoyed the music, I savored the connection between the three girls. Shame burned inside of me over the idea I'd ever thought of Kaitlin as cold, distant, or uncaring.

She was absolutely *none* of those things. The misery in her eyes when she left her dressing room gutted me. Mom had been right there, her anger at all of us palpable. Interestingly, she said *nothing* while Aubrey and Yvette were present. Instead of disappearing into the other dressing room, they'd taken up residence to protect their girl.

Our girl.

And I intended to make sure they had all the room they needed. That she needed. No one was getting close to them. Or bugging them.

"Kaity," Gibs said as she zipped up her hoodie. She still wore her stage make-up. The concert was continuing. I thought they might need the girls for the end but they were only doing the two sets. Well, three if you counted the one Kaitlin had done with Gibs. "I'll call you."

She stared at him for a long moment, then shrugged like she didn't care. Piece by piece, she was putting on a face for the rest of the world. "If you do—I'll answer." But nothing in her manner or her tone indicated she thought he would. Then she turned and there was no mistaking the way she gave her back to Mom when she looked at us. "I'm ready to go, if you guys are."

"Yep," Yvette straightened. "Let's grab our bags." She and Aubrey nipped in to bring out their duffels. I moved with Lachlan and we took the bags from them, Jonas already had an arm around Kaitlin's shoulders. The tired radiating off of her made my soul sick for how upset she was.

"I'll get the car," Dix said. "You do not step outside until I text."

"We'll be fine," Lachlan informed him, irritation drenching every single word. Somehow, I doubted that irritation had to do with the man himself and more for our mother and stepfather. Dix, however, shot Lachlan a glare before he stalked outside.

"Deep breaths," Aubrey murmured to Kaitlin. She or Yvette kept hold of one of her hands. Jonas had the other. The fact she was holding Jonas' hand and not Lachlan's, had to be contributing to his upset. Or maybe he was as annoyed with Gibs as I was.

The time spent waiting with Mom and Gibs hadn't been pleasant. Particularly cause Gibs kept saying "no," whenever she suggested they move away or leave or in any way abandon the spot he was waiting in. Then when Gibs went into the dressing room, Mom looked ready to make a scene. But Yvette and Aubrey hadn't left, and their presence seemed to mute Mom.

Security opened the door. "Ladies," he said. "Your car is here and we've got an audience waiting at the ropes. Do you want to go straight to the car or are we doing autographs?"

Straight to the car? I shot a look toward Kaitlin who had lifted her head and squared her shoulders.

"Autographs?" Yvette seemed to turn the concept over verbally, but her gaze was on Kaitlin. They shouldn't have to do any of this.

"They're waiting and they showed up," Kaitlin said with a sigh.

"We're going to do autographs," Aubrey said. "Do we have enough security out here or do you want us to wait?"

The guy gave a once over. "We have enough. The guys go straight to the cars, you girls will each have an escort and we've got additional on the perimeter."

"I'm staying with KC," Jonas said.

I wanted to stay with her too... "I'll keep watch over Aubrey," I offered.

"Oh, delightful, I get the ninja dick."

Lachlan's glare vanished for a moment when Kaitlin laughed. From the smug look on Yvette's face, I had a feeling that was what she intended.

"How long are you going to need?" More to make sure we all understood.

The girls exchanged a glance. "No more than a half-hour," Kaitlin said, and the decision seemed to settle her. "More acts will be wanting to leave, so we're better off keeping it efficient."

"Then divide and conquer," Aubrey adjusted her hoodie. And it hit me why they'd not removed their cosmetics. Besides the fact that Kaitlin wanted to talk to Gibs, their exits would be photographed.

It made sense to not give the press something to give them hell about. It registered that Kaitlin stared at me. "You okay?" The soft question had me reaching over to squeeze her hands.

"I'm fine. Stick close to Jonas. We'll all meet at the car."

The corner of her mouth quirked, then she nodded. "I'll take left," Kaitlin said.

"I've got right," Aubrey agreed then glanced at me. I nodded even as Yvette shook out her hair before she unzipped her hoodie. She was wearing a spangly crop top under the hoodie.

"That means I'm center stage," Yvette said with a wink at Kaitlin and Aubrey. Her smirk grew when she glanced at Lachlan. "Try to keep up."

He snorted, but he didn't dispute her.

Thirty seconds later, I was right behind Aubrey as she followed Yvette and Lachlan out the door. The girls worked like a team, their strides out to meet the fans who all started yelling and waving. More than one autograph book or piece of paper was thrust out. I kept pace with Aubrey and her security. I didn't get in the way, but I was keeping an eye on everyone else.

Security helped stay between the girls and the crowd, limiting the interactions. I could practically feel Dix glaring at us from where he waited with the car.

It seemed to take forever. Ten minutes after we got out there, we'd barely moved a few feet and Aubrey had already signed a dozen things. They were given gifts, everything from flowers to bears to t-shirts. They were asked to sign even more. I found myself scanning every single face.

Were the people who stuck her in that fridge out here? Were the gossips who posted all those stories about her out here? What about the fire? Was someone here who set that?

"Relax," Aubrey said in a low voice and it dragged my attention to her as she turned away from the rope. "You're glaring. Don't," she continued then patted my chest as she handed me some of the gifts she'd received. "It draws attention and you don't want to do that right now."

I blew out a breath, then nodded as I took the pieces. A moment later, someone from security took them from me. They were collecting all the gifts together. Smart. We weren't taking anything with us. The next fifteen minutes took forever, but then Kaitlin was blowing kisses to the crowd as she headed for the car. Yvette and Aubrey were right behind her and that meant we were too.

Once I settled inside, Kaitlin slid up next to me and I lifted an arm so she could lean against me before I draped it over her shoulders.

"Lemon water," Dix said over his shoulder. "We're a good hour to get clear of all this and then out to Beverly Hills, unless you girls want a hotel for the night."

I glanced down at Kaitlin and she let out a sigh. "The idea of running away to room service and anonymity is amazing—but Jackie took Mom to the house."

Her mother.

I didn't sigh, but I did press my lips against her hair. The smell of her perfume was just under the hints of sweat and hairspray. "What do you need us to do?"

"Just—don't let her chase you out when we get there." Kaitlin knocked her knee against mine lightly. "She'll be in a mood."

"We can handle her," Yvette said as she glanced up from her phone. "Jean-Paul is here, so after we get everything settled, I'm going to steal away for the night."

"Have someone drive you?" Aubrey said.

"Yep," Yvette agreed without any nudging. "Did you hear from Forrest?"

"No," she answered, but she also wasn't looking at her

phone. "I didn't think he would call tonight anyway, and we have plans next weekend after we're back on campus..."

Campus seemed a million miles away. The ride back to the house went almost quiet and when I stole a look down at her, I realized Kaitlin had gone to sleep. Her breathing had evened out and her hand was pressed against my thigh. Eyes closed, she curled into me.

Silence drifted in the dark of the car. Darkness broken up periodically by the passing lights helped to insulate against the rest of the world. The quiet seemed to have a texture, almost like a blanket after the noise of the backstage area and the concert itself.

The lack of sound was a strange thing. It could be comforting or intimidating. Safe or threatening. At the moment, it was none of those things. It stretched out like a vast gulf. Separating all of us while also isolating us together.

Jonas' head was back and his eyes half-closed. Lachlan's eyes were open and his attention riveted on Kaitlin. Not that I blamed him. The evening had been grueling for her. Grueling for all of them, emotionally, mentally, *and* physically.

When we passed through the gates to the Beverly Hills mansion, some of the tension bled out of me. The hush in the car remained and Yvette sat up a little and twisted to glance up at Dix.

"Pull us up to the side," she said in a voice pitched low. "KC's out. Aubrey and I can deal with Jennifer tonight."

"Do you need help?" Jonas asked, smothering a yawn.

"Nope," Aubrey said. "You three get her up to her room. I'd recommend crashing out up there in her suite. Tomorrow will be here soon enough."

Neither waited for us to agree. As soon as Dix stopped and Lachlan had the back door open, they hopped out and headed in.

"You got her?" Lachlan asked as I shifted forward. She was

out, she barely even shifted as I slid an arm under her legs and lifted her.

"I got her." I kept my voice low. We all were. And as I climbed out, balancing her, it was hard to miss Dix's dark stare. "Thanks," I told him. "We got her from here." Then I headed inside.

We were on her side of the house, these doors opened right into her wing and saved us having to go through the center. Right now, I didn't want to spend any time with Jennifer Crosse if I could help it.

Jonas went ahead of me, but Lachlan waited for me to head inside before he followed. Ten minutes later, we had her up in her room and I carried her into the bathroom.

Her groan as I roused her made me feel a little bad. "I'd let you sleep, Siren," I promised her. "But you still have all your stage makeup on..."

And I couldn't imagine that was a good idea. Smothering a yawn, Kaitlin blinked up at me.

"I didn't mean to fall asleep," she muttered. "I have to deal with Mom..."

"Nope," Lachlan said as he let himself into the bathroom. He carried over sleep shorts, a tank top and a t-shirt. "Got you the stuff you like to sleep in. Need to shower? Or just wanna wash your face?"

For a moment, I thought she would argue but then she ran a hand over her hair and then looked at me. "Mom is okay?"

"Yeah," Jonas said, leaning in the door. "She's great. Get ready for bed so we can."

It was a little bossier than he was usually and she summoned a smile. There she was, rallying.

"Okay, I'll shower real fast."

Then she was stripping off clothes. I wasn't the only one helping. Though Jonas shifted to turn his gaze elsewhere, he stuck close. Lachlan got the shower on and I helped Kaitlin get glitter and rhinestones off her face.

When she ducked into the shower, I half-expected Lachlan to follow her, but he just waited—like I did. As unabashed as she was standing under the stream of hot water, she was also tired. It was clear in every sway of her steps. As soon as she finished, I held out a towel for her and she wrapped it around her middle and Lachlan helped her towel her hair.

She fumbled with a braid, but Jonas moved over to help and then I held out the clothes Lachlan had carried in. She chose the t-shirt. I tugged it over her head for her and Lachlan whisked away the towel. Then Jonas caught her hand and walked her into her bedroom proper. She climbed right into the bed and then looked at all of us...

"We can go," Lachlan offered and I knew it had to cost him. At the same time, I was damn proud of him for at least *asking* her for what she wanted.

She stared at us for a long time, me, then Lachlan, and then finally Jonas. He was parked on the edge of the bed.

"Can you guys just all sleep in here? There's room..."

"You sure?" I wanted to make sure it was fine with her.

"I want you close," she said softly, then added, "I don't want to be alone."

"Dibs on the shower when I get back," Lachlan said. "Gonna grab stuff from my room."

"Yep," I said, then eyed Jonas as Kaitlin settled against the pillows. "You need anything?"

He shook his head. When he laid down next to her, she gripped his hand and curled it to her chest. Before Lachlan even made it back, she was out again. I stroked some of the hair back from her face. I rubbed a hand over my face.

I thought she might be too wired to sleep tonight, but the weariness draping her just made me tired. Lachlan ducked into her shower as soon as he was back.

"Mom was trying so hard to make sure they didn't talk," Jonas said quietly and I nodded.

Yeah. I'd gotten that too.

"Is it our fault?" The question made me frown and I glanced at him.

"Is what our fault?"

"Mom wanting to take Gibs away from KC. Do you think she was doing that for us?"

Raking a hand through my hair, I shook my head slowly. "No. I don't think we had anything to do with that choice."

Curled up around Kaitlin, Jonas was mostly out by the time Lachlan emerged.

"Keep an eye on them."

He didn't respond with anything sarcastic, just nodded before asking, "You want to sleep with her or do I get the free spot?"

"Not sure I'm gonna sleep," I told him. "So if you can, go for it."

I bumped my fist against his shoulder before I went for my own stuff. It was quiet in the hall, but I found myself checking the doors and then locking up behind me as I made my way back into her suite.

There were a lot of people in the house, including her mother, and I didn't trust very many of them. By the time I showered, shaved, and changed, the guys were sound asleep, bracketing her on either side.

I settled on the sofa where I could keep an eye on the door and on Kaitlin. Tonight had been great, despite the ambushes and whatever the hell was going on with our mother and hers. At the same time, I didn't want to invite any more trouble. I could sleep later.

Tomorrow would be here soon enough...

Seven

KC

Warmth blanketed me everywhere. A soft snore drifted alongside me where I floated. Gradually, awareness of a hand on my hip and another holding my hand against a chest and the steady thump of a heartbeat penetrated the sleepy fog. My mouth was dry and my lips stuck together.

Morning breath was gonna suck. Movement had me trying to drag my eyes open and I swallowed a groan when it registered that I was cheek to chest against Jonas. It had to be him...the visible tattoo was one of his. Lifting my head, I blinked slowly. The room was cast in twilight.

My room.

Right. We were back at the house. I barely remembered coming in the night before, I'd showered, washed my face, then braided my hair and...

The bed shifted behind me and the grind of an erection against my ass had me twisting just a little. Lachlan.

I was in bed with Lachlan *and* Jonas. With care, cause I

didn't want to wake them up, I glanced around my room. Ramsey was asleep on the sofa. Dressed in a t-shirt and shorts, he sprawled with one arm tucked under his head and his free hand against his abs where the shirt had ridden up.

All three of them stayed with me.

Gratitude fisted in my chest, gratitude and relief. Now that I was awake, my bladder was letting me know I needed to pee.

Bad.

It took a little squirming and care to ease out from between the brothers. I had to eel down the bed without grinding back against Lachlan or forward against Jonas. Though the moment I was eye to groin with him, gave me a little thrill. While I hadn't felt his erection, he was also very stiff and his penis peeked out from his boxers.

Once I made it to the floor, I stood slowly and stretched. Oh, fuck, I was stiff everywhere. Stiff like I hadn't been in a while, cause we'd put on a performance the night before. Extending my hands to the ceiling, I tried to loosen up the tightness in my shoulders and back.

Stealing a look back at the bed, I grinned. The guys hadn't moved. But there was an open space between them. I kind of wanted to crawl back up there or go curl up with Ramsey. But first—I needed to pee.

I was doing a dance by the time I got into the bathroom. Emptying my bladder had never felt so good. After, I washed my hands and my face, then brushed my teeth. My hair was still pulled back into a braid, though there were wisps escaping. When I let that out, I was going to have very wavy hair.

A light knock on the door warned me before it opened and I turned to find Jonas standing there, all rumpled hair, pillow impression on his cheek, and sleepy eyes. I forgot how to breathe. His gray eyes seemed to lock onto me. I wanted to drown in the storm brewing within them. I don't know who moved first, and I didn't really care. I went from standing at the sink to having my arms around him and his mouth fused to mine.

The heat of his palms skating down my sides left a trail of fire in their wake. When he slid his hands under the shirt and gripped my ass, we both paused. Lifting his head, he stared at me.

"Apparently, panties were optional," I whispered and the corners of his mouth curved a little higher.

"I like that," Jonas murmured, before he dropped another kiss on the corner of my mouth. Then his fingers flexed against my skin before he gripped and lifted me. The door was closed and the marble of the counter was cold on my ass when he set me there. "I like that a lot."

The dip in his voice sent a shiver through me and I didn't mind in the slightest when he nudged my shirt a little higher.

I let go of him long enough to tug it up and over. The air was chilly against my breasts, but I was burning up. When Jonas' gaze went to my lips, I licked them and then he cupped my face before he kissed me. I drank in the taste of him as he thrust his tongue against mine.

His kiss was both a demand and a request. The calluses on his fingers were a little rough. They were familiar to me. The calluses of a musician. Then he was kissing from my lips to my throat as he skated his hands down to cup my breasts. My pussy clenched and I was torn between running my fingers through his hair and tugging at his clothes.

"KC," Jonas whispered against my ear as he started to roll one of my nipples before he pinched it. The sharpness of pain had me arching my back. It also conflicted with the shudders passing through me as he nuzzled my ear. "I've never done this before..."

The admission penetrated the haze of want he was filling me with and I dragged my eyes open to meet his gaze. A flush touched his neck and spread up to his cheeks. He glanced down at my breasts then up to my eyes.

"Made out in a bathroom or had sex?" I wanted to clarify because there was a lot of this right now that we hadn't done before. Our kisses had been limited, and he'd not been pushing for sex at all, but the press of his erection against my bare pussy was enough to make me want to lift my hips.

"Both?" Uncertainty filled his eyes and my heart squeezed. I cupped his cheek and the stubble prickled against my palm. "I didn't mean to take your shirt off now but..." He licked his lips as he tweaked the other nipple. Even as he spoke, he kept massaging and teasing my breasts. It was going to drive me a little mad.

"Hot Shot..." A smile pulled at my lips as he flashed me a grin. "Jonas..." It was my turn to lick my lips and I reached out to tug at his shirt. "I'm not exactly an expert, but—I'm more than happy to be your first, if that's what you're ready for right now."

If I hadn't been this close, I might have missed the catch in his breath.

"I wanted to kiss you last night," Jonas said, his voice thicker all of a sudden. When I pulled at his shirt, he let go of my breasts to yank it off. It was funny, sex with the guys had opened up a new way to connect. At the same time, I never really got to enjoy them without their clothes. Jonas had a lot more muscle than he seemed.

It was hard to miss as his arms flexed when he hooked his fingers into his boxer shorts. I pushed off the counter and covered his hands with mine. "Can I?"

He gave a little jerky nod and I tugged them down before I could talk myself out of it. Nerves fluttered in my gut as his cock seemed to spring free. It was red at the tip, flushed a deep crimson, and damp at the slit where a bead of pre-cum escaped. I slid down with his shorts, bringing myself eye to cock as it were.

The flash of heat that went through me on the bed when I'd wiggled my way down returned with a vengeance. I ran my hands over his thighs, the spring of curly hair on them tickling my palms. Lifting my gaze, I whispered, "I really haven't done this before either..." Then I kissed the tip of his dick without looking away from him.

Jonas gripped the counter as I ran my tongue in a circle around his tip, lapping away the bitterness of the pre-cum. I didn't make a face, even with how unfamiliar he tasted, because I wanted him to become familiar.

"That feels good," he told me on a ragged note and I smiled before I wrapped a hand around his base and gave him a slow pump before locking my mouth around him again. I understood the principle behind a blowjob. I wasn't one hundred percent sure I could swallow him all the way into my throat, or that I wanted him to come in my mouth—

We could figure that out later, right now, I reveled in the way his jaw tightened and his eyes widened. When I began to bob my head, he thrust his hips forward. I choked a little and he backed off.

"Shit," he muttered. "Sorry." I gave him an affectionate squeeze then traced my tongue along the bottom of his cock, teasing the vein there before I nuzzled his balls. Every time my tongue touched him, his face seemed to redden more.

"I need to practice," I whispered.

"You can practice on me whenever you want," he said it so fervently, like it was a prayer and a laugh escaped me.

"Yeah?"

"Oh yeah." He touched two fingers to my cheek. "But I want to touch you too, KC."

I sucked at his tip again then let him pull me up. He kissed me, chasing the taste of himself in my mouth and I groaned at every thrust of his tongue. I wanted to make this amazing for him, but I was already grinding. More, I wanted to feel him inside of me.

"Jonas," I whispered against his lips and he pulled back then glanced at the mirror before he looked back at me. "Yes."

"Yes?" The question in that single syllable carried so much weight it threatened to drag me under.

"Yes," I confirmed, then nipped at his lower lip as I gave his dick another stroke from base to tip and back again. "I want you."

"Show me how to make you come," he ordered and then turned me around so my back was to his chest. I locked eyes with him in the mirror as he massaged my breasts. "This? Do you like this?"

"I definitely like that," I exhaled on a sigh. "That feels good. I like it when you—" A little grunt escaped me when he pinched both nipples, the twist and tug added a spicier sense of pain that had me clenching everywhere. "Yes." I told him when he searched my face. Again and again, he tormented my nipples, then I reached up to take one of his hands and pulled it down to my pussy.

His eyes widened as I spread my legs, shifting my stance so I could balance and he could see what he was doing. His hand relaxed in mine as I guided his fingers down to my clit.

"Rub here, slow circles, then get firmer..." I showed him, guiding his hand to teasing my clit. The things that Ramsey had done to me with my vibrator were still fresh in my mind, but I was enjoying Jonas' fascination. He teased kisses along my throat, watching me as he shifted the way his hand moved.

His teasing touch grew more certain and when a whimper escaped me, I tried to swallow it. But the effort was to waste because he grew fiercer in his movements and I was chasing my own orgasm as he teased and stroked. The scrape of his teeth over my pulse made me come and I leaned my head back against his shoulder as he kept teasing my clit even when I groaned.

"I like that a lot," Jonas told me then nipped at my jaw. "Can I come inside you? I didn't bring any condoms."

Heat washed over me at the sweetness in that heady request. "I would love it if you did," I told him and I meant it. "I can try to swallow if you want..." Fuck, I was pretty much willing to do anything right now.

"No, I want to come in here," Jonas told me before he cupped my pussy. "I want to do everything with you."

"How do you want me?" I offered.

Jonas glanced around the bathroom and then he pulled out the bench seat that parked under my vanity. When he sat down on it and tugged me to him, I straddled his lap, one knee on either side of him. We fisted his cock together and teased him along my slit. His breath was coming in pants.

"I don't know how long..." He admitted then shuddered as I slid him into me, just the tip. "Oh, you're hot—KC."

"Right back at you, Hot Shot," I teased him as I put my hands on his shoulders and then sank down on him. I went slow until he gripped my hips. I swore he got thicker as I took him inside, or maybe it was the angle. "Oh, fuck..." I let out another shudder.

"Bad?" Worry coated that word and I sank the rest of the way down before I brushed my lips to his.

"No, you feel—fucking amazing..." I didn't have the words for how it felt, especially the way the wonder in his eyes pierced me as deeply as his cock did. When he shifted my weight, I began to roll my hips, writhing up and then down. My nipples were almost too sensitive, everywhere I brushed against him, it set off tremors.

I flexed around his cock and savored how much it seemed to split me each time I sank to the hilt. It was both torment and a bliss. When Jonas gripped the back of my neck, it dragged all of my attention to his eyes. "I need to move," he warned me. I locked my legs around his hips as he stood suddenly and then my back was against the wall and his hips were pistoning.

All hints of gentleness and ease faded as he ground into me with every thrust. He fisted my braid. The pull lit up my scalp and then his mouth fused to mine. The angle of his thrusts and the position of his pelvis kept setting me off, and then another orgasm rushed over me as his hips stuttered. Heat bloomed inside of me as he came and his shout lifted me even higher.

Then we were just clinging to each other. Sweat made his skin slippery. Dampness trickled down my thighs. The sharp pants of his breath made me smile, not that my breath control was any better.

"I want to do that again," Jonas told me and this time, a laugh escaped me.

"You and me both, little brother," Lachlan said from the other side of the door. Fresh heat swept over me. "You guys are not quiet and that sounded hot as hell."

Jonas locked the door and the distinctive click burst through the silence and I cracked up.

"Asshole," Lachlan called.

"Yep," Jonas answered, then grinned at me. "We're busy—go away."

Eight

LACHLAN

Waking up to the sound of Ace's moans had left me with a hard-on that even jacking off twice in the shower—*alone*—wasn't fixing. I could come, sure, but it wasn't the same without Ace. She, on the other hand, seemed attached to Jonas, so I wasn't stealing her away. At least, not yet.

Fair was fair. I didn't want to let her go after that night in the club either.

Or the car.

The night before, I got to sleep right next to her. I'd take what I could get.

Ramsey had showered right after them and I grabbed one after. They waited while I got dressed. In fact, when I came out of the bathroom, I drank in the sight of her laughing. She'd pulled her hair back into a ponytail. The blue tresses seemed to shimmer in the sunlight spilling in the windows.

Dressed in a tight t-shirt that was not quite a crop top, though it periodically gave us peeks at her tummy, as well as a pair of shorts, she was the most relaxed I'd ever seen her. Considering how exhausting the night before had to have been, I was fucking happy to see it. Folding my arms, I leaned against the doorjamb and studied the way they were all sitting.

She was on the sofa that Ramsey had crashed on, feet propped against the little coffee table, flanked by Jonas on one side and Ramsey on the other. With two fingers on Jonas' arm, she was discussing musical credits and that he would need to sign a release for them and she would make sure he got paid for his work on the song he'd helped to write.

"You don't have to do that," Jonas said slowly. "I just loved that you sang it."

"I don't have to do a lot of things," Ace countered, stretching her legs out one at a time before she crossed them at the ankles. There was a stiffness to her movements. There had been a lot of time on stage and she'd danced, sung, and then had to deal with all the emotional turmoil backstage.

Sliding my hand into my pocket, I pulled out my phone. The messages from Mom ceased sometime around one in the morning. Either she'd given up or she'd been distracted. I needed to talk to Dad before I spoke to Mom again. Too many things weren't adding up.

"Jonas, just go with it," Ramsey said with a laugh. "You did the work, and Kaitlin wants to make sure you get the credit. These are not bad things."

"But I did it because I wanted to help, not because I wanted credit..."

"Those things aren't mutually exclusive," Ace told him and he covered her hand on his arm. There was a fixed earnestness to him. Irritation scraped through me, not because of his need for reassurance from Ace, but because that uncertainty had its roots elsewhere.

"Little brother," I drawled. "Here's the cool part. You did

it to help Ace and succeeded, in spades. Now she wants to acknowledge that and help you in return. Right?"

She shot me a quick grin before turning to Jonas again. "I want to show my appreciation *and* I want everyone to know what a talent *you* are." Discomfort was written all over him. "I know you think it's too much or maybe you don't want the attention... I get that. But I *want* to do this and if you ultimately decide you don't want this eventually, we can work out a pen name for you."

Jonas let out a long sigh, then he surprised me when he cupped her face and kissed her. Irritation flamed through me at the possessiveness in the contact. Since when did Jonas have more luck with girls?

Fuck girls. With *Ace*. Since when did he—Ramsey caught my eye and gave me a bland stare and I shook my head. No, he didn't get to say shit either. The whole thing annoyed me.

"Fine," Jonas said after a minute, pulling our attention. "Thank you." Leaving it at those two words seemed to be almost a struggle for him, but Ace raised her hand and then stroked it through his hair. Some of the tension went right out of him. "I mean it," he added in a quiet voice. "Thank you."

"You're more than welcome." The soft curve to her lips held just a bit of triumph. It wasn't smugness. Far from it. But there was a definite element of pleasure that shut down my envy. She really did want to do this for Jonas. Her smile faded as she leaned her head back. "And I suppose we need to go down..."

"You don't have to do anything you don't want to," I informed her a beat ahead of Ramsey's "No, we don't."

She smiled at me, then lifted her shoulders. "Actually, I do. We have a house full and I'm kind of surprised that no one has come up to get us yet."

"They did," Ramsey told her. "Davina knocked to let us know that breakfast was going to be a late brunch." He checked his watch. "She was holding everything until one and if you need longer, she told me to call down."

Surprise flickered over Ace's expression. "When—"

"When you and Jonas were showering," I commented. Red flushed her cheeks and Jonas' grin actually grew, even if his neck went pink. And I could give them hell, but... "Still, you don't have to do anything you don't want to do, Ace. We can get out of here whenever you want. We can call a car or I can drive one of yours for you."

I hadn't forgotten about what she said with regard to getting cars as presents when she couldn't drive. That shit needed to change and soon. In fact... In fact, when we got back to school, I was going to start her driving lessons. She needed to know how.

"I can't take off," Ace said with a sigh. "And before you guys tell me I can do anything I want, I really can't. Mom is here and I need to talk to her before she makes any more crazy decisions. Yvette and Aubrey are here and we have to discuss what happened last night about Teddy... and we have a couple of interviews we're going to need to do. Then, I want to go see Pen."

The last sentence echoed with how important it was to her. "Can I steal five minutes with you before we head down?" I kept my focus on Ace and not my brothers. Jonas' expression tightened but Ramsey actually looked more thoughtful than annoyed.

"Kaitlin?" Ramsey managed to sum up a lot in the single utterance of her name. I shrugged it off because I did need to talk to her and I didn't want to have the conversation with an audience.

"It's fine," Ace said, brushing a kiss to Jonas' cheek before she twisted and gave Ramsey one. "If you don't want to go downstairs without us, just go over into the sitting room and we'll get you in five?" She raised her brows at me and I nodded.

"I'll try to keep it to five." But it would take as long as it took.

"Behave," Ramsey said, giving me a firm look and I folded my arms even if I mentally flipped him off. His faint smirk said I didn't hide the urge from my expression. Fine by me. I didn't need to make excuses to him.

"Or else," Jonas tacked on and Ace seemed to be struggling with a smile as they trickled out. I shook my head, waiting for the door to close before I focused on my girl.

She met my gaze, head tilted, waiting. Unfolding my arms, I joined her on the sofa and took the spot Jonas had abandoned. One arm on the cushion behind her, I kept my hands to myself. As it was, I struggled to keep my gaze off her kiss swollen lips or the shadow of at least one hickey I could see on her collarbone.

Twisting, Ace bumped my knee with hers as she shifted so she could sit sideways and face me. "What's up?" she asked, breaking the silence while I turned over all the words I wanted to say.

"A lot," I admitted. "More than we have time to discuss right now."

"Okay." The steadiness in those blue eyes of her kept me riveted.

"You really are fucking gorgeous," I admitted and the corners of her lips tipped upwards. "You were magical last night on that stage." Beyond magical. "I couldn't take my eyes off you—but this morning..." Now I gave into the urge to cup her cheek, I kept the contact light. "You're just—you take my breath away." Then I grimaced. "That's cheesy as fuck."

"Nothing wrong with a little cheese," she murmured, then she pressed her hand over mine and some of the tension bled out of me. "Did you really ask me for a private conversation to just compliment me?"

The words were edged with teasing and I grinned. "Not exactly, but you should be told how beautiful you are—inside and out—often."

Surprise flickered in her eyes and I wanted to kick myself. Yeah, I needed to make a point of making sure she knew these things. "No lies, Ace. I've been attracted from the beginning..." I stroked my thumb over her lower lip. "From those smoking eyes to this fuckable mouth—my dick has been hard from day one."

"Felt like that when you threw me in the pond." The reminder stung. "And when you cut off my bra." Hurt flashed across her face. "Or when you insulted my tits."

The last time this subject came up, the porn star punched me in the face. I probably deserved it.

No probably about it.

"I think your tits are magnificent," I told her. "But they aren't what attracted me, Ace. Not kidding here—the spirit, the fight in you, the fact you never backed down from me— hell you didn't back down from any of us. That was sexy as hell and I wanted more."

This close, it was impossible to miss the way her pupils dilated. "Lachlan..."

I pressed my thumb to her lips, more to keep myself from kissing her than silencing her. "I need to say this," I told her. "I need you to know that this isn't just a game for me. I want more than sex in a car or sex in a night club—not that I didn't enjoy those, but I *need* more with you. The way you love your family and your friends? I want to be worth that. If that means I have to prove shit to you, then I'll fucking prove it."

Sucking in a breath, I brought my free hand up so I could cradle her face in my hands.

"I listened to you have sex with my brother this morning and I hated it..."

She swallowed.

"At first." I stroked her cheeks. "But listening to how you sounded? That was hot as hell. Watching them with you? I hated it."

"At first?" The question was a whisper leaving her lips.

"Not all the way there, yet." I could be honest about that. "But I'm working on that—just need you to let me work on it and let me be there for you too."

"Lachlan..."

"I get it, I'm an asshole. Not saying I won't continue to be an asshole." At her pursed lips, I laughed. "You can handle me, Ace."

She scraped her teeth over her lower lip and then she sighed. "You're terrible."

"Yep," I said. "But that's not a denial."

I dipped my head, testing her willingness. When she covered both of my hands with hers, I hesitated.

"Kiss me, Lachlan."

She did not have to tell me that twice. I fused my lips to hers, pouring every ounce of my feeling and want into it. She tasted minty, like her toothpaste and the warm scent of her filled my lungs. Fuck, I wanted her.

The urge to strip her down and have her right here had my hands shaking. I dragged out her lower lip as I made myself let go or we would definitely be here for another five hours if I had my way.

My brothers were not going to give us that much time.

She licked her lips and I grinned. I liked the fact I could still taste her on mine. "I want to take you on a date..."

"You mentioned that," she whispered in a breathy voice. "And I said I had conditions."

"Then set them, but as soon as we're back at school, I

want our date. I'd press for now but there are other things that need your attention."

"You don't want to know what the conditions are?"

"Do your worst," I dared her before I pressed another kiss to her lips. "I know I plan on it."

Nine

KC

From waking sandwiched between Jonas and Lachlan to discovering Ramsey sprawled on the sofa to Jonas following me into the bathroom, I was practically buzzing. Energy hummed under my skin. There was a looseness to my muscles that left me floating. That was definitely the orgasms. A girl could get used to waking up to those.

At the same time, it was more than just the physical contact. The determination in their eyes and the warmth they wrapped around me with their words. Even Lachlan—maybe especially Lachlan. His declaration this morning left me a little off-center, but not in a bad way. Of course, now we had to go downstairs and face the chaos.

Ramsey and Jonas were waiting for us in the hall. This part of the wing was silent. But then, sound didn't carry up and around the curve of the staircase.

Nice architecture.

"Dumb question," Ramsey said, a frown tightening his brow. "Why is there a deadbolt on your bedroom door?"

I shrugged. "To keep people from wandering in my room when I'm in it. Lot of parties here when I was younger." There would typically be parties here *now* except Mom had been off —doing whatever she was doing with her cult boyfriend. *Fiancé* whispered a snarky voice in the back of my mind.

Jonas' scowl deepened, but it was Lachlan who looked suddenly furious. "Someone came after *you* in your *room*?"

"Nothing happened, but after the second time someone just showed up in there, I asked Davina for a fix. The lock was it." Then because it happened a long time ago... "Some parties get out of hand, I just didn't want anyone else deciding my room was where they got laid. So the bedrooms on this floor all got deadbolts and the only ones with keys are me, Davina, Dix and the girls." Since Aubrey and Yvette stayed here.

"Not your mom," Jonas said slowly, cutting a look down the hall then back to me.

"No," I answered that and left it there. Blowing out a breath, I pivoted to face all of them. "Look—Mom isn't perfect, far from it. At the same time, her negligence isn't cruelty. She would never deliberately try to hurt me."

We might not be as close as we once were...

"She has a lot of problems, but I know she loves me and she's done her best to support me when she can." Then because we really hadn't discussed my conversation with Dad, I added, "The gulf between me and Dad, I never had that with Mom. Sometimes, I'm more her bestie than I am her daughter, and it's not always healthy. She loves me and I've never questioned that."

The only competition for her affection I'd ever faced was her own crippling self-doubt when it hit. That was usually when she descended into the bottle, the pills, or poor life choices.

Sometimes all of the above.

"I hate the idea you weren't safe here," Lachlan admitted,

chewing the words over like he had to grind them between his teeth. "That you had to lock the door like that."

I shrugged. "I spent the last few years on tour, before I headed to school. Don't worry about whatever it is you're imagining. That's why the locks were there, so I would be safe. It's why Dix could get in if I needed him too—so I would also be safe. There's security here. The girls are here a lot. Now you guys are here."

Lachlan's expression darkened. I stroked his arm, the contact grounded me. He studied me then glanced at his brothers. Ramsey wrapped an arm around my middle and dragged me back against him. A sigh escaped me, especially when Jonas caught one hand and Lachlan the other.

"So, we're going downstairs," Ramsey said, his voice calm and steady. "What do you need us to do?"

Jonas studied me, his deep gray eyes sober and serious. The strength there promised me it would be all right. Lachlan still appeared furious, but the way he focused on me was almost a hug.

"Don't start any fights and give everyone the benefit of the doubt. And—let me deal with Mom." They didn't need that fight.

Ramsey pressed his lips to the back of my head. "Within reason," he said. "But if they start something with you..."

Leaning back, I smiled up at him and my stomach let out a rather noisy growl that Lachlan's echoed.

"Food," I prompted.

After giving me another long look, Ramsey dropped a kiss on my lips then let me go. Lachlan tugged me right to him and the kiss he planted on me had my toes curling and my heart pounding. The sweep of his tongue demanded access, but it wasn't for long. All he did was take a taste before he lifted his head.

When I glanced at Jonas, he was already moving and I met

him halfway. This time the kiss was as sweet as it was heated. He didn't thrust his tongue in my mouth so much as just hold my lips hostage. Then he pressed his forehead to mine before he released me.

Heat suffused my whole body. The last thing I wanted to do was break up the intimacy and go downstairs. But I'd run away the night before. Exhaustion, physical, mental, and emotional had sacked me out in the car and the guys had just gotten me to bed.

"It's gonna be great," I told them, trying to pep myself up. "Hopefully, we have good news from the show."

We needed good news.

"And I need to call Tracy and check on her and Jackie..." Jackie had taken care of Mom last night, I owed her.

"One thing at a time," Ramsey said, then sighed. "I need to call our mother at some point, but that won't be right now."

Their mother.

That information kind of landed between us like a dead fish no one wanted to touch. I made a face, but it was Jonas' expression that arrested me. Emotion drained out of his eyes and he scowled. "We don't need to talk to her."

"Actually..." Lachlan began but Jonas whirled on him and I gripped his biceps before he could raise his fist. Jonas froze at my touch, but Lachlan didn't back off nor did he look at all upset at the idea that Jonas might punch him. "Ramsey's right. We need to call her out on her bullshit. If I wasn't sure before—last night confirmed a lot of things for me."

"I don't want to talk to her," Jonas said, his tone flattening.

"You don't have to," Ramsey said with a sigh. "But we still need to address some issues."

"Not right now," Jonas argued. "I'm here for KC and we're helping her. I don't care about Mom right now."

My heart twisted for him. "Maybe not now," I told him. "But you might care later—"

"She hates you," Jonas said without preamble as he looked down at me. The tension in his arm relaxed a fraction. "I don't know why and I don't care. She's wrong."

I opened my mouth to respond to that then snapped it shut.

"Ace, we'll deal with our mom," Lachlan promised and I made a face.

"Guys...I remember your mom from when I was a kid. Kinda. It was—a long time ago. And I'm pretty sure my mom tried to humiliate her or did...and I'm pretty sure my dad succeeded. Maybe—if they were seeing each other then." I grimaced and the fact Lachlan made a face almost made me laugh. "Yeah, the less I think about that the better."

"Agreed," Ramsey said from behind me. He wrapped his hand around my nape. The weight of his touch combined with the pressure of massaging the stiffness in the muscles there had me sighing. "We'll deal with our mom. I think there's conversations that we need to have *but*..." The stress on that last word pulled my attention. "But not right now and not anything you need to worry about."

"If it affects you guys...I want to help."

"Ditto, so we're doing this one step at a time." The last he added with a firm look at Lachlan. "We face what's in front of us and we deal with Mom later."

Despite his grimace, Lachlan didn't reject the idea entirely. His phone buzzed and he pulled it out. After one look at the screen, he darkened it and then focused on me again. All at once his expression softened.

"You want to go for a run later?"

"Maybe," I admitted. "Depends on how much chaos is downstairs." My stomach growled again. Firming his grip on my hand, Jonas tugged me toward the stairs and I laughed. Food sounded really good.

Davina's food sounded even better.

Lachlan and Ramsey followed, but they were speaking in low tones. Rather than try to listen, I squeezed Jonas' hand and took point. They'd been to the house before and we were staying here for this short trip, but it would probably be better if I was leading, to intercept any issues like...

"Kaitlin," Mom called, her voice cutting across the silence. She was standing in the sunken living room dressed in a silk dressing gown with feathered sleeves. Her cosmetics were immaculate and her hair artfully pulled up and into a tumble.

She looked more like someone playing a character who'd just gotten out of bed than someone who had actually just gotten out of bed.

"Good morning, Mom," I said. "I hope you slept well." Then because I could see the flush in her cheeks and the way her chin came up, I added, "I didn't get a chance to introduce you to my boyfriends last night."

Yes, I said boyfriends.

Mom's eyes widened and I met her stare for stare. "This is Jonas Dekkar. That's Ramsey Malone. And Lachlan Nash." Squeezing Jonas' hand once, I let him go and crossed to my mother.

Mom opened her mouth then snapped it shut again without a word escaping as I brushed a kiss to her cheek.

"You look good," I told her. She really did. "And I'm starving. Davina said brunch at one, yeah?"

"She did," Mom murmured, then cupped my cheek as she studied me before she glanced past me to the guys then back to me. "We should talk, sweetheart. I'm not happy with what your father pulled last night..."

"Mom—"

"No, I mean it. He had no right ambushing you." She

frowned. "That said, I'm not terrifically happy with you either."

"Well, I can live with that. But it will all have to wait until *after* I have coffee." Cause I could smell the coffee, and the bacon for that matter. "I need to eat." My stomach had been growling upstairs. Down here? It was cramping and all I could smell was the food. "Do you want to join us?"

It was the concession I would make for Mom, cause she was still cutting her gaze back and forth between me and the guys.

When she didn't answer or move, I gave her another kiss on the cheek. "I'll be back after I get something then..."

"Wait," Mom said, catching my arm. "I can't go in there." She said the last in almost a hushed whisper.

"Why not?" I asked, glancing from her toward the dining room and back.

"Because—" Uncertainty flickered across her face and she pressed a little closer to me. I was about ready to take that coffee cup out of her hand. Voice lowering further, she whispered, "Johnny is here."

"Yes, he is," I informed her.

"*Why* is *he* here?" The distress in her voice wasn't manufactured. "We broke up."

"Because he's family, Mom," I told her. "He adores you. He's also been super patient. But he needed someone to look after him too. So, you can stay out here, I won't make you talk to him. But I'm also not asking him to leave..."

"If Roger comes—"

"Him, I will ask to leave," I said flatly. "I don't know why you agreed to marry that man, but I don't like him and I don't want him here."

"Kaitlin." She almost sounded scandalized.

Almost.

"Nope," I said. "He's—there's just something wrong with him. Now, I need food."

I let her hand go and pivoted to head for the kitchen, Ramsey glanced past me to Mom. Lachlan and Jonas seemed almost expressionless, but Ramsey had worried written all over him. I caught his hand to tug him with me.

I pushed open the door to the dining room and hit the wall of food scent, and sound. Johnny rose from where he had taken a seat. Yvette shot me a bleary smile and Aubrey just lifted her coffee cup. I felt every inch of that tired. Dix passed me a freshly made latte. It was probably his, but I wasn't going to argue, I needed it too much.

"Thank you," I said to him and he gave me a quick smile that soured as soon as he glanced at the guys.

Right, not dealing with that before I had coffee.

"There you are," Davina said as she hustled into the room and headed over to the silver tray topped serving dishes. "We have everything laid out and warm. I can start fresh waffles if you'd like, or would you care for an omelet?"

I gave Davina a hug after I had my first sip of coffee. She chuckled as she patted me. "C'mon, sweet girl. Let's get you all fed. You have company coming..."

"I do?"

"Yeah," Aubrey said around a yawn. "Teddy will be here in about ninety minutes."

I made a face.

Johnny pressed a kiss to my cheek. "We'll deal with it," he reminded me. "Food first. C'mon..." then he went still and all of his attention riveted to the other side of the room. I didn't have to look to know Mom was there.

"Go see her," I murmured. "Don't let her push you away."

He dipped his chin, but he didn't move. Johnny adored Mom. Worshiped her. When they were together, she was happy.

I needed her to remember that.

Or at least, look for that happiness and not whatever bag of crazy the guru was selling.

"C'mon Ace," Lachlan said as he picked up a plate. "Tell me what you want."

I shot him a grateful look. Ramsey and Jonas were filtering in there too, buffering me from the room.

"I want everything," I admitted. For once, I could actually say it.

I wanted all of them and I wanted all of the food.

I wanted Pen healthy.

I wanted to maybe build a relationship with my dad again.

Yeah, maybe it was unrealistic to want all of that, but it didn't change my answer.

"Then you get everything," Lachlan said with a playful wink and a laugh escaped me.

He was never going to change.

There must have been something wrong with me, cause I kind of didn't mind...

la Leço Ga
107.

Ten

JONAS

Brunch was—not fun. In fact, I wouldn't even begin to use the word fun to describe anything about the meal. Yvette and Aubrey were both sleepy, but they were also watchful. I didn't miss how they studied all of us. KC seemed at ease all the way down the stairs, into the living room where her mother waited. Even there, she just hustled her mom along and didn't let her comments slow her down.

I kind of admired how smoothly she handled it. Especially since Jennifer Crosse was... I really didn't have words for her. She also didn't seem to know what to make of us. Lachlan didn't like her. Or maybe he just didn't know what to do, especially since Johnny seemed so riveted. I was kind of okay with the fact she didn't talk to us and he had all of her attention.

Food loaded onto my plate, I followed KC over to the table. Johnny and the girls had put themselves at the mid-point on the table, separating KC from her mother. That also left the far side of the table for us and my least favorite person—Dix.

He claimed a chair on one side of KC and I took the other. Lachlan gave him a dirty look as he dropped into the chair opposite him. Ramsey didn't say a word, but he wasn't watching Dix, his attention was on KC's mom.

Davina reappeared with fresh coffee for KC and then she looked at us. "I know everyone else's orders, what do you boys want?"

"Jonas drinks what I do," KC said as she picked up a slice of bacon. "Lachlan prefers a double shot Flat White. Ramsey is a black coffee guy, but he won't mind a mocha if we have the chocolate."

I hid a laugh as Lachlan snorted and Ramsey eyed her.

She tossed him a playful look. "Surprised?" Everything in her tone was a dare. She paid attention. It was one of the things I liked about her.

"Impressed," Ramsey told her. "I don't know why though… you've always been talented at picking up on information."

"Awww," KC said, putting a hand over her heart and pretending to swoon by leaning into me. "You say the sweetest things."

It wasn't long before Davina was back. Jennifer didn't do much, just sat there, drinking her coffee and not staring at Johnny. For his part, the porn star—right not supposed to think of him that way—the guy made no pretense of worshiping Jennifer with his eyes.

A foot knocked against mine. I jerked my gaze over to KC who grinned at me before she took a sip of her coffee. Oh. Yeah. I probably shouldn't stare.

"Sorry," I murmured and she bumped my shoulder lightly with hers.

"It's fine."

Aubrey watched us with a small smile and then she shook her head. Davina was hustling in and out. She put food in front of Jennifer.

"Oh, that's too—"

"No, it's not. You're skinny like some little bird. You haven't been eating properly, I can tell from how pale you are. Now, you'll eat at least half of that and I'll bring you more coffee." Davina patted her shoulder. "That's a good girl. Johnny, are you done? Or would you like more?"

Yvette bit her lip as Jennifer stared at Davina for the longest time before she focused on KC.

"This is your fault," her mother informed her, though it didn't sound nasty. It sounded more—resigned.

"Yep," KC said. "What can I say, Mom, I like it when you're eating and taking care of yourself."

The doorbell rang and Dix rose.

"I'll get it. If it's Teddy, do you want me to take him through to the office?"

KC made a face, then she looked at Aubrey and Yvette. One of the most fascinating things about them was the way they could communicate without saying a word. It was like they had a secret language all their own. It was there when Aubrey was around, but far more visceral when Yvette was.

"Yes, please, Dix." KC stuffed another piece of bacon in her mouth then washed it down.

"Don't choke on the food," Ramsey warned and she actually laughed.

"Are you firing Teddy?" Jennifer asked, she'd finally started cutting into her eggs.

"Maybe. Either way, I want to hear his explanation."

"Me too," Aubrey and Yvette said in the same breath.

"And I want to get the final figures from last night." KC ran a hand over her face. All the worry that had crashed out of her expression was back. She pushed her plate away, but she hadn't eaten much.

"You should eat more," Johnny said. "Let that asshole cool his heels and wait for you—actually, let *me* talk to him." He was already standing and Jennifer looked startled.

Oh, if we were going to threaten the manager, I was down with that. "I can help," I offered. I kind of liked Johnny. Guy was—different. But after he punched Lachlan and ripped him a new asshole, I'd definitely become a fan.

"Why would you—" Jennifer began and they were the first three words she'd actually spoken to the guy since we came in. It was like one of KC's reality shows, only I didn't have any background or previously ons to catch me up.

Johnny paused, smoothing down his t-shirt like it was some kind of button-down or suit. He studied Jennifer and there was no mistaking the absolute adoration in the guy's eyes. It was kind of a kick in the gut. "Because she's KC," he said. "She's your daughter. She's my friend. Because that jackass set her up." Straightening, he cut a look in our direction. "Because, no matter what happens, I'll have your back and I'll have hers."

"Johnny," KC said softly. "You don't have to. We can handle Teddy."

"I know you can," he said without missing a beat. "Jonas and I are just gonna entertain him until you're ready. So eat your breakfast and drink your coffee. You need the fuel."

"I'll be back," I promised KC. I wanted to give her a kiss, but everyone was watching us, so I settled for just slipping a hand onto her shoulder. She touched my fingers and glanced up at me.

"Thank you."

I grinned. "You're welcome. But this is going to be fun."

"Don't fire him," Aubrey said from where she reached for her coffee. "We get to do that."

"You got it." I followed Johnny out of the room, aware of the speculative looks following me. But Jennifer Crosse seemed completely focused on Johnny. I hope that worked out for him cause she was—yeah probably better not to finish that thought.

Johnny knew right where to go. From the dining room, we cut through the more formal living room where we'd encountered Jennifer earlier, then to the main hall by the door and to the right where there was a sitting room tucked away.

I needed a map for this place.

Currently, I knew where KC's room was and that was it. If we came out here fairly often, I really needed to learn the full layout.

"You gonna hit him?" I asked a beat away from Johnny opening the door. He had a really nice left hook. It had knocked Lachlan on his ass.

Johnny shrugged. "Probably not." Then he blew out a breath before he glanced back the way we'd come before focusing on me again. "I doubt the guy was trying to hurt her. Don't get me wrong, he's an asshole. But assholes like him—they aren't about personal feelings or hugs. They're about the bottom line. Getting her on a stage with her dad—it was for the money and the attention. It's a viral clip and it's already making the rounds. It makes both of them relevant, casts more light on the charity and on both of their careers."

Distaste curled through me. "That doesn't—that doesn't make it right."

"No," Johnny said, then he shrugged. "It's not personal for him. It's business."

I didn't like that argument. "It was personal for KC." Hell, it was probably personal for Gibs, but I wasn't gonna defend him. The more layers we tore back the more I had to wonder why *he* didn't do something instead of putting the responsibility on everyone else.

"Yes, it was. But we still have to let her handle the business side of all of this." He stared at me as if waiting for me to—oh.

"I would never step on her business." I wouldn't. "But she matters to me and personal is personal."

"Exactly." Johnny clapped my shoulder once. "I like you, kid. We're going to get along great. Unless you hurt KC, then it's personal."

"I don't want to hurt her." It was the last thing I wanted.

"Like I said, we're gonna get along great. Ready for this?"

Squaring my shoulders, I nodded. Johnny shoved the door open without knocking. Dix was in the room with Teddy, apparently keeping him there. Both pivoted sharply. There was no mistake, we'd interrupted something.

Dix's eyes narrowed. "This is a private meeting for KC and the girls."

"Except you're in here," I said as I leaned back against the door and folded my arms. "They're still having breakfast." Dix glared at me and I just met him stare for stare. The more I got to know him, the more I didn't like him.

He was important to KC. I had to respect that.

But I didn't trust him. He was too possessive.

KC didn't belong to him.

Johnny crossed the room to where the two stood, holding out his hand to greet the manager. I kept all of them in my line of sight. It was how I didn't miss Teddy's grimace at Johnny's handshake.

"Teddy," Johnny said. "I'd say it's good to see you, but not really feeling it today."

"Johnny," Teddy said and his voice had an odd—oh, his jaw was swollen and there was a definite puffiness around his lip. Lachlan had gotten a really nice shot in. "Look, you know the business. None of that with Gibs was personal."

"That's what we like to call bullshit. You can say it's about the bottom line and selling the event, hell, you probably raised a lot of money." Johnny sounded just so—upbeat. There was a smile in his voice and an easiness to his manner. Except, he hadn't let go of Teddy's hand and he was bracing his other hand on Teddy's shoulder, keeping him in place.

"We did better than that, we've got all kinds of interest. The media loves a good reunion story. The whole world knows how much Gibs loved his little girl and they all think that little girl is one of their own cause they love her parents..."

"Uh huh," Johnny said. "You don't have to sell me on the story. I understand business and selling image. I even see how beneficial this was to the fundraiser..."

The manager sagged a little, almost relieved. "It raised a huge profile." He sounded almost giddy. "The morning shows have reached out. A couple of the night time ones too. The label is already reporting increased plays, trending hashtags—Torched is getting a huge lift from this. We dropped the album overnight—their single already had twenty-two million hits."

"Single?" I asked. "The one she sang with Gibs?" 'Cause those were his songs...

"No, none of those were released, though the label is asking because some bootlegs are making it up there—" He really was proud of himself. "This changes the whole game."

"Maybe," Johnny said, letting him go. "But you should have made sure she knew what was happening before you ambushed her."

Teddy rubbed his arm as he retreated a couple of steps. He glanced at Dix but the bodyguard didn't say a word. He also didn't look—

Son of a bitch.

He'd known.

I wanted to launch off the door and beat him until the truth fell out of him.

Even as the thought crystalized, there was a light knock on the door. Dammit. I straightened and opened the door. KC stood there, looking absolutely beautiful. While a part of my mind registered the presence of Yvette and Aubrey, KC held all of my attention. For the longest moment that seemed to border on infinity, I wanted to be back in the bathroom earlier. I'd woken up to find her gone and the first thing I'd done was find her.

I just wanted to see her.

Drinking in the sight of her now, I wanted to steal away.

"Time for business?" I asked when I found my voice.

"Yep," she said, keeping her attention on me as she shifted to let Yvette and Aubrey go in first. "After—we can figure out our plans. I know there's gonna be some stuff I have to do before we leave."

"And you want to see Pen."

Her eyes flared and she nodded.

"We'll make it happen." It was a promise.

She rose up on her tiptoes and kissed me. It was a soft contact, all too brief, there and then gone again but the memory of it was a fiery imprint. "Thank you." Her eyes were intent, the color so vibrant and I kind of wanted to find a way to write music about them. But then the shadows moved across them as she flicked a look into the room. "Business first."

"If you need me…" I offered.

That earned me a flash of a brilliant smile.

"I'll be right outside." I'd rather be in the room, but she had Aubrey and Yvette. I would be close.

Johnny squeezed her arm before he slipped out and then KC glanced at Dix.

"I'll stay if you—"

"I don't," she told him and his expression shuttered. Then she softened a little. "Yvette, Aubrey, and I need to have this conversation, Dix. It will be fine. Thank you."

"Of course."

It fucking killed him to leave and have me still be right there, even if I planned to slip out too.

Asshole.

"Go get 'em," I whispered to KC before I gave her another kiss and she grinned. The light shove was more playful than anything and I closed the door behind me as I stepped into the hall.

Arms folded, I settled in to wait and met Dix's glare.

Yeah, he could go get fucked. I wasn't going anywhere.

KC

"You're angry with me," Teddy said without preamble and I didn't roll my eyes. It was a battle, but I kept them focused on him. Rolling eyes and snorting didn't make us look mature. Something all three of us learned the hard way. When it came to negotiations, we had to be the most mature people in the room. Even when I wanted to stomp my feet, scream, and cry.

Teddy faced us with a sigh, instead of sitting though he stood. He had started to take a seat until he realized that the three of us *weren't* sitting. No, we held our ground. Another lesson, when you were short, standing forced them to level the playing field. Some.

Most of this was performance psychology, but the rest of it was practice. We'd needed Teddy's help a lot, in the beginning. We didn't need it now. Not if he was going to pull shit like this.

"Why?" I fired the single question that had been burning

in me since I walked off the stage and found a way to string thoughts together that weren't aching with hurt or screaming in confusion.

"Because you want to raise money," he said, not sugar-coating it. "Cancer is a subject everyone hates and no one wants to talk about. People like to throw money at it because either they've been affected and they want to help. *Or*—they feel guilty that they've never had the issue and they don't want to face it. Three things make money in this business—platinum singles from established bands, breakout hits no one saw coming, and an emotional gut punch that answers a question people didn't even realize they had."

"So—me performing with Dad...?"

"Hits all three," Teddy said, his tone utterly matter-of-fact. The lack of malice or cruelty didn't make this better. Particularly because there was also a distinct lack of regret or guilt. Clearly, this was what he'd said—business. "I didn't warn you because I wanted—I wanted an authentic reaction. Gibson Crosse doesn't agree to perform without his band that often."

So why did he? I wanted to ask the question, but I saved it for when I spoke to Dad. *If* I did. He swore he would return any message and he seemed genuine about the fact he didn't know about earlier communications. But c'mon, he was an adult, how did he go *years* without talking to me and just presume I hadn't wanted to speak to him? What happened to reaching out himself?

I scrubbed a hand over my face as Yvette clucked her tongue. "So Gibson agrees and you just throw KC out there without a word of warning—"

"To be fair, I didn't realize it would be an issue," Teddy said, his first actual attempt at a defense. "He's your father. He's your sister's dad as well, I'd have thought he wanted to be involved."

Aubrey snorted, and I didn't disagree. "Did you talk to him?"

Our manager sighed. "Briefly. Took a little finagling to get him on the phone. When I said you were hosting a charity fundraiser, he said yes—didn't even wait for me to explain." Teddy stared at me, his expression sober and serious. "KC, he *wanted* to be there. As for the rehearsals—"

There it was—the hesitation. "What about the rehearsals?" Yvette asked, her tone carrying a snap. Impatience streaked through her expression, but I could almost imagine what Dad said.

"He thought if he was there, I'd refuse."

One long exhale, then Teddy nodded.

"Which means," Aubrey picked up the thread, the words coming out clipped and sharp. "You damn well knew there *might* be a problem."

"But you did it anyway," I summed up.

For once, something like chagrin flickered through Teddy's eyes. "Yes." No excuses, just an admission. "I believed it was worth it. The sight of you two on stage together, the very organic nature of that performance and how raw it was? It would go viral, and in turn raise awareness, which could raise money. It did. It *has*." He pulled out his phone and crossed over to us.

Just a flick through social media and there we were— trending. Us. Dad. The concert.

I scrubbed a hand over my face and turned away from him.

"KC," Teddy said. "If you want an apology, then I am sorry. I had no idea that your relationship with your father was that strained. We don't—we don't discuss your personal life unless it's to clean up some story and even then...it's usually more about your mother than your father."

Even when it was Mom, especially when it was her. I

didn't explain anything, I just told him what I wanted to do or say. "You still shouldn't have done it. The lack of rehearsal, the fact we'd never performed together—it could have gone very wrong."

"Maybe, but you're a professional. Something I've learned about all three of you over the last few years. You *always* deliver. Exhausted, overworked, and sometimes when you should have said no and taken a break, you've always come through. I didn't like it when you said you three wanted to take a couple of years off and go to school—but I didn't hate it either. I have to worry about the business side of things...you don't generally like it when I try to worry about the personal."

He wasn't wrong. We had all kept some very clear boundaries on that. Maybe too many. I cut a look at Aubrey. Did she believe him?

The dislike in her expression wasn't hard to interpret. Yes, she believed him. She just didn't want to cut him any slack. When she lifted her chin toward Yvette, I glanced at the third of our trio. No emotion reflected in Yvette's expression as she stared at Teddy.

"No more ambushes," Yvette said firmly. "Period. I don't care if you want an organic response or you aren't sure if something is going to happen. Correction: *we* don't care. You're our business manager, you're there to help us manage contracts and arrangements. Not our lives. You make a decision like this again and don't warn us—you're fired."

"We'll call this a warning," Aubrey continued, catching the lead. "I believe you meant well. I believe you thought this was a great idea and it may be proving beneficial."

"But it could have also gone really, really wrong," I added. "And I did *not* enjoy those moments at all." I'd been raw, exposed, and far too vulnerable. It might have earned me a conversation with Dad. It might even lead to some kind of reconciliation someday—but that wasn't the point.

Others meddling in our communication was already a prob-lem. We didn't need more. *I* didn't need more. "Do you understand?"

Teddy frowned. "I'd say I was sorry, truly. But it would only be half-true. I'm sorry that it hurt you. I'm not sorry that it helped your cause."

As brutal as it was, honesty was better. "But half of it would be true, so I'll take what I can get."

"So—I'm not fired?" Teddy clarified, his voice and expres-sion sober. Which was good, because right now if he smirked, I'd probably give in to that initial urge and punch him.

"For the moment," Yvette agreed in a chilly voice that just made me adore her. "We reserve the right to revisit this should that change. We're also serious, no more surprises."

"None," Aubrey emphasized.

Hands raised, Teddy said, "Understood. Now that I've been handed my ass, can I show you the initial numbers? I think that they will make you a little happier…"

"WE'RE GOING TO HAVE SOME VERY STRICT RULES going forward," I explained to Ramsey as I packed my bag. We were headed to the airport after I spent some time with Pen. The red eye back to the East Coast. "Particularly when it comes to springing surprises, as in he doesn't get to do it again."

"Are you really okay with that?" Ramsey studied me. He'd settled on the edge of the bed, hands locked together and elbows on his thighs. We'd been closeted away with Teddy for the better part of two hours.

"Yes—" I said. Then blew out a breath. "No." I dropped a shirt into the duffle and spread my hands. "I—don't know."

Ramsey caught my hand and tugged me to him and then I

was in his lap and he wrapped a hand around my nape. "It's okay to not be okay."

I glanced down to where he held my hand. His fingers were longer than mine and his palms broader. The weight of his arm around me helped to ground out some of the nervous energy.

"I don't know how I really am. I—I hate that he did it. At the same time, I got to talk to Dad. I mean, really talk to him for the first time ever. Maybe—maybe his not talking to me isn't his fault and at the same time, why didn't he ever just try to reach out to me? I'm not the only one in that relationship."

Not saying anything, Ramsey just kept holding me and a shudder escaped.

"Then he acts like he has no idea about Pen, or Zeke, Allie, Cam—and I know he doesn't know about Tracy." That was a given. Tracy hadn't wanted to tell me because she'd been worried about my reaction, and more worried about what the celebrity status around me would do to shine a light on her. "How the hell does Dad not know about his kids? There are child support payments—"

Payments.

It couldn't be that stupid, could it?

"Hey," Ramsey murmured, the slow stroke of his fingers against my neck easing the tension knotted there. It made me kind of want to curl up and purr in his lap. "Talk to me."

"Just—Mom has accountants and business managers, they take care of all the bills and payments. Then there are the lawyers and the agents. I have them too—there's a lot of stuff they just take care of so no one has to think about it." My eyes drifted shut as he found a particularly tight spot. "It's how I can block the fiancé of hers from getting access to her money and her properties. Not all of it but—enough."

"So, you don't have direct access to your own money?"

"I have a discretionary account. All of us do. It's like petty cash, but our major expenses are all taken care of for us. If we need clothes or instruments or gear—" Just mentioning instruments made my heart squeeze thinking about my guitar. "Tours have a lot of income and expenses. It's better to centralize it. Also—the more money that stays in the business, the better it is for taxes."

I blew out another breath.

"Even emancipated, it's better to have savvy business persons involved to help manage the assets. It helps us to avoid being defrauded but also from being too impetuous with the money."

"But you know where everything is," Ramsey said slowly. "I seem to recall being informed that you managed a lot of your own business, and that you didn't get to where you were by being an airhead."

I grinned. "This is true, and I made it a point to learn. I've been lucky, I have a lot of good people around me. Aubrey and Yvette are the same way. It's one thing to be told something is a good decision, it's another to take all the facts and line them up to make the decision ourselves. I don't—Mom has made a few bad calls before just because she listened to someone else. Then she didn't know how to fix it. Makes me uneasy to do the same thing."

"Okay, so you think that Gibs' management people—his attorneys, manager, label—they've all conspired to keep the truth from him?"

"I don't know," I admitted. "I think that's what bothers me more than anything else. He seemed so—genuine. Course, he was also kind of high. But how do you not know? And he's been with your mom..." I bit my lip. Maybe I shouldn't bring her up.

"And apparently cheating on her a lot too," Ramsey said with a shrug. "I don't know either, Siren. What I can tell you is that I plan to find out. Mom—knows something. That much was clear to me last night. If she has had anything to do with keeping you away from Gibs, someone needs to call her on it."

I wasn't sure I could care about Linzi Crosse and her plans, or why she did what she did. "I just don't want this blowing back on you guys." And I didn't.

Sliding his hand to the side of my neck, he stroked his thumb along my jaw until I tipped my head back so we could lock gazes. "I don't care if it blows back on us," he promised. "I care that I get you the answers you deserve and the ones I need."

The squeeze around my heart was almost painful. "Thank you."

"You're welcome," he murmured, then nuzzled a kiss to my jaw. "Now—what else do you need to pack or need to do before we leave to see Pen?"

Need. Not want.

"I have to talk to Mom. If she's up for it." I made a face. "Is Johnny still here?"

"Yep, he and Jonas are thick as thieves, or they were before I left to come up here." His droll response made me smile.

"I'm glad they are getting along. He's still not a fan of Lachlan."

Ramsey laughed softly. "Don't worry, Siren. Lach can take it."

Made me wonder... where was Lachlan? But I didn't ask. He could be giving me space. Another sigh escaped me. "I guess I should get up then."

"You don't have to do anything," Ramsey assured me. "If you need to sit here for a little longer, I'm not going anywhere."

Another smile tugged at my mouth. "You trying to win friends and influence people?"

"Nope," he whispered, then pressed a kiss just behind my ear. "Just looking after you."

Curling into him, I settled my head against his shoulder. "Then, I'm just going to hang out here for a few more minutes."

He didn't say anything, just tightened his arm around me and pressed a kiss to the top of my head.

Twelve

RAMSEY

Only two visitors were allowed at a time inside the pediatric intensive care unit. Jonas was in there with Kaitlin, leaving me and Lachlan in the hall. We could observe though the window. The four of us—with Dix driving—had come to the hospital so Kaitlin could see her sister before we headed back to school. The last—I checked my watch—sixty-seven hours had blown past us. The benefit had taken nearly all of her time.

The benefit. Her manager. Her parents. I scrubbed a hand over my face. Gibs had never seemed like a guy with feet of clay. While the past few months had been illuminating, the last three days brought it all into sharp relief. There was no way Mom didn't have something to do with the broken relationship between KC and her father.

More, there had to be others in the loop. Gibs never struck me as an especially talented liar. He preferred to get high, be mellow, play his music, and just get along. Pretending to be utterly unaware of how many kids he had didn't seem to fit that. He admitted to three of them.

Tracy. Bronson. Kaitlin.

Kaitlin, though, was the only one he brought up to us regularly. That made sense if Jackie—I was going to need to make a flowchart for all the various members of Kaitlin's family—refused to let Gibs have a lot of contact with Bronson while he was getting high regularly.

That made sense.

I had no idea what his relationship with Tracy had been before. Since she'd been circumspect about contacting Kaitlin the past few years, it seemed a safe bet she wasn't talking to Gibs either. I tracked Kaitlin cuddling her sister. Like Jonas, Kaitlin was dressed in scrubs with a cap and a mask. The baby —well she was more a toddler now—did not like the mask. She kept trying to take it off.

Jonas captured her fingers and Pen tucked her head against Kaitlin's shoulder. I couldn't hear them, but I could see their eyes. Their focus was one hundred percent on that little girl. Just from their gentle sway, though, I'd guess they were singing to her.

"Coffee," Lachlan said and I pivoted to take the cup he held out. "Found a cappuccino machine in the nurse's lounge. I didn't want to go all the way downstairs."

I nodded. "Thanks." It was watery, but beggars couldn't be choosers.

"I figured we can stop on the way to the airport to get the real stuff for Ace." Lachlan took a sip of his own with a faint grimace. We'd had worse. "How are they doing?"

"Fine, I think," I said, following his gaze to watch them. "Can't tell much other than Pen doesn't like their masks."

"Yeah," Lachlan muttered. "Ace mentioned something about that."

I didn't say anything. What was there to say? I didn't

know much about kids. Not much beyond learning theories for teens, which was where my education had been focused. That baby wasn't a teenager. I knew my brothers too.

Didn't really make me an expert.

"What's eating you?" The question pulled me back to the present and I eyed my brother. He wasn't looking at me, but at Kaitlin and Jonas. We had maybe another half hour and then we would need to leave. Yvette and Aubrey would be meeting us at the airport.

"Do you really care?" Maybe not a fair question but I wasn't feeling especially fair at the moment.

"Yes," Lachlan said with a snort, before he flicked a look at me. "And no."

"Well, thanks for clearing that up."

"Don't be a dick," Lachlan advised. "I'm way better at it. You're also really tense and you have on your disappointed face."

"Disappointed face?" Pivoting from the window, I faced him.

"Yeah, it's the look you get when Jonas and I aren't living up to your expectations. Only, I don't think it's us you're annoyed with. Even if baby brother scored with my girl this morning." The possessiveness wasn't lost on me.

"She's not just yours," I reminded him. This argument was also tiresome. We were all damn lucky she spoke to us. The fact she'd said, "please don't hurt me again," would haunt me for a long time. "My mood has nothing to do with you or Jonas. Though if you keep it up, that could change."

Rather than argue, Lachlan grunted. "Fine. So what are you upset about?"

"Same thing you are," I told him before I took another swallow of the watered-down coffee. At least it was hot and it flirted with caffeine. "Mom. Gibs. Their manager. Dix. Her mother. Maybe not all in that order."

"You forgot her would-be kidnappers," Lachlan added, not disagreeing with my assessment.

"I haven't forgotten them. With no way to identify them, I can't do anything about it. Our mother, however..."

"You think she's the reason Gibs thought Ace didn't want to see him—"

"She has to be. How often did she run interference on his calls and messages? How many times did she tell us not to bother him while he was working?" No, it made sense. "She never wanted him disturbed or interrupted. She didn't want anything to take his mind off the work." Or her.

But I kept that last thought to myself.

"Doesn't let Gibs off the hook." Lachlan drained his cup, then tossed it into a trash can.

"No." It definitely didn't. "What I don't get is how she blocked phone calls and voicemails?"

"Gibs is forever losing his phone," my brother said with a shrug. "When he didn't lose it, he used to let the charge run down."

I pushed up my glasses and pinched the bridge of my nose. This whole thing was a mess. "Think he really doesn't know about his other kids?" Because that was another fact I had a real hard time wrapping my mind around.

"Maybe. I don't know. I know he adores Ace. That was clear on his face at the show. However this went down... I don't think he realized. Doesn't excuse him. Not in the slightest. Ace didn't want to talk to me either, but I didn't just disappear on her."

A laugh escaped me that came out more like a cross between a snort and a scoff.

The smirk curling Lachlan's lips just made me shake my head. "You're just as hooked as I am."

"Didn't say I wasn't," I said, still chuckling. "Just never

heard anyone patting themselves on the back for being a stalker."

"Self-deprecating is all well and good, but I know where my talents lie. Communication is a skill and a talent. Maybe I didn't have all the words, but I had the actions." Then his grin widened. "Besides, I need to reframe the whole thing because she's still annoyed with me sometimes. Even if she did agree to date me."

"That would be the possessive side of you, genius. She clearly isn't interested in *only* dating you." I rolled my head from side to side before I glanced down at my coffee.

"For now," he said and the denial was right there in his voice. "Maybe I just need time to make my case. She's not just any girl, Rams. She's—special."

"That's the thing, Lach. She is special. She means a hell of a lot to me." The finer details of that conversation were one I would have with Kaitlin, not Lachlan. "She means a lot to Jonas too—and I know you can see her very clear affection for him."

Lachlan glared at the floor. "I don't like it."

"Too bad," I reminded him. "You keep fighting to separate them and you're going to lose our girl and a brother."

"Does it bother you?" he asked, pivoting to face me. "At all? You're right, she's clearly attached to Jonas. I'd like to think I'm making inroads and you..."

"And I'm?" I prompted him.

"You seem to have something with her, but you're not listing yourself as an attachment."

"I hope she's attached," I told him with a shrug. "But I still have a lot of ground to make up for. I said some shitty things to her in the past." I cut a glance toward the hospital room where Jonas was holding Pen and Kaitlin had her hand on Pen's back, but her focus was on me and Lachlan. Concern reflected in the deep glowing blue of her eyes. She flicked a look at Lachlan then back to me. While the mask hid most of her expression, I could make out the way her eyebrows lifted.

Were we okay?

I nodded, then blew her a kiss. It was a moment of whimsy. The fact her eyes lit up even if her smile wasn't visible told me it was the right one to make.

"You've made up more ground than you think," Lachlan murmured and it was my turn to shrug. "We treated her badly."

"Yes, we did." To my great regret, I'd let my own experiences, prejudices, and my mother's version of things color my view of her. "Can't undo it, can only try to make up for it and make sure it never happens again."

"Ramsey..."

I spared him a look.

"I don't want to lose her," he admitted and he wasn't looking at me or her. Instead, he focused on the floor. "I don't want to fight you two, but I don't want to not fight for her."

I got that.

"Then fight for her," I told him. "Be on her side. But stop making it a choice."

"So, we just date her? All of us?"

"For now," I said slowly. "I don't see a way that ends without someone getting hurt, but she's interested in all of us. She's not keeping secrets about seeing each of us. We're all living in the same cottage."

"But can we make it work?"

"The alternative is losing her," I reminded him. "Could you live in the cottage if we tell her she has to make a choice and she doesn't choose you?" The idea made my stomach bottom out. I wasn't sure how I would react to such an ultimatum. If she dated one of my brothers, I would still be able to be around her.

Could I do that? Could I just be her friend and never kiss

her again? Never make her sigh or gasp or cry out as she came? I didn't like my chances. The idea of walking away didn't sit well with me.

"I don't know if I could," he admitted. "I hate the idea of her *not* choosing me."

"Same," I said. "Luckily, we don't have to deal with it right now, she's choosing all three of us at the moment."

"You just said you didn't see a way this ended without someone getting hurt..." He sounded almost mystified.

"I don't," I said. "But I refuse to give up a chance to have what we want and to see where it goes because I don't see another way yet. Just cause I can't see it doesn't mean there isn't one there."

"You really think that?"

"I know that."

"Huh." Lachlan smacked my arm lightly as he turned away from the window to face me again. "When did you become the optimistic one?"

I chuckled. "The day Kaitlin gave me a second chance..."

Thirteen

KC

Sleeping on the red-eye flight back to Connecticut proved far more difficult than normal. I'd learned how to sleep just about anywhere, but I was still vibrating from the past three days. From the concert to the hospital to Dad to Mom, and Teddy. Fucking Teddy. I couldn't get my thoughts to stop whirling at high speed. Each time I closed my eyes, I just started making lists of everything that could go wrong.

They were working to get Pen strong enough to have her marrow obliterated and then replaced. I hated the description. Tracy was going to stay in Los Angeles. I'd offered her the house but with Mom back, I didn't blame her for not wanting to be near there. As it was, I covered the expenses on the rental Tracy chose. It pissed her off, but we could fight about it later.

Then Mom... Mom and her fiancé. Despite the fact, I blocked the guy from even coming in the house. Mom didn't seem that upset about it. Course, Johnny was also keeping her off balance. Johnny offered to go but I told him he could stay as long as he liked, but—if he was uncomfortable, I would understand.

"I just miss your mom," he said. "Not really a fan of being here to watch her with that rat bastard she decided to hook up with."

"Well," I'd told him with a grin. "Lucky for you, he's not allowed in here. Security will keep him out. Mom isn't fighting that, for the moment, so as long as she doesn't go see him, you won't have to either."

A thoughtful look crossed his face. "You're sneaky."

"Nope. I'm direct. You are one of my favorite people. You adore Mom, all her quirks and all. You care about her, not her money, not her stardom, not her connections. She needs that in her life." It wasn't until I said it aloud that I realized how true it was. Johnny cared about Mom and she needed that far more than she would ever realize. "I know she can be difficult..."

"I've never minded difficult," he admitted and for a moment, his expression shifted to something wistful. "I just want her to be happy."

"And?" I prompted.

He gave me a small smile. "I'd like her to be happy with me, but I don't know that it will happen."

"You don't know that it won't," I said. "I mean—look at me. I've got boyfriends." That was pretty weird.

Johnny dropped a kiss on the top of my head. "Yes you do, that reminds me. I need to go threaten them again."

While I laughed, it didn't escape me that he was one hundred percent serious. Whether he actually threatened them or not, they didn't mention and I didn't ask. I had mental fingers crossed for Johnny. He deserved better than he'd gotten from Mom. It didn't seem to change his mind about her and I wanted them both happy.

Shifting in the seat, I let out a sigh and debated dragging

out my phone. The plane was dark, everyone else was asleep. I could watch a movie or catch up on videos from the show. I hadn't watched any of them. Hell, I'd been avoiding the news. A hand covered mine and I glanced to my right. Ramsey had claimed the seat next to mine on the flight.

"Sorry," I whispered, squeezing his hand.

"Can't sleep?" He stretched his legs and studied me. His eyes were a little red. Unlike me, he had been sleeping.

"No, I think I'm gonna watch a movie."

"Okay." He waited until I had my phone and headphones out before he claimed. "Share one?"

I blinked. "You were sleeping. I didn't mean to wake you up."

"It's fine, Siren," he said then leaned over to kiss me. It was a light kiss, there and gone again but it stifled my objections. "Dreams were boring. I'd rather be awake with you." The offer made my heart flip-flop. So I tucked in one ear bud and he put in the other and then we scrolled through the movies the airline offered on their free WiFi.

"Action movie? RomCom? Horror film?" The offerings were kind of slim, but he snorted at the last and I snuck a look at him. "What?"

"You watch horror movies?" The level of skepticism in his voice made me grin.

"I could watch them," I said. "Maybe."

The doubting look in his eyes just made me giggle.

"I mean, I've never watched one. So—there's a chance I could like them." Picking out a movie often gave me anxiety because what if I didn't like it? What if I picked the wrong one? Which was the right one? That anxiety was kind of why I preferred reality television.

"Well, let's not see if you want the crap scared out of you at thirty thousand feet." Amusement softened his expression and the smile on his lips just left my heart squeezing all over again.

"Okay." I could agree with that. "Action movie then. Something—with lots of noise and explosions."

"Action movie it is." It took us about ten minutes to choose one. Ramsey liked to read what the movies were about and when we narrowed it down to two, we watched the trailers. He was kind of fussy about it and when I cracked up at the second trailer, he said, "That one."

"You sure?" I checked with him. "I've never heard of this one."

"I'm sure," he said. "Now hit play."

"Bossy," I muttered, then he nipped my ear. It was a gentle tug but it chased away my scowl. I hit play and then tucked my head against his shoulder. He didn't let go of my hand but we locked the phone in so we didn't have to hold it and the movie started. I didn't think I lasted ten minutes into the movie, between Ramsey stroking the side of my hand and my focus on the movie, I went right to sleep.

IT WAS A LOT COLDER IN CONNECTICUT THAN IT WAS in California. I pulled on a knit cap before I knocked on Lachlan's door. Jonas was sound asleep in my bed. The door to Ramsey's room was closed. It was still early.

Unsurprisingly, Lachlan answered on the first knock. Dressed in boxers only, he gave me a sweeping look from head to toe. "Ace," he said with a half-sigh. "You're not going to let me persuade you into some more horizontal calisthenics, are you?"

Tongue against my teeth, I just grinned. "I'll give you three minutes. Then I'm going..."

"Mean, Ace," he muttered. "Really mean."

"Tick-tock." Winking, I headed for the stairs. Granted, staring at Lachlan shirtless while he was still rumpled from bed was not a hardship, but I did want to run. The restlessness that always hit after we came down from a show was rioting in my blood. Despite his complaints, Lachlan didn't keep me waiting.

At two minutes, he was on his way down the stairs with his shoes in hand. I did some stretches while he pulled them on. Awareness of his observation skated over me. Once his shoes were on, he pulled on his windbreaker hoodie and zipped it up. I already had mine on. In fact, I was practically toasty.

Stopping next to me, Lachlan brushed his knuckles down my cheeks and I pushed up on my toes to meet the light kiss he gave me. "You really need to run, don't you?"

"Yeah," I said, the agitation was right there. The flight back. Getting caught up on classwork, phone calls to check on Tracy and Pen before we all crashed early because apparently, I wasn't the only one who slept badly on the plane. I wish I could say I'd slept better, but my mind wouldn't shut up and even cuddling the guys hadn't quieted it fully.

Course, it didn't help that I spent a couple of hours doomscrolling TikTok, YouTube, and Instagram. Teddy was right.

Dammit.

The performance with Dad was the highlight of the night. It was *everywhere*.

"Let's go then, Ace," he said, snagging his keys. "Got your earbuds?"

I was already holding one out to him. He winked. Then we were outside. The air was nippy as hell and I jogged in place as he locked up. It took us an extra five minutes to get to the trail from here, but I was ready for it.

"Crank it up," he told me. "Let's see if we can shave time off your mile."

A laugh bubbled up through me. That sounded perfect to me. I hit the music and we were moving. Lachlan matched pace with me and when I added speed, so did he. The cold air was perfect. We hadn't had any snow yet, but it was coming. I could taste it on the breeze.

I did shave time off my miles. All three of them. When we were back at the house, it was still dark and Lachlan raced me all the way to the door. Not that he was really trying to get away, but he did slide to a stop ahead of me and caught me when I would have crashed into him.

"Gotcha," he teased and then I looped my arms around his neck and met his fierce kiss with one of my own. My pulse was pounding and my breath was coming in swift little pants. Lachlan tasted better than coffee.

When he dragged out my lower lip, there was just a bit of a sting from the sharpness of his teeth. "Shower?" I asked, despite the cold, I was definitely sweaty. His grin grew.

Then his eyes narrowed. "That is an invitation, right?"

I laughed as he pushed open the door. A part of me was tempted to tease him, but the run had my endorphins up and helped to calm me down at the same time. Toeing one shoe off and then the other, I tilted my head.

His eyes narrowed as he yanked off his shoes.

"Yes." As quiet as that one word was, you'd have thought I fired a gun. Because Lachlan went from standing still to coming straight for me. I was up and over his shoulder and he took the stairs nearly two at a time.

Laughter bubbled up and despite trying to keep it quiet, I couldn't stop the giggles as he rushed me up to his room. Then we were in his bathroom with the door closed and his expression fierce as he set me down on the counter. I had my hands on his chest.

"Get naked, Ace," Lachlan said, the growl in his voice making my thighs tight. He was dragging the zipper down on his hoodie and I slid off the counter. Cause, he was right. As much as I would enjoy watching him. I'd enjoy being naked more. He turned the water on and thankfully it heated up super fast because he locked his arm around me and half carried me under the spray.

Somewhere in there we found soap and washed, I was pretty sure. But the fusion of his mouth to mine didn't leave a lot of room for oxygen or worrying about rinsing. When he lifted me up and pinned me to the wall, I was wrapping my hand around his dick.

A laugh escaped me as I stroked him and he kissed a path to my throat. "What's so funny, Ace?"

"I'm getting to touch you," I admitted. "And I like it."

He paused to lift his head. "You can touch me any time you want." The promise sent another shiver through me. My nipples were tight and everywhere they slid against his wet chest, they seemed to get even more sensitive. When he covered my hand with his and lined himself up, I forgot how to breathe.

Lachlan was a wild combination of ferocity and gentleness. He never treated me like spun glass. When he nipped at my lip, I focused on him. No, he never treated me like I was delicate. The first thrust was sharp, and stretching. It pushed all the air out of me and then he was nibbling kisses along my mouth, to my jaw, and then to my ear.

"You feel so fucking good, Ace," he whispered and I dug my fingers into his shoulders.

"So do you." The admission cost me nothing and it was true. The first piston of his hips lit me up and when he sucked a kiss against my throat, I soaked it all in. The run had pushed aside the wild tangle of thoughts. Lachlan set them all on fire. Every thrust pushed me up against the tile. He kept one hand on my ass and the other braced on the wall next to my head.

I rolled my hips, trying to keep up with him. Sharp bursts

of pleasure erupted in my system. When I bit down on his shoulder, he let out a low chuckle.

"That's my girl," he hummed. "Dig your nails in, bite me —mark me up."

I dragged my head up to meet his intense stare, then he grinned. The smile was a heart stopper, especially with his haunted forest eyes that seemed to be blazing right now. Would I ever understand his insanity?

"You're crazy," I said in between pants as he drove his hips into mine. It was so hard to even hold onto thoughts, much less words.

"Good thing," he said, his grin undiminished, "you need crazy."

I didn't have time to agree or not, because my orgasm was right there and when he slid a hand between us and teased my clit, I came with a startled shout. The spasms had my thighs flexing against his hips. He swallowed my cries with another kiss and then he came in a hot jet that left me shaken and trembling.

We leaned there, against the wall, panting and holding onto each other. A knock at the door froze me in place. Lachlan lifted his head.

"Fuck off," he called.

"Pretty sure you just did," Ramsey called from the other side of the bathroom door. "I'm making breakfast and I want to see Siren before classes. So finish up."

A giggle-snort escaped and Lachlan grinned. "Morning, Ramsey."

"Morning, Kaitlin. Coffee will be ready for you downstairs..."

"That's cheating," Lachlan yelled but I was already sliding my trembling legs down to try and stand.

"Coffee trumps dick," Ramsey teased. "Maybe you need

to up your game. I'll see you downstairs." Then the sound of a door closing told us he was gone.

I wasn't sure what cracked me up more. The absolute shock stamping itself across Lachlan's face at what Ramsey said or Ramsey's retort.

Either way, I rode that high through the quick actual wash and then slid out of the shower.

"Lach," I said as I wrapped a towel around my torso.

"Ace?"

"Thank you," I blew him a kiss. "For the run and the shower."

He grinned. "Tomorrow, let's stay in bed. We'll have more time."

"We'll see..." Then I was slipping out of his bathroom and his room to head for mine. The smell of bacon and coffee hurried me along, and I made it down the stairs a few steps ahead of Lachlan. Jonas handed me my coffee and I kissed him good morning, then I slid over to Ramsey and gave the cook a kiss too.

It was already looking up. There was a letter on the table addressed to me. Lachlan scowled when he saw it, and I couldn't blame him. "That's..."

"Yep," Jonas said. "They're tapping you again this year."

Knots and Chains. I was not a fan.

"But you guys are members, right?"

"Not anymore," Lachlan said as he pulled a gallon of milk out of the fridge. He had his coffee too. "I quit."

"So did I," Ramsey said.

"I never joined," Jonas told me.

"They aren't worth it." The flatness in Lachlan's tone was utterly at odds from our shower. "Just... not after everything and not after what RJ pulled and wanted to pull with you. We're out."

I picked up the letter then walked over and dropped it in

the trash. Ramsey dipped his head, an approving smile on his lips as he nodded. Lachlan blew out a breath. Did they really think I wanted anything to do with that group?

Jonas pulled a chair for me and Lachlan helped Ramsey serve up the food. It was weirdly domestic and kind of nice.

I reclaimed my coffee. "So... what's the plan for today?"

Fourteen

LACHLAN

Zoning out during the lecture portion of the class left me with only a few notes. Since I read the chapters though, I wasn't too worried about it. I didn't have Ramsey's work ethic or Jonas' ability to hyperfocus, but I pretty much retained everything I read. It made skating by when I didn't feel like taking notes, or listening to some sonorous bore, work.

Still, it didn't keep me from checking my phone for the time or skimming through social media. The chatter about Ace, Torched, and Gibs had increased significantly. Made sense, the concert was still creating ripples. Clips were all over TikTok and YouTube. IG had reels—funnily enough, other people were using the video clips to promote books and other shit.

So fucking weird.

While Ace repeatedly told us to not read the gossip sites, it was hard to ignore the headlines.

Kaitlin Crosse snubs father during first ever performance together

Problem Child is no hero for using fundraiser to relaunch career

Torched in war with label? Or is the problem child looking to break up the band?

Problem Child playing a new game with brothers…

The last headline leapt out at me. I spared a glance at the instructor who was continuing to flip through the PowerPoint presentation. Yeah, they were only on the second chapter of the reading. If he was just gonna regurgitate what he assigned for the reading, I really didn't need to listen.

Clicking the headline, I opened the gossip site and stared at a blurred image of my car with the camera focusing on us in it. That was when we pulled over on the way back from meeting Tracy and she was riding my dick. We weren't naked but it was pretty fucking clear what we were doing.

Anger threaded through me as I scrolled down to the headline *From Topping the Charts to Topping Brothers*. Below that was an even ruder comment about *the Problem Child might be channeling her inner diva while "at school" as rumors allege she is hooking up with brothers…*

It went downhill from there. While they didn't name us, we were all pictured.

Fuck.

Anger threaded through my veins like a wildfire. The article used the words allegedly and rumors like too much salt on the wound. Legal bullshit to cover their ass from defamation per se, I got it. Didn't mean I had to like it.

I scoured the article. Then followed the links. There was one that showed pictures of us with her backstage at the concert. There were more, pictures from the costume party where I kissed Ace for the first time—fuck me that was two years earlier.

Where had they gotten these?

Then there were pictures of her with RJ, Dix, and one side profile of her dancing at a club with the caption "Maybe the problem child is just a wild child and party girl."

Maybe they needed to get fucked.

Assholes.

I barely acknowledged the teacher when the class wrapped, just shoved my shit into my backpack and headed for the door.

"Hey, Lachlan," a blonde said, shooting me a flirty smile. I just lifted a hand in passing as a half-wave and then headed out the door. Weaving in and around the other students, I headed for the Heinritz building.

Ace was just descending the steps with Jonas and Dix as I got there. Fucking Dix. He could get lost now that I was here. She'd discussed replacing him, but it was hard for her. He'd been around forever and his attitude demonstrated he'd gotten far too comfortable.

"I didn't say you shouldn't go," Dix said, his tone frosty. "I said it was a bad idea. You don't always make the best decisions at parties."

Jonas glared and he wasn't alone. "Watch it," I warned Dix. I didn't hesitate to cut between him and Ace.

"Lachlan..." Ace said, putting a hand on my arm, but I shook my head.

"No, not this time. Dix forgets who he actually works for here. You're her employee, not her bestie, her brother, or anything that gives you the right to take that tone with her. You talk to her with respect or you shut the fuck up and say nothing at all."

Expression tightening, Dix got right in my face. Yeah, he wasn't taller or bulkier. The need to hit something fired my whole being and this asshole just stepped into the ring. I would—

"Guys," Ace said, flattening her hand to my chest. The

fact Dix was right there, meant she was practically wedged between us. "Not here. Not now."

"I wasn't starting anything," Dix said. "Your little—"

"Dix," Ace snapped and cut a look over her shoulder. His eyes narrowed. "Not here. Not now. In fact, Jonas and Lachlan are both here so you can go. We'll discuss this later." Despite the clipped nature of her tone, she never raised her voice.

The asshat looked ready to argue, but then he glanced around before taking a step back and blowing out a breath. I took advantage of the moment to slide an arm around Ace's middle and pull her closer to me. The last place she ever needed to be was between me and a fight.

"You're right." Dix said, his expression relaxing. Not that I bought the act. He wore a patently false smile that didn't touch his eyes. "My apologies. Let's get you back to the house—"

"It's fine," Ace told him. The tension coiling through her shoulders seemed to ease as she leaned back against me. "We're all tired and you need a break, Dix. I think we really do need to look into getting you someone to relieve you so you can have some downtime. But we'll talk about that later too."

If I hadn't been watching him, I might have missed the way his eyes flashed and his mouth compressed at her statement. Just when I thought he might offer up another argument, he backed off completely.

"I'll speak to you later then." Then Dix strode away and Ace turned to me. I tracked Dix's path to make sure he kept moving. Gradually, it hit me that we had an audience.

"Hey," Ace said, pulling my attention back to her. "Buy us coffee?"

Coffee?

"Yeah," Jonas said with a faint smile that also didn't reach his eyes. He was too watchful. Great, I came here to warn her about the gossipy bullshit and then managed to create a scene.

Fuck.

"Sure," I said, going for a lightness I didn't feel. "Unless you want to go back to the house..." The longer we were out, the more eyes were on her.

Head tilted, she studied me with those perfect blue eyes. They really were perfect, they seemed to have their very own glow. Her cheeks were a little pink from the cold and so was the tip of her nose. "I'm fine with heading over to Dancing Goats and grabbing something. The walk would be good. I'm a little stiff."

I frowned. The more I thought about it, the more I didn't like it.

"Lighten up," she said, smacking me lightly in the chest. "You're all doom and gloom—" Suddenly her smile evaporated. "Did something happen?"

Did something... "No," I hurried to assure her and shook my head. "Just had a lot on my mind and Dix pisses me off."

"He's under a lot of pressure," she offered by way of defense as I caught her book bag and lifted it off her shoulder before I slung it over mine.

"Ace, I don't care what pressure he's under. He's rude as fuck when he talks to you and he's been getting more assholish by the day." I jerked my head to get her and Jonas moving. "Let's go." We didn't need to hang out here and give the whole damn campus a show.

"You're in a mood," she teased, but I wasn't really feeling playful. Not after those stupid articles.

"Lachlan is right," Jonas said and I blinked.

"I'm sorry, baby brother—what did you just say?"

"Fuck off," he told me cheerfully, before he glanced down at Ace. "But he's right about Dix. I don't like how he looks at you or how he talks to you."

She sighed. "I don't know how to fix it, but we'll figure something out."

I looked over her head at Jonas and he lifted his shoulders in a shrug. I knew how to fix it. Fire Dix. But she was fond of the dick. Fuck, we needed to do more than "figure it out." The guy needed to go.

At the same time, Ace needed protection. Maybe more now than she had before. The last update from the cops on the kidnapping hadn't really been optimistic. They had no leads, and Ace hadn't been able to offer them much info at all.

I hated it.

Throw in everything with her sister and with Gibs—and fuck, our mother—yeah, I wanted to make sure nothing bothered her. Maybe we should increase security on the cottage. All the way through getting coffee and the walk back to the house, Ace kept shooting me looks.

Or she did when we weren't being interrupted. A whole gaggle of the high school freshmen spotted her and then swarmed in to get autographs. Jonas and I blocked them from being able to overwhelm her, but she was so patient and signed everything they handed her.

So annoying.

When it looked like more were heading our way, I shook my head. "That's enough ladies. Technically, this is violating school code. Ace has been super kind, but time for you guys to get back to class."

A round of "awwws" echoed from them but they listened. I didn't really care how disappointed they were. It was making the back of my neck itch to be out here. Not that I got to enjoy our escape for long.

"What's wrong?" Ace asked.

"Nothing," I told her. "Just—there are rules for a reason."

"Uh huh," Jonas said. "Why don't I believe you?"

"Cause you're a dick," I informed him with a smirk.

"Must be it," he said then rolled his eyes.

"Look, let's just get back to the house…" The sun had vanished behind dark clouds. While the hints of snow were on the air, the only moisture to spatter us was more like icy rain. Thankfully, we were almost to the door.

Once we were inside, I took off my shoes and set her bag down.

"I'm gonna grab a shower. Want to order pizza? Or we can fix something…"

"Hey," Ace said as Jonas stared at me. "Are you sure you're okay?"

"Yeah, I'm great," I told her and dropped a kiss on the chilly tip of her nose. "In fact, I've been working out our date. I just need to do a little more planning. You're still up for it, right?"

She had set the conditions. I just needed to find a way to make it all work.

Her smile was quick and it lightened her whole expression. "I thought you'd forgotten…"

"Bite your tongue," I told her. Then I slid a hand around her nape. "Better, let me bite your tongue." Her lips parted as soon as I fused my mouth to hers and she swept her tongue against mine in a tease. I scraped it lightly with my teeth and she chuckled even as I deepened the kiss.

My dick all but stood up to salute and while I would be more than happy to dickstract both of us, I didn't feel like putting on a show for Jonas. I was pretty sure he wouldn't appreciate it. Dragging out her lower lip, I sighed as I studied her and then I kissed her lightly.

"Definitely not forgotten."

"Okay," she said, a little breathless. "Then I can't wait."

"Good." Catching Jonas' eye, I nodded to him. "Keep an eye on our girl, I'm going up to shower. You guys figure out what you want for food."

Once I was in my room, I dumped the backpack and blew out a breath. Fucking gossip, then Dix, and now those girls wanting her autograph. It never let up. I rubbed the back of my neck and headed in to start the shower.

My phone buzzed and it was a message from one of the guys on the team. I still helped out coach with the lacrosse team, not that I'd had as much time this semester. Practices wouldn't really ramp up until spring though.

I stared at the message. Someone was selling a guitar on one of the trader sites. Hadn't I been looking for one? I immediately followed the link and stared as it loaded.

The guitar had been listed for a while and we'd tried to buy it, but the seller chickened out. And there it was, the picture was similar to the other ad—I saved a copy of it then scrolled back in my phone to check.

Similar, but it was a new image. It was sitting on a stand. It had some dust on it. It looked good.

It also had a contact for more info and no price tag. Well, that was annoying.

I messaged Walker back and asked if he could reach out and make an offer. Find out what they wanted and don't say anything about me being the one interested. He didn't keep me hanging. Said he'd do it right away.

Fine.

I returned to the ad and stared at it. I wanted to get that guitar back for her. I also wouldn't mind getting my hands on the asshole who stole it and did all the damage to her room.

The fact I had a lead at all buoyed my mood. I couldn't tell Ace yet, I didn't want her disappointed. But maybe we could get it back sooner rather than later.

Fifteen

KC

"You're in a mood," Aubrey commented as she carried the coffees over that she'd just made. Her place was smaller than ours, but she didn't have to share it with anyone. So the bright, bold geometric patterns were so her. The blue roses were my thing, Aubrey liked everything just so and the harder lines appealed to her.

"Am I?" I asked, tilting my head back. Ramsey had walked me over to her place on his way to tutoring. It had been funny when he said he had scheduled a half-dozen tutoring sessions with students who were struggling. It set off a little ping inside of me—jealousy? Envy? Maybe.

Those tutoring sessions used to piss me off, but on some level I had enjoyed frustrating and challenging him too. So— maybe I was a little warped now.

Hell, I was dating three brothers. I was definitely warped.

Dropping onto the sofa next to me, she pulled her legs up to sit curled up and facing me. "Yes," she said. "You are. You've been brooding since you got here. And while fan mail isn't always fun, we are a little behind…"

I made a face. "It's not the fan mail, though I did forget we'd let so much of it slide while ramping up to the benefit."

Lips quirking, Aubrey raised her cup to me and then took a sip. "Okay, so is it the douchebags three?"

"Well, living with one guy was weird last year but way easier than I expected it to be." Which was true. Jonas and I could be quiet together. Not something I'd ever considered as a positive trait or necessity before, but I liked it. "Living with three guys is…?" I turned the idea over in my head.

"Hard?" Aubrey suggested with a faint curve of her lips even as her eyes danced with mischief.

I groaned.

"C'mon, that's a lot of dick," Aubrey teased me. "If something or someone isn't hard all the time, then they are doing something wrong."

Laughter swelled up inside of me. "Bitch."

"Yep, but I'm your bitch," she said with a grin. "So, tell me—how is it living with all of them?"

"I don't hate it," I said slowly, then took a sip of the coffee. The hit of caffeine and chocolate was exactly what I needed.

"But?"

At her prompt, I glared. Not that it seemed to affect her in the slightest. She just stared right back at me. Then again, why would me glaring be a problem? I groaned again. "Aubrey, I don't know. I don't think it's them. I think it's me."

"Okay, why do you think it's you? And what is you?"

"The problem. Me? I'm the problem." At the quote from the popular song, Aubrey rolled her eyes. "I'm serious. Mostly." Pulling my legs in to sit criss-cross, I bobbed my head from side to side. "I like being with all of them. Jonas is…he helps me be peaceful. He understands the music and sometimes he just seems to get everything and wraps it up in the notes perfectly. Ramsey is... clever and sharp. He's also so good at anticipating what I might need. Is it weird to say I love that he makes a point of seeing that I eat breakfast every day? Even if he isn't cooking, he offers to grab me cereal or pick me up something..."

"No, it's not weird. It's sweet." It was Aubrey's turn to grimace. "He's got that whole caretaker daddy vibe going on."

"Ewww... don't call him a daddy." I shuddered and she cracked up.

"Why not? He's older than you, he parents your other two boyfriends, and since he managed to dislodge his head from his ass, he's looking after you the same way—well, maybe a little kinkier, but you know."

"Oh my god," I said, laughing. "That's awful."

"Maybe, but it doesn't matter what you label it. He's good for you. The fact I can say that tells you just how far he's come. I liked Jonas before. Ramsey's okay. I think he's getting better."

I couldn't argue with that. But the truth was, I liked Ramsey before I knew who he was to them or to me. Except when he was being the douchebag captain, that was hard. But he apologized.

More, he'd made up for some of those choices.

I asked him to not hurt me again and he hadn't. When I just needed comfort, I could curl up with him and he'd hold me. No questions asked. It wasn't always about sex—though the sex was definitely nice. A little shudder went through me.

"That leaves Lachlan," Aubrey circled us back to my last douchebag. "He still fighting for pole position?"

"I don't think so. He makes comments here and there but he's been... off a little the last few days. Something's eating at him but he doesn't want to talk to me about it. I haven't pried and maybe I should, but I feel like we've all got a right to privacy, though I'm worried about him."

"Then talk to him."

"Well, now that we've solved that..." At the wry comment, Aubrey snorted.

"We haven't solved anything. Stop ducking the conversation, you're upset. Is it Pen? Last I heard she was still on schedule for her transplant, right? Tracy passed all the tests and is good to go?"

"They're fine," I hurried to assure her. "I talked to Tracy last night. They have one last doctor who needs to sign off, but the concentration has been on getting Pen strong enough. Jackie has a good feeling about it, and apparently Dad has been to the hospital."

"Oh shit," Aubrey's eyes widened. "Way to bury the lead."

"Well, I don't know how it all went, but Bronson told me that Dad showed up when he was there. Didn't go in to see Pen, but did watch her through the viewing glass and he seemed sober enough to ask about how she was doing."

"Did Bronson talk to him?"

I shook my head. "Not much. He talked to Jackie, and whatever went down between the two of them, she's not sharing." That was strange enough. "I guess I could call him..."

"You haven't called him, have you?"

"He says things will be different but he hasn't called me either. So—I don't want to call him and get ghosted again. If he's gonna show up for Pen, that's fantastic. I don't think Tracy has seen him and I'm not sure if she even wants to at this point. But—I don't want to be disappointed again. I've been doing fine without Dad for years now...and right now, Mom kind of has all the oxygen sucked into her drama..."

"Kait," Aubrey said softly. "If you want to talk to your dad, call him. Maybe he still has feet of clay. Maybe he's still going to disappoint you. But you deserve to have the parent you want and need. So if you want to talk to him, call him. Put the ball back in his court. I'm not defending him, and I never will, but I have to wonder if the reason he hasn't called you is because he's afraid you won't talk to him too."

Setting the coffee aside, I flung myself back and rubbed at my face. "I'll think about it. I can't—I can't deal with all of that or him right now." There was still the stepmother issue and while the guys had all been staunch in *my* defense, there was no escaping that the woman was their mother.

I didn't want to be the person getting between them and their mother. For all of my mother's faults, I wouldn't let them get between me and her. It was a mess.

"One more word on the subject," Aubrey said. "Then we'll move on to the fun of answering fan mail, talking about album and concert schedules, and debating whether we want Chinese or Mexican for dinner."

Aubrey was so damn matter-of-fact sometimes, it made me laugh. "Hit me."

"Talk to those douchebags about this. About what is going on with them and what is going on with you. The reason you had so much trouble with them in the beginning was all the assumptions—" She held up a finger when I opened my mouth. "Ah, their assumptions were *not* your fault, but you still paid for it. So, let's skip any assumptions now. Talk to them, tell them how you're feeling, and find out what is happening with them. Okay?"

"Some days I hate you," I muttered and she leaned over to kiss my cheek just as there was a knock on the door.

"But today," she said with a wink, "is not that day."

A laugh escaped me and I shook my head as she went to answer the door.

"Oh," Aubrey sounded surprised. "I didn't know you were coming over." The smell of pizza drifted inside and my stomach growled. There was also something distinctly cinnamony on the air. Cinnamon rolls? Or one of those dessert sticks?

"Hey babe," Forrest said as Aubrey pulled the door wider. "I know you said you had a fan mail date with KC—hey girl," he called past her with a grin and I laughed as I waved at him.

"Hey, Forrest!"

Aubrey looked amused as Forrest focused back on her. "I thought I could give you both a hand, and even if not, I brought pizza and cinnamon sticks—with extra sweet dip sauce—from your favorite place to give you guys sustenance." He wagged his eyebrows almost playfully. While I was trying not to stare, it was adorable, and a hint of a red flush touched Aubrey's face.

Forrest might be the on-again off-again boyfriend, but I liked that she enjoyed him so much. She glanced back at me with the question in her eyes. Did I mind if he stayed? We hadn't really had much time since we got back to school, and I chuckled.

"Hey, more the merrier. He can do what Jonas did and help us sort." The gentle reminder that we'd had assistance before helped to relax Aubrey's expression. "Fair warning, Forrest, this isn't always 'fun.' Most of the time it's boring."

"I find it hard to believe anything that lets me hang out with the pair of you would be boring." He dropped a kiss on Aubrey's lips as he wandered inside. The pizza smelled fantastic.

"Well, at least with the pizza here, we won't be hangry," I teased and Aubrey chuckled. We took a few minutes to get slices of pizza and then rearranged ourselves in Aubrey's front room and around the flat, oblong coffee table that looked like a reclaimed tree stump of some kind but it had been shined to a polish.

I started going through one stack of mail in between taking bites of the pizza—it was so freaking good. I had skipped breakfast earlier, even when Ramsey offered to stop and grab something on the way here. The pizza was perfect.

Aubrey took a couple of minutes to explain our system to Forrest and then handed him his own stack.

Forty-five minutes and three slices of pizza later, I'd managed to answer a dozen notes while setting aside others just to get a signed photograph. Some needed more personal touches than others.

"Did you ladies ever decide about your next album?" Forrest asked.

"No," Aubrey said. "We've discussed it."

"But it's scheduling and timing. We need to do another album before we schedule another tour..." And I wasn't in the headspace for that right now.

"Unless you want to do a limited run set of engagements," Forrest suggested. "Those are all the rage, it makes it exclusive and gives the fans something special to look forward to and I don't think they'd care if you had new songs to perform or not..."

"Even a limited run," Aubrey argued, "would be time-consuming. Concerts don't just happen overnight and a lot of venues are booked months, sometimes years, in advance. We'd need the band, the backup dancers, and the crew."

"We could downsize," I said, testing the sound of it. "It doesn't have to be the huge showstoppers we did last time...if we're going to do something limited and exclusive. Smaller venues, smaller audience—more intimate performance?"

It sounded good, in theory.

"That would be killer," Forrest said. "Think about it, only make the tickets available to your fans and you could even do it like a lottery, limit how many at each location, then you could throw in meet and greets or something..."

"That was kind of what we did when we were starting out," Aubrey looked thoughtful. "But I don't know that it would go over well now, especially if we reduced how many could even show up. The amount of people who would be upset...versus, you know, a traditional show."

"Except, you're not launching a new album. You'd just be revisiting some of your previous hits and making it a more private evening with your fans. Based on what I'm seeing here..." He held up one of the letters. "I can't imagine there aren't a lot of fans who *wouldn't* want a chance to see you that way. How up close and personal can you really get in a ten thousand strong arena?"

He wasn't wrong but... "I don't know if we're in the right place to plan either kind. We are working on some songs."

"Really?" Forrest glanced from me to Aubrey. "Keeping secrets, babe?"

She laughed. "Working on means not finished. We rarely let anyone hear our work before we finish it. So you'll have to deal with some suspense."

"Damn," he said, snapping his fingers and playing up his mock disappointment. "I'm wounded."

I snorted but he let that go. Still, I couldn't shake the idea and I wasn't sure what I wanted to do. Neither did Aubrey or Yvette. We were all kind of in a holding pattern...

Maybe that was the problem. It was well into evening when we finished and I stretched. We'd killed all the pizza and the dessert sticks. We'd also made a couple of goofy videos for TikTok while answering our email. Forrest was funny, but he had some good ideas.

"You want me to walk you back to your place?" Forrest offered just as there was a knock on the door.

"No," I said, heading over to answer it. As expected, Jonas was there. "Come in a sec, I gotta get my coat."

He nodded.

"I didn't realize she called you," Forrest said, lifting his chin to greet Jonas.

"We arranged it earlier," Jonas told him as I dragged on my coat.

Aubrey leaned in to give me a hug. "You good?"

"I'm fine," I told her. "Tired... but I had fun. Thanks for putting up with me."

She snorted. "Look after our girl, Jonas."

"I will," he said and I gave her a gentle shove before heading for the door.

"Night and thanks for the help, Forrest," I said, and he surprised me when he caught me in a sideways hug. Okay.

"Night KC," he said. "Thanks for letting me help."

Jonas held out a hand as I got to him and I clasped it. Then we were out. Hopefully, Forrest took Aubrey to do something fun. We descended the steps into the chilly night air and headed for one of the paths. The campus was kind of quiet. Not that I minded.

"I'm surprised Dix wasn't the one who showed up," I said. As we strolled, he released my hand and slid his arm around my shoulders.

"Didn't tell him," Jonas said. "I wanted you to myself." He cut a look at me. "That's okay?"

I grinned and leaned my head against his shoulder. "More than okay."

Sixteen

JONAS

"Thanks, Dad," I said as I sat up on the sofa. I'd been sprawled, catching up with him. "I know, I owe you a visit. It's been a busy year..."

"And there's a girl," Dad said, his tone dry and vaguely sarcastic.

"She's not *just* a girl." KC was so much more.

"I'm beginning to get that...let me guess, she's a reference for one of your new tattoos."

I debated answering. Lachlan was in the shower and Ramsey hadn't returned yet. He and KC went to pick up food. Probably both so he could spend some time with her and because we hadn't picked up any groceries this week. Thanksgiving break kicked off the day after next, and we were on a flight the next evening.

"She's—important to me, Dad." That took a lot more effort. "Really important. I'm sorry I haven't visited. I know I keep putting it off..."

"Jonas," Dad said, his voice dipping a little. "Ease up. I was just teasing you. Normally, you're like clockwork when you come to visit. Always on time, sometimes staying for longer than planned. I like hanging out with you, but you're also eighteen—"

"Nineteen," I corrected and he chuckled.

"Stop getting older," he admonished me. "My point, you're an adult. You need to chase what you want to do. Just —promise me one thing."

Cautious, I considered the way he phrased that. "What?"

"Don't make every decision in your life about a girl. She can be the best thing that ever happened to you, but if you make her the focus of everything—it's going to end in tears. For you. For her."

I frowned.

Dad sighed. "It's hard to explain this when you're young, but you need to be happy with yourself. You need to find fulfillment that isn't just her. I chased a woman for my happiness, that didn't work out because I made her the center of everything and when she got bored and moved on...it took me time to recover. Sometimes, I'm not sure I have. I don't want that for you."

"You're talking about Mom." We didn't talk about her. Not that often. Passing comments, small talk, but nothing in depth.

"Yeah, I am."

"KC isn't Mom." This was an important distinction. "Mom—Mom has issues. I get that. And I'm sorry she did that to you. KC isn't going to get bored with me."

"You sound pretty damn sure there."

I shrugged. "Because KC is different. She—she's my friend. She was my friend first. Now she's my girlfriend." That sounded a little strange to say, but at the same time—so very right. "Music is our language. We communicate really well that way. I know you're worried, but I'm not."

Not about that. KC's loyalty was unquestionable. More, her commitment to her family and her relationships? She was all in. I couldn't do any less.

"I hope so," Dad said. "I really do. Maybe you can bring her to meet me."

I chuckled. "I'd like that. Need to get these tattoos finished and we aren't done with my lessons."

"See, I'm still useful." His tone was a lot lighter by the time we said goodbye but I needed to make a point to go and see Dad. Maybe after everything with Pen was settled. Right now, her surgery and health was the most important. KC wasn't going to be able to focus on anything else until then. I needed to be there for her. She carried too much.

"They back yet?" Lachlan called downstairs and I twisted to see him leaning out of his room, hair wet and wearing boxers only.

"Nope," I said.

"I gotta make a call," he said. "If they get back before I'm down, just tell them I had to talk to Coach for a bit."

"Are you talking to Coach?" Cause that didn't sound right.

"Talk to him most days," Lachlan said, then closed the door to his room. I shook my head. He seemed weirder than usual lately.

There was another Knots and Chains letter on the table. I hadn't said anything to Lachlan about it. It was for KC. If she wanted to toss it, she could. One would think they'd get the point that she wasn't interested.

Flopping back on the sofa, I tapped through some of the social media apps. I didn't like most of it, but I wanted to know what people were saying about KC. I hated the gossip sites, but I also needed to protect KC. The pictures and stories had doubled since the concert.

So had the speculation about who she was dating. There

were pictures of us. If Dad followed any of this, he'd probably seen these articles too. I didn't want to discuss the gossip with him, but I did want to keep an eye on it. Should have thought about that earlier...

Ugh.

The sound of the lock turning had me sitting up. The door opened with Ramsey ushering a laughing KC inside and I swiped off the site I'd been reading. She didn't need the gossip. Light glittered off of her hair and her knit cap, her eyes were bright.

"It's snowing!" She sounded positively giddy.

"Just a dusting," Ramsey said as he nudged her in and closed the door. "But it does look like it's sticking."

KC laughed as Ramsey carried the food bags into the kitchen. "I love it. I wasn't sure we would get to see any before we headed for L.A."

"Go for another walk after dinner?" I offered and her smile warmed me.

"Oh, yes please..."

CLASS WRAPPED EARLY WHICH WAS GOOD. LACHLAN would be out soon too. The only one not done before one would be Ramsey. He still had classes right up until four. Then he had to lock in grades.

"We're leaving for the airport at six?" I verified before scooping up KC's bookbag for her.

"That's the plan." She checked her phone. "No one has changed it. I want to go by Aubrey's before I head back to the house. I already packed."

"I'll walk you over," I told her. We were making sure one of us was always available to escort her. It seemed to really grate on Dix, but he'd also seemed to have calmed down some since we started this. Whether it was because he didn't think she went anywhere or because he was getting the message, I didn't know and I didn't care.

"Are you sure it's okay for all of you to come to Thanksgiving in California?" KC asked as we left the academic building and headed for the dorm apartments where Aubrey was living.

"Yes," I said. "Why wouldn't it be?"

The snow crunched under our boots. It had been more than a dusting, four inches had actually fallen overnight. They were predicting another three for later this evening. We'd miss that but from the looks of it, we'd have plenty of snow by the time we got back to classes.

"Just..." She trailed off and I glanced at her a couple of times, waiting.

"Just?"

KC sighed and paused.

"You okay?" Concern filtered through me and I gave a sweeping look at the area around us. I didn't want any of her little fans to show up for autographs or videos or worse. One sentence I'd said about how she liked her coffee had ended up in some article. I didn't trust anyone around us anymore.

"I'm worried that you guys aren't seeing or talking to your mom because of me." That was literally the very last thing I ever expected her to say.

"Mom?"

Our mom hated her. That much was clear. No, I hadn't spoken to her in months but that wasn't...

"Yeah. I mean—you guys looked close a couple of years ago and look, I know my mom has issues. But she's still my mom. And your mom is still yours. I don't want to be the reason you guys don't see or talk to her."

I wished Ramsey or Lachlan was here. They would know exactly what to say. Holding out my hand, I kept glancing around to make sure we were still alone. When her palm slid over mine, I closed my fingers around hers. "You need gloves," I reminded her. Her hands were freezing.

"I forgot them," she admitted.

I nodded. I wasn't wearing the right jacket or I'd just give her mine. But even with the snow, it hadn't been that cold earlier.

"KC," I said, squeezing her fingers and turning to walk. She fell into step with me. I was trying to line up my thoughts.

"I'm sorry, I shouldn't have just launched that at you."

"You should," I told her. "I just—words are Ramsey and Lachlan's thing. They are better at wording these things than I am."

"You're not terrible," she informed me and I stole a look at her and smiled.

"I'm not terrible with you," I could admit that much. "But I am still not good with words."

"I don't need it to be pretty, I'm just—I worry about you guys. I've been taking up a lot of oxygen in this relationship."

"You can have all the oxygen," I told her. "I want you to have it. You're worried about so much. I just worry about you."

Her face flushed. When she slowed to a stop, I faced her, still holding her hand.

"Jonas..."

"It's true," I said. "You're worried we're not talking to Mom. But we didn't talk to Mom that much before. I didn't. I talked to Gibs more. I still message him, but it hasn't been the same since he took the song."

"You didn't talk to her before?"

"They were always touring or busy. Gibs always came first. So, most holidays when we were with them, Ramsey was usually in charge. Probably why he's bossy."

Laughter spilled out of KC and I grinned. "He is a little controlling."

"Just a little," I agreed. "But I don't mind so much. So...us not talking to Mom isn't *only* because of you."

"Okay," she said slowly then blew out a breath. "I know she doesn't like me."

"She hates you," I said, then I shrugged. "I don't know why. It's probably stupid reasons. She owes you an apology." On so many levels. Then something Dad said tickled in the back of my brain. "Are you worried because we're making our plans around your schedule and not ours?"

She winced, shifting her stance as she lifted her shoulders. "A little. I mean, I didn't go all the way to California our first Thanksgiving here. I went to Massachusetts to hang out with Yvette. This year, I want to go because of Pen."

"Do you want us to stay here or go somewhere else?" Because if she was worried about that, I could do that. I wouldn't like it. I didn't want her on her own or left with only Dix to "protect" her.

"No." The vehemence and lack of hesitation made me grin. "I want you guys there. I love that you want to go with me. You've...you've been great. I was just worried about you."

"You don't have to worry. We want to be there. Lachlan *really* wants to be there." I rolled my eyes and she laughed. That was exactly what I'd hoped for. "Ramsey wants to be there too. I know they do. And if you need me to tell you, I can. *I* want to be there."

Her grip on my hand tightened and tears shimmered in her eyes. "I needed to hear that."

"I will tell you every day if you need it," I promised. At my light tug, she came right to me and I hugged her tightly. She clasped her arms around me. I didn't care if someone took our picture. If she needed a hug, she was getting a hug.

"Hey, Jonas," she murmured against my ear. "I think you had really nice words."

I smiled. "Good." Letting her go, I studied her. "Better?"

She nodded slowly, exhaling a shaky breath. "Way better. I didn't realize how much that was bothering me."

"Good. If it bothers you again, tell me. Still want to go to Aubrey's?"

"Yes, please." She clasped my hand again and we continued across campus. Aubrey must have been watching because she had the door open before we got there.

"Wait for one of us to get you both," I reminded them. "Lachlan and I can grab your luggage too, Aubrey."

They both saluted, then laughed as they waved me off. I waited until the door locked, then I headed back down the stairs and cut across campus to the house. I needed to tell Ramsey that KC was worried about us and Mom.

Me telling her I wanted to be there was good. But she needed to hear it from them to... I was almost to the house when I caught sight of someone closing the front door. The shadows cast by the trees made it hard to see them, especially with the patchy clouds. It couldn't be Ramsey. It didn't look like Lachlan...

Hitting speed dial on my phone, I was happy Lachlan answered on the first ring. "What? I just got done."

"Where are you?"

The guy wasn't on his phone.

"At Grace Hall—why?"

I hung up and sprinted forward. The guy was already cutting away toward one of the running trails. "Hey," I called and pushed to run faster. But no sooner did I make it through the tree break and he was gone.

I spun in a circle, searching. My phone buzzed in my hand as I doubled-back to the tree line and checked. Did he cut in and then back out? But there was no one.

My phone buzzed again and I hit answer, panting.

"What's wrong?" Lachlan asked.

"Someone was at the house," I told him. "Coming out of it. Wasn't us."

"Where's Ace?"

"She's with Aubrey." I was really glad I dropped her off now.

"Wait for me," Lachlan ordered. "I'll be there in three minutes."

He hung up, probably so he could sprint, though it had already sounded like he was running. I headed toward the house and stared at the steps. We'd swept them that morning. The walk had been cleaned too.

There was some crusted snow on the doormat.

KC and I were the last to leave that morning. The mat had been clean.

I pivoted to stare around again. Lachlan needed to hurry, I wanted to know what they'd done inside *before* KC saw it.

Seventeen

KC

"F uck," Tracy swore and I had to bite back a smile. "I didn't think about the time difference. It's what? Five there?"

I grinned as I stared up at the ceiling. "It's two, we got in last night." Her groan almost made me laugh a little harder. I pitched my voice lower cause Ramsey was sound asleep next to me and I didn't want to wake him up. "It's fine. I used to call you on the road in the middle of the night all the time." I smothered a yawn. "And I need to get up to go running in a few hours."

"You and that running, you need a hobby," Tracy scolded, but the laughter in her voice softened it. "I would have hoped you'd found something else to try and take those edges off. You haven't toured in more than two years..."

I shrugged, not that she could see it. "I know, but I like running. I feel the difference when I don't run, you know."

"Maybe I should take up running," Tracy mused. "Though I'm not a fan of running in general. I'd love to go down to the beach...except there are people and they want me to continue to keep everything as healthy as possible. Which means using the treadmill in this very nice rental you set me up in and that's just a little boring..." There was just a hint of frustration in her voice.

A restlessness I understood.

"I'm sorry," I murmured, stretching one leg out from under the comforter. "You've basically had to put your whole life on hold and we're in this waiting game..."

"Don't," Tracy said, her tone firm and unyielding. It was more than a scold, it was almost a snap. "One, I wouldn't be anywhere else. I'm only sorry it took me so long to return your messages and find out what was going on. Pen is *my* sister too. Two, this is what big sisters do, we take one for the team and we are here for our siblings. If you were a match, I don't doubt for an instant you would have walked away from everything else to do this too."

She blew out a breath.

"And furthermore," she continued before I could respond. "You have put tremendous resources into this and carried so much of the weight, from finding the medical teams to throwing your influence to the concert and Dad..." The last word ended on a real scoff before she took another beat. "And coping with that Dad ambush—God, I still can't believe it and I watched it happen on the broadcast. You were a fucking rock star."

There was another beat and a giggle escaped me as Tracy groaned. Even putting a hand over my mouth to smother the sound, didn't quiet it fully.

"I can't believe I just punned like that." Her mock protest just made me giggle harder because she absolutely did that on purpose.

"I can, but it's okay," I assured her, smiling hard enough it made my cheeks hurt. "I actually like that description and the dad thing—" I sobered a little. "I really don't know what to do with that yet. I mean…Jackie and Bronson both said that he's gone to see Pen. He's asking questions. That's something, you know?"

"I don't know if it's enough," Tracy admitted, giving voice to the same doubts that I had. "For Pen's sake, I hope he's a better father than he's been to you or me. But I don't need him anymore. I stopped needing him a long time ago. So did you."

Had I?

Maybe.

"Bronson…I don't think he ever needed Dad. He's so damn grounded and together it's annoying." The sibling disgust just made me grin. Tracy wasn't wrong.

"He's a good big brother," I reminded her and she chuckled.

"He's a good little brother too." She yawned. "Okay, I'm going to shut up and let you go back to sleep. I'll talk to you for Thanksgiving…"

"I wish you could come."

"I do and don't," Tracy admitted. "It's better for me to keep isolating so nothing holds up her surgery when she's ready. And as much as I want to come and hang out with all of you, there's enough drama, you know?"

"Video chat? I can send dinner over to you and we can have a private siblings only turkey day on Friday?"

"Deal."

Then she hung up and I smothered another yawn as I stared at the phone. The blue light seemed almost too bright even in night mode. There was a buzz and a message popped up from her with a selfie of Tracy making a face and crossing her eyes. I grinned, then a sigh escaped as I shut the phone off.

A hand skated along my side. The gentle feathering of his fingers not quite tickling but still sending a shiver over my flesh. My nipples pebbled as he rolled onto his side and then his leg covered mine.

"Sorry," I whispered. "I didn't mean to wake you up."

Ramsey chuckled softly, then pressed a kiss to my temple as he wrapped his arm around me and tugged me into him. The slow stroke of his hand over my arm was like he was soothing away all the rough edges. "We have to get up in a few hours for you to run anyway…"

The soft reminder of my smart-ass comment to Tracy made me laugh. I covered my mouth with my hand to check my breath before I twisted to face Ramsey. It was too dark to make out his face, but I could feel the soft tease of his exhales on my cheek. When I traced my fingers over his brow, he swooped in to kiss me.

The massage of his lips to mine was both an offer and invitation. I sighed against his lips. Morning breath was overrated. We'd been exhausted when we got in the night before. Or at least, I had been.

Dix had flown with us. Yvette and Aubrey were on the same flight, but we took different cars back to the house. Aubrey was getting me a break from Dix's irritated vibe. The guys weren't even attempting to suppress their dislike for him, nor was Dix doing anything about his radiating disapproval for them.

It made my jaw ache from how hard I had to bite my tongue. I wanted them to get along but it seemed to be a rapidly losing proposition. We'd eaten almost quietly together, then we'd all split off to sleep. Davina had gotten the other suite of rooms right next to mine ready so that there were extra bedrooms. Yvette and Aubrey took the suite at the other end of my wing.

The weirdest and sweetest part was how natural it all felt to say goodnight to the girls and head to my room. Lachlan and Jonas both kissed me goodnight but they didn't follow me into my room. They'd both been in a mood before we left, so I could hardly blame them for being tired. When I was brushing my teeth, Ramsey slid in to brush his.

It was just nice. And now, with Ramsey kissing me and the soft sweeps of his tongue stroking mine as he slid his hand under my shirt to cup my breast, I sank into the contact. A sigh escaped me as he began to kiss a path along my jaw that turned into a gasp when he twisted my nipple. The sharp bite of pain a delicious wake-up that chased away any trace of sleepiness.

"I like this," I groaned when he reached my throat. The scrape of his teeth over my pulse point had me tugging at his shirt. I wanted to feel his skin. He bit me again, this time sucking a hickey right at the edge of my shirt's collar before he half-sat up and then my shirt was being dragged up and over. I had to let him go, but he didn't pull my shirt all the way off, he just tangled it around my wrists.

"Shh," he whispered when I groaned. "I want to play." Something dark and sensuous slid under those words and it had my thighs rubbing together. Then he kissed a path down my chest. The rasp of his stubble added a sting that I half-forgot when he locked his lips around a nipple.

And by play, he meant tease and torment with tiny licks, nibbles, and kisses as he moved between my breasts. When he slid his hand into my panties, I almost wept in relief because all I wanted was him to—

He stroked his thumb in a circle over my clit and my hips jerked upwards because it wasn't quite enough pressure. It was killing me. I wanted *more*. Another stroke, this time lighter than the first and a sound of protest escaped from my throat. Then Ramsey laughed and the sound sent a cascade of shivers through me.

"Someone is eager," he murmured, biting my lower lip as he continued to delve his fingers along the seam of my pussy.

Not quite giving me enough contact to do anything other than tease me that he was there.

"Ramsey…" I groaned out his name. The scrape of his teeth as he bit my lower lip again and held onto it offered a sting that grounded me. Rolling us over, Ramsey eased his fingers away before tracing my lips with the dampness that left me smelling and tasting myself. Fine, whatever, I wanted him… and then his thigh was between my legs, the pressure almost just there.

"Make yourself come," he told me, flexing his thigh as he dropped his hands to my hips. "Come on, Siren… make yourself come for me."

It took a moment for what he was demanding for to sink in. "You want me to…"

He flexed his thigh again and with his hands on my hips, he ground me against his leg. "I want you to come…and I want you to make yourself do it… Take what you want, Siren."

I braced my hands on his chest as he gave my hips a squeeze. I rolled my hips forward, he wanted me to grind on his leg. Could I do that? Heat swept through me like a hot desert wind. It was dark in the room, I couldn't see him but I could feel him.

Rotating my hips as I rolled them, I searched for the right amount of pressure. Ramsey had muscled thighs, so when he flexed them it changed the tension. A whimper escaped when I was almost there and he shifted his thigh again and I lost the tension I craved.

"You can do this, Siren." The dark encouragement was almost a taunt and I slid a hand down his chest to his boxers. His dick was already peeking out of the top, hot, hard and silky soft. The swift inhale made me smile.

"Keep your leg tense," I half-ordered and half-begged as I flexed my fingers around the base of his dick and began to stroke. The dribble of dampness at the top provided a little lube. At his barely suppressed groan, it was my turn to chuckle.

He locked his thigh again so I could use the ridge of the quadriceps to get myself off. I rewarded him with a stroke for each time I managed to ramp my own tension up. I was almost there. Practically shaking, I fought to go faster and tease him at the same time. The first spasm left me trembling and then I was off his thigh, my panties were gone and he lifted me right onto his rock hard erection.

There was no patience in either of us as he mounted me on him and then I let out a shriek as he thrust all the way in. The stretch and burn pushed me the rest of the way over the edge. At some point, we were writhing together and I ground down to meet his every thrust and then his mouth was on mine and he came with a stutter of hips as I continued to shake from the climax.

Clinging to Ramsey, I rained kisses down on his face and to his jaw, then to his throat. His pulse beat as hard as mine. When he began to squeeze and massage my ass, I sighed. I swore his dick twitched and then I was on my back, his shirt was off and he loomed over me.

"You're still thinking really hard, Siren," he told me in a rough voice. "I don't want you thinking about anything else except me... except us... right here and right now."

By the time he kissed a path to my abdomen, I was already squirming. My nipples ached in the best way and he used his thumb and forefinger to tease my swollen clit, obliterating my thoughts.

We didn't get back to sleep for another hour, by then, I was too boneless to do more than wrap around him and sleep. Dawn's grayish light edged the windows when I woke up and I was sore, but in the most sensual way when I slipped out of bed. A quick wipe after I peed and I got dressed. I'd need a shower after my run anyway.

I pressed a kiss to Ramsey's jaw on my way past and chuckled when he caught my arm. "Going to run—in the gym," I tacked on so he didn't think I was leaving the house. "Go back to sleep if you want."

"I'll come..." He murmured before he yawned and I grinned.

"Pretty sure we both did...a few times."

He gave me the lightest of swats on my ass. "You don't have to wait for me, but I'll be there..."

I was still giggling as I headed out into the hall. I debated waking Lachlan, but if he was asleep then he should rest. Ramsey said he'd come and join me and I was okay with running on my own. The downstairs was quiet. Mom hadn't been up, or at least she hadn't been downstairs when we got in, so I'd check on her later today.

Through the doors and across the patio and around the pool, I savored the quiet breeze and the cool air that was a far cry from the ice and the snow back at school. I'd just gotten the gym door opened and the lights turned on when someone clearing their throat jerked me around.

David Ranier was the last person I expected to see, his expression grim and filled with disapproval. "It's about time you and I had a conversation, Kaitlin."

Eighteen

RAMSEY

Sex with Kaitlin definitely took the edge off for me. I wished it helped her more, but the agitation that finally seemed smoothed away when she went back to sleep was back with force when she headed out to run. While I wasn't Lachlan, and I didn't embrace early morning runs, I could and would do it for her.

If we weren't at the house in Beverly Hills with its security and gates, I'd have asked her to wait. As it was, I made quick work to wash up and get dressed. I needed to shave so I could spend an hour or two eating her out later. Maybe if we gave her enough orgasms, we could ease some of her stress.

The closer we got to the surgery date the more tightly wound she'd grown. Worry for her sister occupied most of her waking moments. It was the only reason I agreed with Lachlan regarding what *might* have been a break-in at the house.

We hadn't been able to prove anything. Nothing was missing that we could tell and nothing had been disturbed. I'd filed a report with campus security then I'd requested a security upgrade. It would be installed before we were back.

In the meanwhile, we would make sure one of us was with Kaitlin at all times. That in mind, I cleaned my glasses before I slid them on and then I was heading out to go downstairs. I glanced at the door to the room Lachlan and Jonas crashed in.

I could wake them up, but then I'd have to share Kaitlin. Between my schedule and hers, I hadn't spent as much time with her as I would like. So, they would be awake soon enough.

When I circled the pool on the way to the gym, I expected to hear music playing and the sound of the treadmill running. Instead, David Ranier stood in the doorway, practically looming over her.

"You need to be more receptive," Ranier was saying. "Your mother values your opinion and the suppressive tendencies you're expressing are closing her down. This is not good for her and it won't be good for you."

I didn't care how he dressed it up, the implied threat echoed resoundingly.

"I don't know how the hell you got in here," Kaitlin informed him, not an ounce of fear in her voice. "But you're leaving."

"I am here at your mother's invitation," Ranier said. "You don't get to decide—"

"Actually," I said as I closed in on the guy. "Kaitlin lives here. So yes, she does."

Ranier pivoted, surprise on his face, and I invaded his space the way he'd invaded hers.

"Let's get another thing straight, Mr. Ranier," I told him as he backed up a step and hit the doorframe. "You think you have the right to say anything to her, you don't. You might be her mother's guest, but that gets you exactly nothing where Kaitlin is concerned."

"You misunderstood—" the man began but I cut him off with a slice of my hand.

"I didn't misunderstand anything. I can read body language. Even if I couldn't, the moment you decided to corner her in the gym, in the dark, while she was alone, you crossed a line."

Kaitlin had her phone in her hand, so I kept my focus on the guy in the doorway.

Ranier straightened. "As I recall, Mr. Malone, you have a bit of an inappropriate relationship of your own with our Kaitlin."

"I'm not your anything," Kaitlin said from behind him. "Yes, this is Kaitlin Crosse, we have an intruder at the gym and I need him removed from the property."

Good girl. I wanted to beam with pride. She called security. Ranier tried to pivot to face her, but I gripped his shoulder and dragged the man backwards. He wasn't that muscular, more on the lean side. Despite the fact he could loom over Kaitlin, I had at least an inch on him. That worked for me.

He wanted to use his size to intimidate, I'd be happy to return the favor. The man struggled as I dug my fingers in, but I grasped his arm to force him out of the doorway. He jerked away from me and then went stumbling through the open gate to the pool area.

That was fine. It put more distance between him and Kaitlin. I stalked after him. All I wanted this morning was time with Kaitlin, a chance to make her smile, and see what I could do about easing her worries.

Instead, we get this prick.

Whatever his game was, he wasn't going to—

Ranier took a swing at me. I avoided it easily enough. Lachlan and Jonas were a lot faster than this asshat when it came to throwing punches. I responded, the crack of bone in my hand when I hit hurt like a bitch. Still, my fist plowed into his face and he went staggering right into the pool.

Kaitlin rushed up next to me. When she wrapped her hands around my bicep, I nudged her back behind me, while Ranier flailed in the water before catching the side. Two guys in security uniforms appeared from the other side of the pool and the floodlights kicked on.

I squinted against the sudden brightness. Ranier glared at me as the guards ordered him out of the pool.

"Miss Crosse," a third guard greeted her as he circled the pool toward us. The man was easily my height but he had to have another fifty pounds of muscle on me. He was also giving me a distinctly unfriendly look. "You all right, ma'am?

"I'm fine, Bryan," Kaitlin said, relief in her voice. "Thank you. This is Ramsey, he's made sure that Mr. Ranier backed off. Then Ranier took a swing at him."

The guard—Bryan—relaxed at the description. He nodded. "Are you sure you want us to escort Mr. Ranier out?"

"Yes, please. He can go right out the gate as is. I'll ask Davina to have someone on the staff pack up his belongings. We'll send them to wherever."

"I'll take care of it," Bryan said, then the guard glanced at me again. "Your hand all right, Mr...?"

"Malone," I supplied and I flexed it slowly. No, it was definitely sore and I'd broken the skin on one of my knuckles. I hit the guy a lot harder than I meant to—then again, he deserved it. They'd fished him out of the water and he was protesting their not so delicate handling. "What happens after you show him the gate?"

"We'll call him a car," Bryan told me. "We'll also inform him that he's trespassing if he doesn't leave. If he continues to refuse, we'll hold him and call the police department. Then he becomes their problem."

"And if your mother...?" I glanced down at Kaitlin and she gave me an encouraging smile.

"Mom would have to be awake to protest, but it doesn't matter. He tried to assault you, I saw it. And I don't feel safe with him here."

"Then we're removing him now." Bryan's expression gentled. "We'll have one of our guys up closer to the house this week, make sure there are no more incidents."

"Thank you, Bryan. I hate to ask for more over the holiday."

"Not a worry, that's what we're here for." Then Bryan gave me a nod before he strode around the pool to where his guys had Ranier. The man hadn't quite started truly protesting but he raised his voice when Bryan got there.

Kaitlin leaned into me and I lifted my arm to wrap it around her. My hand throbbed but it felt good at the same time. Worth it. Ranier glared at Kaitlin, but whatever Bryan said to him shut him up and then they were escorting him out.

"Fuck," Kaitlin said as she blew out a breath. I squeezed her a little tighter. "Mom is gonna be pissed... and I can't believe she invited him here. Well, I can, but Davina didn't say anything."

"Maybe she didn't know," I suggested. Because based on everything I'd seen, Davina would go to war for Kaitlin. I didn't think any of that was an act. I pressed a kiss to the top of her head. "C'mon, let's get your run in. You'll feel better."

"Your hand," she protested as I turned her around to walk her toward the still open gate.

"My hand will be fine. I can clean it up after your run. It's sore, not gonna lie, but I enjoyed that way too much to ruin it right now."

Her sudden laugh was worth every ounce of the bruising. "This from the guy who wouldn't let me punch Teddy." I resembled that remark.

"These hands?" I reminded her as I nudged open the door to the gym, then caught one of her hands to lift up and kiss. "Are infinitely more valuable than mine. Besides, Jonas and Lachlan both hit like freight trains. They were going to do more damage."

Light kindled in her eyes as she tilted her head and looked up at me. "Thank you."

"For?"

"For—this morning and earlier this morning." Pink flushed her cheeks and I dropped a light kiss on her nose.

"Believe me, both were my pleasure." Then I sobered as she frowned down at my hand. "I'm going to be fine, I promise. How long was he out here?"

"A couple of minutes," she promised. "I was more surprised than anything else." That wasn't totally true. She let go of my hand and fixed her pony tail before she met my gaze. "Okay, I was also pretty creeped out too."

I nodded. "We'll make sure security keeps him out and you're not coming down here by yourself."

"This is my house, Ramsey." The protest wasn't because of me, but because she should feel safe in her own house.

"It is," I agreed. "But with your mom here, and Thanksgiving, there's gonna be a lot of people in and out. I'd feel better if one of us was here with you. Lachlan already likes to run with you."

She made a face. "I know. I just—" All at once, her expression tightened and the air around her turned positively electric. This was just one more thing she had to deal with.

"I can't fix it all," I said, cupping her cheek with my uninjured left hand. "I wish I could. You're carrying a lot right now, Siren. Let me help where I can."

After kissing my palm, she let go and put her hands on her hips to pace away. The gym was a nice one and there was more than one treadmill, but she didn't look at any of the equipment.

As much as I wanted to push, I didn't. She was already dealing with so much…

Finally, she pivoted to face me. "Okay."

That was it.

I raised my brows. "Okay?" I wanted to be clear on what we were agreeing to here.

"Okay, I'll make sure I come out here with one of you guys. We're already in each other's pockets all the time. But I don't feel like you should have to be with me twenty-four seven."

"That's fair," I agreed. "But maybe we want to be. I mean, Lachlan's just dying to be your one and only. He'll love the chance to have you all to himself as much as possible."

The teasing remark worked. She rolled her eyes, then a real, if reluctant, smile curved her lips.

"Thank you, Siren," I said. "I know we keep asking for a lot and you keep giving us so much."

"You don't ask for as much as you could," she informed me before she turned to get on the treadmill. Instead of starting it right away, she glanced over her shoulder at me. "You keep mentioning what Lachlan wants or Jonas…"

I nodded, then tested my fingers. As stiff and sore as my knuckles were, I could flex them all and curl them into a fist. I didn't think I'd broken anything, even if it had sounded like I had. Maybe I got lucky and broke something in the jackass's face.

"What do *you* want?" The question pulled all of my attention and I met the seriousness in her eyes.

"You." It was the easiest answer. "I need my brothers in my life and I need you. If that means we are all dating you, then we are."

"But—" She hesitated, then shook her head.

"But?" I prompted.

"What about what happens later? What if—I don't want to pick? Even later?"

"Then you don't," I said, before closing the distance to where she stood on the treadmill. "Do I know what I'm saying? Yes. I love my brothers. I know how much they want you. You're good for Jonas—"

"That's not what—"

I closed my eyes for a moment, grimacing. "I know, what I said before, about you being bad for him. I was an asshole. I— let what I read and believed from bad sources dictate what I thought, even when the evidence right in front of me denied all of it. You are *good* for him. You are good for Lachlan. And you are the absolute best for me."

She swallowed and the shimmer of tears in her eyes made me want to kick my own ass.

"Did you really think I still thought you were bad for them?" I stepped up onto the treadmill with her, then cradled her face in my hand.

"Do I sound pathetic if I say, a little? Sometimes? It's like I can hear it in the back of my head? And I am the one who is so focused elsewhere, and you guys..."

"Are right where we want to be," I told her firmly. "Are we working on figuring things out? Yes. Has it been easy? No. Do I regret anything?"

The last question I left right there until she let out a shaky breath.

"The only thing I regret is how I made you feel. If it takes me ten months or ten years, I'm going to make that up to you."

She leaned her cheek into my palm then she was wrapping her arms around me, so I picked her up as I held her. "I'm a mess," she whispered.

"Well, that's fine, I like you just the way you are." The

embrace lasted for a long time, but I wasn't in any hurry to let her go. When she finally pressed a kiss to my throat and eased back, I set her down. "Ready to run?"

She swiped away the tears from her cheeks and nodded. "I think so—" Huffing out another breath, she shook her head, then dipped her chin as she studied me.

"What?"

"You're just—really hot...and I thought so even when you were my teacher."

I chuckled. "I didn't notice."

"No, I pretty much thought you were a douchebag too..."

That made me grin wider.

"Okay," she said, getting it together. She had this way of just pulling herself together and shaking off the emotional damage like it hadn't happened. That wasn't always healthy, but it was damn impressive.

I moved to the other treadmill and got it started, waiting for her to warm up. Ranier could be a problem. With everything else we had going on, she didn't need that. I needed to talk to Lachlan's dad and maybe mine. We needed help.

We needed her safer than she'd been, and that meant dealing with some of these problems now.

Nineteen

Tossing David Ranier out the day before had some drawbacks. One of those drawbacks had poured herself a drink and stood out on the back patio smoking a cigarette. She'd quit drinking and smoking many times, this was more to quiet her nerves than because she had a real need.

At least, I hoped so. Johnny wasn't a big fan of when Mom drowned her problems, and he hadn't objected to the pitcher of Martinis she'd prepared before heading out here. Yvette and Aubrey had both shot me questioning looks, but I shook my head.

I needed to talk to her. Mom hadn't been thrilled about the guys being here, the fact she kept shooting them dirty looks hadn't been lost on any of us. Jackie and Bronson called, they would be heading over shortly.

Davina and I already arranged for dinner to be sent to Tracy and we talked earlier. There would be time later in the day to go and see Pen during visiting hours. I had sent presents to my other siblings, along with their favorite pies.

Thanksgiving didn't need to be a formal occasion, but I loved the idea of having everyone together for the holiday. It was also good for Bronson to get to know the guys. Jackie wanted her own look at them. They'd earned some of Davina's approval—that much was clear when she served their favorite coffees at breakfast.

Johnny caught my arm before I stepped outside. "Be gentle with her," he said quietly. "She argued with David this morning."

I frowned. "He's not supposed to be here."

"He wasn't," Johnny promised. "He called her before dawn to demand she either invite him back in or to leave and join him."

Before dawn... Johnny was there. I tried not to smile, but the corners of my lips twitched. "Thank you for looking out for her."

"I always will." The firm tone allowed for absolutely no disagreement. "I'll look out for her *and* for you. So is she. He wants her to cut all ties with you, and that was when she hung up on him."

Tears burned in my eyes and a lump in my throat threatened to leave me choking. Blowing out a shaky breath, I nodded. "Thank you."

Johnny didn't have to tell me any of that. I didn't want him to break Mom's confidence, but at the same time...? It made me feel a little better. He gave my arm a squeeze and I slipped out to the patio.

It was sixty-five, sunny, and damn near perfect out here. The high for the day was seventy, and it was going to be amazing. I considered inviting Lachlan out for a drive after food. He'd been—distant wasn't the right word, but definitely not as engaged as he usually was.

Worry filtered through me that I'd been too preoccupied with my own stuff. I needed to remember to check on them more often. Putting a pin in that for now, I padded over to the patio table where Mom had set herself up.

She was dressed in a filmy white gown over silk pants and a classic spaghetti strap camisole. With her white blond hair styled in a simple updo, she looked like a throwback to the Hollywood actresses of the forties and the fifties. Classy, curvy, and unattainable.

"You're staring, Kaitlin," Mom said before blowing out a stream of smoke.

"You're beautiful," I admitted, crossing the patio to take the seat opposite her. Unlike Mom, I was dressed in capris, an oversized sweatshirt—it was one of Jonas' that I'd stolen—and my hair was just up in a ponytail. Our definitions of casual were two very different things. "Sometimes, I forget how much."

Surprise flickered across her face as she blinked at me. Yeah, I really hadn't expected to say that either. Maybe I needed to remind her more often that she was more than the image she projected. "I..."

"Look great," I told her. "Thanks for going to the effort for Thanksgiving. It's not your favorite holiday."

Mom snuffed out her cigarette then picked up the Martini glass. "I—wasn't really planning to be here for the holiday."

"I know," I said, propping my chin on my hand. "You had plans with Ranier..." Lips pursed.

"Well, not anymore," Mom stated firmly. "I won't have him threatening you. So, that means I will be here for Thanksgiving. Davina mentioned Jackie was coming, along with her son."

Her son. "Yes, she's bringing Bronson."

Mom nodded. "And those boys in there?"

"They aren't boys, Mom."

She narrowed her eyes. "One of them is too old for you and the other two are—"

"Wonderful. They're all wonderful." Then, because her nostrils were flaring and after she took a long drink, I added, "Don't get me wrong, they are still guys. They aren't always great. But I like having them around more than when I don't have them."

Mom said nothing for a long moment, her gaze on the doors to the house. Everyone left us alone, which I appreciated. They could have moved out here, followed with conversation, but they hadn't. Yvette and Aubrey were used to indulging Mom and distracting her.

I didn't need her distracted today. I wanted— "Mom," I said, pulling her attention back to me. "I want to be different."

"We've always been different, darling. You have made a small fortune on being different... your image, your talent, and how you manage both? They make you different and exceptional."

The compliment floored me. She loved our music, that she'd never hidden, but she didn't make a big deal out of what I did. Only when it was a reflection of her, then she embraced it.

"Thank you," I said. "I try. But I meant I want to be different as a family. You and me? We have all these people here who care."

"Well, you do," Mom corrected and I snorted.

"Don't play the pity me card," I told her flatly and she jerked like I'd slapped her. "You have me, Yvette, and Aubrey without trying. You have Davina and Dix. They both care. Then there's Johnny, a man so crazy in love with you, that he wants to protect you even when you were dumping him for another man."

"I didn't dump him for David," Mom corrected. "Johnny and I were broken up before I even met him." She drained the Martini before reaching for her cigarettes. "Johnny and I..."

I waited, letting her sort her thoughts out. Half the time I didn't know what I needed either. Could I sum up my relationships with the guys?

"Johnny is young and ambitious and full of plans." That wasn't what I was expecting. "He sees all these possibilities for us."

"You don't?"

"Kaitlin... darling..." She released a sigh so heavy, the weight dragged at me. "I've made terrible decisions before. I'm not always a good person. Sometimes...sometimes I don't know how to not be selfish."

"Okay."

Fresh surprise flickered in her eyes. "Okay? I confess that I'm a bad person and you just say okay?"

"First of all, you didn't confess to being a bad person. You confessed to being human. You're not perfect. Newsflash— neither am I. You've never been perfect, Mom. I've never expected you to be. But you are passionate about the things you love and you are passionate about your work."

The words hardly mollified her. "That doesn't sound too bad, or too good for that matter"

I lifted my shoulders. "It sounds like you're human. Look...did I sometimes wish you would do more mom like things when I was little? Yeah. I can admit that. Did I wish you and Dad had been able to work it out? What kid from divorce doesn't? But here's the thing... you're my mom. Good, bad, or indifferent, I love you. I love the things we've done, I love dress up days and high tea days. I love going to awards shows with you and gossiping about what the other stars are doing."

A smile curved her lips and I grinned.

"I love cheering on your roles, even when they take you away, because you love what you do. Maybe we don't always get along, because we don't really get to see each other or know each other anymore…"

"Maybe," Mom said slowly, then she put her pack of cigarettes down. "I'm sorry about David, sweetheart."

"Thank you, but as long as he's gone for good and can't hurt you anymore, I'm fine."

"You stopped those financial transactions," Mom commented, tapping a finger against her lower lip. "I didn't even know you could do that."

I dipped my chin and she nodded.

"Thank you," she said softly. I didn't need anything else. When I reached over the table to clasp her hand, she gripped mine tightly.

"Now it's Thanksgiving," I told her and she looked to her cigarettes and her pitcher.

"Maybe we should go join our guests…"

I grinned. "Maybe."

The next couple hours flew by as the scent of dinner roasting drifted out to tease us. Instead of throwing on a movie, we dragged out a board game. That led to us all pairing off to do Pictionary.

Jackie and Bronson arrived in the middle of the first round so we pulled them right into it. Even Mom was laughing as she and Johnny worked together.

It was hilarious.

I was still laughing when the doorbell rang and I did a quick survey of the room. You could only get up to the house if your name was on the list, and I'd given security the list of who I invited. Dix wasn't here—maybe he wanted to come in the front.

"I'll be right back," I told Jonas as I headed for the front door. Lachlan was a half-step behind me. I would have teased him about not letting me out of his sight, but the guys were really serious about it.

After I swung the door open, I faltered.

Dad stood there, his long hair brushed back and secured at the nape of his neck. He was dressed in jeans and running shoes, but his shirt was a button down. Next to him, his—wife—looked stricken, like she'd rather be anywhere but here.

"Hey," I said slowly as Dad let go of Linzi's arm to step toward me. He was telegraphing the hug, so I met him half-way. It was awkward as hell. "I didn't know if you would come..." I admitted.

He gave me a little squeeze then backed up a step. His pupils were a little swollen. He'd probably had to get a little high for the courage. I was kind of wishing I had something at the moment, as it was, Lachlan caught my hand.

"Gibs," he greeted him, and offered him his free hand, they shook briefly. Then Lachlan glanced at Linzi. "Mom."

"Good to see you," Gibs said to Lachlan before he focused on me. "I—you invited me—us. It's still good, yeah?"

"Yes," I admitted. I'd added his name to the list because... honestly I never thought he'd show up. "Come in..."

I backed off and thankfully, Lachlan stuck with me and I took all the support from his hand on mine. As Gibs and Linzi walked ahead of us, I looked up at Lachlan. "Did you know?" Even whispering seemed too loud.

"No, Ace, I had no idea." Then he pulled me a little closer. "You didn't even tell me you invited him."

"I didn't tell anyone," I admitted. "I didn't think he'd come." And I didn't know what to do with it since he had.

"Hey Gibs," Bronson greeted him.

"Gibs?" Mom's voice climbed a half-note.

"Jackie," Dad was saying. "Good to see you. And Bronson, you're looking good."

The room seemed to spiral out in front of us as Dad went around the room greeting everyone. Jonas and Ramsey were both on their feet and Johnny moved closer to Mom. Linzi said next to nothing.

She hadn't even greeted Lachlan.

What a bitch.

I wasn't even sure what to say or to do. When Dad got to Mom, I forgot how to breathe.

"Hello, Jennifer," he said slowly. "Happy Thanksgiving."

Mom's withering expression had blanked away as she stared at him. For one brief second, she glanced at me then back at Dad. Finally, she stood and I clenched Lachlan's hand as fiercely as I could.

"Gibson," Mom said, holding out her hands. He took them and she greeted him with a kiss to his cheek. One he returned. "Happy Thanksgiving."

Wow. That was...

"I see you brought the whore..."

Twenty

LACHLAN

Brought the...

"Jennifer," Johnny said before anyone, least of all Mom, could respond. The tension sharpened in the room. Ace's grip on my hand turned into a vise. "Not the time, my darling. Especially with *all* the children here."

"Yes, her children, who are seeing *my* child," Jennifer's cultured voice took on a distinct edge, and I wasn't the only one who noticed. Ramsey and Jonas stood when Mom walked in, but Jonas moved toward us, not Mom.

"Mom," Ace said as she loosened her grip on my hand.

"KC is right," Jackie joined in the interruption, her no nonsense crisp tone lancing right the bubbling tension. "We've discussed this. One doesn't have to like someone to be polite, and it *is* the holiday. Maybe, for the afternoon, we can put aside old animosities."

Jennifer canted her head as if she actually needed to consider the choice. "All right, I actually think it's time for a round of drinks. Davina said food would be ready in a half-hour." She turned to Johnny. "Help me?"

"Absolutely."

And as one the whole room let out a collective breath. I shook my head as my phone buzzed in my pocket. Ramsey had moved on an intercept course for Mom and Gibs, I wanted the hell out of this room.

But I wasn't going to abandon Ace.

"I can't believe he came," she said in a soft voice. Jonas rubbed her shoulder and I moved to block Mom's view of them. She was watching via one of the mirrors.

"It's a good thing that he came, right?" I checked with her. Cause if it wasn't, I could talk to him and get him to take Mom and go.

"I think so," Ace said, then blew out a breath. "Actually, I'm going to go and check with Davina and make sure we have enough place settings."

"I'll go with you," Jonas offered and I nodded to him. Good plan. Ramsey had gotten Mom and Gibs away from the central part of the room, while Yvette and Aubrey seemed very focused on Jennifer.

Good.

Keep them all apart. Pulling my phone out, I caught Bronson eyeing me and I met him stare for stare. Ace's brother wasn't certain of us, but that was fine.

We weren't dating him.

The other guy just shook his head and pushed to his feet before he squared his shoulders and headed toward Gibs. Better him than me. I thought the tension when we came down for breakfast and Jennifer radiating disapproval had been bad.

That seemed almost idyllic by comparison.

WALKER:

> I got a number. They are willing to talk price with the buyer only. No texts. No emails. Only voice calls. They responded via an encrypted server, but their account is already gone. So we have the number and that's it. What do you want me to do?

Fuck.

We'd been playing cat and mouse with the seller for the past couple of weeks. They wouldn't commit to anything. Walker had upped the bid to the max I could pull together without involving Ace.

ME:

> Did they give you a time frame?

WALKER:

> Just said if I wanted the guitar as badly as I seemed to, then I would call.

Not helpful.

Walker: I don't mind calling. I'm at my parents place, but it's insane with my sisters and all their kids here, so I just need to head out to do it.

I shook my head.

ME:

> You've done enough. Send me the number. I'll take it from here. I owe you.

WALKER:

> No problem. Though, if you decide you could hook me up with one of your girl's bandmates, I wouldn't say no.

I snorted.

Right, not making any promises.

The number flashed up on the screen. I glanced around

the room. Ace and Jonas weren't back. Ramsey was giving me a look, but he was stuck with Mom and Gibs. Yeah. This was as good a time as any.

Heading for the doors to the patio, I let myself out and took a walk. I wanted some privacy for the call. I hesitated to press dial right away, because my phone wouldn't exactly protect who I was...

Right. There were VPNs and dialer services. It took me fifteen minutes to set up a spoofed number via an app that would let me do WiFi calling. So whatever number the other person saw wouldn't be me.

Shooting a look at the house, I added the number into the app and pressed dial.

It rang twice, then answered. Silence greeted me, but it wasn't dead air.

"Hello?" Impatient with all the hoops, I wanted answers. The person wanted a call. I was calling.

A soft chuckle greeted me and I frowned, pacing off the patio and heading toward the path that had more shade.

"I'm glad I entertain you."

"Lover, you've always entertained me." The voice made my skin crawl.

"Payton." I almost spit out her name.

"Awww, you missed me, didn't you?" Nails on a chalkboard would have been more welcome than her cooing voice.

"You took her guitar," I said slowly as the memory of the destruction in her room washed over me. The shit on the bed. The absolute carnage done to her clothes.

"Did I?" It wasn't like her to play coy, but then she played at everything else. "We're just two old lovers playing catch up, Lachy babe."

I made a face at the nickname.

"Give me one good reason to not just hang up." I glanced back at the house. I wanted privacy for this call. "Let me be one hundred percent clear, if it doesn't involve the guitar, then this conversation is over."

"You want it, don't you?"

"Not hearing a reason," I gritted out. My jaw ached from how hard I fought against clenching my teeth.

"See, Lachy, this is where I know you better than you know yourself. It's always been the chase. You love to catch your prey..."

"Get the fuck over yourself, Payton. You were a mistake. One I would love to go back in time and erase. It has nothing to do with pursuit..."

"Oh, you thought I meant me?" She laughed and it was a nasty little chuckle. "No, I'm talking about how you and your brothers are all chasing the same girl and you want the edge... that means you'll do anything to win. You're very competitive..."

Curling the fingers of my free hand into a fist, I cracked two knuckles. "You don't know shit about us. Don't play with me."

"I have what you want so you can edge out your brothers. The only question you have to ask is what will you do to get what I have?"

That wasn't my only question. "Not playing this game. Goodbye, Payton—"

"Wait," she said abruptly. For the first time, the smirky sarcasm was absent from her voice. "What do you want, Lachy?"

"I want the guitar," I told her flatly. I also wanted the bitch in jail, because if she did all of that *and* stole the guitar. She'd assaulted Ace. "How much?"

"A night with me."

What? "I didn't hear you correctly."

"You heard me fine. I've missed you and we were good together. One night with me and I give you the prize to win the rock star. Your choice..."

I almost pulled the phone away to stare at it. She was insane.

"You might need a little time to think about it. See you soon, Lachy." She ended it with a kiss and then hung up.

Was she insane? I half-wanted to just throw the phone across the pool or smash it into a wall. I'd never wanted to hit a woman before. Right now, I would cheerfully punch her.

If she had anything to do with Ace getting hurt...

Anger was a knotted ball in my gut. She could be playing a game. Lying. Except... this wasn't the first time the guitar had been up for sale. We knew whoever took it had to be someone at the school. Someone who knew Ace. Knew us.

It was why we used Dix initially. Then they shut down and disappeared. Scared off. Because they figured out it was us?

And now this? How likely was it that phone number would be any good after today?

Fuck—I needed to know if she had the guitar. That meant I had to see her and if I saw her...

"Lachlan?" Great. Another person I'd rather not talk to. When I pivoted, I found Mom standing there, staring at me. The pinched expression on her face just radiated disapproval.

"Mother."

Eyes narrowing, Mom folded her arms. "Mother? I haven't seen or heard from you in months and all you can say is Mother?"

I shrugged. "I thought it was a polite greeting. I can go back to saying nothing at all." That would be fine by me.

"Lachlan..."

"What?" I didn't want to talk to her. I didn't want to deal with her at all. Right now, I was already pissed at Payton and I really wanted to break something. If Mom wanted to step into the ring for a fight, well... bring it the fuck on.

"Why are you being so rude?" The faint scandalized note almost hit the right beats. Almost. Except...

"Oh, I don't know. Would you like it alphabetically? Or numerically?"

"You've been spending too much time with that—"

"You think very carefully about whatever label you're about to apply to Ace. *Very* carefully."

"'Oh, so you'll defend her, but when her mother called me a whore...''

I shrugged. "That's between you and Jennifer."

Her eyes rounded. "You think I'm a whore?"

I didn't sigh, but I did shake my head. "Not what I said. If she called you a name, that's between the two of you. She also changed the subject. Considering you showed up at *her* house for Thanksgiving... I think you should just count yourself lucky she didn't throw you out."

I had a headache.

"I can't believe you. First you choose that—that girl. That girl who treats her father—"

"Stop," I snapped. "Stop. Stop. Stop." I fired off each sylla-ble, barely able to keep from spitting the words at her. "Just *stop* with the lies and the bullshit. I don't know why you think coming between Gibs and his daughter was something you needed to do and you know—I don't fucking care. You have painted Ace with this negative brush for as long as I can remember..."

Shock stamped across her face and I didn't care.

"But she's not like that at all. And she did not deserve you getting between her and Gibs. You are always going on and on about how cruel and thoughtless she is. How she ignores him. How she cut him out of her life. But maybe you should look in the mirror—at how cruel and thoughtless you've been. From everything I've seen, he *wants* to see her, or why else would he even be here?"

Because Ace invited him. After the ambush at the show and their confrontation where the pair actually talked, he was responding to her.

"You didn't even care that she'd been kidnapped. You decided she was just playing some game. You wanted us to make her go away." That, I would never forget. I doubted I could forgive it. "Worse, you filled Gibs' head with that. He almost didn't pay the ransom."

I sucked in a breath, I was flexing my hands. Opening and closing them as I fought to get my temper back under control.

"She—"

"She what?" I snarled. "She was a kid who needed her dad and you made sure that didn't happen? Did you know about his other kids? I mean—you probably did. You manage every-thing else. Did you know about that baby fighting cancer? Did you make sure Gibs didn't know about her too? Is that who you are, Mom? A woman who cuts children out of her husband's life—why?"

She practically trembled as she stared at me. "I will not stand here and be spoken to this way."

"Then leave," I told her. "Go do whatever it is you do. I don't think anyone is going to miss you."

"Why do you hate me so much?" she asked, and I had to laugh. It was laugh or it was scream.

"Lachlan?" Ace. The soft, lyrical nature of her voice pulled me around. Worry filled her expression. Worry for me. Worry for the family. I hated being something that caused her worry but at the same time...I wanted to mean something to her.

"What's up, Ace?" I shoved my phone in my pocket and left Mom to walk over to her. Gibs was a few steps behind her and his expression was guarded as he studied me then past me toward Mom.

"Davina is calling everyone to dinner," she said and I

caught her hand when I was close, kissing it once before I slid my arm around her.

"Then let's go eat. I'm starving." I was going for light, but she searched my face. "It's okay," I said in a lower voice. "It's fine, let's go back to having fun, yeah?"

She frowned but I wanted her to keep enjoying her day. Gibs was here and surprise or not, it had meant something. Her mom was here and despite some tension, they seemed to be getting along.

C'mon, Ace, I tried to encourage her mentally. Just let it go and let's enjoy ourselves.

She leaned into me and slid an arm around my waist. "Okay." Then she glanced at Mom. "Linzi, I was just thanking Dad for coming. Not sure if you have any food allergies or anything, but Davina can answer any questions."

Mom looked at us and then past us to Gibs. Yeah, time to go. I did not want to be here for this part and Ace didn't need to be either.

"Go on in, Sweet Kaity," Gibs said. "Linzi and I need to talk for a minute..."

Definitely our cue to go. I nodded to him and then hustled Ace to the doors and inside. Once the french doors were closed, she turned to face me.

"How much did you hear?" I asked.

"Enough," she whispered. "So did Dad." Sadness etched in her eyes.

"Well, then you know I'm on your side. I don't know why Mom did the things she did or what she wanted to accomplish. But she doesn't get to do it anymore."

Ace pushed up on her toes and then her lips were pressed to mine. I wrapped her up and half-lifted her so our heads were even, and I drank in her kiss.

My dick went to stone at the first touch. Fuck, she could burn me alive with just the promise of her lips. I dragged my head up when all I wanted to do was find us a spot to get naked.

"I'm going to earn sainthood," I informed her. "Because I'm going to put you down and we're going into that dining room to enjoy all the food, drama, and family chaos."

Her eyes shone. "Sainthood, huh?"

"Yep. Cause I really want to give in to all my demons, but I'll put those aside for now."

"Raincheck?"

"Hell. Yes."

Her smile was worth it, then she nuzzled another kiss to my lips. I savored it but made myself put her down.

"Sainthood," I repeated, reminding us both. Then the little devil winked at me before she turned to head for the dining room, and there was a definite sway to her hips.

"Killing me, Ace," I muttered. "Killing me."

<h1 style="text-align:center">Twenty-One</h1>

The sun barely edged the horizon as we left the airport. I'd tried to sleep on the flight back, but I'd been making lists. We were all tired. Even Dix. Probably why he agreed to letting me just use a car service. He was riding with Aubrey and Yvette while I piled in with the boys. We hadn't had that much luggage, but still a few cases and duffels between all of us.

Smothering a yawn, I went through my messages. Thanksgiving had been packed with chaos, good food, and a lot of near-miss arguments. The best part though had been Mom and Johnny. Johnny had been right there for her the whole day. Each time Linzi or Dad spoke, Mom's expression would begin to tighten and Johnny would swoop in with a teasing remark or a whispered comment to make her laugh.

The tension with Linzi had been ridiculous. The only one of the three of them that even seemed to talk to her was Ramsey. Lachlan kept his comments short, direct, and then switched his attention. Jonas said nothing.

It was awkward and bizarre, yet we still managed laughter. Frankly, when was the last time Bronson and I had managed to be at a table with *both* of our respective parents for a holiday? Like—ever?

I'd been even more grateful that Bronson got Jonas talking to him. Then Yvette or Aubrey would serve up softball topics to keep us going. The concert came up twice, including Johnny congratulating us on the money raised.

That prompted the question of, were Dad and I considering actually recording the songs we'd performed. Clips from the concert were super popular but, I managed to defer —for now.

By the time the day was over I'd been exhausted. Dad had given me a hug before he left. He also spoke to Bronson for a few minutes. Then he took Linzi and went. Whatever went down between them after Lachlan and I left, I had no idea.

Friday, I'd spent at the hospital visiting Pen and dropping off presents for Tracy. Then we handled a business meeting on Saturday before we went to the airport.

Classes kicked back off on Monday, so we wanted to have one day of recovery—Ramsey definitely needed it, because he had grading to do.

I needed to see if I could move one final, then I was flying back to California for the surgeries. We hadn't booked the flights yet, but I would take care of it soon. Thankfully, it didn't take long to get to the cottage. I was happy to see the cozy little place.

Weird how quickly it had become home. Yvette was just going to crash on campus with Aubrey this week. Hopefully, it wouldn't be a big deal. What the school didn't know they couldn't complain about.

Lachlan claimed my bag before I could get it and Jonas snagged my backpack. Okay, I could carry my phone. Ramsey caught my hand and then we were heading for the house.

"Run?" Lachlan asked.

"Maybe," I said, before a yawn cracked my jaw. "I might need it."

"Coffee first," he suggested. No argument from me. Ramsey let go of my hand to unlock the door then he was disarming the security system. I frowned at it before I walked in farther.

It was a different system...

"Upgrades were done over the holiday week," Ramsey told me. "I figured it would be less disruptive if they did it while we were traveling."

"Oh." It was hardly my first alarm system, but it was still weird.

"Come get changed, Ace," Lachlan said as he climbed the stairs. "Jonas, you wanna make coffee?"

"Yep," he said, smothering a yawn of his own.

"I can do it when I come back down." But Jonas just gave me a sleepy kiss for my protest and headed to the kitchen. When I glanced at Ramsey, he had his phone in his free hand.

"Just checking email. I have a lot of grading to do and two tests to write."

I grimaced. "Should we have come back earlier?"

That earned me a bland look. "No, you needed the time there and I wanted to be with you. Now go get changed. I'll be here when you come back down." The scold held just enough playfulness to make me smile.

"Promise?"

Rolling his eyes, he chuckled. "Cross my heart."

"Yay!"

I headed up the stairs. Jonas still had my backpack but I didn't need it. As I passed his door, I heard Lachlan's voice. He was talking to someone. Irritation laced his tone, but I kept walking. If anyone called me this early, I'd be irritated too.

Lachlan had set my suitcase down just inside the door to my room.

It took me all of ten minutes to strip out of plane clothes, do a swift rinse off in the shower and splash some cold water on my face. That did wonders to help wake me up.

A peek out the window showed there was snow on the ground, but it wasn't deep nor on the sidewalks. The running trails would probably be fine. I got out my insulated running gear anyway. Once I was dressed, I stuffed my knit cap and gloves in my pockets and then headed downstairs.

"That's not the point," Ramsey was saying. "We can't keep everything—"

He broke off as I came into the kitchen. I slowed my step. "Am I interrupting?"

Jonas frowned, but his expression softened at my question. "No," he said, then held out my coffee cup to me.

The scent of it was a siren call all its own. I was kind of surprised that Lachlan hadn't beaten me downstairs, but then he'd been on the phone. The first swallow was pure decadence and I let out a sigh.

"Never leave me," I murmured and Jonas grinned.

The tension bubbling around Ramsey also seemed to pop as he shook his head at me.

"Didn't you say something about coffee beats dick before?" I challenged and that got me a sudden, genuine smile and Jonas laughed.

"Yes," Lachlan announced as he descended the stairs. "He did. I just think he's not using his dick right if he thinks that."

"Pretty sure I was referring to yours, smart-ass," Ramsey retaliated and a giggle escaped me. This was a *weird* conversation, but I liked it.

Lachlan had his running clothes on and he glanced around the kitchen before he pinned a look on Jonas. Not missing a beat, Jonas shrugged. "Your dick doesn't do it for me either."

I had to lean into the counter as I laughed. Flipping him off, Lachlan headed to the coffee maker to get his own. I wiped at the corners of my eyes. All the knots inside seemed to loosen some. Catching Jonas' eye, I grinned before pushing up on my toes to give him a kiss.

The droll humor was the best.

"Before we go run and then we all rush back into everything we have to do... I want to fly back to California next week, probably a week from Tuesday. If I can change my finals and pull any others up, I might try to go earlier."

Sobering, Jonas nodded. "Just tell me when. Everyone has signed off on the transplant?"

I nodded. "They have one more set of tests but all the surgeons and specialists that needed to sign off have. Pen is doing great." I couldn't shake the nerves for it. "I just—one day at a time. I want everything to go exactly as planned, but they always have caveats."

"I can't leave that early, but I'll look at booking a flight out right after finals are finished." Ramsey's mouth compressed. "That might mean I'm still here when the surgery happens."

"We'll be with her," Lachlan said. "You gotta be all adult and shit."

"Just let me know when you're free and I'll book the tickets—"

"Kaitlin," Ramsey said. "You do not have to keep paying for everything."

"Well, except we're going back for my sisters..."

"You are," Ramsey said, closing the distance between us and cupping my chin in his palm. "I'm going there for you."

I couldn't help my smile. "Maybe I want to pay for it...and I can afford it."

"I know you can, but I don't want to feel like we're using you for money."

I blinked. That... "I didn't think you were at all." Still, I glanced from him to Jonas to Lachlan. "Do you guys really think, I think that?"

"No," Jonas said even as Lachlan commented, "Not all the time," and Ramsey sighed.

"I don't," Jonas reiterated and shook his head. "I want to do more, but I can't afford the constant flights—we do have miles though."

"To be fair, Ace," Lachlan said, before raising his finished coffee for a sip. He let out a little sigh. "You don't generally give us an opportunity to pay. You just kind of do it or ask your manager to do it or Dix…"

"And we're not complaining," Ramsey said firmly. "I mean it, Siren. That's not a complaint. I—we don't want you having to do everything. You're used to carrying everything for everyone…we want to be able to do that for you too."

"What he said," Lachlan said with a laugh. "Teamwork, like me punching your manager for you. More than happy to take up that slack."

"I can do that too," Jonas said.

"You've all been helping me," I reminded them. Tilting my head back, I blew out a breath. "I do charge in and just—start doing things." I always had. Mostly because if I didn't do something, it didn't happen. Aubrey and Yvette were good at tackling their parts, but… "I'll try to include you more in the decisions?"

That seemed a fair compromise. Hopefully.

"Conversations like this are fine," Lachlan said, then he slid over to wrap an arm around my middle and pulled me back against him. "I'm totally willing to work off my flight costs in trade."

"Oh my god," Ramsey muttered with a groan and rolled his eyes. A laugh escaped me as Jonas just shook his head.

"How about we work it off in miles?" I elbowed Lach, but he just pressed a kiss to my throat.

"You got it, Ace. You ready to go?"

I was. Coffee finished, I gave Jonas a kiss and then another to Ramsey. "We'll be back in an hour... or two." I was already pulling my hat out as Lachlan snorted. Ramsey caught Lachlan before I reached the door, so I waited while those two put their heads together.

Jonas leaned around to roll his eyes about them and I grinned. Then Lachlan finally joined me.

The brisk air seemed chillier after the warmth in the kitchen. Despite that, I was almost craving the cold. I wanted the bite of the air so I could push myself.

"Hard or soft run?" Lachlan asked as he caught my hat and eased it down onto my head, making sure my ears were tucked in.

"Is my restlessness showing?" I had been trying to not pace or overthink everything, but it was hard.

"Maybe, but only a little." He touched his finger to my nose lightly before he pulled on his own hat. Our breath frosted and what sun there'd been earlier had vanished behind gray clouds.

Dampness hit my cheeks, and I angled my head back to gaze up at the sky.

"It's snowing..." It wasn't a lot, but it was definitely snowing.

"You're adorable," Lachlan murmured and heat flushed my face. "C'mon, Ace. You can catch snowflakes on your tongue while we run."

He matched my stride as we headed for the running trail. It was so early on a Sunday, the campus was quiet. The hush would be broken with kids coming back to school. Right now, it was just me and Lachlan. I craved the isolation and the solitude. Even more because Jonas and Ramsey were waiting for us at the house.

We'd just gotten to the trail when Lachlan muttered and

pulled his phone out. He glared at the screen then closed it without answering.

"All good?" I wanted to check. He'd been on the phone earlier, so it was entirely possible it was related to that. Or it could be someone else. He had other friends and family.

"Yep," he said. "Just a spam call. I got on some stupid list so I keep getting them."

I made a face. "I block most of the unknown numbers these days. It's just easier."

"Good," he said. "Left or right? Ace's choice."

I grinned. "Let's go see the pond..."

His groan cheered me on as I started jogging. "You're never going to let that go, are you?"

"Someday," I promised him over my shoulder. "Just not today." Then I winked. "Keep up. I'd hate to lose you."

"You're never losing me." The very visceral declaration should probably not be as comforting as it was. At the same time, the words sent a shiver through me.

"Promises, promises," I teased, but something remarkably like happiness pierced through me. There was comfort in knowing he was right there and going with me. There was security in the idea that he wasn't going to let me get away.

Somewhere along the way, I'd begun to rely on them—my douchebags—and that was scary as hell.

"C'mon, Ace," Lachlan taunted with a grin as he matched me. "No time for slowpokes. I thought you were after a run, not a mosey..."

"Ass," I said, but the grin actually hurt my cheeks. I shoved all those doubts aside and pushed myself to run. He was right. That was what I wanted.

A run with him.

Twenty-Two

JONAS

Finals week was both more brutal than I expected, and somehow not that difficult. The classes and the exams weren't hard. It was almost sad how easy the tests were in the first two classes. The tough part was making sure one of us was always with KC.

Neither Lachlan nor Ramsey wanted to mention the potential break-in.

"One," Ramsey said. "We don't know for sure if it was a break-in. Could have been someone knocking on the door, or maybe another note... we don't know."

"Telling her," Lachlan said with a sigh. "It'll just worry her. Maybe for no reason and right now, she has so much on her mind that I don't want her having to think about this too."

"But we don't know that it wasn't a break-in," I argued. "How does she protect herself if we don't warn her?" I didn't like secrets. We got into trouble before because we knew stuff about her that she didn't. I really didn't like the idea of her getting hurt either.

"Until we know for sure," Ramsey said, his tone decisive and his gaze firm. "We exercise caution. We stick close to her. Dix is still here on campus, whether we like him or not, he is here. He can be there if for some reason one of us can't be."

"What about Aubrey?" I asked. "Yvette is still here too."

"Again, they have enough on their minds," Ramsey said thoughtfully, but he didn't look comfortable about it.

"Little Brother," Lachlan said. "She's already having trouble sleeping. She's focused on Pen twenty-four hours a day. We can worry about this part for her."

I still didn't like it.

Maybe that was why I was making it a point to be wherever KC needed to be. If she wanted to go for a run, I went with her, whether Lachlan was going or not. I didn't like running as much as they did, but I didn't like it when I couldn't see her.

I liked it even less when I spotted a guy who looked like RJ heading into the food court as we were leaving. But even when I doubled back, I couldn't find him. Twice I thought I saw him in the library, but both times it turned out to be just some high school junior who looked like him.

Didn't like it though.

The new security system had cameras that let us check the doors and windows. There was another camera in the living room. The ones outside had motion detectors that sent alerts to our phones. The one inside we had to check manually.

That was fine. We shouldn't need the one inside unless we got the alert that something was activating outside. It still grated on me. While I told myself I wouldn't use the living room camera to spy on anyone, I found myself checking it a dozen times the day Aubrey and Yvette came over to work with KC and I went to get us pizza.

The three of them were there alone and I wanted to make sure they were okay. The fact I kept seeing RJ everywhere was grating on my nerves. In between study sessions, I looked him up.

He was arrested, there was even a record of it and a booking photo. Then he was released on bail. There was a court date pending and that... was it.

A court date pending. They arrested him forever ago, why the fuck wasn't he in jail? I'd kind of hoped finding out what happened would help, but no dice.

"Hey," KC said as she slid onto the sofa next to me and I blinked up at her. "You okay?"

The weight of her hand on my shoulder was like a brand that went all the way to my soul. I covered her hand with mine, then tugged her the rest of the way over to sit in my lap. I had to shove my laptop away to make the room, but I'd rather have a lapful of KC than the computer.

"I'm better now," I promised her. She was dressed in pajama shorts, fuzzy socks, and my sweatshirt. It was one I'd cut the sleeves off of. "You look nice."

Laughter filled her eyes as she twisted to straddle my lap and wrapped her arms around my neck. "This old thing?"

I skated my thumbs down her back to just above her ass. The muscles right there were always tight. Her neck was tighter and her shoulders were sometimes locked up like steel. Rubbing my thumbs in slow circles, I began to work against the tension on either side of her spine.

Her eyes drifted half-shut as she sighed. "You can stop that never."

It was my turn to laugh. "Never, huh?"

"Hmm... well in a few hours if you need a break." I found a particularly tough knot and she made a face as I worked it. "You have a musician's fingers," she half-moaned the words.

That gave me pause, particularly because that sound was

just—intoxicating. Particularly when it came from her throat while she half-rolled her hips on my lap. My semi went erect in no time.

"A musician's fingers is good?" I didn't think anyone had ever called my fingers that.

"Amazing," she admitted, then teased my earlobe with a kiss. The tickling sensation of her lips sent a shudder right through me. "Admittedly, I've only ever heard rumors. You're my first musician."

I was her first...

Need burned right through me as she traced her tongue along the whorls of my ear. It was both too light contact and too much. I pressed my thumbs into another knot. She nipped my earlobe then sucked on it until I moved my hands up under the shirt to her skin.

She was all warm and soft, liquid heat pressing down against me. "KC..."

"Hmm?"

The words escaped me. So much I wanted to tell her. Why did I always have to struggle with the right way to say something? She sucked against my earlobe then kissed along my throat. When she hit my pulse point, I was the one groaning.

"Do you want a hickey?" The question sent another hot lance of need bouncing through me. I wanted nothing more than to peel away our clothes and fuck up into her. So it was taking me a moment to even process the question.

"Are you giving it to me?" I wanted to congratulate myself for forming a sentence.

KC lifted her head and stared down at me with sleepy eyes and tousled hair. The sexiest thing ever. "Did you want it from someone else?"

"Fuck no," I said, moving one hand from her back to slide up her side and then I was pushing my sweatshirt up and off of her. She stretched her arms up, helping me out and then all I could see were her breasts.

They were flushed and rosy, the same shade as her pink cheeks. The nipples were darker, and tighter. I licked my lips.

"You're so pretty."

"So are you," she whispered and I had a palmful of breast as she leaned in to kiss at my throat. I wasn't quite ready for the hard, sucking pull and burn as she left her mark. But fuck if I didn't want her to do that everywhere.

In fact...

When she lifted her head, and looked pleased, I moved my hand to her hip and lifted as I pulled her forward. I locked my lips over her nipples. Teasing it with my tongue, I traced the beaded bumps as it pulled taut. Her soft little gasps were all the encouragement I needed. Teeth, tongue, and lips, I used all of them to get a reaction.

Her moans intensified and she fisted my hair, so I moved to the other nipple. "I like your breasts," I whispered before tracing my tongue in a slow circle around the second nipple. "I love how you taste and feel."

Another catch in her breath had me glancing up to find her staring at me as I used my teeth to catch the nipple. No force, just a gentle scrape before I laved at the engorged tip with my tongue.

With two fingers, I hooked her sleep shorts and dragged them down. I wanted to taste her pussy, and play with that. Oh, yes, that was exactly what I wanted to do. I got my laptop off the sofa and flipped her over onto her back.

She stared up at me breathlessly, nude except for her fuzzy socks, she was... perfect.

"Can I...?" I asked, tracing my fingers down between her breasts, then along her abdomen to her hips and to where she spread her legs at my touch. I hadn't really had a chance to sit and study her pussy. It was pink, and glistening, and looked delicious.

That delectable pink flush seemed to deepen and she spread her legs a little wider. Oh, that was even better. "Yes."

One syllable. A soft gasp. Then I lifted her leg and slid it up over my shoulder before I nudged her to scoot back a little more toward the other arm. Better, I could sprawl facedown between her legs.

Teasing the labia apart with my nose, I took a deep breath. There was just something rich and intoxicating about how she smelled. Her shampoo had one scent, her soap another—they complimented each other. I loved sleeping in her bed, where I could be surrounded with her scent.

But her pussy?

Hmm... "I could write a song about this," I said, and her strangled laugh had me flicking my gaze up. Her mouth formed a little 'o,' that was perfect. "It would start something like this..."

I traced my tongue from her entrance to her clit, then began to draw circles around it. The heady scent hadn't remotely prepared me for the flavor. I couldn't quite decide if it was sweet or salty. Maybe a little of both.

A hum escaped me and she gave a little jerk. Oh, I checked to see her startled expression. "Good?" I wanted to make sure.

"Oh yes," she said with a sigh. "That—that was like the best kind of shock."

I resumed my teasing exploration, humming again when I circled her clit with my tongue once more. Her muscles flexed and clenched. I teased my fingers along her and then eased one inside her. She damn near soaked my hand and I lapped at the release to soak it up.

Her squirming intensified over the next hour as I teased, nipped, licked, and sucked. Whenever I curled my fingers she would buck. When I curled my fingers, sucked on her clit, and hummed, she let out little screams of sound. I loved the way it felt when her inner muscles flexed around my fingers. I had three inside of her by the time she was thrashing.

As much as I wanted to keep playing, I let her drag me up and then she had her hand around my dick and we were lining me up. Her gaze fixed to mine as I pushed inside of her. She shuddered and bucked, I had to fist the sofa to keep from just slamming into her.

When she opened her mouth to my kisses, I savored the way she tasted as she licked herself off my lips. I didn't last long, a few thrusts and my spine was going liquid. My balls dragged up and I tried to fight it but she dug her nails into my back and pushed up to meet me.

I came in one long heated rush, but she didn't let me go. The kiss seemed to go on forever, the duel of tongues another reminder of eating her out. I just wanted to repeat it all again.

When the shocks finally slowed, I buried my face against her throat. While I wasn't remotely cold, the sweat on my skin had begun to cool me off as the air brushed over us.

She combed her fingers through my hair. "You know, I didn't mean to distract you from studying."

Laughing, I lifted my head. "You are a thousand times better than studying. I'd rather study you and play with you and taste you..." I wanted everything. "You're better than music, KC."

Surprise flickered through her eyes.

"I mean it," I traced my fingers down her cheek.

She swallowed then tugged me down to her until our lips crashed together. Yes, I could do this too. Kissing was a lot like music. You could communicate with it.

So much better than words.

Twenty-Three

KC

Curled up on the sofa with music sheets in my lap and my fingers itching for my guitar, I wasn't even working on Jonas' latest creation. I was texting with Tracy. She'd had an appointment that morning and gotten the final clearances. She'd be admitted to the hospital in a couple of days in prep for the surgery.

While I needed to bite the bullet and just buy a new one, it just made me twinge to even think about it. My stomach bottomed out each time the thought crossed my mind. So as much as I wished I had a guitar right now, I shoved it aside.

ME:

Do you need anything?

TRACY:

I'm good. I'll see you next week, right?

I grinned.

ME:

Can't keep me away.

TRACY:

I know, I wouldn't try. Even if I think you should take a real vacation sometime soon.

I stared at the message for a long moment. That's—

ME:

We've been on a break from touring for a couple of years. We're just now discussing putting together a new album for real.

She didn't respond right away and I flipped to the notifications of secure messages from Pen's medical team. I kept waiting to see one more update. One more delay.

One more... something.

Then a message from Tracy flashed up on the screen.

TRACY:

That is not a vacation. You've been going to school. You're dating three boys. You're dealing with Dad and the Stepmonster.

I made a face at the last description.

TRACY:

You're worrying about all of us and taking care of Pen. I also seem to recall there's been drama with your mother. So no, KC, this is not what I would call a vacation. When I'm all recovered, I'll take you on one.

I laughed.

ME:

Deal. But you have to get all better first.

She sent me back a crazy face emoji and I leaned my head back on the sofa. It was... I hated that I couldn't do anything more. It was all on the doctors, Pen, and Tracy now. Flipping to email, I stared at the latest updates.

Teddy had been providing almost up to the minute numbers to show how well we were doing. Maybe he thought that if he kept showing me higher and higher numbers I'd get over the ambush.

The question was, had I gotten over it yet? Dad and I were talking again—sort of. He'd come to Thanksgiving. It had been awkward and uncomfortable, but he'd been there. I chewed my lower lip.

The house was quiet. For the first time in several weeks it seemed, I was on my own. Ramsey had classes to grade, finals to administer, and a full-time job to see to, as well as tutoring. His hours had all been long this week.

Lachlan was at his last final. Jonas and mine was the following morning. I kind of wished it was today so it could just be done. Jonas had gone to one of the music rooms to work. I should have gone with him, he'd invited me, but I just—

I glanced down at the sheets of music and sighed. The words weren't there nor was the desire. Collecting the sheets together, I set them on the table then rubbed my face.

Maybe later. What I needed was a run. Shoving off the sofa, I headed for the stairs. It was only early afternoon. We still had plenty of light. I could get in a couple of miles and it might make me less restless.

Lachlan would be done with his final soon, I hoped. If not, I'd just let them know I was going. I couldn't stand just sitting here.

My phone rang, with a ringtone I hadn't ever heard, as I hit the top step . Turning it over in my hand, I stared at the contact info that appeared on the screen. Surprise rippled through me.

Swiping right on the answer bar, I put it to my ear. "Dad?" Was that actually him?

"Hey, Sweet Kaity," he said in that liquid drawl that made him a killer performer and entertained fans for decades. "How's my girl?"

I was... How was I? I pushed open the door to my room and crossed over to the unmade bed. Jonas had been wrapped around me this morning. He slept like he was a koala and curled around me. I'd thought it would be suffocating, but I rather enjoyed the security.

Dropping to sit on the edge before I flopped back, I said, "I'm okay." It wasn't a lie. I was okay. For the most part. "How are you?"

Silence held me suspended for a moment, then he chuckled. "I'm okay too." Then, he added, "You sound surprised."

I sighed.

"Wasn't trying to make it a thing, Sweet Kaity, just—you answered the phone like I was some kind of scam caller."

"Scam callers call all the time," I countered, then slapped a hand to my face. "I'm not—trying to make it a thing either."

"You have the right to make it anything you want. I haven't really called you that much."

"But you're calling now," I countered. "That means something."

"Yeah?" Was it me? Or did he sound as uncertain as I felt? "I like that."

"I—" I didn't want to lie to him or myself if I could help it. "I think I like it too—though... did you call just to say hi or...?" We hadn't talked since Thanksgiving beyond a couple of text messages.

"Well, I'd promised I'd call and then..."

"Yeah." We both went quiet and then I had to laugh. At

my broken chuckle, he let out a quiet huff of laughter as well. "We're really bad at this."

"You're bad at nothing, Sweet Kaity. I'm not giving you anything to work with. I know how to throw a lead and I'm feeling..." He trailed off like he didn't have the words for how awkward this was. Not that I could really blame him, I had no idea either.

"Okay—let's try this," I suggested. "I was getting ready to go for a run. Have one more final before I can fly back to California. What are you up to?"

"If you were going for a run," he said slowly. "I should let you go."

"Dad," I cracked out the label swiftly. I didn't want him to hang up before I could stop. "The run can wait. I mean... I'm restless, but the run really can wait. If it gets dark, I can go to the gym. This campus has a nice one."

"Make one of the boys go with you," Dad said. "I don't want you going on your own."

The corners of my lips pulled higher as I grinned. "They aren't here right now, but they usually go with me all the time. Lachlan does, but Jonas tags along when he can. Ramsey tends to use the gym late when everyone else is asleep." Especially the past month or so between all our traveling and his own work.

"Good." He blew out a breath and there was a sound of something squeaking. Maybe a chair wheel. "I'm in the studio. Been here tinkering. The muse has been fighting me a lot the last few years, always seems to get harder to even get the notes to come, much less the lyrics."

I felt that.

"Came back from Thanksgiving though and finished two songs."

"That's awesome," I applauded him. "Did you lay all the music and the lyrics?"

"Yep." He had a kind of bemused pride underscoring the

single syllable. "Not sure either are any good, but it felt damn good to put it down."

"You needed to write it then," I suggested. Not that I didn't understand that because I absolutely did. "Jonas has been working on a lot of music, we're co-writing one right now but the words just aren't hitting today."

"So you were gonna run?" Dad sounded genuinely interested.

I shrugged, despite the fact he couldn't see me. "Not sure. Just...waiting on the final confirmation for Pen's transplant. They've been eradicating her marrow and it's taking a toll."

"The doctors told me that's normal," Dad said, seeming to feel his way around each word. "I went and saw her yesterday. She seemed really different. More tired, wan... I don't like it."

"I don't either." What I didn't say was how much I hated it. "But they are adamant this is the way to go. She needs the bone marrow transplant, but before they can do it, they have to destroy what she has, which means she gets worse before she gets better."

I needed her to get better.

I needed it like I needed my next breath of air.

"When you come out," Dad began, then hesitated like he needed to gather his thoughts. Or maybe he just needed a little practice to say it in his head before he admitted whatever it was aloud. "I was hoping you might stay with me at the Morton downtown. I have two full floors. So you could stay on one and I'll be on the other."

That was almost kind of sweet.

"It's a whole floor, but I guess if you want privacy..."

"Thought you might want it. It's closer to the hospital than your mother's place and might be more comfortable for us to get caught up with each other than there."

"Mom might appreciate it if I didn't invite you again." I could hardly fault Mom for being angry.

"Might be wise. Jen's—she hasn't been happy with me in a while."

We were both kind of dancing around the subject, so maybe I should rip the Band-Aid off. "What about—Linzi?" I did not want to call her my step-mother. Even if Tracy labeled her that. The less I reminded myself that I was dating my step-brothers, the better.

"She's gone to stay with some friends in Banff for a week or so."

"Oh."

"Sweet Kaity, I know you don't like her—"

"To be fair," I interrupted. "I don't know her. I've only met her a couple of times before and.. to be honest, what I have learned about her hasn't been that positive."

"She's... I can't make excuses. I mean I could, but I won't. She thought she was doing the right thing and she wasn't. We've—discussed that at length. Right now, she's visiting friends and I'm going to be here for my girls."

The squeeze on my heart threatened to leave it battered and bruised. "Dad?"

"Yes?"

"Why didn't you ever just call me?" All the messages I'd left, until the day I gave up.

"Thought you were busy. Sometimes Linzi would call or maybe she just told me she called and left you a message."

Bitch.

I closed my eyes. "So she's been lying to you about us? Me, Bronson, Allie, Cam, Zeke...?"

"If those are the names of your other siblings then, I suppose yes, she has been—manufacturing or at least—carefully selecting what pieces of information she shared with me. But I can't blame her for everything."

"I can," I said flatly.

"And you have that right," he agreed with me. "But I'm an

adult, Sweet Kaity. I know how babies are made. I just never checked...apparently the attorneys have a form they fill out when a woman approaches them about me being the possibility of the dad..." The disgust in his voice was pretty evident. "I... was careless. I let her handle everything because I didn't want to. And when it came to you, Sweet Kaity...I thought you didn't want to see me. So I was trying to respect that."

I groaned, rolling onto my side where I was able to grab the pillow and curl up around it.

"Not a lot of real excuses here, my sweet baby. I fucked up. I fucked up real good. I hate to say it but I think sometimes your mother was right about me."

I grimaced. "Dad..."

"Don't make me feel better." It was almost an order.

"I was going to—I've been angry at you for a long time. But I've missed you even longer."

"Then you'll come and stay with me? You'll have your own floor and you won't need to do anything and if you want your privacy or the boys do—" He hesitated and I had to bite my lip to keep from laughing. "I don't know if you need privacy with them but if you're doing what I think you're doing, then you will and I think that's just better for me to not know what you're doing... or who you're doing it with."

"I'll make you a deal," I offered, losing my war against not laughing even as tears ran from my eyes. "I won't talk about my sex life and you don't talk about yours."

"Done."

His chuckle at the end made it worth any embarrassment. A door opened downstairs as we were hanging up. That had been kind of a record call, but I was even more restless than I had been earlier.

"Ace...?" Lachlan called from downstairs and I sat up. "Get your gorgeous ass down here. We're gonna go have a driving lesson."

Driving lesson...?

I could do a driving lesson. We could still use the gym to run after if I needed it.

"Coming!"

"Not yet," he retaliated. "But we can do that *after* you spend some time learning to throttle..." the drawn out pause made me roll my eyes. "... in the car."

"That was terrible."

"And you loved it." He stared up at me with a teasing grin and a light in his eyes that had been all too absent the last week or so. "C'mon, get your shit together woman. I don't just let anyone touch my car."

"I've touched your dick." Or did he not remember?

"That's my dick," he informed me. "My car is a whole other level, Ace."

I mean... yeah, but... Wait, I wasn't going to have that argument. There were things about who touched his dick and his car that I didn't want to know except...

"Lachlan?"

"Yes?" The impatience in his sigh demanded I move it so I snagged my jacket and socks and headed back down the stairs.

"Am I the first girl to drive your car?"

"Not yet," he said, then winked. "But you will be."

Twenty-Four

RAMSEY

Not even one full day—fuck, not even a few hours after Jonas and Lachlan left with Kaitlin, Aubrey, and Yvette to head back to California and the house was far too quiet. It wasn't like we played host to house parties or got noisy but...

The hum of conversation. The laughter. The sounds of Jonas' keyboard or Kaitlin humming as she looked at a music sheet... These were all sounds I'd grown used to and very fond of.

I hadn't even taken them to the airport. Dix had driven a rental car. Lachlan's car was in a secure lot away from the winter weather. My car was in the employee lot. I'd rented one for the semester and I'd return it when I drove myself to the airport in a week.

Students were already beginning their winter break exodus to head home. College students and elementary students were among the first to go. My students had two more exams this week and then they would be dismissed for three weeks. We would be returning just after the new year.

My phone buzzed with a message.

SIREN:

Miss you. I wish you could have come with us.

I smiled, but it was only fleeting. There was an ache in my chest I'd been trying to ignore with their absence. I was used to the guys heading off to see their dads on various breaks. This was normal.

But since we'd gotten Kaitlin back, I hadn't been away from her for any significant time at all. Even nights she slept with Jonas or Lachlan, she was right down the hall or right next door.

ME:

I'll be with you soon. It's a promise. I'm here if you need to talk whenever.

SIREN:

Is it weird that it feels so weird?

Then...

SIREN:

Does it feel weird to you?

For all of her confidence and beautiful spirit, she was still prone to flashes of insecurity. I wasn't sure Lachlan or Jonas ever noticed, but I did. Those were the moments when she would look to me, and I liked being able to steady her. I liked...

Fuck it, I just adored her and everything about her. Even those pieces that had frustrated me once upon a time. I rubbed my arm and then fired off a response.

ME:

> It feels weird to know that when I go to sleep tonight you're going to be thousands of miles away. It feels weird that I won't see you first thing in the morning. I don't like that it's gonna be this way for the next six or seven days.

ME:

> I missed you before you left. I just miss you more now.

She deserved to know this and to hear it, even if I could only type the words.

SIREN:

> That felt good to read. I know I already said it, but I really do miss you. Lachlan is making faces at me right now. We're supposed to be watching a movie. But he can't just decide on one.

I snorted.

ME:

> For Lach.

I included a middle finger emoji.

She fired back a laughing face which had been my intention.

ME:

> Make him watch all the Fast and Furious movies with you. He likes cars and girl butts. Lots of those in the movies.

I waited a beat, grinning stupidly at the message.

SIREN:

What's in it for me?

I could almost hear the smile behind the words.

ME:

Tell him he has to work it off in trade.

That got me more laughing and crying faces and then Lachlan messaged me.

LACHLAN

Nice, even when you're being a dick.

I snorted.

ME

I could have suggested the Alien movies.

He didn't answer, not that I expected him too. Not with her right there. While I wanted to ask how she was doing really, I didn't want to with her right there. It was one thing to check in, it was another to feel like we were talking about her behind her back.

Didn't mean I wasn't worried. She was literally an open, vibrating nerve at the moment and I wasn't sure she saw it or not.

SIREN

He picked Jumanji. The new one. He said the new one, which means there's a first one. But we're negotiating.

I grinned.

ME:

Make him work for it.

SIREN:

I will. And I'll call you after we're at the hotel tonight before you go to bed.

ME:

You call me whenever. I don't care about the time. If you need me. Call me.

She sent me back a heart and I nodded.

I flipped to Lachlan's messages, then to the group message with both of them. Nothing new. They still had another four or five hours in the air, then they'd have to get their luggage and off to the hotel.

The hotel was gonna be its own kind of stress. I liked that Gibs seemed to remember how to be a father after how long? I rubbed my jaw as I scrolled through my contacts to one that I rarely ever used.

While she may not have gotten WiFi on the flight, it would pop up for her once she was there. Was it crossing a line to reach out to her? I wasn't one hundred percent positive one way or another but...

ME:

Worried about Kaitlin. If she needs me, can you let me know?

Aubrey wasn't always thrilled with us, but she seemed to have softened some over the last few months. Yvette on the other hand? She didn't pretend to trust us. I had a feeling as long as we didn't fuck up it would be fine.

If we did? She was going to slit our throats. I could respect the loyalty and the protectiveness. It would be patronizing to encourage it, but I liked that they put *Kaitlin* first. That they always would also pleased me.

Putting that aside for now, I went back to working on finalizing the final for the rest of my classes. I'd altered the final for all four class periods. Blue Ivy students were clever, and while academic cheating was frowned upon, it happened.

Too many wealthy, privileged students who liked to buy their way past the rules. The test modifications meant it didn't matter what one class period told another, they wouldn't find cheating easy.

More work for me, but I busted my own ass getting through this school and put in the time and effort. It would be a good life lesson for my students to do the same.

By the time I finished, I was starving. We really had bare-boned down the kitchen at the house. A couple of microwavable meals, coffee, and soda. None of us wanted to deal with spoiled food.

I headed across campus to the dining hall and the food court. There was only a handful of options opened with classes winding down. Kaitlin messaged me that their flight had landed just as I got to the doors.

SIREN:

Heading for luggage claim. Dix is picking up a car. Then we'll be on our way. Traffic is bad though. Could be a couple of hours.

ME:

Send Jonas for coffee while you wait for luggage and make sure Lachlan stays with you.

She sent me back a laughing face.

SIREN:

Jonas already headed to the nearest one.
Great minds and all that.

Good boys.

Aubrey messaged while I was chatting with Kaitlin.

Right, just sent her a thumbs up because I wasn't going to rock that boat. Done, I scanned my options and headed for the sandwich shop. I ordered two large sub sandwiches and got a couple of bags of chips and some fruit. I'd take the extra back with me and I could have the fruit for breakfast along with the other sandwich.

"Hey, Ramsey." I didn't recognize the voice and it took me a minute after I turned to identify the owner of it who was greeting me.

He was familiar...

"Walker," I said, excavating the name from under a dusty list of stats from when Lachlan played lacrosse. He was still assisting the coach, but his interest in the game seemed to have waned this year.

Not that I blamed him. I'd rather spend the time with Kaitlin too. Walker... I couldn't remember his last name. But he'd been a good player and while he and Lachlan weren't the best of friends, they had a decent relationship.

"Been a while," I said by way of greeting and offered him a hand.

He grinned, clasping my hand for a brief shake. "Yes, sir..." Then he shook his head. "Sorry, you were the TA in my sophomore year so it still feels like I should say sir."

I shrugged. "It's fine. You don't have to, but I appreciate it." Then his presence struck me as odd. "Aren't you a freshman on the college campus these days?"

"Yes and I haven't gone home yet because I blew a midterm and one of my profs let me make up some work so I could retake a second mid-term after the final. That way I didn't lose my position on the team." The word vomit spilled out of him. "Works out, I can be on campus for a few more days in case Lachlan needs me to keep running interference..."

Interference? "That's good. I'm sure he appreciates it." It was Walker's turn to give his order so I retreated a step or two so he could do that while I waited. What interference was he running?

Better to play along like I knew, since he seemed to be assuming that I did. It could just be team politics, but Lachlan volunteered. There wasn't anything he should need covered unless...

No, no unless. I couldn't think of anything that would be an issue for him. Not to mention games really didn't ramp until spring.

When Walker finished paying for his order, he returned to where I was waiting. My sandwiches were almost done so I wouldn't be here much longer.

I weighed the option of fishing for more information against respecting Lachlan's privacy. Then again, we all had a lot going on and we were all worried about Kaitlin. If I could take something off his plate too, I was happy to do that. "Lach's already—"

"Yeah, I know," Walker said easily, folding his arms. "We talked. He just wants to make sure the salty bitch doesn't know he's off-campus."

The salty...

"I get it," Walker continued. "Don't tap crazy, but with his new rock star girlfriend, keeping those two as far apart as possible is a good plan."

With *his* new... We didn't advertise the fact that all three of us were dating her, particularly since we were living together and we had a tangled weave of family relationships. At the same time, what the hell was Walker talking about?

"No gossip at all would be the best plan." In fact, it would probably be even better if Walker wasn't talking about whatever this was at all.

"I hear you," Walker said, then lifted his chin toward the counter where they were bagging up my order. "Don't worry, I'll cover for him. Hopefully we won't hear from Payton until the spring and he's back on campus."

Payton.

Webber?

It took every ounce of self-control to *not* react to that name. "Don't mention it," I suggested and fortunately, it didn't come out as strangled as it felt. "Like, really, don't mention it."

"Sure thing." Walker saluted and I just nodded and lifted a hand in farewell as I grabbed my bag. I was back outside into the icy darkness and on my way back to the house as I turned that bizarre conversation over in my head.

Walker was Lachlan's *friend*. I knew him. Not once in our acquaintance had he ever struck me as an asshole. Sometimes stubborn and bull-headed, but not an asshole. He also seemed genuine in his plan to keep Lachlan covered.

They didn't want Kaitlin to know about Payton.

Was he—no, there was no way Lachlan would be that fucking stupid. He'd made no bones about his interest in Kaitlin. The fact he was even willing to play nice about us seeing her had been a huge step for him.

Did he want her to himself? Probably. But he wasn't fighting us or fighting her. That was important.

So what the hell was he doing with Payton Webber?

Nothing good ever came where that girl was concerned. All I wanted to do was call Lachlan but he was with Kaitlin right now.

Dammit.

I had no appetite by the time I got back to the house and I didn't know what to think. The only thing I knew for sure was I needed to get my temper under firm control before Kaitlin called.

She did *not* need to know anything about this. Particularly when I had no idea if there was anything to know.

C'mon Lach, do me a favor, don't be a dumbass now.

It was going to be a brutally long few days.

Twenty-Five

KC

It was surgery day and I hadn't slept all night. I was up when Ramsey woke up for the day and talked to him for an hour. The hotel had a gym so when I couldn't stand it anymore, I dragged Lachlan downstairs with me. Dad secured us two whole floors and that wasn't as weird as it could be, but the gym was on a public access floor. You still needed a room key to get in and we could request it be closed for us, but that was the kind of diva behavior I liked to avoid.

Thankfully, Lachlan didn't protest even once when I told him I needed to run. One brief moment of resistance when I said we were too far from the beach or a good running trail. If I'd told him I wanted to go out, I think he would have tried to make it happen. As it was, when I brought up the gym he relaxed and gave me a hard kiss.

He threw on clothes and shoes, and five minutes after I woke him, we were in the elevator. His hair was rumpled adorably, not that I planned to tell him I liked the bedhead.

Most of the time, he was too cocky as it was and yet, I couldn't deny that his cockiness wasn't part of my attraction.

"You're staring, Ace," he commented as he keyed us into the gym. It was empty and I wasn't going to pretend that it didn't relieve me. "See something you like?"

I grinned as I pivoted to walk backwards. The mirrors made it easy to not trip over something. "Actually..."

I took the time to sweep my gaze over him before I licked my lips. Really, he was pretty even dressed in an old t-shirt and loose sweats that played peek-a-boo with his abs. Maybe it was the swagger or the way the muscles rippled as he stretched, but I really was enjoying just looking at him.

"I just might." Surprise flashed in his eyes and I had to hide a grin when I winked before I pivoted to head for the treadmill. Did I add a little extra sway to my hips? Yes, yes I did. My capris were more spandex than cotton with their moisture wicking material. They were practically painted on. I'd gone for a workout bra slash tank that bared my midriff because I really wanted to run. Sweating was a necessary by-product. I could feel the fire of his gaze as he tracked it over me.

"Oh," Lachlan hummed the syllable before he wrapped an arm around my waist and dragged me back against him just before I could step onto the equipment. The shirt and sweatpants might disguise his erection, but there was no mistaking it right there where it ground against my ass. "We can both play that game, Ace," he warned, before he nipped my earlobe.

The tension cording my muscles released even as anticipation coiled tighter in my stomach. "Is that a threat?" I asked, meeting his gaze in the mirror. "Or a promise?"

Flattening his hand against my bare abdomen, he smiled slowly then ran his tongue up the length of my neck. It was the lightest of touches, a caress that lit me up inside and out.

My nipples went hard and he paused just behind my ear where he pressed a butterfly kiss.

"Who says it can't be both?" The whisper had my pussy clenching and a shudder rippling over me. "You need a distraction today, Ace?"

Leaning my head back against his shoulder, I closed my eyes and soaked up his nearness. Did I? They'd be taking Tracy into the procedure in just a few hours. Pen's marrow had been eradicated as they prepped her for the "graft" and "transfer" process. Today was the day we'd been working toward. Two years, or almost, since we'd discovered something was really wrong with Pen. From baby to toddler and she'd spent more time in a hospital than out of it.

"Yes," I almost pleaded. Cause I needed the help and it fucking killed me to ask for it. But Lachlan would do it if I asked or not and that—I needed that almost as much as I needed to know he would listen. "Please."

"Done," he whispered the oath like I needed to hear it. Then he lifted me up and put me on the treadmill. With one hand, he smoothed over my ass before he slapped it once and the sting made me jump. It pulled me out of that foggy place. "For now, we're running. So let's get these miles locked in, then you're showering and we go to the hospital *after* you eat."

The orders washed over me, sinking into my bones.

"Okay." I could do all of that.

"We're not *staying* at the hospital," he continued. "You will check on them, you will get updates, then we're coming back here."

I was making my selections on the control board of the treadmill and I blinked at him. "Then what?"

"Then you'll shut up and take it like a good girl."

That startled me and sent a very unsettling and absolutely enticing shiver through me.

Lachlan chuckled and it was as wicked as it was sensual. It definitely promised all kinds of dirty things that I actively wanted to discover. "For now—you focus on what's in front of you, Ace. You need to run. So let's run. Then we're going to tackle it one step at a time, and I've got your back. Understood?"

I blew out a breath before I studied him for a long moment. "Lachlan?"

"I'm here," he promised, the playfulness in his eyes fleeting as he sobered and returned my gaze. "I'm not going anywhere."

"Thank you."

"You *never* have to thank me."

"Yes, I do," I said, then cupped his cheek and gave him a gentle brush of a kiss to his lips. "You can be such an ass."

"You like that though."

"I really shouldn't," I admitted and his slow grin did even more devilish things to where my thoughts were going.

"Woulda," he teased. "Coulda. Shoulda."

Eyes rolling, I laughed and turned to focus on the panel. What was I picking for speed? Lachlan climbed onto the treadmill next to mine. In no time at all, we were both jogging. The pace was a warm-up. We'd pick it up here soon...

"Ace?" Lachlan pulled my attention. "It's going to be okay."

Fuck I hoped so. I nodded, then focused on the run. I could control my speed and my pace. These were things I had power over. For the rest?

I had to trust everyone else.

The run, the shower, the breakfast—they all helped, but nothing really sanded off the edge of my nerves. If anything, it just seemed to give me enough respite that when the anxiety hit again it was a thousand percent worse. Aubrey actually suggested I asked Dad to order me alcohol.

Maybe.

I dismissed it, but Lachlan admitted he could get it if I really needed it. As nice as that sounded on some levels, I didn't need or want to rely on any substances. Though to be fair, getting high kind of sounded good too.

Again, I didn't want to rely on anything else. Besides, if anything happened—I needed my wits about me. Dad joined us for the drive to the hospital. The quiet in the vehicle seemed to vibrate with all the things we weren't saying. When he mentioned that we should visit with "Trace" after the procedure, I'd stared at him a beat.

He and Tracy hadn't done more than spoken on the phone since Dad got re—well there was no "re,"—since Dad got involved with the whole procedure. Tracy hadn't talked to him about her choices. That was her choice, when, how, and *if* she decided to read him in.

That said, I kept it even and didn't correct him on the misgendering. Jonas had given me a faint questioning look. Had Tracy told Dad? I shook my head. As far as I knew, no, she hadn't. Until she did, we would keep what we knew to ourselves.

He answered with a nod and the guys, like Yvette and Aubrey, followed my lead. As the limo pulled into the hospital, I scanned the sidewalks. No press. No gathered crowds. Nothing. We didn't go through the main entrance, but still pulled into the back through a secure lot and into the parking structure.

Pen's age and HIPPA laws helped to keep things as quiet as possible. The medical center was also familiar with handling celebrity patients and their families. Jackie and Bronson were already there when we climbed out of the car.

"Come here," Jackie said as soon as we walked into the waiting room. She wrapped me up into a tight hug. The familiar tickle of jasmine in her perfume relaxed more of the tension in my back and I held onto her. "They are both going to be fine," she said. "We're right here, we're going to wait for word from the doctors, then you're going back to the hotel to rest. Because we won't know everything today."

When she pulled back and gave me a stern look, I summoned a smile. "Yes, ma'am—I just..."

"I know," she told me, rubbing my biceps. "I do know. Because I am hoping and praying for all the same things. We've done everything we can, it's up to the doctors now and they are very confident."

"Besides," Bronson said, wrapping an arm around my shoulders before he pressed a kiss to my temple. "I brought Cards Against Humanity and Mom said she'd play with us..."

Disbelieving laughter swelled through me. I wasn't sure what I expected to do for the next few hours, but that definitely wasn't it. Dad glanced at us and I could almost feel his desire to join us. Instead of invading our space though, he waited for the three of us to move to where they were and then he gave Jackie a very sweet kiss on the cheek before he clapped Bronson on the shoulder.

Right, the awkwardness did not improve all that much. Still, I sandwiched between Jonas and Lachlan, so we could play. By the third round of the most ridiculous responses, we were all laughing. From the awkward to the absurd to the just flat-out amusing. I threw myself into the game.

The moment the doctor stepped inside, I climbed right over the back of the sofa to meet him.

"Miss Crosse," he said. "So far, everything went like clockwork..."

Relief swamped me and it was like someone sliced my strings and I half-collapsed, even as Lachlan wrapped an arm around me from behind and kept me on my feet. It was so smooth, I barely stumbled.

"So let's talk about what's next."

WHAT WAS NEXT WAS ME BEING BANISHED FROM THE hospital. Jonas said he would stay, so did Aubrey. Yvette had an appointment but she would be back. "We'll do it in shifts," Yvette suggested and Jackie agreed so easily, it was clear they'd all planned it. "That means one of us is always here and we can be your eyes and ears."

I didn't protest, though I did stop by the observation room so I could at least see Pen. She was half-asleep and I didn't want to wake her up. The next few days were going to be tough for her. Tracy was in recovery. Jackie tackled distracting Dad, and Bronson said he'd visit Tracy as soon as she was awake and then he'd be heading out on his break.

Dix wasn't our driver, in fact, we didn't have one at all. Lachlan surprised me with a rental car Dad had delivered for us. He drove us back to the hotel, one hand on my thigh with my hand on top of his. I sent a series of messages to Ramsey filling him in, though he promised Jonas had briefed him too.

Once we got to the hotel, Lachlan turned his key over to the valet and then we headed in the private entrance to the private elevators. Privacy was the key here and I was almost boneless from the relief that I didn't mind taking advantage of all the benefits of Dad reserving both floors for us.

Back on our floor, Lachlan didn't turn us to the suite I'd been sharing with him and Jonas. Nor did we stop at Aubrey and Yvette's rooms, instead he took me all the way down to the other end to another suite. "Close your eyes for me?"

I could ask, but what had he said earlier? I was going to

shut up and take it like a good girl. I could do that. Closing my eyes, I squeezed his hand.

"That's my girl," Lachlan murmured before ghosting a kiss to my lips. Then he guided me inside. Hints of vanilla lingered in the air and the room was cool and quiet. There was low piano music playing. Was he going to give me a massage? Goosebumps raised across my skin as he navigated me through a room.

"You can sit here," he said softly and helped me to ease back until my legs encountered a chair. "Good girl," he praised again. "Now, give me a count of thirty then open your eyes, okay?"

"Okay." Another kiss and then the breeze of him passing brushed me. At thirty, I opened my eyes and stared at the room around me for a moment before I blinked at the frosted pane of glass and wall that seemed to bisect the whole room. I was—alone.

"Lachlan?"

He appeared on the other side of the frosted glass. "Hey," he said. "I'm here. I believe you requested a pod date where we talk and flirt and play—but can't see each other?"

Love is Blind.

My jaw fell...

"So, I thought I'd start by introducing myself..." he continued as I gaped. "I'm Lachlan. I have an affinity for blue-haired sweethearts with sexy voices and sassy mouths... how about you?"

Laughter bubbled up through me and I spotted the drinks and snacks he'd set out.

"Ace?" he prompted when I continued to say nothing. "This is okay, right?" It was the first time I'd ever heard him sound truly uncertain and my heart squeezed. He'd set up this date because it was what I'd asked for and it was...

"This is perfect." I promised. "More than perfect..." I took a deep breath then grinned almost stupidly. "And it's nice to meet you Lachlan, I'm KC. I—I keep telling myself I want to be normal and that I like normal."

"Normal is overrated," he told me and I couldn't stop smiling.

Because it absolutely was. "Tell me more about you?"

"I thought you'd never ask," he answered and I leaned back in the chair, the butterflies in my stomach taking flight. "I wish I could say I'm an only child, but that's only because I never want any competition where you're concerned."

"It's not a competition," I told him. "It's family..."

And every single day, they were rapidly becoming the only one I wanted. All of them.

LACHLAN

The date went far better than I could have imagined. I still didn't get the appeal of the show she and Jonas seemed to love. That said, when I'd asked her out on that date a few months earlier, she'd described the pod idea to me. The idea of dating someone you couldn't see or touch wasn't that farfetched, but it hadn't seemed like something we needed to do when we were already close.

Still, I got Jonas to point me to her show and I'd done my research. The people who volunteered to do that were ballsier than me. If Ace wanted a date in a pod, then a pod date she would get. Gibs and Aubrey both helped out with making arrangements at the hotel. Ace's reaction made even the sillier parts worthwhile. Surprise followed by genuine pleasure.

We talked for hours about everything and nothing. If you'd told me that I'd savor that time with her when I couldn't look at her or touch her, just talk to her? I'd probably have laughed. Yet, the date was *perfect*. Just like her.

One nice thing about staying at the hotel, we only had to

see Gibs when we planned to. He didn't come down to this floor. Even better, we didn't have to deal with our mother or Ace's. I didn't ask about Mom and Gibs didn't volunteer any information.

Jonas said she was visiting friends and he thought that maybe they were on a break. It bothered him more than me, but I wasn't sure what part of it bothered Jonas. We could talk about it more when Ramsey was there.

Speaking of which, three days post procedure, everything *seemed* to be going well, and I was on my way to the airport to pick up Ramsey. Even with the billboards along the freeway advertising Christmas sales and the decorations on some of the cars, it really didn't *feel* like Christmas.

Sunny, with gentle breezes, and not a spec of snow except in the distant mountains? Yeah, it didn't feel like the holidays. Or at least, it didn't save for the cautious optimism from the doctors. So far, Pen hadn't rejected the marrow and stem cells.

Tracy had been discharged from the hospital, she was back at her place. I'd dropped Jonas and Ace off first thing this morning. She wanted to spend the day with her sister and Jonas was going to stay with them.

They'd either take a ride share back or I'd pick them up later. I had time before Ramsey's flight landed, and it was my first time truly alone in a few days. Time to check on what Payton was up to. She'd been playing this game with the guitar.

While she teased me about having it, she didn't quite commit to *actually* having it. Sometimes she suggested she could help me get it and other times, she just wanted me to admit that I wanted it.

Her price, however, had not changed. She wanted sex, from me specifically, and she wanted it on her terms. The fact she'd always been a little crazy used to appeal to me. I couldn't even tell you why now, except it seemed that she'd do whatever, without an ounce of reservation or inhibition.

Not as attractive a quality as I would have once thought. The fact she'd started sending me suggestive pictures just made it worse.

Today's batch? Nudes.

Straight up, full on nudes.

I'd deleted the first set but the second set gave me pause. She wasn't alone in the pictures. They were us—

When the fuck had she taken pictures of me going down on her? It was nauseating. All I could hope was they were photoshopped.

Parked in the cell phone lot, I got out the new burner phone I'd picked up and I called her "new" number. She'd sent it to Walker a few days earlier right as she began her nasty campaign of porn-a-grams.

It rang three times then went to voicemail.

"You know the drill. Leave me a message. You know you want to."

What I wanted to do was throttle her. Hanging up, I didn't bother with a message. I wasn't leaving her any recordings for her to use.

Bitch.

Walker didn't have any new details. The last time I spoke to Payton, I told her I wanted proof. She could try to manipulate sex all she wanted, I'd rather castrate myself than touch her again.

Time and distance had more than illustrated to me what a mistake she'd been from the beginning. If she just let go and moved on, this wouldn't be a problem. But the idea she'd taken the guitar *and* attacked Ace just took this to a whole other level.

We needed proof.

Incontrovertible proof.

When I had that, not only could I get the guitar back, but I could get rid of her and eliminate the threat to Ace once and for all.

My burner rang just as a message from Ramsey hit my phone.

BRAINIAC:

Landed.

I sent him a thumbs up and told him to tell me when he had his luggage. I wasn't leaving the cell phone lot until then. We had enough of a drive once we left LAX to get back to the hotel.

I didn't answer her call. Instead, I just let it go to voicemail. Time to piss her off and frustrate her. She wanted to play games, she needed to learn she wasn't in control.

Payton tended to be susceptible to rash and impulsive actions. Particularly when she was angry. It was why she'd acted with such malice toward Ace. She'd been jealous of her from the beginning. I let my own stupid irritations blind me to it.

Head back, I closed my eyes and waited for word, silencing the burner when she called again.

Go ahead and leave a message bitch, you know you want to...

~

IT TOOK RAMSEY ALMOST THIRTY-FIVE MINUTES after he landed before he texted to say he had his luggage. I was pulling up to the arrivals area ten minutes later. He shoved his backpack and suitcase in the backseat before he climbed in the passenger.

"Welcome to Los Angeles," I greeted him and he scrubbed a hand over his face before he pulled his seatbelt on. As soon as it clicked, I was moving. Traffic was sluggish, but I followed it out of the airport. "Good flight?"

"It was fine," he answered in a clipped voice. "How is Kaitlin?"

"Better, I think. She's been stressed. Still not sleeping enough." We'd have to be deaf, dumb, blind, *and* stupid to miss how strained she'd been. "She and Jonas are with Tracy today. She was practically vibrating when I dropped her off. We've gone to the hospital every day and we're still taking it in shifts."

"Still all good news?"

"So far," I said and flexed my hands on the wheel. Each time the medical team said everything seemed to be going well, I had to fight against doing a fist pump. The simple fact was, we wouldn't know for a while yet if this was successful, or if Pen would even have to do it again.

They'd harvested enough from Tracy to let them do a few grafts of cells as needed. I just wish we had confirmation *now*.

"Good," Ramsey murmured, continuing to rub his jaw as I drove. He wasn't looking at me but out the window. "We're going to the hotel now?"

"That was my plan. Ace knows you were coming in today and she said she was coming straight back after she visited with Tracy for a while. She hasn't been able to see her since Tracy started isolating ahead of the procedure."

Another nod, but this time he didn't comment. Not really.

"You're being pretty non-verbal," I said, after another couple of miles passed without him saying a word.

"I'm debating an unpleasant conversation and how to begin it," Ramey admitted and I cut him a side long look.

"Just rip the Band-Aid off. There's enough stress and tension right now for Ace, she doesn't need any more from you." Big Brother would do well to remember that. She'd been leaning really hard on her messages to and from Ramsey.

I'd half-thought it would make me jealous, but it hadn't. When she talked to him, he made her feel better. She always seemed a little lighter, a little more up, when they exchanged messages. As much as I might hate to admit it, she needed him.

Needed him.

Needed Jonas.

I wanted to be her everything but what I did for her was different too. I had no idea how any of this shit would work out but—

"Are you actually still seeing Payton?"

The question was so out there, I damn near jerked the wheel as I cut a look at him. "What?"

"Payton Webber. Blonde. You dated her for a couple of years. I know you were sleeping with her."

"And she showed up in your bed naked, uninvited. I know who she is—why the *fuck* are you asking me that?" What had that bitch done?

"Answer me first," Ramsey said, his tone as stern as it ever was when he played the role of a disappointed father figure. Some days, I wished he would remember he was only four years older than me. Just barely four years.

"No, I'm not seeing Payton fucking Webber." Anger swept through me. "I get you don't think much of me, but I'm not a complete asshole. I want Ace. I've made no bones about that. I dumped Payton a long time before I started seeing Ace, and I haven't looked at another girl."

He said nothing. The silence in the car turned turbulent as he kept his thoughts to himself all the way to the hotel. As long as the drive had been, I was glad we were at the hotel and *not* Ace's house. That would have taken even longer to get to.

As soon as I could pass the vehicle off to the valet, I slammed out of the car. Ramsey followed at a more sedate pace. I should have fucking left him in the lobby, but I had the keys for the private elevator.

The air was electric with everything we weren't saying. As soon as we got to "our" floor, I strode out and headed straight for the suite. I had my phone out and I sent a message to Ace.

I needed to know she wasn't back already, especially before I walked in there with Ramsey.

ME:

Got Ramsey and back at hotel. You good?

She didn't keep me waiting long.

ACE:

I can't wait to see him. I'm doing Tracy's nails and we're catching up on some reality television. I might get Jonas addicted to a new show.

I chuckled.

ME:

Let me know when you're heading back?

ACE:

We will. Promise.

The door to the suite closed and I pivoted to face my older brother. He set his bags down and then eyed me. There was fatigue around his eyes and a five o'clock shadow on his jaw.

"You look beat," I admitted, keeping a firm grip on my temper.

"Tell me again," Ramsey said. "To my face, that you're not cheating on Ace."

"Every part of that is an insult..."

"And if you thought I was cheating on her, you would demand the same thing," Ramsey countered.

"I'd *never* think you were cheating on her. They'd have to bring me pictures and even—" Pictures.

Ramsey locked his gaze on me, a muscle appeared to be ticking in his jaw.

"You got pictures." That *bitch*.

"Tell me to my face, Lachlan. Look me straight in the eye and tell me you aren't cheating on Ace. Especially not cheating on her with Payton."

"Just tell you and you'll believe me?"

He closed his eyes and I almost felt guilty. Almost. Except he was acting like I *was* guilty. "Yes, I will believe you, because you've never lied to my face. I don't want to think this is true now. But... I need to see and *hear* you tell me you're not."

"I should slug you." Aggravation rifled through me. Goddamn Payton. Goddamn her.

"Maybe. Right now, I could slug you. I've waited five days to ask this question. I waited until I could stand in front of you and I am doing you the courtesy of *asking* instead of accusing. Stop fucking around and do me the favor of *answering*."

"I'm *not* cheating on Ace," I snapped out each word. "I would never. I am *definitely* not sleeping with Payton Webber. I haven't laid a finger on her since I dumped her ass out of your suite when she tried to show up in my bed naked—and if you're tracking when that was, it would be *before* you slept with Ace. And *before* we were seeing her."

Ramsey blew out a breath. "So you've had no contact with her...?"

He really did look relieved.

It pissed me off that he thought I could do that to Ace. Did he really think that little of me? "No, I've talked to the cunt. But I'm not touching her. Ever again."

His eyes narrowed. "Why are you talking to her?"

Goddammit.

Twenty-Seven

KC

Wrapping my arms around Tracy, I hugged her carefully. She laughed at me and squeezed me a little tighter. "I'm not that delicate," she chastised me. Pulling back, Tracy tapped my nose gently. I'd always kind of envied her height. Hers and Bronson's both, but it also made for the best hugs. "I'm sore, but I've had much worse."

"I'm glad you're okay," I told her. "I mean, really glad. I thought..." I worried. "They told us all the drawbacks and the possible side effects and any surgery has a risk—"

"Kaity," Tracy shook her head, her expression softening. "You worry too much. But I adore you for it."

"I know." I didn't even try to deny it. As I took a step back, I bumped into Jonas and he wrapped an arm around me to keep me from tripping. I glanced up at him with a grin and he pressed his lips to my temple. Comfort and support. He communicated so much with a single gesture.

Tracy sighed softly. "I like him," she said with a glance at Jonas. "I do like you, but I'm keeping my eye on you."

"Okay," Jonas said easily. "Do you need anything before we go? Dix will be here in ten and KC will feel better if she knows you have everything you need."

I could argue, but he wasn't wrong and Tracy shook her head, exasperation written all over her face. "Don't you start too. I'm fantastic. Full fridge, along with ready-made meals courtesy of Jackie and Davina. There are a dozen gift cards here for every meal delivery service in Los Angeles and..." Tracy laughed. "And Dad has been sending me some of my favorite childhood meals."

"Oh." I made a face. "Do you still like them?"

"Most of them," Tracy admitted as she moved slowly to walk us to the door. I wanted to offer her help or urge her to rest, but I didn't. She didn't need me to fuss, she needed me to be supportive. "But I could live without the corndogs."

I burst out laughing. Corndogs. "I—"

"He made them for you too, huh?" Tracy teased and I lifted my shoulders even as Jonas glanced between us.

"When I was little. Used to make Mom crazy when I would ask for them at home, but when I was at Dad's, he used to buy the—"

"—microwavable kind and they were kind of sweet, but you could easily overcook them?" Tracy was dead on accurate.

"Yes, but mustard fixes everything."

She snorted, then caught my hand. "Well, I have four boxes of the frozen kind if you want to take some back with you."

Giggles actually escaped me. I really hadn't... "You don't mind?"

Delight curved Tracy's smile and she winked. "Take them all—I can't eat them anymore."

"Ooh, okay. One sec." I let go of Jonas and darted into the kitchen. We'd been in here earlier to make lunch. Jonas knew a surprising amount about the perfect grilled cheese sandwich and after he'd made us a stack of them, I knew exactly who'd taught him.

Juliet had made these kinds of sandwiches at Dad's place, and they were wonderful. I had no idea it involved mayonnaise though. When Jonas had murmured a quiet apology at my question, I'd kissed him. Nothing to be sorry about, but he needed to make grilled cheese more often.

Stacked neatly with the labeled Tupperware containing prepared meals were four boxes of the exact same kind of corndogs Dad used to make when I was little. I pulled out two of the boxes. "You sure you want me to take all of them?"

"Please," Tracy called back. "I just—I tried it a couple of times after they got here, but it's really not the same."

I pulled out the other two and then carried them with me. Jonas relieved me of the boxes and slid them into one of the bags we'd brought things over in for our visit. Only I'd brought some books, games, and five different kinds of polish. While we'd hung out, I'd also done Tracy's nails.

It had been fun. Jonas teased me about giving him a manicure and I promised I would. I actually liked being able to do things like this, it was—nice.

"Do me a favor," Tracy said as my phone buzzed. Dix was there to get us. "Take it easy. Christmas is coming and there's plenty of time for visiting and hovering, but make time for fun."

I made a face. Christmas *was* coming. "I will do my best. I need to get some shopping done."

"Call me," Tracy said before she opened the door. "We can plot to spoil the little ones."

I grinned. "You get me."

"Yes," she told me, with affection and amusement in her voice. "I do. Now shoo—and I expect you to look after her, Jonas, and make sure she relaxes."

"I'll try," Jonas said, then he tracked his soulful gray-eyed gaze right to mine. "But KC needs to make sure everything is done or she won't rest."

I wrinkled my nose. "I'll rest—someone is going to teach me how to take a vacation." At his smile, I glanced at Tracy. "Love you. Talk to you soon?"

"Yes," she said, gripping the door handle. "Now get out. Both of you."

The smile in her eyes and on her face robbed the words of any sting and I laughed as we headed out to where Dix waited with the car. He stepped out as soon as we appeared and opened the back door for us.

"Hey, Gorgeous," he greeted me. "And Jonas."

I didn't laugh, but Jonas just stared at him. "Hey, Dix," I said. "How are you doing?"

"Good, was starting to think you'd replaced me." There was just an element of accusation under the lightness in his tone. "I haven't seen you since you took the car to the hotel after we got here."

We had separated. I'd told him to go home, take a break. "You were due some days off," I reminded him. "The hotel has been providing cars and the guys can all drive. So—it was just easier."

And it meant he wasn't staying on the same floor with all of us. That was more a bid for peace than anything else.

"Hmm," he said, canting his head. "You look tired."

"I am a little tired," I admitted.

"Home?" He kept his focus on me and not on Jonas who hadn't moved to get in the car. They were both waiting on me.

"Hotel," I told him firmly. "It's closer to the hospital and I need to talk to Mom and Johnny about Christmas."

Disapproval flickered in his eyes, but he just gave me the barest of nods. "All right. I've had plenty of time so you don't need to keep relying on other people to get you around."

"You're sweet, thank you," I said, then added, "But I think

we'll go the way we have for now then revisit *after* we relo-
cate." I wasn't sure if going back to Mom's was the right plan
or what. Should I spend Christmas with her? Or with Dad?
Or maybe with neither?

That was just a stress to even turn over and over in my
head. I climbed into the car and Jonas slid in behind me. Dix
didn't quite slam the door but it gave a distinct thump. I
grimaced and shot Jonas a look, but he just put his hand on
my thigh.

"Seatbelt," he murmured against my ear and then reached
past me to snag it. After he buckled me in, he did himself, then
put his hand back on my thigh. I covered his fingers and
leaned my head back.

All at once the tired slammed into me. Tracy really did
look good. She looked good, she sounded good, and we had a
good time. Closing my eyes, I smothered a yawn with my free
hand. Jonas turned his palm over and threaded his fingers with
mine. Shifting, I tucked my head against his shoulder.

"Gonna nap a little," I murmured.

He kissed the top of my head. "Go to sleep, I'll wake you
up when we get there."

I'd been fine before we came outside. Hell, I'd been fine
until I climbed in the car and now, I couldn't keep my eyes
open. I barely seemed to even blink and then we were there.
Jonas woke me with care and I groaned. Dix had to pull into
the portico for guests at the main entrance, so I needed my
game face on.

Jonas exited the car first, with the bag of frozen corndogs
in one hand. He held out his hand to me, not letting Dix help
me out. I squeezed his hand and found a smile for Dix.
"Thanks for coming to get us."

"Anytime," he said, then gave me a stern look. "You need
to get more rest."

"I will..."

"Call me if you need me?" It was both a command and a request.

"I will," I said, more to just end the discussion than because I thought I would. Dix was one of my oldest friends in a way, but the last few months—hell the last couple of years, something had shifted and it had all grown more strained.

When Jonas gave me a light tug, I went right with him and headed inside. The lobby was huge and there were a lot of people coming and going. Some guests were seated around the foyer area, others were heading into or coming out of the bar or the restaurants. It was a busy hotel.

We didn't pause or linger, just went to the private elevators and Jonas scanned his keycard to even call the elevator. We'd have to scan it again inside, before we could choose the floor. They had a lot of similar security measures in place. Didn't mean there weren't also paparazzi hanging out somewhere down here, so we always moved swiftly through the lobby and onto the elevators.

The blue hair stood out. If I didn't love it so much, I might even consider changing it. But I didn't want to. The day I dyed it blue the first time, I'd fallen in love with it and didn't want to go back. Maybe someday in the future.

Maybe.

Not now.

As soon as the doors closed, I leaned into Jonas again and he wrapped an arm around me. "You that tired?"

It wasn't worry or fussing, but a kind of gentle care that I craved. It was hard to put it into words, so I tucked my head against his shoulder. "I feel like we just finished a five hour concert where we lost track of our sets."

We'd done that before.

"I was fine until..."

"You really relaxed and realized that Tracy was definitely alright?"

"She looked great, didn't she?"

Jonas nodded, putting his hand out to brace the doors when they slid open. "Yes, she did. I think you're worrying her now."

Was I? I frowned, straightening. "I'll talk to her."

"Later," he suggested. Since he already had his key out, he unlocked the door. "After you get some sleep."

The suite wasn't empty. Lachlan and Ramsey were both there, standing on opposite sides of the room, not quite glaring at each other. But there was no mistaking the tension crackling in the air. "Ramsey..."

Some of my tired fled in the face of the fact he was *here*. Lachlan had messaged earlier but it wasn't the same as seeing him. I strode straight to him and he met me halfway. He picked me right up when I hugged him and I took a deep breath, inhaling his familiar scent and hugging him tightly. It had barely been a full week but it felt like eons.

"Hey, Siren," Ramsey said against my hair before he leaned back and then cupped my face with one hand. The light kiss was like a downpayment on the kiss I wanted but I was too damn happy to see him.

"I missed you," I promised him and his smile eased some of the tension around his eyes.

"Missed you too..." He let out a sigh and hugged me to him again. I held on and closed my eyes to just drink in his nearness. "Good visit with Tracy?"

"Yes." I barely got the word out before a yawn tried to strangle it and he set me on my feet. "Sorry... she's great."

"Good." He gave me a wordless stare. "How are you doing?"

"Tired," I admitted. He glanced from me toward Lachlan, his expression tightening again and I glanced between them. "How are you? You guys okay?"

"Fine," Lachlan said almost too quickly even as Ramsey said, "For the most part."

"Actually, Ace," Lachlan said. "Why don't you go take a nap? You look like hell."

Jonas snorted. "Smooth. I'm gonna put the corndogs in the freezer." Thankfully, our suite came with a full kitchen. It was a very nice hotel.

"Thank you."

But the tension between Ramsey and Lachlan was so thick, I could cut it with a knife.

"Are you sure you guys are okay?" I wasn't as positive.

"Just brotherly stuff," Ramsey said after a long pause, then he focused on me. "Do you want to go and take a nap?"

I glanced at the time then made a face. "If I go lay down now, I might crash all night." It was barely six. "And you just got here..."

"We have plenty of time," Ramsey reminded me. "And I'd rather you got some rest. I can come curl up with you in a bit, if you want."

But not right now. Right, he wanted to talk to Lachlan. Jonas came out of the kitchen with a bottle of water that he held out to me. "I'll fill them in," he offered. "Go to bed. Sleep, and if you sleep all night, that's fine. We can sleep in there if you want or you can have the bed."

I chuckled. "I like sleeping with you guys." I rose up on my tiptoes to kiss him, then gave another to Ramsey before I turned to go to Lachlan. His jaw was tense but he softened enough to give me a kiss. I didn't like the dark look in his eyes.

"If you need me..."

"We all need you," Lachlan said. "But we're okay and you need rest. So, go on... and if you feel like sleeping naked, none of us would complain, I'm sure."

Jonas snorted and Ramsey blew out an exasperated breath, but neither of them actually denied it. "I'll think about it," I told Lachlan, then winked. "I'm sure whoever comes to sleep with me will find out."

"I like goals," Lachlan said, then wrapped his hand around my nape before he gave me another hard kiss. "Go be a good girl."

That sent a very delicious shiver right through me. He'd said the same thing about our date and that had been—a really good date.

I couldn't help but glance at them again before I slipped into the suite's largest bedroom. Lachlan and Jonas had slept with me every night since we'd gotten here. I wasn't sure how that would work out with Ramsey here now, but I was fine with figuring it out.

No sound drifted through the door, so whatever they were discussing, they were keeping it quiet. Maybe the tension was nothing. Or maybe I was just reading too much into it cause I was tired.

I got ready for bed, stripped out of my clothes as requested and climbed into the middle to curl under the covers. One quick look at my messages with the latest positive update for Pen and then my eyes were closing whether I liked it or not.

Twenty-Eight

JONAS

The silence rippling out as KC disappeared into the room we'd been sharing with her deepened as the door closed. The click of the latch echoed through the room and I swung a look at my brothers. Before I could open my mouth though, Ramsey shook his head once and pointed to the patio doors.

I nodded as they picked up their drinks and strode toward them. I paused to secure the main door to the hall, throwing the deadbolt. KC had a habit of doing this at night before we went to bed.

If she was going to be asleep in here by herself while we were going to be out on the balcony, I wanted it doubly secure. Other people in the hotel had keys to the various rooms. We weren't risking her.

Not again.

Snagging a drink of my own, I followed them out onto the balcony. The earlier tension was back in full force. They were standing five feet apart, the area between them an open moat lined with all non-verbal spears they weren't actively throwing at each other.

Or at least not right now.

"Someone want to fill me in?"

"It's nothing—" Lachlan began but Ramsey's low growl was a sound he only made when we truly aggravated him. I used to think it was funny.

I got most of the temper. Lachlan got the rest of it. Ramsey? He was a well of calm and reason. Even when I lost my shit, he could keep everything around me calm until I could get a grip.

Probably wouldn't have survived high school without him. KC helped me keep my temper in check more and more these days. The work my psychologist had me doing had also helped. The homework. The meds. My people.

"Fine," Lachlan said. "I was just telling Ramsey that I got a lead on her guitar again."

I straightened. That missing guitar was an open wound she didn't want to discuss, but we all wanted to get it back for her as soon as possible. All our previous attempts had gone nowhere. "What's the lead?"

"One of the guys on the team found it on one of the auction sites. I had him reaching out to do all the negotiation. Every other time we've done this it fell through, so I tried to keep my distance and let the seller think he was the only one interested."

"And?" Ramsey prompted, his tone so testy it made me want to verify I hadn't fucked up.

"And he got me a number, so I called it to make contact and complete the transaction."

"We know the seller." That had to be why they were waging whatever this cold war was. "Please don't let it be Mom."

That earned me a pair of sharp looks, and I shrugged.

"Don't pretend it didn't occur to you too," I said. "Mom hates her." It pissed me off every single time I thought about it. "She barely looked at her over Thanksgiving, and I got the distinct impression that was the last place she wanted to be."

Hell, she'd said all of five words to me. I was pretty sure she said way more to Lachlan, but he didn't share and I hadn't asked. Ramsey spoke to her and to Gibs, but he'd been playing peacemaker.

Better him than me. I still couldn't wrap my head around the idea that Mom *lied* to us. Us. Gibs. And by extension, KC.

"The seller isn't Mom," Lachlan said with a sigh and he raked his hand through his hair. "It's Payton."

"Webber?" I stared at him. Was he for... "That bitch broke into our room and trashed KC's things?" I hadn't forgotten that nor the fact that... "She *hurt* KC?"

"That's a solid question," Ramsey stated, folding his arms. He transferred his gaze to the suite doors briefly before focusing on us again. Yes, we were outside and there were closed doors, but we were keeping our voices down. The last thing we needed was to be overheard. "Payton kept sneaking into my suite at the dorm."

I frowned. "She had a master key."

It was the only explanation that made sense. Ramsey nodded once. "She had to have copied mine. Not sure when she got her hands on it..."

Both of us looked at Lachlan. "I was not sharing keys with her, even when I was seeing her. So don't act like this is my fault."

"You fucked her," I commented. I used to think Payton was good looking, until she opened her mouth. Then I wanted nothing to do with her. "She used to be in our suite all the time." I'd seen her naked more than once and I didn't think it had ever been an accident.

I also didn't accept her offer.

Ever.

"Don't remind me," Lachlan said with a grimace. "And I mean it, don't remind me ever. I'm putting that down to insanity..."

"Except," Ramsey interceded. "It's not just that she has it."

"What does she want?" The fact she was talking to Lachlan at all was a good thing, right? "Or are we just waiting to turn her into the cops?"

"It doesn't matter," Lachlan retorted. "I don't have confirmation that she *has* the guitar and she is playing coy about providing it."

"Because we could turn her in," I muttered and Ramsey actually took a step forward and braced his knuckles against the table. Despite the fact it was December, we were all outside in shirt-sleeves. The sun had gone down, and it was chilly but it was far from cold.

Connecticut and Tahoe were generally not this warm. Hell, neither was Denver when I went there. December usually meant coats and gloves. Instead, we were just out here.

"There's more to it than that... whatever she wants she must really want because..." Ramsey slid his phone onto the table and I picked it up. There were pictures on it.

Photos of Payton—at least I assumed it was her, the angles were all on her breasts, her pussy, and her ass. Most were close-ups that I could have lived without seeing.

KC's were much nicer.

I thumbed through the images, swiping them from one to the next...

"Why the fuck is she on our sofa?" That was the sofa at the cottage. My keyboard was on the coffee table. I'd packed and brought it with me.

"Really good question," Ramsey said. "I didn't even realize she was back on campus."

"Stop looking at me like this is my fault," Lachlan snapped back. "I didn't invite her. If anything, I've been working to keep her away from Ace. I just wanted to get that damn guitar so I could wipe away those shadows in Ace's eyes whenever it comes up in conversation."

Genuine anger underscored every single word. I believed him.

"I want to believe you, Lach," Ramsey said. "But you have to admit, you're keeping secrets and these photos..." he motioned to me. "They are pretty damning."

I scrolled through a few more. Payton coming in and heading out from the house. More than one of her coming down the stairs.

The sloppy nude mess of her on the sofa, I could have lived my whole life without seeing. Was she fucking someone in our living room?

I supposed the idea was we would blame it on Lachlan, maybe? For what? If he was cheating on KC I'd—

"Wait, who sent these? And who were they meant for?" Cause it would piss me off. It clearly pissed off Ramsey.

But this had the power to *hurt* KC and that was unacceptable.

"Good question," Ramsey said as he took a drink. "It was delivered this morning before I left for my flight. I didn't bring the originals with me because the last thing we needed was having them floating around."

"Would Payton send them?" They were dropped off with Ramsey *there* not here. But maybe they didn't know we were *here*. We'd been pretty circumspect coming and going. Gibs and KC weren't checked in under their own names.

Both of us turned to Lachlan. He unscrewed the cap on his water then drained the whole thing before he said, "Maybe. But it makes no fucking sense to threaten me. She's not close to getting what she asked for and she hasn't produced any proof of the guitar. Sending those? That's just designed to piss me off."

"Or maybe it's a threat," I said and the fact the pair of them glanced at each other confirmed it. "Or did you think I wouldn't see it?"

"No," Lachlan answered before Ramsey did. "To be honest, I just don't want you getting angry and flying off the handle or charging in and doing something impulsive."

I snorted. Not because he was wrong, but I would prefer something to punch in the face. "Wait—" Looking at the images again, I frowned. "These are almost all from the same angle."

"I noticed," Ramsey admitted.

"Someone has a camera in our house?" Fury blew through me. *Now* I was pissed.

"Maybe, or maybe she set it up to look like that," Lachlan said. "First step, I need to talk to her and find out what her game is..."

"What did she ask you for?" Ramsey demanded. "That's the one thing you've been very careful to *not* tell me."

I wasn't sure how they were that calm. "I don't want KC going back to this place if there's a camera in there..." We'd had sex on that sofa.

Had someone taken pictures of us?

She and Ramsey had sex in that house. As far as I knew, so had she and Lachlan. They'd been up in his bathroom but...

Would they sell those images to the paparazzi? I did not want to be used to hurt her.

"Agreed," Ramsey said. "We're going to take care of that. But whoever came and went did it before our cameras were in place. That's—something..."

Our cameras hadn't been in place for long. We were stupid. We should have had better security for her period. "Maybe we move off campus..."

Maybe we shouldn't go back. What had Yvette said about the school? She hated how much KC had suffered there.

The rumors.

The gossip.

The bullying.

The fire.

The assault.

The robbery.

The kidnapping...

"What did Payton want, Lachlan? Is it something we can just give her so she can crucify herself?"

"She wants me back in her bed," Lachlan said flatly. "That's *never* going to happen."

"Fuck," Ramsey said with a groan and leaned against the railing as he pinched the bridge of his nose. "This is..."

"Exactly," Lachlan said, folding his arms. "I can take care of it. It's just going to take time. She doesn't trust me to meet in person..."

"How exactly is she planning on riding your dick if she won't meet you in person?"

"Because I want to meet in public," Lachlan spoke to me like I was a child. I wasn't, but sure, he could keep that shit up. "She wants something more private and exclusive. The kind of thing where she could set me up. I'm not interested, and as much as I want that guitar back for Ace, I'm not willing to touch Payton for the remote chance she actually has it."

"Then lie," I said flatly and I had both brothers staring at me. "She wants something from you. Something she's playing this stupid game for. Lie to her. You don't have to fuck her to make her think you'll show up and be willing... You used to not have standards."

"Thanks for that," Lachlan said, glaring at me and I shrugged.

"He's not wrong," Ramsey said slowly, pulling Lachlan's glare to him.

"Fuck both of you, I'm not doing that to Ace."

As much as I hated to say it... "If she doesn't know..." I groaned. "Do you think Payton actually has the guitar? For real?"

Neither of the other two said anything, but it was Lachlan who blew out a long breath. "Yes, I do think she has it. I think she's had it from the beginning..."

"Which means you have to think she also attacked KC." Because KC had been assaulted in our suite. Someone had bludgeoned her.

Lachlan's jaw practically clicked when he snapped his teeth shut.

He wasn't disagreeing.

"Then we need to set Payton up. She has to pay for that. I don't want her to be a threat to KC anymore."

"I hate her," Lachlan admitted. "I hate her for who I thought she was and who she actually was. I hate her more for what she put Ace through..." Then he grimaced and spit. "What—she and I both put Ace through. Because if I hadn't been interested in fucking with her, Payton may not have."

"You don't know that for sure," Ramsey told him but the thing was, Lachlan was probably right.

Everything I knew about Payton said she was a narcissist and a self-involved diva. She may not have liked the attention KC got, but she would have hated the fact that KC got attention from Lachlan *and* Ramsey.

"If she was jealous of your focus on her, I didn't help when I invited her to join the tutoring sessions with Kaitlin..."

"Why the hell would you do that?" Lachlan asked and it was Ramsey who appeared embarrassed and I shook my head.

"He wanted to rattle her by throwing someone in her face she didn't like and who didn't like her."

"Didn't really work," Ramsey admitted. "Except she told me off and ripped me a new asshole." A faint smile touched his lips. "I deserved it."

"Well, bully for you," Lachlan said. "This doesn't change the situation."

"No," I said. "It doesn't. We need to set her up—that means you need to make her think she's getting what she wants. Then we can get what we need to make her go away."

And maybe get the guitar back for KC.

"Ace can't know," Lachlan said firmly and Ramsey nodded once.

"Keeping it a secret is a bad idea," I told them.

"Telling her is just gonna stress her out," Lachlan countered.

"Right now, we don't have everything to tell her," Ramsey said and that decided it for us. "When we have proof, then we can tell her."

Essentially, when we gave her the guitar back.

I hated this plan and at the same time... KC was exhausted.

"Fine, we don't tell her immediately, but we're not keeping this a secret forever."

"No," Ramsey agreed. "Not forever." Then we both looked at Lachlan.

"Fuck," he muttered. "Fine, I'll make arrangements for after we're back in Connecticut. I'm not ruining Christmas with Ace by calling that bitch here."

Couldn't really argue with that.

"I'm sleeping in KC's room," I announced. "So you two decide who gets the other spot." With that, I turned to head back inside.

"Did he just call shotgun for her bed?" Lachlan asked and Ramsey chuckled.

"He did, and I'm taking the other side. You've both had her all week. Now you have to share."

"Woah..." Lachlan protested, but I closed the door on them and left them to argue about it. I wanted to check on KC and finish working on the song I was writing her for Christmas.

Nudging the door open to her room, I peeked in. She was curled up right in the middle of the bed and the soft sound of her steady breaths drifted over to me.

She was sleeping peacefully. That sight relaxed the ball of tension in my gut. I drank in the sight of her and then closed the door softly. She hadn't been sleeping that much, that she was now? *That* was a good thing.

A very good thing.

Twenty-Nine

KC

By unanimous decision, we decided to have Christmas at Mom's. It was big enough for everyone to come and stay. Dad offered Tahoe, but I didn't want to be that far away from Pen. When it came down to it, none of us did. As it was, the day before we checked out of the hotel, Tracy came to see Dad.

While she hadn't asked me to, I'd gone up with her and said I could hang out, back her up, or do whatever she needed. The first few minutes of conversation with Dad had been brutal. He didn't get it.

Not at first, you could practically see the wheels turning as he tried to reconcile what she was telling him with what he'd thought he'd known. Finally, he'd said...

"She/her?" The single question made Tracy raise her brows briefly, then she nodded slowly. "No more he/him. Just she/her." Dad rephrased it like he needed to verbalize it. "Tracy—not Trace?"

Tracy smiled then. "Preferably, though Trace can be short

for Tracy so if you slip... it's okay. Mom still has moments periodically. She asked for the labor exclusion."

I wasn't the only one who gave her a puzzled look and then Tracy laughed.

"She was in labor with me for fourteen and a half hours and I dislocated her hip when I was born. That means she gets all the time in the world to get the name right and at the end of the day, if she fucks it up, it's not because she's doing it on purpose."

"Oh." I made a face because that all sounded very uncomfortable, but Dad laughed.

"Can I get a stoned exclusion?" Dad asked, rubbing his jaw. "So that when I'm high and I slip, I'll try to catch it, but —yeah. This isn't my first rodeo. Just—you've always been Trace to me."

"Take your time, Dad," Tracy told him. "But it's important to KC that I come to Christmas and I didn't want to do this there."

"Oh... does Jennifer know?" He looked at me curiously and I shrugged.

"I haven't told her specifically, but I don't think she's gonna care one way or the other." I shot Tracy an apologetic look before focusing on Dad again. "I don't know that Mom really paid attention to the gender of your other kids."

Half the time, I wasn't sure she remembered Bronson was my brother, even if she knew about Jackie and Bronson now. Then again, maybe she genuinely didn't care about Gibs' indiscretions. Particularly post-divorce.

As much as I didn't want to ask the next question, I went with it. "What about Linzi?"

Dad sighed. "I've asked her for some time. So she won't be there."

Tracy and I traded a look. Some time? Did that mean

divorce? Should we ask? Should we leave it alone? I wasn't one hundred percent sure on any front. Shit.

"I'll deal with Linzi, girls," Dad said, and the fact he delivered it in his easy, relaxed drawl made me grin. "Just make sure Jennifer knows I'm coming?" The last Dad directed at me.

"I can do that. I'm going to ask Davina to set up the pool house for you..."

"No," Dad said with a shake of his head. "Me being there for the day is enough for your mother and Jackie to put up with. I can stay on here at the hotel. I think I want to book some studio time near the new year when the guys are back in town..."

He'd been struggling for the last couple of years, so I raised my eyebrows. "Feeling the urge to record?"

"A little," he said. "More, starting to hear the music again."

I understood that so much. When the music went quiet, the hush on the world was too much. It was why I ran, why I went to clubs to dance...and why, without his guitar, I'd struggled the last few months.

Maybe it was time to let it go.

We were in a better place. Did I really need the guitar to remind me of the dad I lost? When I'd found him again?

Dad bumped my shoulder with his and pulled me to the present. "Feel like maybe doing a session or two in a studio before you go back to school?"

"Dad," Tracy said before I could answer. "Let's get through Christmas first, yeah? You guys shouldn't be working."

"Well, it's not exactly work," I admitted and Dad grinned at me. Tracy just rolled her eyes. But, I could see her point, so I raised my hands. "Fine, we'll talk, okay? In the meanwhile, I'm going to finish packing. We're heading to Mom's today, with Yvette and Aubrey. Tracy, you are more than welcome to come stay as well."

She was already shaking her head, but opened her arms as I gripped her for a hug. "I'll be there for Christmas," she promised. "But the whole craziness of all those people *and* your boyfriends in one place is stressful enough for one day."

A laugh escaped me as I leaned back and I didn't miss Dad's grimace or the look Dad and Tracy shared.

"Neither of you get to start," I said. "I like my boyfriends just fine. And the rest is—kind of fun." It was. Even with the chaos and Pen in the hospital. I loved having everyone around.

"Uh huh," Tracy deadpanned, then she tapped my nose. "We'll see you in a couple of days."

That was that. The shift from hotel to the house was more welcome than I realized. I hated going through the lobby, but I also didn't like being further from Pen. Out of the hotel, the guys seemed to relax a little.

Which was good, Ramsey had been on edge since he arrived, though he denied it. He and Lachlan were also fighting, but they never said a word about it to each other when I was there.

"Let them disagree," Aubrey recommended when I escaped to her and Yvette's room. She'd been on the phone with Forrest when I came in and Yvette had patted the bed next to her. Curling up there, I tucked my head to her shoulder and she shifted her phone to show me the TikTok videos she'd been watching.

Dog and cat videos fixed everything. We watched those while Aubrey talked to Forrest. It had been a nice way to spend a couple of hours. Especially when it hit me that I had not purchased a single Christmas present. The panic was real. Yvette, however, dragged out a laptop and we hit every website and paid a small fortune to get super-fast shipping.

When the boys came to find me, they seemed far less tense. So maybe they had worked it out. The sudden adrenaline dump of realizing I'd been so focused on Pen and Tracy that I hadn't even thought about the actual holidays left me more than a little shaken.

Dix arrived to get us all not long after and take us back to Mom's.

The house was hosed down in Christmas. The scents of pine and peppermint scented the air with a holiday kiss. A huge tree filled the entranceway, adding the woodsier scent while a second, classic blue spruce dominated the living room. Everything said the *holidays are here and you will celebrate.* Homey *and* dramatic.

Johnny descended the stairs to welcome us sporting a Santa hat to go with his Hawaiian shirt and shorts. It was adorable. Even better, Mom drifted down behind him, her expression far more relaxed than our last visit. She also kept shooting Johnny fond looks.

Mental fingers crossed they were working it out. Presents were still a day or two out from arriving. We ended up spending the rest of the afternoon by the pool. The weather was perfect and the pool heaters were on, so the water was warm. I kept half-falling asleep.

I was in no way prepared for the call that came in mid-afternoon. Dad was on the call, as was Jackie, Tracy, and Bronson. They waited for me and by extension the rest of us, so Pen's doctor could give us an update.

One full week since her infusion and they had just finished their first full round of tests.

"And?" I asked when the doctor paused.

"First, I want to tell you this is just week one..." Yeah, all the caveats because nothing could ever just be a straight answer. "We've still got a ways to go, and we're going to keep you all updated regularly..."

At some point, Ramsey covered my hand with his and I was digging my nails into his palm. Jonas had slid onto the lounger and wrapped an arm around my middle and tucked his head against my shoulder. Lachlan locked his hand around my ankle.

The shaking didn't translate at first, but it was there.

"Doc," Dad said. "We get it. You can't give us anything concrete because you have to cover your ass, but what are the results telling you?"

I could have kissed Dad. That was *exactly* what I wanted to know.

"I understand, I just don't want to over promise anything. That said... we're very pleased with the results. No signs of rejection. Her counts are up..."

I missed the rest of it as the doctor's relieved description seemed to sink into my bones. Pen was doing better.

Across the board.

She was doing *better*. While they couldn't commit beyond that, the results were everything we could have asked for and more. The world went wavey as tears splashed down my face and hit my thighs. Ramsey pressed his lips to the side of my head and Jonas squeezed me tighter. Even Lachlan flexed his hand around my ankle.

The shaking and the tears redoubled in force and suddenly Ramsey picked me up and wrapped me up tight. The guys were all there. Someone—maybe Aubrey, took the phone. Probably good, 'cause I lost it. I couldn't see for the tears filling my eyes and I couldn't even suck in a deep breath.

My nose was clogged, my throat hurt, my chest spasmed, and each time I thought I had it under control, I started crying all over again. Ramsey murmured nonsense as he rubbed slow circles against my back.

The next time reality surfaced for me, my eyes were so sore, I could barely open them.

"Nope," Lachlan said from somewhere when I started to sit up. "Stay."

He pressed a hand against my shoulder and caught the damp washcloth sliding off my face.

"What...?" I winced as he replaced the first washcloth with a second one. "That hurts."

"I'm not surprised, Ace, your eyes are almost swollen shut." Ouch, really? "Now stay there. Ramsey is downstairs getting food sorted out for you and Jonas is showering. When he's done, I'll take mine and then we're going to hole up in here."

In here...? "My suite?"

"Yep," Lachlan murmured, before he pressed his lips to my forehead. His kiss was cool against my overheated flesh. "You need a break. We'll see everyone tomorrow."

I wanted to argue but Lachlan began to massage my hand, his thumbs easing tension from my palm.

"Pen is okay?" I hadn't imagined the call, right? She really was?

"Yes, she is," he said softly. "We double and triple checked. Even Gibs messaged after, from the hospital..."

"He did?" I wanted the washcloth off, but my eyes hurt so bad when I opened them.

"Yes, he did." Lachlan held up his phone and there was a picture of Pen on it, her eyes shining and her smile huge. Dad was dressed in a surgical gown and he was holding her. His smile was almost as big as Pen's.

My heart spasmed again.

"Now," Lachlan said, shutting off the phone before he draped the washcloth over my eyes again. "Take it easy. Everything is being taken care of and you're going to rest."

"Or what?" I sniffled, not that I wanted to fight but he was in full bossy mode.

"Or nothing," he said, pressing a kiss to my palm. "You're going to be a good girl for me, or I'm going to fuck you into this bed until you can't move."

A shudder rippled through me.

"I'm not sure if that's a threat or a promise." Cause I kind of—no kind of about it. I pulled the washcloth off and reached for Lachlan. One hand around his nape and I tugged him gently. He didn't make me work for it. His mouth crashed into mine and I drank in his kiss.

It was salty from the remnants of my tears, but I savored the way his tongue swept against mine and how he devoured my lips. I needed this.

I needed him.

A door opened and a soft chuckle reached me as Lachlan lifted his head. "Fuck off, Jonas."

"Nah, I'm good right here." There was laughter in Jonas' voice and when I tilted my head I could see him standing in the door to the bathroom, dressed only in boxers. He was a sight for sore eyes and my eyes were definitely aching.

My heart though—it was better for seeing his smile. When I held out a hand to him, he crossed over to the bed and caught my fingers. "Hey."

"Hey," he murmured, then traced his fingers down my cheek. Lachlan had one hand and Jonas the other. When Jonas dipped his head to kiss me, I sighed against his mouth. As much as I needed to close my eyes, I wanted them open.

I wanted to savor having them right here.

A soft groan intruded as Jonas teased my tongue with his and Lachlan snorted. "Get in line, Big Brother, Jonas already stepped on my moment."

I couldn't help giggling as Jonas grinned then lifted his head. "You won't hear me complaining," Jonas said and then he winked at me. My heart did a little flipflop, but he moved to give Ramsey room and then Ramsey was there, two fingers against my cheek, he studied me.

"Feeling better, Siren?"

Yes... yes I was. Tears burned in my eyes again but I blinked them back. "I am," I confessed. "I am better than ever."

All three of them were right here, Pen was doing better, Tracy was okay, and I had my dad *and* my mom back in my life.

Jonas was right. No complaints at all.

Thirty

RAMSEY

"I'm not sure whether I should be happy or annoyed," Kaitlin announced as she eyed the family arrayed in front of her. Honestly, the fact they had all gathered on Christmas Eve to sit her down and have this conversation could have gone badly.

Running my knuckles along her arm pulled her attention to me.

"Et tu, Ramsey?"

I chuckled. "Not exactly," I said, keeping my tone even.

The fact she'd half-collapsed after getting good news had just reiterated to me how much of all of this she'd been weathering on her own shoulders. Thankfully, her whole family also recognized it.

"But," I continued before she could latch onto that fact. "I don't disagree with a single person here. You have been doing too much."

"Darling," Jennifer Crosse said as she leaned forward, her perfectly manicured hands clasped together. "Your father and

I have been talking..." Gibs nodded once from where he was standing. "We have to face some hard truths—all three of us."

I narrowed my eyes. The last thing Kaitlin needed to be doing right now was shouldering more of the burden. Period.

"And that would be?" Kaitlin asked as she placed her hand over mine on her arm. When the family called us down for drinks, the last thing I'd expected was the ambush they'd planned.

Led by Jackie, Bronson's mother, they were all calling Kaitlin on the carpet for taking on too much. But they weren't accusing her or trying to corner her, what they were doing was demanding she let them all help. They were divvying up the responsibilities.

Despite the fact the planned "intervention" caught me off-guard, the fact Aubrey and Yvette were in the middle of it *with* the rest of her family promised me it was necessary.

As protective as Tracy and Bronson were about their sister, they had nothing on Yvette or Aubrey. I admired those girls, I also respected their absolute loyalty and love for Kaitlin.

"We're your parents," Gibs said slowly. "It's about time we acted like it."

The corner of her mouth jerked upward, a half-smile, and then Kaitlin shook her head. "I—"

"Have been doing everything," Jackie said, and her tone held not one element of scolding to it. "You are not remotely afraid of the hard work or the uncomfortable truths. You put yourself out there, take on the weight of every single person you love—but now, you're going to let *us* do the lifting."

"Yep," Tracy said with a little pop. "Pen is doing great. She's going to keep doing well. Soon, she's going to move back home with Jackie..."

"And we're going to get back into a new routine," Bronson added. "Davina has volunteered to help us with childcare and Dad..." He glanced at Gibs.

"I'm going to make a point of being around more. I should have been doing more to begin with. There's a lot I've missed out on over the last few years."

"So," Jennifer said, seemingly picking up the thread before Johnny took her hand. "Johnny and I are also going to volunteer our time and effort. While Gibs and I don't need to spend more time together than absolutely necessary, we are capable of getting along for you. Something we should have done a long time ago."

"That means we'll be working together to get along for Pen," Johnny said with an easy grin. "Your little sister is going to be well loved, KC, and you're going to focus on your life and your career and get to be a daughter, a sister, and a friend again."

"Not the one who has to look after everyone else," Davina added as she joined us. "Family takes care of each other. You're going to let us do this and let those boys do their part too."

Kaitlin put a hand over her mouth then glanced around at the gathering of people who loved her so much, before she stole a look at me.

"I'm on your side," I reminded her softly, and her smile chased away the earlier unease. "But I don't think they're wrong. I'd like to help you focus on other things too."

Whether those other things were school or a tour or music or whatever? It didn't matter. I wanted Kaitlin to have what she wanted. That list started and ended with her being happy. Mostly, I just wanted to be there with her and to help her get wherever she was going or whatever she wanted when she got there.

"Now," Davina continued. "We're not going to scold you anymore, we've told you what we thought and what we want to do. Next is celebrating—who wants hot cocoa?"

Everyone raised their hands and Gibs rose to go and help Davina. That was odd. Even odder? Johnny went with him, and the two were talking. I caught Jennifer staring after them just like I was and I shook my head.

This was not the Christmas I could have imagined. Mom wasn't here, and while Gibs didn't stay the night, he did plan to come back the next day for food. I debated on asking about Mom but she'd been pretty quiet. I'd call her the next day after I called Dad.

Wish them both a good holiday. In the meanwhile, I tracked Kaitlin as she and the girls started divvying up the presents from under the tree. I was right where I wanted to be.

~

Unfortunately, as much as I would like the holidays to last, they didn't. We had to be back on campus sooner rather than later. At least *I* did. I had classes to prep for, students to assess, and a whole new semester ahead of me. Well, ahead of all of us. Jonas and Lachlan had spring classes they'd signed up for, as had Kaitlin.

The girls planned to finish the academic year and then decide whether to continue with school or go back to recording. I got it, neither of them were really committed to a college degree.

Frankly, none of them were. Which *almost* entertained me because Lachlan had had far more serious plans before. Now? He wanted the freedom to hitch his schedule to Kaitlin's. Where Jonas could write music in his pursuit with or without a degree, Lachlan needed plans of his own.

Plans, I needed to give him a friendly shove on *before* he set himself up for failure. Sadly, that was not the priority or why we elected to head back to school a couple of days ahead of Kaitlin.

"Are you sure it's okay that I'm going to be a few days more here?" Kaitlin asked, while sitting on the bed as I packed.

Lachlan and Jonas had already finished their packing. Lachlan had calls to make and Jonas went down for Kaitlin's coffee.

I checked my watch. Normally, we went back on the red-eye, but we'd booked an earlier flight. Sliding my hand against her cheek, I cupped her face. "It's more than okay. You need time here with Pen. If I could stay longer, I would—"

"I know," she told me, covering my hand with hers. "I just feel weird that you're all going back and I'm staying here."

"Just for a few days," I said. "We'll see you before next weekend, right?" I hated leaving her too. But we'd been trying to resolve this Payton issue, as well as get the guitar back. To do that, we needed to be back in Connecticut. I'd rather get it all sorted *before* Kaitlin was back there.

"I promise," she said, crossing her heart. "Dix is gonna fly back with us and before—I know we need to have someone else do the bodyguard work but he's been working on his attitude. He's not being so—pushy about everything."

"And you know him," I finished for her. "It's hard enough for you to trust people, but new people are much more difficult."

She winced. "I know it sounds terrible..."

"Siren, it does not sound terrible. You have a right to feel comfortable with the people in charge of your safety."

"But you guys don't like him."

I shrugged. "Not a fan, no. But I also don't have to like him if he does his job and is respectful with you." Lachlan was the one who had a real problem with Dix. "And to be fair, I'm never going to like anyone who thinks they have a right to say you can't see me, or shouldn't."

She dipped her chin, pushing some of her hair back behind her ear. She'd gone the day before to see Anastasia and I'd gotten to meet the mysterious hairdresser who took care of her blue tresses. The woman was definitely interesting.

I'd also ended up getting a hair cut. So I couldn't really

complain. "Well, on the upside," Kaitlin said. "Dix at least seems to be getting used to you guys too—so maybe it will all work out?"

"We'll see," I promised her. "For now, what are you girls planning for your last few days of freedom?"

She made a face, glancing to the right with a wince before sneaking a look at me again. Guilt was all over her face and it took enormous self-control to *not* laugh at her.

"We decided to get some studio time for a few days and see what happens," she admitted finally and made a face.

"Okay," I said slowly. "I know Gibs asked you about maybe working with him."

She shook her head slowly. "Not sure I'm ready for that yet." That took a lot of effort for her to admit so I nodded again. "And that's it? I tell you we're going to work and you just say okay?"

Indulgence unfurled within me. "Siren, you like music. You love your girls. You love working with them." These weren't questions or guesses. "So, you just said you're going to spend a few days doing something you really enjoy."

"Oh." She tilted her head from side to side. "I didn't really think of it that way."

I chuckled. "Never be afraid to tell me something, okay? If you want to work, then I might want you to take it easier or look after yourself, but I'm always going to support you."

Her cheeks flushed, and she dipped her chin again. With care, I nudged her chin up so I could see her eyes.

"That said, I am going to miss you. When we're back at school and after we've all got a grip on our schedules, will you let me take you out?"

"Out?"

"Yes, Siren, out, for a real date. You and me. Maybe dinner. Maybe a movie. Something fun, off campus and away from my brothers, at least for an evening." It had begun to sink in over the last few days, I'd never taken her out.

I'd tutored her. Picked on her. Rescued her. Had sex with her. Did my damnedest to look after her. But I'd never taken her out.

"You're seeing all of us and I'm okay with that. I know you have sex with them, and I'm fine as long as they look after you. But I want to take you out on a date, Siren, just us."

The shock and surprise giving away to wonder was damn humbling.

"I don't—I haven't really dated that much."

"Then we fix that," I informed her sternly. "You deserve to be treated like a queen."

"Well, they say pop princess or problem child," she teased, a spark of impish humor in her eyes and I shook my head.

"I don't give a damn what they say, only what you do." The press could go get fucked as far as I was concerned. Let them print all the bullshit they wanted, I knew the truth. So did a lot of other people.

Her smile grew. "I would love to go out with you," she said. "I think Jonas has taken me on a date—-but I wasn't sure we would call it a date then."

"So, what I hear you saying is light a fire under them." Her laughter had been exactly what I wanted. "I like to lead by example."

"I'm going to miss you," she said before she pressed a whisper of a kiss to my lips.

I couldn't really argue with her on that. I wrapped her up tight, holding her at least until Jonas came back up with her coffee. Then I made myself let her go to finish packing. It took some persuasion, but she stayed at the house rather than going to the airport with us.

The flight itself was long enough, but none of us rested. We spent too much time working out how we were going to deal with Payton. After realizing that the pictures suggested cameras in the house, we wanted to get back there and identify if there were cameras and *where* they were.

Hiring someone to come in and do a security sweep had felt a little like overkill. That was before he found one camera five minutes after walking inside. I wasn't prepared to find three cameras downstairs. Worse was when he went upstairs and found the one in her bedroom.

Thirty-One

KC

Six days. Six days without the guys had been forever. I texted with them frequently, which was great. Talked to them every night before they went to bed. The three hour time difference sucked. Yvette and Aubrey enjoyed teasing me, especially when I sent music clips to Jonas. Then I caught Aubrey sending one to Forrest. The laughter took the pressure off.

We recorded one full song and two partials. We weren't really sure about either of the partials, but we were toying with them. Dad came to spend one afternoon with us in the studio and it was both weird and kind of wonderful. I wasn't sure I wanted to record with him. Just going from no contact to talking regularly was going to take time.

Yvette elected to stay in California when we headed back to school. She'd been debating the move from Boston. In part because she wasn't going to school and in part because Aubrey and I weren't committed past this semester. Did we want to finish college? Or not?

I wasn't sure. Did we need a degree? Did I want one?

The only thing I was certain of, I loved working with them back in the studio. We spent one whole afternoon just mixing it up, remixing, then jamming out. When was the last time we just jammed and let the music *flow*? The benefit concert was continuing to produce capital for cancer research. The "live" album had dropped a few songs here and there but the full album was dropping right after the new year.

I agreed to letting the songs Dad and I performed together be added to the final compilation. We talked about it that afternoon he came to the studio, then again at dinner that night when it was just the two of us. I didn't realize how much I needed the others to run interference until we sat there in what had been a kind of awkward silence.

"You know, Sweet Kaity," Dad said, breaking the silence. "It's okay to be quiet with someone. I think—when you can be quiet with someone, it's better than someone who fills the air with a lot of nothing."

"It doesn't bother you?" I had to ask. "I feel like—I feel like I should have more to say."

"It only bothers me that you're upset." He lifted his shoulders. "I like that I can see you. I like that you want to talk to me. If you don't have much to say, that's all right too."

A laugh escaped me. "It's weird, I feel like we're strangers."

"Well, we are." Until he summed it up that way, it hadn't truly hit me how right he was. We were strangers. We'd been strangers for years. "That just means we have time to get to know each other, yeah?"

"I'd like that." At first, I thought it was bad that we didn't know each other but—we didn't. I wanted to know him. "I'd really like that."

His smile promised me he wanted the same thing. Still, despite how much I enjoyed the time with Dad, the time with the girls, with Pen in the hospital and even time with Mom and Johnny—I was *ready* to go back to school.

No, I was ready to get back to the guys. I missed them. The day before we left, I went to get waxed and got my nails done. Ramsey wanted to take me on a date. I couldn't wait to go running with Lachlan or maybe another driving lesson. Jonas had sent me some snippets here and there of music. He'd also offered a couple of suggestions for the jam sessions I'd sent him.

Instead of the red-eye, I booked us on an earlier flight. Aubrey teased me, but I was just ready to see my guys. I didn't let them know about the booking change because I wanted to surprise them. Dix flew with us and he'd made all the arrangements for a car. On the flight, I emailed back and forth with Frankie about updates to Bound Hearts recording schedule.

Meeting Frankie Curtis was one of those fortuitous moments you couldn't plan for or expect. When we met her, she was just a fan who'd come to one of our concerts with her boyfriends and her best friend. Ian wrote music, something Frankie had shared with us. I offered them a chance to listen. To be another ear. Nine times out of ten, a fan never takes you up on the offer. Frankie had.

Even better, I *liked* her. She'd never expected anything and asked for even less. When they came out to London on the last leg of our tour, it had been a delight to get them to perform with us. While I didn't get to see them that often, we emailed —a lot. She was in her junior year of college and her mother had died not that long before. Throw in the tour they'd been on and I could see it being a lot.

Now, they didn't want to spend as much time on the road. It wasn't just her and Ian, though they were the only two in *their* band. Frankie had three other boyfriends. Those boyfriends didn't go on the road with them. I got that. But touring, I wrote, was an important part of connecting with the fans. So they needed to decide what would work for them and commit to it. Then again, they had so much going for them and while she loved the music, it was because she loved Ian, not the other way around.

I was far more into the music. Could I give it up to stay in one place? Hmm... I had for the last couple of years. But if anything, the role music played in my life was too vital. Maybe I wouldn't be touring year in and year out. Maybe I could have both a life on and off the road, but I loved performing.

I loved immersing myself in music. If we decided to tour again, there was a real chance Jonas could go with us. But Ramsey was a teacher. He had a career. Lachlan? I wasn't sure what his plans were. Did I want to go on the road for months at a time and be away from them?

Or was I getting ahead of myself?

I was nineteen. Lachlan was twenty? Almost twenty-one? What was I even trying to plan right now? It was crazy and I kept obsessing. My mind was going in circles. By the time we landed, I was jittery as hell. I stuffed my hair under a knit cap to hide it before we went to collect our luggage.

Thankfully, we walked right past a coffee place literally on our way out of the baggage claim area as we headed out to pick up the car. It didn't take us long to get everything into the car with our coffees, which I was grateful to have cause it was freezing outside. Between the bite in the air and the kiss of ice on the sidewalks, we were definitely *not* in California anymore.

Aubrey texted with Forrest all the way back to the school. He was going to pick up dinner for them and he'd meet her at her place. I told Dix to drop Aubrey off first. I offered to walk across campus to the cottage, even with the suitcases it wasn't that far. Still they both shot me dirty looks, so I hushed.

Excitement threaded in my veins as we pulled up to Aubrey's building. I climbed out to give her a hug as Dix got her suitcases out. Forrest showed up as we were saying bye and he grinned as he took one of her cases. "Hey, Forrest," I greeted him and then Aubrey winked at me. "You two have fun!"

"You too, KC."

It was just after seven, dark and frigid, so I climbed back into the car. "Thanks, Dix," I told him when he slid in behind the wheel again. "Hopefully, you'll get a break now that we're back."

He'd been great about all the running around we'd been doing this past week. "Anything for you, gorgeous. You know that."

I did, actually. I smiled at him and then blew out a breath as I tracked our progress around campus. The closer we got to "home," the more excitement bounced through me. I was so ready to see them. As soon as we pulled up, I scooted over to let myself out.

"I'll be right back for the suitcase," I said and half-skipped up the path key in hand. The stupid grin on my face was going to be a dead giveaway, but I didn't care. I was so ready to see them.

Pushing the door open, I locked eyes with Lachlan. My smile expanded as he straightened.

"Ace..."

The uncertainty in his tone gave me pause, but that wasn't what made my smile falter. No, that was the blonde sitting on our sofa, half-nude, her shirt open and breasts on full display. "Do you mind?" Payton drawled as she reached a hand up to Lachlan. "We're a little busy here..."

I cut my gaze from Payton on *our* sofa to Lachlan where he stood beside the sofa. His belt was undone and his hair was mussed. What...?

"Are you deaf?" Payton drawled as she stood, walking her hand up Lachlan's chest. "We're busy."

The scrape of a shoe behind me yanked me out of the

blank reverie and I jerked my gaze from Lachlan and Payton to Dix, who glared past me toward them. Then the sound of a door opening upstairs pulled me around and Jonas was just there.

"KC..."

Surprise filled Jonas' expression, but not at his brother and Payton. No, he looked surprised to see me.

"I guess I came back too early..." Surprise rippled into shock before it tumbled into hurt. It crashed into anger somewhere along there but I—

"C'mon," Dix said as he gripped my arm. I wasn't sure whether to yell, to scream, or to punch Payton in her smug face. She looked so fucking triumphant. And she was still touching Lachlan and still half-naked in my—well, I guess it wasn't my house.

Dix hustled me backwards, all but shoving me out the door before he yanked it closed, cutting off my view. It was like the string holding me prisoner yanked tight and then snapped. I choked back a breath and then half-stumbled down the path as Dix nudged me into motion.

"Let's go, gorgeous," Dix said, one arm around my waist as he got me moving. Where the hell was I going to go? Back to the car?

No, I needed to walk back in there and punch Payton, then Lachlan.

Maybe Lachlan first *then* Payton.

Dix's arm tightened as he half-lifted me. "Keep moving," he said. "I'm getting you out of here."

"No..."

Thirty-Two

LACHLAN

The sound of the locks tumbling open had been a godsend. Ramsey was back. That was what I was waiting on. As it was, I'd had to peel Payton's grabby fucking hands off my groin twice as she rubbed up against me. I wasn't going to kiss her and make out. I played the arrogant card. She wanted to seduce me, she had to work for it.

The whole point of the exercise was to backtrack what she had and where she had it. If she had the guitar, it would link her to Ace's assault. Campus security could deal with her from there. Murray Creglin had listened to every single word of our story, and with Walker to corroborate, along with receipts for every electronic interaction, we set the trap.

The only way to make it work, though, was to keep Payton one hundred percent distracted. I was chum for the sharks in this play and if it were for anyone but Ace, I'd have said fucking no. As it was, I'd rather get my groin waxed than let her get anywhere near it. Thirty minutes into this farce, the door opened. Instead of rescue from Ramsey and campus security, it was my worst goddamn nightmare.

Ace.

Her beautiful eyes were frozen, like the rest of her expression. The soft smile on her lips died, leaving pain that raked poisonous claws across my chest. Payton said something, but the grating sound of her voice faded behind the roar in my head.

Ace was not supposed to be here.

She was due in the morning.

We'd been pushing to get this done so we'd have answers for her and instead...

"I guess I came back too early..." The absolute emptiness in her voice shredded me. Dix appeared in the doorway and then he was tugging Ace out with him. The moment her gaze left me, I moved.

Payton grabbed at me. "Lachlan..."

I peeled her hand off my arm and shoved her away. "Don't touch me," I snapped. "And button up your shirt." Then I was plunging outside into the icy air. The biting chill barely registered as only the faint frosting of my breath as I headed straight for Ace. She was with Dix near a car.

Correction, she was *struggling* with Dix. Anger struck a match inside of me and I dashed over the crackling snow to yank him off her. The other man came around swinging. I ducked his fist, but struck upward, swift and hard with a punch of my own. His head rocked back.

"Get the fuck off of her," I snarled. Ace slid against the door and dodged when Dix crashed into me.

"Cheating bastard," Dix snapped back and his fist slammed into my side once, twice, and the third one really fucking hurt. I cracked my head against his. Blood flooded my mouth but it sent Dix staggering backwards. The blow left a white hot ache pounding in my skull.

"Spying asshole," I retaliated, cutting him off before he could get anywhere near Ace again.

"Stop trying to cover up," Dix growled. "You're the one feeling up another girl while KC was away. Maybe you shouldn't have invited her over to get naked."

"Is that how you get your jollies? Spying on Ace? Spying on us? Enjoy getting your eyefuls that way?" Ever since we found those fucking cameras, I'd been trying to figure out who could have placed them and why.

The television though—that clinched it. Dix always brought in her television. He always set it up. He was the only one who had free run of her room, whether it was in their first dorm, the second, when she moved in with Jonas, or when we moved in here.

Mother fucker had been *spying* on her. Infuriating as it was, we'd had to sit on this knowledge. Sit on it and use it...

I just didn't expect it to be *tonight* or—

"What the hell is going on?" Ace appeared between us and Dix snaked a hand out to grab her. I was technically closer and caught her arm. I barely got her closer to me when she slammed her elbow into my gut and I grunted. "I didn't say touch me... I asked what the hell was going on?"

"Lachlan's clearly tired of you, sweetie," Payton announced as the cunt descended the steps from the cottage. Thankfully, she'd buttoned up her shirt but she had her arms folded as she crossed toward us. "He invited me over—told me to make myself at home like I had before."

The slow curve of her cold, cruel smile had me curling my fist. Punching women was not okay. But holy shit I wanted to knock that smug fucking look off her face.

"Let's go, Gorgeous. The last thing you need to deal with is these cheating boys and their piece of ass," Dix ground out the words after he spit blood to the side.

"We weren't cheating," Jonas announced as he stalked past

Payton. His attention wasn't on her, or Dix, or even me. He was looking right at Ace. "The only reason she's here is she has your guitar. She's the one who took it."

Payton snorted but Jonas didn't slow down until he was standing right in front of Ace.

"We should have told you," he said. "Lachlan's never stopped trying to get it back. None of us stopped looking. He got a lead. We'd had them before, but every single time we got close—the seller disappeared again."

"Because you're making it up," Payton scoffed.

"Because she didn't want *us* to know it was her," Jonas said and I kept one eye on Dix before stealing a look at Ace.

I thought the hurt in her expression was the worst. But I'd take that over the blankness visible there now. In the half-dark with only scattered illumination from a handful of path lights to highlight her expression, the lack of emotion gutted me.

"She broke into our suite," Jonas said. "The same way she was getting into Ramsey's at the dorm. She had a master key. Probably stole it at some point and made a copy—I don't know. I don't care. I just know she hurt you."

He raised a hand to her then dropped it again when she backed off a step.

"KC, I promise—I'm telling you the truth."

"We both are," I said, backing him up. "He wanted to tell you before. I thought it was better to get all the answers and not give you false hope—especially since *she* was involved."

"She doesn't believe you," Payton said with a throaty chuckle. "She'd have to be a fool to believe you. Then again... I supposed with all three of you sniffing after her she was bound to give it up sooner or later."

"Shut. The. Fuck. Up." I ground out each word. "In fact, go the fuck away. As much as I want her guitar back for her, it's not worth having to deal with you."

"You're so full of it," Payton countered and once again, I

had to ask myself what the hell I'd ever seen in her. "If she hadn't shown up, you'd have your dick down my throat or up my ass like you always did…"

It was enough to make me want to vomit.

"You're the one who keeps throwing your naked ass at everyone," I countered.

"I can't do this…" Ace said, shaking her head. "I don't want to do this."

"Smart girl, finally getting a clue," Payton taunted her.

"Be quiet," Ramsey's voice rang out as he *finally* appeared from the far side of the cottage, and he wasn't alone. Striding toward us with an expression of pure fury, Ramsey carried a guitar case in his hand. It was a familiar one, right down to the tour sticker on it.

Son of a bitch.

He found it.

Right behind him was Murray Creglin and two members of campus security.

"Where did you get that?" Payton demanded. "How did you—" Then she clamped her jaw shut as if realizing what she was saying. Vindication scored its way through me. Lying. Thieving. Cunt.

"Miss Webber," Creglin was saying. "I'm going to ask you to come with me. We have some questions for you regarding possession of stolen property, trespassing, assault, and a few other charges I'm sure we'll be able to file before we're done."

"I don't have to do anything," Payton whirled to stalk away but she didn't make it far because I cut her off and then one of the security people with Creglin took her arm. She lashed out, slapping the hand away from her.

"Ma'am," Creglin said, his tone vibrating with pure warning. "One more step and I'll add resisting arrest, and assault of a public officer—"

"You're just campus security," Payton retaliated. I bit back a bitter smile. Because that was her mistake. "Do you know who I am?"

"Yes, I do," Creglin told her. "Payton Webber, you're under arrest..."

"You can't arrest me," she said. "You're not even real cops."

"Unfortunately for you," he continued, "You have the right to remain silent, I suggest you exercise it, because anything you say and have said, can and absolutely will be used against you."

Triumph fisted through me as they actually put handcuffs on her. Granted, they were the zip-tied kind and not steel bracelets, but she deserved it.

"Lachlan," Payton said suddenly, whirling to me. "You know I didn't do this—this is a set up. You're just trying to cover your ass with the girlfriend..." Her voice grew more strident as they walked her away and I was still grinning when I pivoted to face Ace.

Dix needed to be dealt with but Ramsey had Ace's guitar. He was joining us and Creglin hadn't left with the security. Instead, he glanced from me to Dix to Ace. "Miss Crosse..."

"I—" she said, holding up her hands. "I can't do this—I don't want to." The hurt in her voice

"I understand," Creglin said, sounding almost sympathetic. "But I do need you to identify the guitar, Miss Crosse. It was yours and you were the one who reported it stolen."

I reached out to her but she jerked away again and I curled my fingers into my palm. "Ace..."

"I said don't." The command landed like a verbal slap. The words couldn't hurt anywhere near as much as her wounded eyes or the way she held herself apart from us. She retreated even from Jonas.

"Ace, Jonas wanted to tell you..." She needed to know that, but she turned from me to face Ramsey and he exhaled a long breath before he opened the case. It was too damn cold out here. She ignored us as she edged closer, arms folding tight to her chest as she looked at it.

The bruise in my chest expanded.

"It's your guitar," Ramsey said quietly. "It's even got the scar on the case from when you were trying to get it out from the fire."

She reached forward with so much hesitance and ran her fingers over the wood. Then she withdrew like it had stung her. "Yes, it looks like mine."

Creglin nodded. "I need to take it in, process it and then I can return it to you."

She gave a shrug like she didn't care, but that wasn't remotely true. I just wanted to—

"I'll get it back to you as soon as possible," Creglin stated. "Do you need an escort somewhere?"

"No," she said. "I don't need anything—except, I'm going to just go." She pivoted.

"Siren..." Ramsey's sigh echoed in my soul but it was Jonas' torn expression that threatened to gut me for real. Baby brother's expression was every bit as pained as hers. Fuck my life...

"I'll drive you," Dix said, but Ace just held up a hand.

"No." She gripped her suitcase.

"Gorgeous I get that—"

"I said *no*, Dix. No to you. No to them. No to everyone. Leave me alone. All of you." Then she set off with the suitcase bouncing along the uneven ground as she moved. She was heading across campus and Dix started after her and I went after him. He barely turned in time for me to slam into him and we went down. I didn't have to look to know she didn't glance back.

I'd be damned if I let this son of a bitch follow her. "You're not going anywhere," I told him. "We have questions... starting with the cameras you installed."

Creglin sighed. "Mr. Nash... please get off Mr..."

I ignored him. I ignored all of them. Only getting off Dix when Creglin was there to block him. I tracked Ace as she vanished into the cold night.

Goddammit.

Just—god-fucking-dammit. I turned to Jonas, half-hoping he'd punch me.

But he did worse.

He walked away.

Thirty-Three

The front door of Aubrey's apartment opened and I glanced over from where I was curled up on the sofa. She slipped in with two huge coffees and a bag that had to have some kind of pastries in it. At least, I thought it must be based on the scent. She'd left earlier with Forrest. They'd been very quiet as they slipped out, trying not to "wake" me, but it wasn't like I managed to go to sleep.

I'd interrupted their reunion with my arrival, but all Aubrey had done was pull me inside before she sent Forrest back to her bedroom. Then she curled me into a hug that I didn't realize just how much I needed. I clung to her, holding on tight. I had no idea how long we stood like that before she got me to sit down, or when I told her what had happened.

Aubrey had been incensed, but she didn't rush off with a bat or even start plotting their destruction. She'd just hugged me. Eventually, she'd gone to bed. I wasn't ready to talk about it any more than I already had. So I pretended to try and sleep, then spent the rest of the night trying to figure out what the hell I was going to do.

The emails that came first thing that morning, however, were enough to just make me pack it all in. They were from Murray Creglin. The chief of campus security had been amazing each time I met him, direct and blunt in an almost comforting way.

The information he sent me on the report the guys filed, including the information about Payton and the guitar just left me aching. All that time, it had been Payton. She destroyed all my things, crapped on my bed—bitch—and stole my guitar. She'd also assaulted me, though Creglin indicated he couldn't really tell me if she admitted to anything as yet.

My guitar, however, would be available for me by the end of the day. I was more than welcome to come and collect it or he could make arrangements to have it returned to me. It was a kind offer. That guitar—I'd missed it so much. Ached for it. It had taken a while to accept I probably wouldn't ever see it again and after the night before, I kind of wished I hadn't.

The night before kept playing on repeat in my head like some kind of horror movie slasher I couldn't escape no matter how many doors I slammed.

"Hey," Aubrey said in the gentlest of tones as she came to sit on the sofa next to me. I pushed the blanket down to just rest in my lap as she handed me a coffee. Wrapping my hands around it, I craved the warmth that couldn't quite seem to penetrate the iciness cloaking me since the night before.

"Hey," I said, and it came out more of a croak. It was like all the effort I put into not crying the night before seemed evident in the strain of my voice. "You should read this..." I passed her my phone after opening the second email from Creglin.

I didn't think anything could make all of this worse. I was wrong. Aubrey set her own coffee and the bag of pastries down on the table before she turned the phone to read it. Sliding off the sofa, I walked over to the table where she had her stack of books, notepads, sticky notes, and other supplies. I picked up two of the sticky notes and walked back over to her television. I covered the camera lenses on the television and then glanced around the room.

The security camera was there, now that I knew what to look for, sitting on her bookshelf tucked up next to one of the art pieces. After I covered it, I walked back over to the sofa and met Aubrey's worried stare.

"Son of a bitch," she exhaled the words and leaned back, her focus on the television more than a little horrified. "Dix put fucking spyware on the televisions?"

"And other cameras, apparently." I sank back onto the sofa and stared at my coffee cup before taking another sip. "They found them in my room. The living room. The television."

I'd had sex on the sofa.

More than once.

How many times had Dix been watching me?

Or in my room?

"Fuck, he was watching us in our first dorm, wasn't he?"

I lifted my shoulders. "He always programmed the televisions, he did—everything." The betrayal cut deep. The sting of it was like a burn on my flesh that left welts.

"Kait..." The sympathy in Aubrey's voice brought all the tears back to the surface and I had to blink furiously. "This isn't your fault."

"Are you sure?" I said, sniffling. "The guys did this whole plan to lure Payton out and get her to confess she had the guitar. A plan that apparently involved her being naked, or partially naked, with Lachlan while he did—whatever."

He acted like he'd done nothing and to be honest, I wasn't sure you could manufacture the level of disgust he'd displayed. At the same time...

Why would they do that in the place we shared? They wanted to get my guitar back. They'd been hunting for it. They'd pursued leads. I knew about the ones in the beginning, but I didn't realize they'd kept looking.

I had no idea that they'd gotten *new* leads. No, they'd kept all of that to themselves.

"Kait," Aubrey dragged my attention back to her and I sighed. She waited for me to meet her gaze, then she leaned back against the sofa. "Do you believe them?"

"The guys?" I lifted my shoulders. "I think so." Maybe. I wanted to believe them. "Does that make me an idiot?" They wanted to get the guitar back, *for me.* Getting it back had been important to them because I was important, right?

But that image of Payton seemed indelibly imprinted in my brain, a memory scarred there forever.

"I don't think that makes you an idiot," she said slowly.

"But?" I prompted.

"But... you're used to losing out on attention from your mom and your dad. You're used to being the one who has to do everything for everyone. You hate to be taken care of because you don't trust others to do that. You expect rejection."

I hated that description, but that was what had come up during their intervention. Maybe not that exact wording. No, they'd been far kinder then. "Do you think I expect rejection?" I coughed, the last word sticking in my throat. I hated this so much.

"I think you've made yourself *be* okay with it," Aubrey admitted. "It's easier to brush aside how much it hurts if you get angry with yourself for not expecting it."

I grimaced, disgust curling through me. "That makes me pathetic."

"No, it makes you human," Aubrey countered. "It makes you the person who wants to be worth other people, but I don't think you're ever going to see how amazing you really are. I could kick all three of them in the balls for this even if it's not *entirely* their faults."

Not entirely... My sniffle turned into a snort that turned into a laugh. "I never in a million years thought I'd hear you taking their side."

Aubrey grunted. "I'm not taking their side."

"No?"

"No," she countered. "*However*, those losers clearly adore you and they've actually grown on me. Kind of like a fungus."

I didn't laugh, because it wasn't funny.

"Even Lachlan." That almost was. "Doesn't mean I wouldn't like to inflict the kind of pain on them they caused you."

After downing a swallow of coffee, I wrestled with all these feelings. "I really missed them..."

"I know you did," she said, looping an arm around my shoulders to hug me sideways and we both sat there just staring at the coffee table.

"Dix is fired," I said, trying to summon up some energy.

"Oh, so fired," Aubrey agreed. "He better be under arrest. That's stalking and so disgusting."

Really disgusting. "I trusted him." Goddamn those tears, they were back. "I trusted him with you and with Yvette..."

"We trusted him with you," Aubrey countered. "This is on *him*, not you." Closing my eyes, I tucked my head against her shoulder.

"I hate him so much." The words ground out on a wave of misery and rage. All the way out of the cottage the night before, Dix had hustled me to the car. He wanted me to get in and then what...? Was he planning on driving me off somewhere away from his cameras? Was I supposed to pretend that was okay?

I went to take a drink of the coffee and my stomach

bottomed out. Had he known before I went inside what was going on? Scrubbing a hand over my face, I glanced at Aubrey. "I need to shower and…"

"And nothing." She pointed to the bag. "You need to eat and you need to sleep. We don't have to do anything else today. I mean, we can even wat—" She paused and we both stared at the television. Her grimace resonated with me so much. "There is *one* thing we need to do today. I'm ordering a new television and I'm going to ask Forrest to come and get rid of this."

"I'm sorry," I murmured and she gave me a look before she went back to her phone.

"Not you," she told me. "Absolutely, one thousand percent, not you. Perverted dickhead." She thumped her head back against the sofa before she sighed. "Right, I'll send a note to Creglin to see if he wants it and if he doesn't, *then* Forrest can take it out and destroy it or whatever. I'd donate it but there's no way I can donate this perversion."

I didn't blame her. While she ordered a new television, I poked around in the bag. The pastries smelled fantastic, but I just didn't want to eat anything. The coffee tasted both heavenly and like ash.

"I'm going to shower," I said and Aubrey lifted her chin. "I'll be here."

Fifteen minutes later, I padded back out in Aubrey's pajamas and fuzzy socks. I'd forgotten to take my suitcase back with me. She just patted the sofa next to her. "I paid extra to get the television here today. We'll have a new one soon. They're gonna take this one with them too. I think we'll order pizza when it gets here, until then…" She pointed at her laptop and I had to laugh even if I was a little misty-eyed. "We'll go old school for watching something."

"Any idea what you want to watch?" I asked, not arguing when she handed me one of the danishes. It was a cream cheese one, and normally one of my favorites, but I had no idea what to do with it. Sighing, I took a bite while Aubrey scrolled through our options.

For the first time, Love is Blind held absolutely no appeal. That was the show I watched with Jonas now. It was the pod date that Lachlan set up. It just added to the sting.

When I shook my head at the option, Aubrey didn't question it. She just kept right on scrolling. What I needed was a distraction, not more reminders.

"Aub..." I studied the danish and not her. "What's wrong with me?"

"Nothing is wrong with you..."

"I wanted to come to this school because I wanted to be normal."

"So?" Aubrey asked.

"I'm not normal."

"And we've never held that against you." The ease of the response pulled the first real flickers of a smile. "But you wanted normal experiences and there's nothing wrong with that."

"But so much has gone wrong..."

"And a lot went right."

I made a face at her.

"You graduated high school," she said, ticking it off on her fingers. "You got your first kiss. Went to your first dance. Proved to some douchebags how fucking awesome you are. You reunited with Tracy, you helped Pen, you helped your mom..."

I sighed.

"You fell in love for the first, the second, and I'm pretty sure the third time."

Did I love them? That... they were so important to me and at the same time...

"While I can say a lot about those douchebags and *have*,

especially about some of their dumbass decisions and opinions, I don't think their hearts were in the wrong place."

"What?" It was my turn to gape at her. "You're taking their side?"

"No," she said, meeting my gaze. "I'm *always* on your side. Yvette and I both are. That said... I think they are too."

I didn't have the words to respond.

"Something to think about." She nudged the pastry again. "Now eat that while I find us something to watch."

Thirty-Four

I wanted to go after KC the moment she left. But she didn't want us. Not right now. Anger shimmered in the air around her like the heat rising off the hot summer pavement—only it was winter and her absence left me freezing.

Lachlan and Ramsey were there with Creglin and Dix. They would make sure Dix didn't leave. The head of campus security already had a report on him. I left them and went the other way, cutting around the cottage and then taking part of the trail to run parallel to the path KC had taken. I knew her destination, but she didn't take any of the easier paths.

No, she stormed across the snow-and-ice-crusted landscape where the wheels on her suitcase kept jerking and more than once she partially slipped. But she didn't slow down. Following her was absolutely *not* what she wanted any of us to do.

Letting her vanish with no one to back her up wasn't

something I could do. So I kept my distance, but I also kept her in sight. The last time we lost sight of her, truly, she'd been taken.

It might have been months before, but I hadn't forgotten. I would never forget. Trapped inside that fridge...shaken, pale, and lost?

No. I could keep my distance if she wanted that, but not when she was out and exposed. Not when... The cold air lashed at me, I should have grabbed a jacket, but I didn't care if I was cold.

Not telling her was our first mistake. It could very well be our last one at this point. I could suffer from the cold. I followed her all the way to Aubrey's. I knew that was where she was going.

Where else would she go?

The moment the uncharitable thought landed, I hated myself a little for it. If she was in this corner, we'd definitely been the ones to help put her there.

I waited until Aubrey pulled her inside and the boyfriend grabbed KC's suitcase. Then I found a spot out of the wind to keep watch. For just a little bit. Just to know...

After an hour though, I knew she wasn't coming back out. I pulled out my phone a dozen times to send her a message and a dozen times, I put it back without writing the message.

Finally, I had to make myself leave but I sent a message to Aubrey.

ME:

> Hate me if you have to, but tell me if she needs us. I don't want anything to happen to her.

I didn't think twice about it, I just sent it. If Aubrey wanted to come for us, I'd stand still so she could punch me. I just wanted KC safe. She'd read the message when she did and she didn't have to respond to me. Aubrey would look after her best friend.

Maybe better than we had.

Back at the house, Lachlan and Ramsey were glaring at each other when I let myself back in. Ignoring them, I headed for the stairs.

"Did you follow her?" Lachlan asked, blocking the stairs themselves.

"Yes," I told him.

"And?"

I just stared at him. And nothing. I wasn't going to answer the question. I made sure she was safe.

"Look, you're pissed at me, be pissed." Lachlan crowded closer to me. "Take a swing if you have to, just tell me she is all right."

"She's not alright," I told him. "She's hurt. *We* hurt her."

"No, *I* hurt her." His jaw tightened and his fingers flexed. For a moment, I thought he might hit me. I'd be okay with that. I could live with the pain of a fist to the jaw much easier than what we'd already done. What *I* had done. Sure, Lachlan had come up with the plan. His rage at Payton was real and he wanted her to *pay*.

Even with Payton facing potential arrest and the guitar back—she wasn't the one who was really suffering right now. KC was.

We'd done that.

I'd done it.

I should never have agreed.

"We all did it," Ramsey said, his tone brooking no arguments. "We give her space."

Whirling, Lachlan glared at him. "That's a terrible idea. She thinks I actually cheated." Rage eddied in the air around him. "How are you so fucking calm? I thought you *cared!*"

"Don't," Ramsey ordered and when Lachlan opened his

mouth again, Ramsey sliced his hand through the air. "I meant it, don't. You don't get to judge my feelings for her any more than I do yours. We made mistakes..."

"You mean I did," Lachlan was damn combative. Anger and derision sanded his words.

"I said we," Ramsey reminded him. "Stop putting words in my mouth or hers. In fact, stop period. As much as I hate it, she has asked for space and she couldn't have made it more clear than telling us—all of us—" He drew a circle that included all three of us in the claim. "She can't do this right now. She didn't want to do it. Does the fact she's hurting gut me? Yes."

"Then why aren't we doing something?" The demand echoed the one in my own soul.

Leaning against the railing on the stairs, I studied my brothers. I wanted to be where she was. If I thought it would do any good, I'd still be outside of Aubrey's place and I'd keep watch. But if she saw me, especially after the way she'd left...

Well, she could always go where we couldn't follow and what good would that do us then?

"We just earned her trust in the last few months," Lachlan argued. "She kept me at arm's length a lot longer than she did you two assholes." Anger blended with frustration there. "She let me in, I'm not ready to let go of that."

"You do know that part of the reason she held you off for so long was that you *never* listened to her?" The scolding echoed my own feelings on the subject. Lachlan stalked her, followed her, invited himself along and what did she call it? Ninja kissed her?

She was the one thing that had ever truly made me want to kick the crap out of either of my brothers.

"You do know the only reason she ever let me in is I didn't go away?" Lachlan countered.

I rolled my eyes. I didn't want to listen to this debate anymore. Cutting around Lachlan, I went upstairs. The fact she wasn't in her room but wouldn't be in mine or theirs tonight poured salt into the already open wound. I ignored Ramsey and Lachlan both when they called my name.

Leaning back against my door, I closed my eyes and then dug my phone out again. The message to Aubrey showed read, but she hadn't responded. Right. I switched to KC's message thread and stared at it for the longest time.

Tomorrow.

Except...

I needed to talk to someone today. KC would be my first choice. My brothers were the second. Dad was already not thrilled with some of my choices and I didn't want to explain our relationship with KC. As unconventional as it seemed, all three of us dating her had worked.

Until now.

I found Gibs contact information and pressed it before shoving away from the door to fall on the bed.

"Hey kid," Gibs said when he answered. "How you doing? Sweet Kaity get in okay?"

"Yeah, she's here," I said, staring up at the ceiling. "Came back early." If we'd known...

"She was missing you boys," Gibs said and guilt disemboweled me. I'd missed her too. The only reason I'd agreed to come back early with Ramsey and Lachlan was to clean up the whole mess *before* she got here. This was not the welcome home I'd intended to share. "Probably a good thing you called, I wanted to talk to you boys about something..."

Shit, did he already know how much we'd screwed up?

"Linzi and I are taking a break," Gibs said slowly. "You know we didn't spend Christmas together and I said we were taking a little time."

I remembered... "You said you just needed to figure out what you both wanted to do."

"Yeah," he punched so much emotion into that single syllable. "But...we talked yesterday. For a couple of hours. First time we've been in the same room since just after Thanksgiving."

I winced.

"First things first, we're not getting a divorce. At least not yet."

Not yet didn't mean ever. "Okay."

"I'm not giving up on her, but Linzi—she made some choices I'm not really okay with and I don't know that I ever will be."

"I get that," I said slowly, because I did. "Mom and I haven't talked but...what she did to KC..."

Course, were we really any different? Mom made bad choices because she hated KC, for reasons I didn't pretend to understand. We made bad choices to protect KC, and I knew it was a bad choice but I did it anyway.

"Yeah well, she's still your mom," Gibs said. "You take the time you need but you have to have boundaries. I need them. She needs them. You need them. My kids—all of you—you're more important. We're going to figure this out. But I gotta put you kids first, you boys, my boys—my girls." He laughed then. "I thought I had three kids who couldn't stand me and I got six that I haven't been there for—nine counting you boys."

"You were there for us," I reminded him.

"Maybe so...the thing is, talking to Jackie, talking to Jennifer even—and to Melinda, she's Tracy's mom—I haven't been there the way I needed to be for the kids and for their moms. That's on me. Linzi, sure, I'm not happy with what she did, but at the end of the day—I'm Dad. I should have been there for my kids."

"You're working on it now." Hopefully, he did a way

better job than we did. "I know that KC has been happier getting to know you." I'd seen it. Even when fear and the uncertainty crept in. She wanted Gibs in her life, but she was scared of it too. Who could blame her? She'd been abandoned.

Goddammit and did she think we were abandoning her now?

"Do something for me," Gibs said. "If my sweet Kaity is the girl for you, for your brothers—I'm not going to pretend to judge or tell you what is right, but if she is the girl for you boys—don't ever let her think otherwise."

Well, we fucked that up already.

"You hear me?" Gibs prompted, making me focus on where I was and who I was talking to.

"I hear you," I said. "You know—I hope you and Mom can figure it out, but if you can't—you're still family."

Maybe Gibs needed to hear that too. I needed to say it.

"Don't want you to think otherwise."

Gibs chuckled. "Thanks kid. I mean that. How's the music going?"

"It's...not bad. I have a new piece I was working on." Music. It was the language I shared with KC.

"You ready to share it?" Gibs asked.

"No," I said slowly. "Not yet. I'll let you know."

We talked for a few more minutes then I hung up. I didn't tell him about our fuck-up. He wasn't the one I needed to talk to anyway. No, I needed to confess it to KC. I needed to apologize to her. I needed to let her know she was important and I wouldn't do this again.

Ever.

My keyboard was still stored, so I went and got it out. Then the music sheets. I'd started on something before Christmas, but this needed to be more.

A lot more.

Putting my phone on the bed where I could see the screen,

I stared at the keyboard as the notes began to dance in my head. It wasn't going to be elegant, but it would be honest.

That was the important part.

Honesty.

She needed it from us and I needed to give it to her.

Thirty-Five

I took the train down to Manhattan. The first couple of days at Aubrey's and all I was doing was second and third guessing myself. I talked to Creglin. Then to the state police. There had even been an interview with the FBI. Between Dix and Payton, the legal ripples were going to haunt me for a while.

Davina had been horrified when I called her and filled her in. Then she'd been *furious*. Our security guys were going to be sweeping everywhere in the house in California, the apartment in Manhattan, and more. Aubrey and I had also briefed Yvette. It was kind of funny, she'd gone on a rant in French for more than ten minutes. I only tracked about a third of what she said but it was still beautiful in its own way.

Beautiful fury.

I was going to write a song about that. Maybe.

The thought of working on music immediately summoned Jonas to mind. Jonas, who'd sent Aubrey a message and asked her to look after me. It was both sweet and infuriating. But more sweet. Ramsey and Lachlan both kept their distance, but I swore I could *feel* Lachlan watching me.

That was why I decided to go to Manhattan. I just needed to get away from everything. Classes were coming. A part of me just wanted to leave Blue Ivy. Again. The thought of running away left a horrible taste in my mouth. I didn't want to leave them but I wasn't ready to talk to them either.

Not—not when I kept seeing Payton's smug bitch smile as she sat there on our sofa, boobs out and touching Lachlan like she had the right. Then I wanted to throw up or cry. Neither were desirable so I made myself wait. Aubrey said I could stay with her and she'd even gone to get my backpack and laptop. Or maybe the guys had dropped it off.

I hadn't seen them and I hadn't asked.

Yes, I was absolutely being a chickenshit. The only bright spots had been the regular updates on Pen and her continued improvement. She would be home with Jackie soon. There was a real chance that the next time I was there I could play with my sister without all the medical isolation garb between us.

I couldn't wait.

My new bodyguard traveled with me. The service had come highly recommended both from Frankie and her guys, but also management. John Porter did not blend in. At six foot four, he cut an imposing figure. When I said people were going to notice him, he'd smiled.

"I want them to notice me," he said. "I want them to be very aware of just how much it's going to cost them to be stupid around you."

That was hard to argue with so I'd just shaken his hand and off we went. He didn't try to chat or have a conversation on the train. The only time I needed to get up to use the restroom, he'd stood to "stretch" but also to keep an eye on me. Then he waited for me to take my seat before he sat again.

The only objection he showed on the whole trip was when I intended to get a cab once we got into the station. He had a private car come get us instead. That was fine. He wanted the security of a background check on the driver. Again, hard to argue. I could have gone to Mom's apartment, but I headed to a different address entirely.

Frankie opened the door the moment I rang the bell. Dressed in a sweatshirt and jeans with her hair up in a ponytail, she was a sight for sore eyes. All the way into the city, I wrestled with what I would say or do.

Although a couple of years older than me, Frankie had always been more of the mentee than the mentor in our friendship. I knew the business, and music. I was more than happy to share with her and by extension, Ian, her partner. "Hi," I said and she opened her arms.

She enveloped me in a hug that chased away the loneliness, the tears, and offered me a safe place. The warmth in her hug made me want to cry and I was sniffling as she pulled back. "Come on," she murmured, before glancing past me to John.

"This is John Porter," I introduced them. "My bodyguard." The fact I had to have one wasn't even a question anymore. "If you don't mind, he's going to want to do a quick sweep and then..."

"Absolutely, we don't mind. This is Miss Abigail," Frankie said, introducing me to the black lab who waited patiently for us to step inside. "She has to sit and stay until you're inside, Jeremy's rules."

I chuckled as John waited for us to step all the way in and then he followed. Once he closed the door, he shook Frankie's hand and then greeted the dog before he glanced at the house.

"Four levels," Frankie said. "Five if you count the roof. We're the only ones here, except for Jeremy, who is out on the back patio with his morning coffee."

"Thank you, ma'am," John said, then gave me a firm look.

I waited with Frankie and she bumped my shoulder as John climbed the stairs, he did his sweep then came back to join us. "All good. I can go wait with the car if you want..."

"Don't be silly," Frankie said. "Jeremy would scold me if I sent you out there to wait. If you don't mind hanging out down here with him and Miss Abigail, KC and I can go upstairs."

Once we got them sorted and I got a chance to say hi to Jeremy, Frankie made us coffee and then we escaped to her room on the fourth floor. I was kind of surprised the guys weren't here and once I settled on the window seat, and she curled up into a chair, she said, "I sent them to the gym and said we needed some girl time."

"Oh."

"One," Frankie continued. "Because you sounded so unhappy and if it's boy trouble, I need to know how much before Jake and Ian find out. Because Ian may very well want to go up there and beat them up."

I had to bite back a smile.

"Jake won't wait, he'll just go and Coop will probably go with him. So—talk to me. Nothing you say is going to leave this room unless you want it to. I'm all yours..."

"I don't even know where to start," I said softly. "There's been—so much. Just so much."

"Then start at the beginning," Frankie encouraged.

I met the kindness in her green eyes and had to swallow back the urge to cry all over again. "The beginning..." Where did all of this start? So I went all the way back. I talked about Dad. Mom. The craziness with Linzi. I told her about meeting the guys at school. I'd told her about them being my step-brothers after that first year when I found out.

"Assholes," Frankie commented easily. "I remember."

"Douchebags."

"That too." Her smile helped even more and a laugh broke free from me.

"You know, they really are, but in some ways they're my assholes—my douchebags..."

"And you still want them." The absolute understanding buoyed me.

I really did. So I pressed on. When I described the fire, Frankie glared at me.

"You never told us it was that bad."

I lifted my shoulders. "There wasn't much to be done at that point," I countered. "Still... they—they came through for me. Ramsey saved me. When Aubrey and I got stuck with Payton for a possible roommate, Jonas offered me the extra room in his suite." Which brought us to everything that happened in my senior year.

We'd kept everything about the kidnapping out of the press. Horror filled Frankie's eyes at my confession. The six or seven months since then seemed to have been an eternity and no time at all. Bringing up everything that happened over the summer to the autumn to the holidays and Pen's surgery took another hour and the rest of my coffee.

When I got to the revelations about Payton and Dix, the shock on Frankie's face morphed into fury. "Wait... Dix spied on you?"

"Or something." I guess I should be glad he never sold any nudes anywhere, and at the same time... "I haven't even figured out what to do with that. He was spying on me. On Aubrey. And—the guys didn't like him and Jonas used to say he was jealous, but Dix was never like that with me. Not really."

"I never liked him," Frankie admitted with a wince and I frowned.

"What?"

"I just—I thought he was kind of creepy. He's a lot older

than you and I didn't like how he looked at you. But I've never been the best judge of guys. Ian didn't like him either."

"Why didn't you tell me?" Then before she could answer, I sighed. "Not that it may have made any difference. Dix was family. I should have known that didn't mean I could always count on him and at the same time..."

"It sucks," Frankie summed it up and I summoned another smile. "The Payton thing though..."

"I—I don't know what to do with that. I *hate* that she was there," I admitted. "I hate, hate, *hate* that Lachlan ever touched her, I knew they dated before but I didn't think about it and now—it's all I can see."

She reached forward and caught my hand. "You can't do that to yourself."

"I don't want to but...how do I not?"

"By choosing what you think about when you think about him. Her? She can get fucked. I personally hope she goes to jail. But the thing with Lachlan—I don't know him. I'm not going to pretend that I do or that I know what he was thinking. Rachel's right, guys can be dumb. But since I can be dumb too—I had to learn to forgive it and to let it go."

"Your guys would *never* do this to you." All four of them were absolutely insane for her. They loved her so much. It was beautiful. "You got so lucky."

At her absolute snort, I raised my eyebrows. Then she laughed as she shook her head. "I did get lucky, absolutely. I love them...I can't tell you how much I love them. But it wasn't always easy and they did some really stupid shit. Like —-" Frankie blew out a breath. "They had girlfriends before me. Quite a few for some of them."

"What?"

"My turn to tell you a story..." When she was done, I really didn't have the words. Never in a million years could I imagine a single one of those guys with another woman. Like—ever. The way they looked at Frankie, she was their everything.

"How?" I had to know. "How did you get past it?"

"We talked," Frankie admitted. "A lot. We fought...I mean, I thought for forever that no one was interested in me. They were my best friends, but I knew when they lost their virginity. I knew who most of the time too. And I had no idea all that time they were dating other girls and making out that they wanted me. I knew they'd blocked others from asking me out, I didn't know why they did it, just that I'd tried to be the best friend, the supportive one, and they were out there sabotaging me. If not for Rachel—they might have kept it up and I'd never have found out, of course, maybe I would have because I met Mathieu and he asked me out and it pissed them off."

There was actual glee in her voice.

"True confession," Frankie admitted. "Apparently, I don't know when guys are flirting with me. I'm getting better, I really am... but—the guys swore they asked me out. They tried to date me and I never noticed."

I frowned.

"It doesn't matter now, the point is—they aren't perfect. But neither am I. There were things I didn't know because I didn't see them. There were things they didn't tell me cause they just assumed that I knew." She blew out a breath. "I don't know what your guys were thinking or what they were trying to do. You don't either."

"I saw—"

But she held up her hand and I stopped. "You don't know because you're going based on what you saw, some of the pieces, and what that bitch said. The rest of it is an assumption. I'm not saying you're wrong. But I'm not saying you're right either... the only way to know for sure is to talk to them."

"The only way?"

"Well," Frankie said. "Groveling is good too. But Jake can

always go beat them up. I meant what I said earlier, and after what you told me, I'm not wholly opposed to it."

A giggle escaped me and I had to clap a hand over my mouth but Frankie's smile grew and then she laughed. Her laughter triggered my laughter and vice versa. I don't think it was anywhere near as funny as it felt, but the laughter was so much better than the crying.

In the end, she said, "Stay for the weekend. The guys would love to see you. You can take some time to decide what you want to do. The kick their ass offer is on the table, always..."

"I'd love to stay," I said slowly. "But I think I need to go back."

I needed to talk to them.

"I thought you might say that." Frankie's grin made me chuckle all over again. She gave a little shrug. "I may not get flirting, but I do get forgiveness."

Yeah. She did.

"You get fighting too."

"Oh yeah," she hummed and then checked her nails. "I have a really good left hook."

Grinning, I looked at my own hands and then over at her. "Am I crazy?"

"Yes." Frankie nodded. "Doesn't mean you're wrong though. Sometimes—crazy is perfect."

Sometimes.

Crazy was perfect.

Thirty-Six

RAMSEY

"**B**e sure to review your syllabus and the reading list. Don't leave it to the mid-terms to realize you are weeks behind. Lack of fore-planning on your parts, can and will, lead to failing grades." I tracked my gaze across the room, studying each student in turn. "Office hours are posted. Your homework is also listed in the syllabus. Plan ahead. Just because you miss a class doesn't mean you can fail to turn in your work."

We repeated this every year. Every year, there was always a student who wanted to plead they were a special case. Each year, it was up to one of the teachers to disabuse them of this —especially the legacy students. That said, I checked my watch.

"I'll see you all tomorrow." The bell rang as perfect punctuation, signaling the end to the final class of the day. I kept my expression as pleasant as I could and my focus on the class. I had a mental bet on who had paid attention and who hadn't.

"Mr. Malone," Brian Tyree said as he approached my desk.

"There are a dozen books on the syllabus for this semester, but it indicates only six will be covered on the tests. How are we supposed to identify which six?"

"You don't identify them," a silky siren's voice answered before I could. "You just have to finish reading to the end of the syllabus where he tells you to choose the six you're planning on reading. Everything beyond that will be extra credit."

Relief flooded my veins as I glanced to where Kaitlin stood in the doorway. Tyree glanced from the papers in his hand to me then to her and back before he did a double take. "Holy shit, you're Kaitlin Crosse."

"Language," I said almost absently as a smile softened Kaitlin's mouth. She was so indulgent with fans. Even when— especially when she shouldn't have to be. "We also don't gawk."

"I wasn't gawking," Tyree argued as he fumbled with his papers. "Just—I heard you went here, but I didn't think I'd meet you."

Tyree wasn't the only student staring at her. Alison Dimont, who'd been waiting to talk to me, glanced at her pen then at Kaitlin.

"No autographs," I reminded the class. "Go on guys, read the whole syllabus, not just the bolded parts. Trust me—it will be worth it." They could leave now, particularly because maintaining any kind of neutrality when I just wanted to drink in her nearness proved a challenge.

One by one, the students filed out of the door and more than one shot her a smile or a nod as they passed her. For her part, Kaitlin waited until the last student was gone before she glanced into the hall. "Do you need to look before I can close the door?"

A man I didn't recognize stepped inside and I straightened. He swept the room with a look before he glanced at her then focused on me.

"John Porter, this is Ramsey Malone. Ramsey—this is John. He's taking over as my bodyguard on campus and while I'm traveling."

Traveling.

My gut clenched. I took two steps toward him and offered a hand. "Look after my girl."

"That's the plan." The guy shook my hand briefly, then motioned to a closed door. "Access to another room or a closet?"

"Closet. But feel free to check if you want."

He nodded. It took him a handful of seconds to complete his search. "I'll be outside," he told her before he moved out into the hall and closed the door.

Alone, finally, I faced Kaitlin and it took every ounce of my self-control to stay where I was and not stride across the room and pick her up. I wanted to kiss her so bad, I burned with the desire. More, I wanted to just hold her, breathe her in, and remind myself what it was like.

The past few days had been hell.

"Hi," Kaitlin said.

"Hi," I exhaled the single syllable. "Are you okay?" Was that strategic? I had no idea and I didn't care. What I wanted was Kaitlin and I *needed* to know she was all right.

"I've been better," she said slowly. The very audible swallow punctuated the sentence. Then her calm expression crumpled. "I—can I have a hug?"

I was already moving, meeting her more than halfway. She crashed into me and I picked her up, wrapping her tight. The tickle of her breath against my throat added to the visceral reminder that she was *here*. I had her. I hadn't lost her.

Hopefully.

The pound of her heart beneath my palm echoed the thunder of my own. "I'm so sorry," I whispered against her hair. "Everything we did—we were trying to fix things, to make it better, and to get back your guitar. We wanted to drive her away. All we did was make it worse…"

Beyond that…

I pulled back, still cradling her and lifting a hand to cup her face. At my hesitation, she leaned her cheek into my palm. "We hurt you. I hurt you. I am so sorry, Siren. So goddamn sorry."

Tears shimmered in her perfect blue eyes. One blink, and that tear drifted down her cheek before it slid along my finger. Her pain clawed at me.

"I love you." The words escaped me in a rush. "I love you so damn much. If you believe nothing else, please believe that."

She ran her tongue over her lips as if she needed to wet them and I got that. My throat was parched. "I—"

"You don't have to say anything," I hurried to assure her. Telling her I loved her while standing in my classroom having just dismissed class was probably not the way to reveal my feelings, and yet—I didn't want to lose another chance. If I only got to see her this once, I had to make it count.

I had to tell her.

"Ramsey," she whispered and there was so much emotion tangled up in the syllables of my name. When she pressed her lips to mine, I took my first real breath in five days. I inhaled her, drank in her kiss, and devoured the headiness of contact. Her tongue was tentative, but I sucked it against my teeth on her first sweep.

Fisting her hair, I tilted her head as I spun her around and pinned her right to the damn whiteboard. She wrapped her legs around my hips and the urge to grind against her was right there.

Still, I fought that, settling for inhaling life through her. When her nails scraped lightly over my scalp, I dragged my mouth from hers.

"Hi," she whispered, her lips wet and a bit swollen. The hint of redness to her cheeks reminded me that I needed to shave.

"Hi, Siren," I murmured, nipping that lower lip. I wanted to indulge the need to see it darken to a heavier pink. The blood pounding south in my body thickened in my cock. The gentle squeeze of her legs had me bumping my hips into hers again. She let out a little gasp. "Yeah," I said, torn between chuckling and groaning. "I've missed you."

"I've missed you too." The confession cut at me. "I needed —I needed time."

"You can have all the time you need." Whatever she needed. Wherever she needed it. I wanted her right here, in my arms and in my bed. If not that, then I wanted to be able to see her, talk to her, and make sure she was safe. "What can I do, Siren? How can I fix this?"

Leaning her head back against the whiteboard, she teased her fingers along the nape of my neck. "I need to talk to you— I want to talk to you. I guess I should have asked if you had time."

A grin pulled at the corner of my mouth. "The answer is always going to be yes..."

"Are you sure about that, Mr. Malone? I mean, I don't want you to think I'm not doing the homework."

The playfulness in her voice wrapped around my cock and stroked it. "I would never imagine you as someone not willing to do everything, Miss Crosse."

Her smile was sharp and brilliant. She sighed, eyes half-closed as her legs tightened around me again.

"Did you need something else from me, Miss Crosse?" Yes, it was both tease and provocation.

"I'm kind of wishing I'd worn a skirt," she admitted and I groaned at the mental image that inspired. "Next time I visit you in class... I promise."

"I like how you think. Not sure that wouldn't get me fired, but..." Then again, I had to grin. "What a way to go."

Her laughter was as unexpected as it was welcomed. I pulled us away from the whiteboard, carried her over to my desk. Sitting her on it, I rubbed her thigh until she gradually unlocked her legs. Then I planted a hand on either side of her on the desk, all of my attention focused on her.

"You wanted to talk to me," I prompted.

"I do," she said, then paused. The scrape of her teeth over her lower lip was a show of such vulnerability my heart bruised for her. "But—you said you loved me."

"I do love you," I told her. "I've been in love with you for a while. I should have told you before but..."

"But there was a lot going on," she whispered.

"There was, but I was going to say, I was an idiot." That earned me another brilliant smile. "Not being an idiot right now. You're here. I love you. You should know."

"I—I worried...I have been worried." She spoke slowly, as though searching for every nuance of each word she chose. "Did we rush things? I was dating all three of you, was that the problem? Then...were we dating? Or just living together? I felt like maybe we skipped some steps but—I can't imagine going back."

Closing her eyes, she groaned and tipped her head back. I kept my hands planted on the desk.

"Talk to me, Siren," I beckoned to her. "I can't help you if I don't know what you're thinking."

"That's the problem," she admitted. "I don't know what I'm thinking... I went to New York..."

She had left campus. We'd wondered, and it had taken a lot of cajoling, bullying, and outright standing in their way to keep Lachlan and Jonas from chasing after her. No way they weren't checking on her, but neither mentioned knowing she was gone, so maybe they hadn't realized?

"Hence the bodyguard," I said.

"That's part of it. Part of it is..." She told me about the cameras in Aubrey's stuff. So Dix, the fucking pervert, hadn't just been watching Kaitlin. He'd also been watching her best friends. I wanted to punch the guy.

For real.

She described her conversations with the cops, campus, state police, and the FBI. "With everything going on, it just seemed prudent that I not ignore my security. Especially when Payton apparently told them that RJ was the one who kidnapped me. Or at least admitted that she helped him, but she's trying to spin it as he blackmailed her."

She did...

The cops hadn't told us that. Creglin said nothing.

Rage vibrated through me.

"I went to see a friend of mine in New York." She'd mentioned Frankie and Ian before. But when she described the conversation there, and the advice—not to mention the friend was also dating four best friends and living with them, I got it. And I found a measure of hope in all of that. "I think I still need some time, but—I also needed to see you. To talk to you. I can't get that image of Payton out of my head."

"I swear to you, Lachlan wasn't cheating. He wants nothing to do with that girl. None of us do. We wanted your guitar back. We wanted peace of mind. We—we tried to be cunning and to do it while you were safely on the other side of the country."

"Then I came back early," she said, sadness encircling every single word. "Because I missed you and then... spoiled your plans."

"Siren, I'm sorry. I truly am. We weren't keeping it a secret forever and I wish with all my soul that I could erase what you had to have seen when you walked in that night."

"I know," she said and it was my turn to bow my head in

absolute relief at her acceptance. "I do know. You—you guys have been amazing. It's just been a lot. Payton. Dix. Everything."

"If I can do anything…"

How the fuck did we fix this?

"You already are," she told me and she put her hand over mine on the desk. "You're listening to me. You're—letting me have more time."

"I meant it when I said you can have all the time you need. Anything you need. I just—maybe throw Lachlan and Jonas a bone. You have no idea how badly I needed to see you. I know they aren't any different."

Her chin dipped and her smile turned adoring. "You're an amazing big brother."

"Yeah well, I like the little shits even when I want to throttle them sometimes."

Her laughter was its own reward. "Me too…"

I wasn't ready to let her go yet but I glanced at the door then at her. "You have time for coffee?"

"I'll make time."

Make time.

I liked that.

"Just—John has to go with us."

"Well, I can live with that." I pressed a kiss to the corner of her mouth. "But he can get his own coffee."

Thirty-Seven

KC

After coffee with Ramsey, I let him walk me back to Aubrey's, along with John. The school had made arrangements for John to have a place on campus but he wasn't actually in Aubrey's building. So, when I wanted to go somewhere, I gave him a heads up so he could meet me. I also had a panic button. When—*if,* but probably when cause I did miss my douchebags—I moved back into the cottage with the guys, we would make other arrangements.

While it was just John on campus at the moment, he would have two others that he rotated with—one who was a woman, so I kind of liked that too. Also something to be dealt with *later.* Aubrey had given Ramsey a long look when he walked in with me then she flicked a look at me.

"We're good with him being here? Or am I kicking him out?"

Adoration for my bestie swarmed through me and I winked. "We're good with him being here. He's not staying for long, but—I did want to talk to him for a bit longer if you don't mind."

Her pleased smile was so sweet. "I don't mind at all. I'm gonna go shower and get ready for my date. Also—douchebag number three dropped off a present for you." She winked before she pointed to the guitar case sitting next to the sofa.

Ramsey pressed his face against my hair, but the huff of his laughter made my own smile grow. The guitar was here. Lachlan had brought it straight here. I blew out a shaky breath. "Thanks, Aubrey."

"Yep." She pointed to her eyes then at Ramsey before she blew me a kiss and vanished back into her room.

After her door closed, Ramsey wrapped his arms around me and I leaned back against his chest. Eyes closed, I sighed. "I'd ask if you wanted to stay..."

"No," he said gently. "Do I want to? Sure, but that's not what you need right now."

Tipping my head back, I gazed up at him.

"You came to see me, Siren. You opened the door and you're talking to me. I can be a very patient man for you."

A smile tugged at my lips. "Thank you."

"You never have to thank me."

"Maybe I want to." I needed and wanted to make sure I acknowledged others, showed them appreciation, and... well, and remembered the people who were worth the trust and the affection. Ramsey was all of those things. They all were, I just—I needed to get some of those images out of my mind.

"Well, I will not stop you." His eyes lightened. "Now, I'm going to go and you're going to lock that door behind me. If Aubrey is out, you have your panic button?"

"I do." I held up two fingers like a scout making a promise. Ramsey chuckled then he pressed the lightest of whisper soft kisses to my lips. "I'll be okay, thank you."

"You're welcome," he murmured, then another kiss. "If you need me—for anything—call me?"

"I promise. Maybe we can get coffee tomorrow?"

He smiled. "Anything you want."

"Anything?"

"Behave." His wink delighted me, but he was already letting go of me to head for the door.

"I'll think about it," I teased as I pivoted to face him and he laughed. "I'll send messages to Jonas and Lachlan too."

"Good. Talk to you tomorrow..." And then he was gone and I blew out a shaky breath. If he hadn't taken the lead on that, I didn't think I would have pushed him out the door. Going to see him had been both terrifying and so fulfilling. He was exactly who I wanted to see. Who I wanted to talk to— and the guys?

The guys.

I opened my phone and fired off individual messages to Jonas and to Lachlan. They weren't the most eloquent, but they deserved to know I missed them and that I was thinking about them. I also thanked Lachlan for the guitar.

Their responses were so swift that I winced. I should have reached out sooner, but at the same time—I didn't even realize how ready I was to see Ramsey until I saw him. Seeing him...

A soft chuckle interrupted my sigh and I turned. "What?"

"You have that dreamy look on your face," Aubrey said, her indulgent smile growing. "I've missed that look."

"It's been a weird year."

"You can say that again." Pushing away from her door, she met me halfway across the room and I sank into her hug. "I love you."

"Love you too—now go see your boy toy and get laid, I'm going to go and think deep thoughts and..."

"Pull something," Aubrey teased and I pinched her as she laughed.

"Bitch."

"For you?" She wagged her eyebrows. "Totally. Lock the door behind me. I have my phone. I'm gonna just stay over with Forrest tonight. So use the bed if you want." She blew me a kiss as she headed for the door.

I wolf whistled as she pulled on her coat and she shook out the fall of her dark hair. Then she was out and I followed behind her to lock up. Smothering a yawn, I turned back to where the guitar was sitting. Crossing over to it, I touched the case. The stickers on it. The damage to it.

They were intensely familiar to me. Trailing my fingers over the rough texture of the case, I shook my head. It seemed almost a lifetime ago when she disappeared. More than a lifetime ago... So much had happened since then. With care, I popped the latches and opened it slowly.

A note fluttered out and I picked up the slip of paper.

> Ace,
> I cleaned the case, the guitar, and checked the strings and the tune.
> I miss you.
> Lachlan

I picked up my phone and took a photo of the guitar, then a selfie of me blowing him a kiss before I sent both to him with two words.

ME:

Thank you.

Setting the phone down, I pulled the guitar out and ran my fingers over the wood. It was almost alien in the smoothness. Moving to the sofa, I checked the tune, playing each key the minor chords, then the major ones. Just little adjustments here and there.

He tuned the guitar.

I blinked. "Lachlan knows how to play guitar..." That made sense, but why it hadn't occurred to me before made me laugh. Jonas was gifted with music. It was entirely possible Lachlan was too.

"You and I are going to have a conversation, Mr. Nash," I murmured to myself as I started to play. I wasn't trying to tease out any one specific song. Instead, I just let my mind and my fingers wander. The music was always there. Closing my eyes, I let the notes surround me even as images played out against my eyelids.

When I told Aubrey the past year had been crazy, it didn't really describe how dramatic it had all been. School. Normalcy. Revelations. Pen. The attacks. The kidnapping.

I shuddered.

Ramsey.

Lachlan.

Jonas.

Shivers skated through me. Much more pleasant ones.

The benefit.

Dad.

Mom.

Tracy.

Jackie.

Bronson.

Opening my eyes, I stopped playing. The music was all there, I could hear the notes I hadn't played, see the lyrics that needed to be written.

For more than two years, I'd been fighting to be what I thought I needed to be instead of who I was. Instead of who I wanted to be.

Who do I want to be?

Tracing my thumb against the grain of the wood, I traced it down to the tiny nick that had been there from the first year after Dad gave me the guitar.

I wanted to be a sister, a daughter, a friend, a member of Torched...

I wanted to sing.

I wanted...

I wanted my douchebags.

For the next hour, I just played and let my mind wander to all those places. Some made me smile, others made me ache—all of them, though? They all fit. They fit me and I wanted to fit them.

By the time I packed up the guitar I'd begun to put together the kernels of a plan. I needed to talk to the girls and I'd need to talk to my douchebags. It would take some time, some patience and some coordination, but —I could handle the work.

The work had never frightened me.

It was still early, but I was exhausted on so many levels. I needed to get some sleep. In the morning, I was going to ask Lachlan to go running. Then ask Jonas to meet me for breakfast.

With Aubrey out, I went ahead and showered, then combed out my hair before I blew it dry. The new television was out in the living room, but I found some videos to watch on my phone and listened while I got into my pajamas. It was dark outside when I did one last sweep of the locks. I sent a message to John to let him know I was officially going to bed.

Smothering a yawn, I burrowed down in the blankets and for the first time since getting back to campus, it wasn't a struggle at all to go to sleep. I didn't even remember falling asleep when a hand curved over my breast and a warm body tucked up against my back. The arms around me didn't even register at first.

A distant part of my brain roused, sounding the alarm that I'd been alone when I'd gone to sleep, and that splashed cold reality onto my sleepy mind. Snapping my eyes open, I frowned. The body cradling mine was definitely male.

Lachlan—

I was all set to roll over and scold him before I kissed him when lips touched my throat. That—those weren't Lachlan's lips.

It wasn't Ramsey or Jonas either.

Panic scrabbled through me as a hand clamped over my mouth before I could scream. "I've waited a long time for this."

That—

Forrest?

What the hell was he doing?

He rubbed his nose along my throat, then mouthed kisses against my pulse. My pulse raced faster and faster. I couldn't suck in a breath with the way he kept his hand over my mouth. The edge of his palm pressed against my nose and all I could smell was him.

Why was he here? Where was Aubrey? Was he drunk?

"Do you know how long I've waited for this?" He asked, then ran his tongue over the whorls of my ear and I shuddered. Revulsion burned through me. I tried to squirm away and he locked his arms tighter. The force pushed the air out of me as he ground a very real erection against my ass.

"It's okay, KC," he practically crooned. "It's just you and me. I've been your forever fan for so long and I've been patient. So patient for you. Finally, you're here and so am I— and we can be together."

I wanted to scream.

I needed to scream.

Then he dragged me over, hand still on my mouth and he loomed above me in the darkness, pinning me to the bed. The panic button was on the nightstand. I stretched out an arm but I couldn't quite brush the wood with my fingertips.

"It's just us," he whispered, before he pulled his hand away and then his mouth was on mine. Panic crystallized and I pushed my hands against his shoulders but he wouldn't move and then he was shoving his tongue in my mouth.

That was when I bit him.

I bit him.

And I screamed.

Thirty-Eight

LACHLAN

You know, stalking isn't dating right?

Jonas' smart-ass comment drifted along with me as I followed the running path. It was dark, it was cold, and I didn't feel any of it. I kept my focus on the trail ahead. The temperatures had been below freezing all week. While there was some snow, we hadn't had a lot of precipitation. That meant while there were little hints of ice, I didn't have to worry about it too much.

The minute I hit the running trail, I knew where I was going. I just made myself take the long way. I'd dropped by Aubrey's earlier to deliver the guitar. I'd been gratified that Aubrey hadn't kicked me square in the balls. That said, she hadn't been that forgiving either.

"Sucking up?" She almost smirked, but the lack of humor in her eyes kept me from retaliating with snark of my own.

"Yes," I admitted. "And no. We did everything we could to get this back for her."

"Even things you really should have thought three or four more times about." Aubrey folded her arms and I sighed.

"You're not wrong. She is due every apology. More than that —she deserves everything. If I could go back and change it—"

"You wouldn't," Aubrey said with a shrug. "You're an impulsive, hot-headed asshole. You wanted to be the one who got it. Didn't matter what you had to do... on the one hand, I get it. On the other, she shouldn't have had to see that."

No. She shouldn't have. On that, we were in total agreement. "I can't undo it now."

Aubrey sighed. "You don't deserve to hear this, and if you quote me on it, I'll say you're lying."

"Okay." I raised my eyebrows.

"You're good for her—most of the time." That stunned me. "You're good for the part of her that wants to be normal so badly. She's spent her whole life under a microscope. My parents are popular and involved in show business. So are Yvette's. We've never attracted the kind of attention Kait has. All Kait's ever wanted was to be accepted for her and to be wanted for her."

"She's the only one I do want and it has nothing to do with Gibs, her mother, my mother, or your band."

"I know," Aubrey said before she took the guitar case. "Don't give up on her. If you want her, you're going to have to fight for her—and that means fighting some of your dumber ideas too."

"But you aren't telling me this."

"No," Aubrey said. "I'm not." Then she shut the door in my face.

That earlier text messages from Ace had been the balm my soul craved. The urge to just go straight to her had flamed to life inside of me like a bonfire. But Ramsey was right—the asshole.

Our choices—*my* choices—sent Ace storming away from us. Aubrey was right too. I still would probably have made the same damn dumb decisions. Those decisions netted us the guitar and got Payton arrested. Payton *and* that mother fucker RJ. I still couldn't believe those two assholes had been behind her kidnapping.

Ramsey dropped the nugget when he got back from *seeing* Ace himself. The envy that flooded me was no less violent than it had been when I discovered Ramsey had sex with her, but it dissipated a lot faster.

He'd *seen* her. He'd *spoken* to her. As jealous as I was, I was also relieved because it meant that Ace was okay. That she had contact with one of us and maybe, just maybe, we might have a chance to win her forgiveness.

All of these thoughts were a tangled knot inside of me as I ran. Since she stormed off and left us, I'd been running twice a day. It was the only way I didn't show up and corner her. Leaving the trail close to Aubrey's place, I slowed to a walk. I needed to cool down and I just—I just wanted to check on her.

I needed to know she was okay. The simple truth was, I felt better when I could see her. It didn't hurt anyone if I was there just to keep an eye out. The lack of a bodyguard was something we'd all been hyper aware of. How could we not be?

Dix—the fucking pervert—had offered some sense of security with his presence. The fact it turned out to be yet another lie didn't make me feel any better. I hated the guy, but more because I thought he wanted *her*. I had no idea that his desire for her turned him into the worst kind of deviant.

Spying on her.

How long? All of her life? The cops weren't telling us what they found on the hard drives but the reality was, for most of their acquaintance, *Ace* had been under eighteen. A child.

If I ever saw that piece of shit again, I was gonna rearrange his face. Still, Ramsey said there was a new bodyguard, but he wasn't living with the girls or staying super close to them. That meant no one was looking over them.

Didn't hurt anyone if I parked myself close. Campus security was supposed to keep an eye on her too. But I didn't see anyone out near the building. If anything, it was almost eerily quiet.

I checked my watch. It was close to midnight. That made sense. I hadn't realized how late it was. Movement pulled my attention and I tracked someone crossing out of the lot and onto the path heading on a direct route for Aubrey's building.

It wasn't until he passed under a lamp that I recognized Forrest. Aubrey's boyfriend. Lucky bastard headed right up the steps for the door. He didn't knock. He didn't even glance around as he pulled out a key and let himself in.

No light spilled out and I sighed. Damn. I'd been hoping that maybe Ace would answer the door and I'd just get to see her. A boyfriend showing up to spend the night, at least Forrest had the right to do that.

Rolling my head around, I glanced from the once-again closed door to the path Forrest had followed then back to the door again. At least Forrest being there meant the girls *weren't* alone.

That was good, right?

The last thing I wanted was for them to be there alone and exposed. I dug out my phone and checked the messages. Only one—from Ramsey.

BRANIAC:

Don't be a dick. Trust her.

It was like having a psychic for a brother. I had zero intention of being a dick. Except—I scrolled to her messages from earlier and stared at the photo of her making a face and the playful smile in the selfie she sent me. She'd thanked me for the guitar. Even better, she'd rewarded me for sending it.

Missing her was a raw nerve in my system.

Right.

Don't be a dick.

I pivoted to head for the running trail. I could come back in the morning. Maybe she would want to go for a run...

Not even five steps later, I hesitated and glanced back at the door. Goddammit. Go, I told myself. Trust her. Trust Ramsey.

Go.

Let her have her space...

Then again, would knocking real quick and seeing if she was awake really be intruding? Forrest had just gotten there—I checked my watch again—twenty some odd minutes earlier. They were awake, right?

Couldn't hurt.

It might hurt.

Fuck it.

I headed for the door. If she wanted to yell at me, at least she'd be talking to me and I could put my eyes on *her*. Not just her picture or hearing from Ramsey that he'd seen her. I wanted to see my girl.

My ace.

I raised a fist to knock on the door when a sound echoed from within. Raised voice? It was there and gone. I glanced at the shaded windows. Aubrey had curtains on them too so it wasn't like a lot of light escaped.

It had been dark when Forrest went in. Maybe they were watching a movie. I knocked once before I could talk myself out of it. Truth was, I wanted to kiss that beautiful mouth of hers. Sometimes, it was fun to see if I could talk myself around her temper.

No one answered and I glanced down at the phone. Well, I was already in for a pound. I fired off a quick text to her.

ME:

I miss you too, Ace. Just—want to stick my head in and say hi. Open the door?

All true. More than true. Another sound echoed from within and I turned my head. It was too muffled to make out, but it sounded like something breaking. What action movie were they—

A scream cut through all of it. A real scream. The volume loud and clear as it conveyed real terror. That wasn't a movie.

I slammed my fist against the door, pounding. It shook a little but no one came. I lifted a foot and slammed it against the door. One kick.

Two.

The door barely budged.

I backed up and charged at it. My shoulder went numb when I hit it. Withdrawing, I charged it again and hit harder. The frame gave a little.

The third time, the whole door flew inward and I couldn't feel my right hand. The screams were coming from the bedroom and there was the sound of more shattering. I dashed through, hitting the bedroom door with the same kind of force. It shattered the frame and the door slammed open, bouncing against the wall before it came back to me.

Three things hit me at once.

There were only two people in the room.

One of them was Ace and she was fighting the guy on top of her.

The guy on top of her jerked his head up.

"Get your fucking hands off of her…" I couldn't feel my hand but it still responded as I grabbed a hold of Forrest's hair and his arm as he flailed out at me. I dragged him off the bed. There was broken glass on the floor.

I ignored it as Forrest turned into me and started ramming his fist into my sides. We were grappling, and I ate the blows as I shoved him into a wall. He pushed back at me as he hit it and I got an overhand blow in but he slammed his head back into my face.

Blood filled my mouth.

Mother.

Fucker.

He wasn't a small guy, but then neither was I. And I was furious. I let my anger fuel my blows. My right eye burned. So did my nose. He was shoving me backwards and then we hit the bed.

Thank fuck, Ace was already out of it and had moved as I used our momentum to keep tumbling over to the other side. Something else shattered as it hit the wall.

"We need help..." Ace was saying, the very real sound of her tears just pissed me off even more if that was possible. Something crunched under me and then I got Forrest flipped over and I was on top.

I slugged him.

One.

Two.

Three.

The stench of copper and sweat filled my nose but I didn't know if that was from his blood or mine. He got his feet up and kicked me, shoving me back to crash into the dresser and then I staggered.

Ace caught me.

"No," I told her and gave her a shove into the bathroom. "Lock it."

"Don't you fucking touch her," Forrest bellowed. "She's mine...they're *mine*."

The fuck she was.

I met his charge and went low, slamming my already abused shoulder right into his mid-section as I picked him up and drove him across the room. We hit the window. The blinds rattled, the glass cracked and then we were tumbling out of it and down.

I was gonna kill this son of a bitch.

Thirty-Nine

KC

The weight of him pressing me into the bed coupled with the way he tried to suffocate me sent me spiraling. I was in the fridge again. Only instead of the ties lashing my wrists to my legs, it was Forrest's grip on them pinning me down. His mouth was the mask, the heat from his wet kiss even more sickening than the cold oxygen.

Internal panic gave way to raw terror.

I didn't want to be trapped in here.

Not again.

Not with him.

No...

I bit him and he jerked his head back, then gathered both of my wrists in one hand before he gripped my face. I let out a scream but he was too fast. The bite of his fingers into my cheeks hurt, then his mouth was on mine again.

Was he bleeding?

Was I?

Thrashing, I kicked but we were under the covers and it

was like I couldn't escape him. "I'm so glad you waited for me," he said and for a moment the words froze me in place. "Aubrey is such a doll, she made all the arrangements so I could stay close. It was so good of her. And I had to be patient, but I knew it would be worth it. She gave herself to me. Now you... then we'll get Yvette and I will have all of you."

Was he *insane?*

"I need you," Forrest said in between more licking kisses along my face as I tried to turn away. But the more I fought, the harder he gripped my face. "Then you came here. You showed up. So you were done and ready for me...when Aubrey said you'd have this bed tonight, I knew you were both ready for it."

"Have you lost your fucking mind?" I demanded as I bucked at him to try and get him off of me.

"Don't be upset, my love," Forrest said. "I've never missed a single performance or message. Then you came here—to my school. To me."

A whole new kind of fear crystalized inside of me. "We came to your school?"

"You did," he said, a smile lighting up his whole face. "I couldn't believe that you were just *here*. I've been your fan forever. I write to you all the time. Then I saw you had my letters...and I knew. You came here for me."

Bile burned up my throat. "I need to pee..."

"What?" Forrest tilted his head as he ground himself against me. The urge to vomit hit me again.

"I really need to pee, Forrest," I said, softening my voice. You needed to be kind to crazy people, right? Be gentle with them? "Please?"

He frowned then glanced down at me before he nuzzled his nose to my ear again. My skin was going to crawl off my body. "You feel good," he whispered and I fought the urge to flinch.

When he let go of my face and slid his hand under the covers, I was ready to scream again.

"It won't feel good if I pee," I told him abruptly. "Better to pee—you know, before we do anything. I don't..." I could do this. "I don't want to miss anything."

He groaned as his fingers hit the edge of my panties. "I don't know, I don't think anything you can do wouldn't be sexy..."

My heart fisted so tight I couldn't breathe. I didn't say anything. I wasn't sure I wouldn't just puke on him if I opened my mouth, and he finally levered himself up. His grip on my wrists loosened.

"Let's go in there, I want to watch..."

As soon as his weight was off me, I grabbed for my panic button but he knocked it away before I could touch it and then the lamp went flying. It smashed against the wall, glass spraying everywhere.

Half-screaming, I twisted and punched him right in the nuts. He groaned and I shoved at him as I tried to get away, but I barely made it off the bed before he fisted my hair. My whole scalp lit up in pain and I screamed again as he threw me back onto the bed.

"No," he snarled, but there was someone banging on the door and I screamed louder, kicking the nightstand. The wall. Anything to make noise.

It seemed to go on forever and then Lachlan was there. I'd never been so goddamn glad to see anyone. One minute, Forrest had me pressed into the mattress, suffocating me and the next he was off. They were punching each other, slamming into things and I scampered to get off the bed.

The light came on in the bathroom and I was looking for my phone. The panic button. Something. Forrest was beating on Lachlan, then Lachlan was punching him. When Lachlan shoved me into the bathroom and told me to lock it, Forrest lost his mind.

One moment they were in front of me and then they were crashing out a window. I found the panic button and squeezed it even as I saw my phone. I grabbed it and hit the first contact on the screen, which was for Ramsey.

"Siren?" He answered the phone in the middle of the first ring. "What's wrong?"

"They're fighting—Ramsey—Lachlan is fighting Forrest —he got here and he got him off me...you have to help—I need to call security. I don't know where Aubrey is." The words spilled out of me in a torrent.

"I'm coming," Ramsey said. "Are you safe?"

"I'm inside..." The cold air poured in from outside and I couldn't see Lachlan or Forrest anymore.

"Are. You. Safe?" Ramsey fired off each word, then, "Jonas —get up. Siren needs us. Now."

"What happened?" Jonas' voice was there but Ramsey sounded like he was moving.

"I don't know," I answered finally, looking around the room. I didn't have anything—not even a baseball bat. "I can't see them..."

The door to the living room crashed again and I screamed as John appeared. He had a gun in his hand and he scanned the room.

"Siren?" Ramsey demanded.

John looked from me to the open window then back. "What happened?"

"Forrest was here...I woke up and he was in the bed. He said he's forever fan and then Lachlan was here...and he got him off me and they went out that window..." It spilled out of me in hiccups and broken syllables. "I don't know where Aubrey is..."

"Breathe," John said as he grabbed a blanket off the bed,

shook it out and then wrapped it around me. "Just breathe, get out of this cold, come on..."

"Ramsey..."

"I'm here," he said, though he was huffing. "We're coming, Siren..."

John took the phone from my fingers. "I'm here, you're coming?" He nodded as he moved me out of the bedroom and into the living room. The door to Aubrey's room was broken. There were people outside. Neighbors.

Phones.

John glared at them. "I'm hanging up and calling Campus Security, do not just charge in the room, knock." Then he hung up the phone. "Sit," he told me and not once did the gun go away as he pushed the door closed.

What seemed like an eternity later, there was a knock on the door frame. The door itself wouldn't close. "It's Ramsey and Jonas," Ramsey called and I was already standing as John opened the door.

Then Ramsey had me up and off the ground. I was clinging to him. Jonas was there and they were both hugging me.

"Lachlan..."

"He's fine," John said. "He'll be here in a moment."

What? How did he know?

I couldn't stop shaking. Jonas wrapped me back up in the blanket, then picked me up and I was sitting in his lap.

"You're bleeding," Ramsey said and I glanced down at my feet where blood seeped between my toes.

"There was glass." The syllables came out shaking. Then the door opened and Lachlan was there. My vision wavered. "Lachlan..."

"I'm here," he said, as he crossed right over to the sofa. Blood leaked from the corner of his mouth, red marks littered his face and his jaw. There was puffiness around his eye and his knuckles were scraped and bleeding.

"Where is that son of a bitch?" Jonas demanded.

"Security has him," Lachlan said and then he fell onto the sofa next to me. I climbed out of Jonas' lap and right onto Lachlan's. He grunted then winced. "Easy, Ace. Pretty sure I've got some cracked ribs."

I started to pull back but he hugged me to him, Ramsey loomed over all three of us, his attention on the door, and then Creglin was there. More cops. There were red and blue flashing lights outside. So many people.

Paramedics insisted on looking at my feet. Then at Lachlan. There were statements and questions.

So many—

"Here," John said as he cut off the others and thrust my phone at me. I took it in trembling hands.

"Kait...?"

Aubrey.

The tears spilled out of me as a sob escaped. "You're okay?" I demanded. "Where are you?"

"I'm not okay, but I will be." The words were slurring a little. "We're going to the hospital...Kait, Forrest..."

"I know. I'm coming..." I looked at my guys. "We're coming."

It took time, too long in my opinion, but we were all on our way to the hospital. We made Lachlan ride the gurney in the ambulance and I sat with Ramsey. Jonas followed us with John.

Aubrey was already there when we got there and we all had to be seen, but they put Aubrey and I in bays next to each other. Lachlan refused to stay in his, and came to sit with me. It took hours.

So many hours.

Phone calls.

Interviews.

But the guys didn't leave us and when Aubrey finally fell asleep it was curled up next to me. In a bed in one of the hospital rooms with the guys on guard. John had more people brought in. During their date, Forrest had drugged Aubrey and told her everything he was going to do before he left her tied up and unconscious at his place. Then he came to me.

They found more pictures of us. Apparently, not all the cameras had been Dix's. Only some of them. Forrest had been watching us for nearly as long. It was so gross and Aubrey's heart was broken.

I couldn't bear to leave her and no one made me. I couldn't sleep either. Every time I closed my eyes, all I saw was the inside of the fridge or felt the weight of him crushing down on me.

Nightmares could wait. My best friend needed me.

Yvette was coming.

Of course she was. She was so mad. Listening to her rant on the phone made me burst into tears all over again.

"You need to sleep," Jonas told me as he sat in the chair closest to my side of the bed.

I shook my head and he put his hand on mine. Lachlan had finally gone to sleep on a rolling cot they'd brought into the room and Ramsey sat next to the door. John and his men were outside it, but neither Ramsey nor Jonas were sleeping.

"No one will get to either of you," Jonas said, stroking my hair back. "I promise. We'll be right here. We won't let them."

I had no idea if I could. Honestly, I didn't think it possible. But Jonas kept stroking my hair and my eyes grew heavier.

"I want to come home," I whispered. "I want you guys to be there..."

"We're not going anywhere, Siren," Ramsey promised. "We're with you."

"Every step," Jonas added.

"Can't get rid of us," Lachlan mumbled. "Stalking for the win."

"You win, Douchebag," Aubrey mumbled. "You definitely win."

It was the most ludicrous pair of comments. A snicker escaped me that twisted into a sob and then a laugh. Aubrey tightened her arms around me and so did Jonas. Then they were both laughing.

Or maybe we were crying.

It didn't matter. They were here.

She was safe and so were they.

Yvette was right. Blue Ivy was cursed.

Honestly. Or maybe I was finally starting to hate the damn school.

Forty

KC

THREE WEEKS LATER...

"Let me get this straight," Yvette said. "Forrest was our forever fan—for like forever. He was writing to us even *before* you guys went to the school and he thought because you were at the school..."

"Pretty much," Aubrey said. "Then he asked Aven to hook me up with him or at least introduce us. And I fell for him."

Aubrey and Yvette were in California. After everything that happened, Aubrey needed a break from the school, from Connecticut, from everything. I really couldn't blame her. If not for the boys, I'd have been on the flight with them.

Still...

"I'm sorry," I murmured. "I can't begin to tell you how sorry I am."

"You have nothing to be sorry about," Aubrey scolded. "I brought him into our lives..."

"No, you didn't," Yvette said with the most impatient if loving sighs. "That asshole brought himself into our lives. Tell me he was at least good in bed because otherwise, you and I are going to find you a cleansing the palate lover..."

There was dead silence on the phone and I had to bite my lip. I was back in my room at the cottage. With RJ and Payton now both firmly in jail, and their various bails either revoked or not offered, I didn't have to worry about them. Forrest was under psychiatric evaluation. But we'd been given assurances that he wouldn't be getting out any time soon either.

Dix?

Authorities were dealing with him, but I had him served with a restraining order and our legal team was making sure he couldn't come near us again. In the meanwhile, Aubrey and Yvette now had full time bodyguards as well. No more games. No more taking risks.

There was still a question about how a door had been jammed during the fire, but we'd all kind of come to the conclusion that we might never know. That—that might be something we had to live with.

Dad came to the school the week before to check on me himself. I nearly fainted when I came back to the cottage with Lachlan and found him sitting on our sofa. Even weirder, we had to call Mom while he was here, along with Jackie. They all wanted proof of life.

"I think I'm gonna take a break from the dating game," Aubrey said. "Maybe for a year or two, maybe a decade."

"It's gonna get better," I promised her. "I don't know how or why I think that, but you deserve the whole world. It will get better dammit." I didn't care what we had to do.

"What she said," Yvette agreed. "For now, we've got your back."

"We do."

Aubrey sighed. "I want to come back but…"

"No," I said. "If you were really up to it, I wouldn't argue. Right now though, I need you looking after you. And I need to work on me. Jonas talked to his therapist and got me a couple of recommendations. I'm starting next week."

"Wow," Yvette said after a long moment. "How are you feeling about that?"

"T.B.D." But the nightmares were getting worse, not better. I couldn't go to sleep without at least one of them in the room with me if not in the bed. I preferred to have at least two. Even then, the nightmares woke me up. "I just—I need to do something. I need to get a grip on this. I refuse to let *any* of them have this power over my life."

"The douchebags are still looking after you?" Aubrey asked, though the level of affection she applied to "douchebags" had begun to rival my own.

"They are, I promise. They are doing everything to help me and we're talking—a lot about a lot of stuff."

"You're still dating all three?" Yvette's turn to confirm it.

"Yep." Then… "I love them." It had taken me a while to even admit it to myself. "I love them more than I thought it was possible and yeah, I know I don't turn twenty until later this year but… I want them in my life." I looked at the filled heart on the side of my hand. The heart I'd had tattooed there for Pen.

I was going to add a new set of tattoos. Three of them.

One for each of my guys.

Jonas and I were talking to his dad about it and I was going to meet his dad over summer break. I was going to meet all their dads this summer.

One step at a time.

"Don't think that means you're getting rid of me," I reminded my girls. "We have an album to write and a tour to plan." The quiet this time was filled with all the things we never needed to say because they were all so wildly true for us.

They were my girls. My family. They were Torched.

So was I.

"Does that mean we're taking boys on tour?" Yvette murmured. "I like the idea that we can send them out for things... Especially if they're still struggling to impress me. That could be fun."

Aubrey's groan turned into laughter and I chuckled.

"Anything's possible," I said, and downstairs a door slammed. "Speaking of possibilities, it sounds like Ramsey is home from classes. I have a dinner date with all three of them and a planning session."

"Oooh," Yvette teased. "Kinky."

"Stahp," I elongated the word. "You're terrible."

"Well, yes," Yvette agreed. "Go on, I've got Aubrey. We'll talk to you in a couple of days."

"Love you both."

"Love you," they answered in almost unison and then I ended the call. Rising, I slipped into the bathroom to check how I looked. Most of the bruises had healed. My feet were better, they had to dig glass shards out of them. And a couple had been pretty deep. I'd almost decided to cut my hair on an impulse, but the guys all talked me out of it.

For now...

A gentle knock pulled me around. "I'm coming," I called.

Jonas waited for me on the landing with a bunch of wildflowers in hand. I blinked at the bouquet and he gave me the shyest, sweetest smile.

"I love them."

"I love you," he said, as direct and blunt and sweet as always. My heart did a little flip. "Lachlan brought dinner. Ramsey got wine. I got the flowers."

"Thanks for that," Lachlan said from downstairs and I

glanced past Jonas to Lachlan stood at the bottom of the steps. "I also got dessert, so that the chocolate orgasm you have later will be one hundred percent courtesy of me."

I had to bite back a smile.

"And if we're taking score," Lachlan continued. "I'm also in love with you. I just—prefer to do acts of service like beating the shit out of assholes for you."

"I'm better at that," Jonas commented. "I did that for you the first semester we met."

"You want to get technical, Jonas?" Lachlan retaliated.

"Oh for the love of—it's not a competition," Ramsey announced. "Shut up, both of you, and let her come downstairs for dinner." Then he glanced up at me and grinned. "Good evening, Siren, you look beautiful."

"Suck. Up." Lachlan rolled his eyes.

"Hmm, maybe," Jonas said as I took the flowers. "But he's not wrong. You are beautiful."

The laughter spilled out of me as all three of them grinned. I hoped they never changed. Whether they were giving me shit or each other—they were perfect.

"You want to know a secret?" I asked and all three of them stared at me. I sniffed the flowers then leaned over to give Jonas a soft kiss before I carried them downstairs with me. Lachlan stared at me, waiting, but I just gave him a kiss before I drifted past to where Ramsey waited in the kitchen. They'd even set the table.

It was...

Perfect.

I tilted my head back as he dipped his head for a kiss.

"Secret?" Lachlan prompted as he pulled out my chair and I giggled.

"Hmm... I'll save it for after dinner. You guys have all worked really hard to dazzle me."

"Killing me, Ace," Lachlan complained as I slid into the

chair, but then he pressed a kiss to the top of my head. "Don't ever stop."

Ramsey threw a napkin at him and Jonas grinned. Dinner was all seafood from one of our favorite places and it smelled fantastic. Halfway through the meal though, it was Ramsey who broke the rule of no serious discussions while eating. "I said I'd wait but...you talked to Aubrey and Yvette?"

"Oh my god," Lachlan gripped a hand over his chest. "Who are you and what have you done with my rule loving brother?"

"Shut up," Ramsey told him before he looked at me. "You mentioned it this morning. I haven't stopped thinking about it..."

"Just finished before Jonas came to get me." I had a sip of the wine. It was sweet and perfect and a lot like Ramsey. "And we're going to do it."

Jonas exhaled. "So, a new album?"

I met his gaze. "Help us write it?"

"Yes," he said, his grin almost joyous. "Whatever you want."

"It has to be what you want too..."

"That means a tour," Lachlan said slowly, leaning back in his seat.

"Not until the album is ready but probably next year, yes." I stole a look at Ramsey. "We—that means..."

"I'll let the dean know I'm taking next year off and maybe the one after that."

I blinked. "Ramsey..."

"No, you need to do this. You need to record. You need to tour. I'm in. I've spent most of my life at this school. But I'm planning on spending the rest of my life with you—I can get another job later. Whether it's here or California or wherever..."

"Same," Jonas said. "I don't really want to stay here

without you anyway." His whole focus was on me. "I want to see what we can write together."

"I just want to play guitar," Lachlan said. "And have sex with you before every show…"

Ramsey put a hand over his face. "I swear he was raised better than this…"

I couldn't help my laughter. Were we really having this conversation? "Look, guys, I want this to work. I want to know what we can be, but…I'm not always good at this relationship stuff."

"Bullshit," Jonas said before either of his brothers responded. "That's totally bullshit. You—you keep your whole family together. You, Yvette, and Aubrey are a family unto yourselves. You made us work together. You're the *best* at relationships because you know how to care about people more than you ever care about yourself."

"Jonas has a point," Ramsey said, fixing his gaze on me. "Your problem, Kaitlin, is that you always put yourself last and everyone has been letting you down for so long that the only ones you really know how to trust are Yvette and Aubrey."

I blinked back the sudden burn of tears as Ramsey seemed to be gazing into my soul.

"We see you, Siren. I see you. If it takes time for you to learn to trust us that way, then we'll take the time. But I have every intention of proving to you that we're going to be there for you."

"Rams is right, we're going to earn it." Lachlan said. "Nothing you do will ever make you lose me. I'm too damn good of a stalker for that."

He deadpanned it so perfectly that laughter exploded out of me. Yes, it was funny, but he was absolutely serious.

"You are the perfect stalker," I told him.

"Perfect for you, Ace," he said, then reached over to put

his hand on mine. Ramsey covered his hand and then Jonas covered his.

"We're in," Ramsey said.

"Wherever it takes us," Jonas continued. "Preferably as far from Blue Ivy Prep as we can get."

"Agreed," Ramsey and Lachlan echoed the sentiment with vehemence.

We held there for the longest moment and then gradually we retreated to our spots. Dinner was perfect. My guys were perfect.

"Ace?"

I glanced over at Lachlan.

"Secret?" he prompted.

I grinned. Yeah.

I loved these guys.

My douchebags three.

Mine.

KC

"So," Bronson said as he fell onto his side on the bed, he was home from college and doing really well. He would be graduating the following year, sooner if he had his way. His interest in veterinary medicine continued to grow. The more he studied, the more he wanted to do. "What day is it there?"

"It's your tomorrow..." We'd arrived in Auckland the week before to film a video *before* we officially kicked off our new tour. "How does it feel talking to the future?"

He snorted. "Hang on..."

"KC!" An adorable little moppet said excitedly and Bronson's phone swung around to reveal Pen rushing into his room. She was already on the bed and Bronson laughed. "KC!" Pen's smile was the sunniest damn thing ever. "Where are you?"

The demand and excitement were the hug I needed. "I'm still in New Zealand," I told her. "Bronson showed you, right?"

Her face screwed up into a scowl. "You need to come home."

"In a few weeks, I promise." I crossed my heart.

"Then Disneyland."

"I think we can do that."

Pen threw her arms up and bounced before she sobered. "Can you come home sooner?"

"I already told you she can't, Peanut." Bronson tweaked her nose. "Don't be a brat."

"Not a brat," Pen informed him. "I'm a Crosse."

"Yes, you are," I said, still grinning at the impudence in her expression. The changes over the last year had been *amazing*. She would be able to start kindergarten soon and that seemed bizarre enough, but full remission was more than we could have asked for. I still delighted with every single sign of her continued improvement.

"Pen!" Jackie's voice drifted in from the background.

"Oo, brownies!" Then Pen blew me a kiss and she was gone.

"Well, thrown over for brownies," I said and Bronson crossed his eyes at me.

"Happens to the best of us." He smirked and then we both stuck our tongues out at each other. "And she's fine," he reminded me. "She's fine. Tracy's fine. Harmonization surgery went really well, she's still recovering and with the swelling she's refusing any photos or anything until it's better."

"She told me," I said, with a little huff. "I called her yesterday when I had a break. No video, but she pinky swore that she was okay."

"She is," Bronson insisted. "Mom and I have been checking on her. I'm glad she decided to stay out here for the surgery."

"I wish I could have been there." The surgery had been

rescheduled twice and when this date coincided with our already booked concert launch, she'd insisted we go. She promised to come to the concert when we came back to the States.

"She knows and so do I. But Dad's been coming through too so, maybe it's okay to let us handle it." The not-so-gentle reminder made me stick my tongue out at him again. "Just saying..."

"I know and I have been getting better about trying to not do everything."

"Better is relative," he teased. "But I will say about six percent improvement. I need your boyfriends to make better distractions."

"Ass."

"Brat," he retaliated and we both grinned.

"How is Dad?"

"Eh, he's fine. We got an invitation to your mom's movie premiere." His grimace was adorable. "Um, would it be bad if I didn't go?"

I laughed. "Mom just wants you to feel welcome." Johnny and Mom were going strong and I couldn't be happier about that. "She invited Jackie, too, right?"

My brother snorted. "Did you ever imagine them becoming friends?"

"Nope, but I can't say it's not a good thing. Jackie's been great with Mom."

"Weirdly," Bronson said. "I think Jennifer's been amazing for my mom too."

We both made faces. I checked my phone for time then glanced at him again.

"You gotta go," he said and it wasn't a question.

"Yeah, Ramsey and Jonas went to get coffees for us and Lachlan just got out of the shower. We have a two hour ride down to Waitomo. We got the last bit of permission and

licensing to do the shots we need in the cathedral caves there—
I can't wait for you to hear how it sounds."

"KC?"

"Yeah?"

"Happy looks good on you," he said with a wink, then glanced past me. "Look after my sister, Lach."

"Can't keep me away if you tried," Lachlan drawled and Bronson snorted. Then he was gone. I turned to face Lachlan with a grin. He had on jeans and no shirt, he raked a playful look over me. "You ready for this?"

For what came next...

"Oh yeah." I was more than ready. This tour?

This tour was going to rock.

Afterword

And...that's all folks!

Or is it?

It's funny sometimes, actually, it's funny all the time that I think I know exactly how it's all going to go and at the end of the day the story says, "But do you? Really?"

From the day I realized I was going to write Blue Ivy Prep, I knew it was going to be a journey. Not just one into adulthood but into the potential of who we can be.

KC was all of that and more. The girl who seemed to have been born with what someone else wanted, in some cases, what everyone wanted.

She's a rock star princess. A Hollywood nepo baby. A rock star in her own right who got "lucky" and was in the right place at the right time with the right idea. Her parents are celebrities and she's lived her whole life in the spotlight. She has a lot of siblings whom she adores, two of the best friends a girl could ever have, and a lot of supportive people in her corner.

All she wanted was to be "normal." So of course, that prompted the, what is "normal" conversation.

Do I think I answered it? Maybe. I think KC answered it for herself and that's the important part.

Of course, it also begged the question, how Ramsey, Lachlan, and Jonas fit into her life and I think the answer to that is "rather beautiful."

While her journey at Blue Ivy Prep is very much done, I think there's still more to *her* story, hers and her douchebags three. And yes, before you ask, I know, what about Aubrey and Yvette?

I don't have their story.

Yet.

xoxo
Heather

Reader group:
    facebook.com/groups/heatherspack
    Spoiler group:
    facebook.com/groups/teammadatheather

I *love* books. Not just a little bit, but a lot. Books were my best friends when I was growing up. Books didn't care if I was new to a town or to a class. They were always there, my trustiest of companions. Until they turned on me and said I had to write them.

I can tell you that my own personal happily ever after included writing books. I've always said that an HEA is a work in progress. It's true in my marriage, my friendships, and in my career. I am constantly nurturing my muse as we dive into new tales, new tropes, new characters and more.

After seventeen years in Texas, we relocated to the Pacific Northwest in search of seasons, new experiences, and new geography. I can't wait to discover what life (and my muse) have in store for me.

Maybe writing was always my destiny and romance my fate. After all, my grandmother wasn't a fan of picture books and used to read me her Harlequin Romance novels.

Friends to lovers, enemies to lovers, friends to enemies to lovers, you name it, I love them and love to write them. I started with Earth Witches Aren't Easy, the first in the Chance Monroe trilogy, but my characters and I have traveled a long way since I created that urban fantasy world.

One of the series I hear my readers recommend the most is the Untouchable series followed in quick succession by the Vandals, and that just delights me. No lie, whenever one of my readers brings up my wolves, I do a little a fist pump.

I'm active on social media, and I love hearing from readers.

Feel free to tag me with a question about any of my books, or just say hi!

www.heatherlong.net
TikTok

Also by Heather Long

82nd Street Vandals

Savage Vandal

Vicious Rebel

Ruthless Traitor

Dirty Devil

Brutal Fighter

Dangerous Renegade

Merciless Spy

Reckless Thief

Fierce Dancer

Always a Marine Series

Once Her Man, Always Her Man

Retreat Hell! She Just Got Here

Tell It to the Marine

Proud to Serve Her

Her Marine

No Regrets, No Surrender

The Marine Cowboy

The Two and the Proud

A Marine and a Gentleman

Combat Barbie

Whiskey Tango Foxtrot

What Part of Marine Don't You Understand?

A Marine Affair

Marine Ever After

Marine in the Wind

Marine with Benefits

A Marine of Plenty

A Candle for a Marine

Marine under the Mistletoe

Have Yourself a Marine Christmas

Lest Old Marines Be Forgot

Her Marine Bodyguard

Smoke & Marines

Blue Ivy Prep

Problem Child

Mad Boys

Party Crashers

Money Shot

Bravo Team Wolf

When Danger Bites

Bitten Under Fire

Cardinal Sins

Kill Song

First Chorus

High Note

Last Word

Chance Monroe

Earth Witches Aren't Easy

Plan Witch from Out of Town

Bad Witch Rising

Her Elite Assets

Featuring:

Pure Copper

Target: Tungsten

Asset: Arsenic

Fevered Hearts

Marshal of Hel Dorado

Brave are the Lonely

Micah & Mrs. Miller

A Fistful of Dreams

Raising Kane

Wanted: Fevered or Alive

Wild and Fevered

The Quick & The Fevered

A Man Called Wyatt

Heart of the Nebula

Queenmaker

Deal Breaker

Throne Taker

Lone Star Leathernecks

Semper Fi Cowboy

As You Were, Cowboy

Magic & Mayhem
The Witch Singer
Bridget's Witch's Diary
The Witched Away Bride

Mongrels

Mongrels, Mischief & Mayhem

Shackled Souls
Succubus Chained
Succubus Unchained
Succubus Blessed
Shackled Souls (Omnibus)

Space Cowboy
Space Cowboy Survival Guide

Untouchable
Rules and Roses
Changes and Chocolates
Keys and Kisses
Whispers and Wishes
Hangovers and Holidays
Brazen and Breathless
Trials and Tiaras
Graduation and Gifts
Defiance and Dedication

Songs and Sweethearts

Legacy and Lovers

Farewells and Forever

Wolves of Willow Bend

Wolf at Law

Wolf Bite

Caged Wolf

Wolf Claim

Wolf Next Door

Rogue Wolf

Bayou Wolf

Untamed Wolf

Wolf with Benefits

River Wolf

Single Wicked Wolf

Desert Wolf

Snow Wolf

Wolf on Board

Holly Jolly Wolf

Shadow Wolf

His Moonstruck Wolf

Thunder Wolf

Ghost Wolf

Outlaw Wolves

Wolf Unleashed